Paprika

PAPRIKA

YASUTAKA TSUTSUI

TRANSLATED BY ANDREW DRIVER

ALMA BOOKS

ALMA BOOKS LTD
London House
243–253 Lower Mortlake Road
Richmond
Surrey TW9 2LL
United Kingdom
www.almabooks.com

PAPURIKA (PAPRIKA) by Yasutaka Tsutsui
Copyright © 1993, 2009 by Yasutaka Tsutsui
Original Japanese edition published in 1993 by Shinchosha, Co., Ltd.
English translation rights arranged with Yasutaka Tsutsui
through Japan Foreign-Rights Centre & Andrew Nurnberg Associates Ltd
This translation first published by Alma Books Limited in 2009
Reprinted 2011
Translation © Andrew Driver, 2009

Printed in Great Britain by CPI Antony Rowe

ISBN: 978-1-84688-077-3

Paprika

Part One

1

Kosaku Tokita lumbered into the Senior Staff Room. He must have weighed at least nineteen stone. The air in the room grew hot and stuffy.

The Senior Staff Room of the Institute for Psychiatric Research had five desks but only two regular occupants – Kosaku Tokita and Atsuko Chiba. Their desks jostled for space near the window at the far end of the room. The Senior Staff Room was separated from the Junior Staff Room by a glass door, but as the door was always left open, each just felt like an extension of the other.

The sandwiches and coffee she'd brought from the Institute shop were still sitting on Atsuko Chiba's desk. She had no appetite today; it was always the same old thing for lunch. The Institute had a canteen, used by staff and patients alike, but the meals it served were like horse feed. Looking on the bright side, Atsuko's lack of appetite meant she never had to gain weight or compromise her good looks – looks that had TV stations begging for her on an almost daily basis. But then again, barring their merits when treating patients, Atsuko had no interest at all in her own good looks or her TV appearances.

"The staff are having kittens," Tokita lisped as he lowered his bulky frame next to her. One of the therapists had gone down with paranoid delusions. "They say it's contagious schizophrenia. None of them want to touch the scanners or reflectors."

"That is a worry," said Atsuko. She herself often had such experiences. After all, psychiatrists had always been afraid of catching personality disorders from their patients; some even claimed that mental illness could be transmitted through the mucous membranes, like herpes. Ever since psychotherapy or "PT" devices had first come into use – particularly the scanners and reflectors that scanned and observed the inside of the psyche – this fear had come to assume an air of reality. "It's the ones who don't like identifying with their patients, the ones who *pass on*, who tend to worry about that kind of thing. Pff. You'd think an experience like that would give them a chance to self-diagnose as psychotherapists."

"Passing on" meant blaming it on the patient's mental disorder when a therapist was unable to forge human bonds with a patient. It had been at the very root of schizophrenic diagnosis until just two decades earlier.

"Oh no! Not chopped burdock with sesame and marinated pan-fried chicken *yuan* style, AGAIN!" Tokita thrust out his thick lower lip in disgust as he opened the lid of the *bento* lunchbox prepared by his mother. Tokita lived alone with his mother in one of the Institute's apartments. "I can't eat that!"

Atsuko's appetite was duly aroused when she peered into Tokita's sizeable lunchbox. For this was surely a *nori bento* – a thin layer of rice at the bottom, topped by a single sheet of dried *nori* seaweed moistened with soy sauce, with alternating layers of rice and *nori* on top of that... A classic *nori bento* from the good old days! To Atsuko, the box was crammed full of the home-cooked delights she craved, the taste of her mother's food. She hadn't always been one to skimp on meals, after all. In fact, she actually felt quite hungry now.

"All right, I'll eat it for you," she said decisively, her hands already stretched out to receive. And with both of those hands she went to grab Tokita's large bamboo lunchbox from the side.

Tokita's reaction was equally swift. "No way!" he cried, pinning her hands down on top of the box.

"But you said you didn't want it!" Atsuko protested as she tried to prise the box from his grasp. She had a certain confidence in the strength of her fingertips.

Apart from this lunchbox, there was nothing at all in the Institute that could satisfy Tokita's appetite or suit his palate. He too was desperate. "I said no way!"

"Oh dear, oh dear, oh dear." Torataro Shima, the Institute Administrator, stood before them with a frown. "Our two top candidates for the Nobel Prize in Physiology or Medicine, fighting over a lunchbox?!" he said with a hint of sadness.

Toratoro Shima had a habit of getting up from his desk in the Administrator's Office, casually strolling around the Junior Staff Room and speaking to anyone he found there. Some of the staff would jump up in fright when he suddenly spoke to them from behind; some pointed out that it was not terribly good for the heart.

Even addressed thus with such distortion of mouth and such heavy sarcasm by the Institute Administrator, the pair refused to relinquish their grip on the lunchbox, and merely continued their struggle in silence. For a few moments, Shima simply stared at the spectacle with an expression of pity. Then he gave two or three little nods of his head in resignation – as if he'd just remembered that genius always goes hand in hand with infantile behaviour.

"Doctor Chiba. Please come to my office later," he muttered, then clasped his hands behind his rounded back, turned and started to walk aimlessly around the Junior Staff Room as usual.

"Anyway, it can't be good for people who are supposed to be treating patients to have the same disorders as them, can it," Tokita continued after reluctantly sharing out half of his lunch into the lid of the box. "Tsumura misunderstood the patient's attempt at transcendental independence as an attempt at *empirical* independence. It's not uncommon for a patient's family to have the same delusions as the patient. This is similar, I think."

In that case, the danger was even greater. Because, in the eyes of the patient, it would certainly have been seen as an attempt to deceive – just as patients feel tricked by family members who express understanding of their condition. Atsuko realized she would have to analyse the therapist called Tsumura.

* * *

Atsuko only ever went to the Senior Staff Room for her lunch. Her laboratory was so full of PT devices as to resemble the cockpit of an aeroplane; she couldn't relax there, with assistants incessantly walking in and out. The same was sure to be true of Tokita's lab.

As she made her way back, Atsuko could see, through the open door of the General Treatment Room, four or five staff members clamouring loudly as they stood around Tsumura. This must have been what Tokita meant by "having kittens" – and it was a fair description of their appearance. Tsumura had his right arm raised as if in a Nazi salute, and some of the others who surrounded him in altercation also did the same. Atsuko felt sure that there would normally be nothing to make such a fuss about; something unnatural was going on.

Back in Atsuko's lab, her young assistant Nobue Kakimoto was peering at a display screen with a helmet-shaped collector attached to her head. She was monitoring the dream of a patient who slept in the adjacent examination room. Nobue's expression was vacant; she was quite unaware that Atsuko had returned.

Atsuko quickly stopped the recording, then pressed the "back-skip" button two or three times. Switching the machine off altogether could have been dangerous, as Nobue might then have been trapped inside the patient's subconscious. The picture on the screen started to flip backwards through the patient's dream.

"Oh!" Nobue came to her senses and removed the collector with some haste. Noticing Atsuko, she stood up. "You're back!"

"Do you realize how dangerous that could have been?"

"Sorry." Nobue seemed unaware that she'd strayed into the patient's dream. "I only meant to be an objective observer…"

"No. You were being counter-invaded. It's dangerous to wear the collector for long periods when monitoring dreams. I've told you that before."

"Yes, but…" Nobue looked up at Atsuko with an expression of discontent.

12

Atsuko laughed aloud. "You were trying to copy me, weren't you! Going into a state of semi-sleep?!"

Nobue reluctantly returned to her seat and began to watch the reflector monitor. "Why can you do it, but not me?" she said dolefully. "Is it because I haven't had enough training?"

The truth of the matter, quite decidedly, lay not in training but in Nobue's lack of will-power. Some had the will-power to become therapists, for sure, but were not adept at time-sharing patients' dreams or transferring emotions into their subconscious. If they were to attempt this, they would merely become trapped inside the patient's subconscious, unable to return to the real world.

"Perhaps. Anyway, please be careful. Tsumura was affected by a patient's paranoid delusions just by looking at the reflector. You must have heard."

"Yes. I heard."

The patient in the examination room was a man of about sixty. He was dreaming of a busy street reminiscent of central Tokyo some decades earlier. The street in the patient's dream was vulgar, charmless, desolate. By transferring emotions to the patient using the collector, that busy street could be turned into a pleasant, desirable place, one that could be linked to the innocent erotic desires of his youth. Or the scene could take him back to a past time when he'd enjoyed a positive relationship with society, symbolizing his need to reforge bonds with the people around him.

Atsuko was about to ask Nobue to call Tsumura when young Morio Osanai walked in. Dangerously handsome, unmarried and already a Doctor of Medicine, he was the target of fervent gossip among the Institute's female staff. But he had a poor reputation, for all that, as he tended to neglect his research in favour of politics. Nobue appeared to dislike him.

"Doctor Chiba," he started unceremoniously. "About Tsumura. I wonder if the problem isn't Tsumura himself, but lies rather in the reflector?"

"Of course it does. Tsumura would never have gone that way if he hadn't messed about with the reflector."

"Right, right. So there are some therapists who *aren't* affected by a patient's paranoid delusions, even if they mess about with the reflector?" Osanai answered with a smile, as if to say "*I knew you'd say that*".

"You know that already, so don't bother saying it," Nobue spat out with venom. She had almost complete faith in Atsuko.

But Atsuko had no desire at all to become embroiled in such a low-level debate. "You won't be forgetting the governing principle of our research here, will you," she said, measuring the words out slowly and deliberately.

"To, develop, PT, devices. Why, yes. I know all about that," Osanai said slowly and deliberately in imitation of Atsuko, completely ignoring Nobue. "What I'm talking about is the actual effect of us observing the subconscious of a schizophrenic as an image on a screen. Schizophrenics make no attempt to disguise their subconscious, as psychopathics do. On the contrary, they express their subconscious as it is, in loud and sonorous voices. They play it out as it is. And in any case, I can't see there's any great value in peeping into their subconscious."

"Their subconscious is the subconscious of the schizophrenic. Surely we have to investigate the abnormal way in which they associate *signifiant* with *signifié*? As you say, these patients are expressing their subconscious as it is. Therefore, we won't know what meanings are tied to their words unless we 'peep into their subconscious', will we."

Atsuko was getting serious now. Having had his say, Osanai merely looked out of the window with a smile, pretending not to listen at all. Outside the window lay about an acre of lawns, beyond them a plantation of trees designed to hide the Institute's perimeter fence, and beyond that, clusters of high-rise buildings in the centre of the metropolis.

"Well, that's your theory," said Osanai, with the implied addendum "*and I think it's rubbish*".

"Now wait a minute," said Atsuko, controlling her anger. Controlling anger was part of Atsuko's self-training as a top-grade psychotherapist. "It's not just a theory, it's the very foundation of our work. It's a theory that's been proven and certified. I don't see why I should have to stand here and explain it all to you. That's it. Now please bring Tsumura to me. I'll treat him."

Osanai straightened his face. He seemed to have remembered that no one could better Atsuko when it came to ironic repartee. "No, no. It's not so serious that we need bother you. Hashimoto and I will cure Tsumura. We're his friends, you see."

Osanai hurried out of the room. Atsuko felt sure that it was he who'd spread the rumour about schizophrenia being contagious. But his intention in coming all the way to her lab and circulating it there, when he knew very well that the dangers of the reflector could be avoided, was still unclear to her.

"Curing him alone won't do," Atsuko muttered. "I'll have to analyse him properly."

"He seemed awfully scared that you would easily analyse and cure Tsumura, didn't he," said Nobue.

2

Rising from his desk in the Administrator's Office, Torataro Shima invited Atsuko to sit in an armchair in the reception area. He himself sat at one end of a sofa diagonally to her right, where he reclined backwards with his body almost supine. The result was that Shima's face became positioned diagonally next to Atsuko's, only a little below hers. Then he merely had to lift his face to find himself gazing at the beauteous visage of Atsuko Chiba from very close quarters. Shima made no secret of his admiration for her.

"So you had a visit from young Osanai, then?"

"What? You mean he came here too?" Atsuko was decidedly unimpressed with Osanai's sense of priorities.

"He said our researchers needn't all subscribe to your theory and help you win the Nobel Prize," Shima said with a chuckle.

"Just as I thought. He came about Tsumura, didn't he. I suppose he yapped on forever with his doubts about the PT devices?"

"Yes, he opposes them. But who cares? The simple fact is that they've cured some patients. That's good enough for me." Shima furrowed his brow ever so slightly. "In fact, half of the patients have even gone as far as remission. That's something we could never have dreamt of until now, anywhere. Isn't that right, Doctor Chiba? So your theory must be correct, mustn't it."

"Well, it's mostly down to Tokita – he's the one who develops the devices. All I do is use them. Oh, and by the way. About two-thirds of the schizophrenics are already in the remission phase. Not half."

"Oh yes. I remember. Well, that's wonderful of course…" Shima pulled a sour face. "But why is it that so many patients in the remission phase identify with the head of their institution like that? Some of them mimick me most grotesquely, without a hint of emotion. Just seeing them makes my skin crawl."

"Those are patients in the so-called malleable-vulnerable phase," said Atsuko, laughing with abandon. "All they're looking for is transcendental independence. Anyway, doctors and nurses are often mimicked by their patients."

Momentarily transfixed by Atsuko's laughing demeanour, Shima finally recovered his composure. "Osanai didn't say anything unpleasant, did he?" he asked somewhat anxiously.

"Not particularly," Atsuko lied, somewhat calmly.

"He was talking about the effect PT devices can have on doctors," Shima continued. "Using a lot of technical terms, you know. So I said, wouldn't it be better to discuss this with Doctor Chiba? Or don't you have the balls to? And he said, all right, I'll tell her, and walked off in a huff. So then I felt I might have done you a disservice. But I'm from the old school, you see. I can't keep up with all these new theories. There was nothing else I could say, really."

"Don't worry about it," said Atsuko. She took a glance around the office. Though suitably well appointed, it was rather on the shabby side – she could have expected more from the Administrator's Office of a research institute that was now receiving worldwide attention. The office was austere, spacious, laid out in the old-fashioned style. Bookcases lined three of its walls, their shelves stacked with classical works of psychiatry. There were original texts by Kraepelin but no recent publications at all. Surely this would create a bad impression on visitors? Atsuko wondered if it was time to replace some of the books.

"I think Osanai's up to something. Please be careful," she said, concerned for the position of her well-intentioned boss. "Of course, he can't do anything by himself. Someone else is pulling the strings. They want to make my failure a fait accompli."

"You mean the Vice President?" Shima shifted his body uneasily, as if he was embarrassed that Atsuko should allude to such inner-circle shenanigans. For as well as being the Institute Administrator, Shima was also President of the incorporated foundation that owned the Institute. "Now you mention it, there is a rumour that Inui has his eye on the President's chair…"

It was no mere rumour. Even Shima must have known that Inui had met the other directors and appeared to be plotting something. But Shima seemed happy just to let it go. Tokita had thoughts for nothing but his research; Atsuko was the only one who seemed concerned about it at all. In an environment so beset with enemies, she and Tokita had much to thank Shima for. It was down to him, after all, that they could concentrate so fully on their research. More than that, though, Atsuko had immense affection for Shima's personality and felt duty-bound to protect him.

Shima misinterpreted the look on her face. "Look, I didn't call you here to discuss such trifling matters," he said, hurriedly adjusting his position and straightening his back.

Atsuko lifted her face in some surprise. To her, it wasn't a trifling matter at all. Their eyes met. Shima was lost for words. It was as if there was something he wanted to say, but he didn't know how to say it. This was clearly going to be difficult.

In the end, Shima got up and returned to his desk. Atsuko smiled. Only when he wanted to convince someone of something did the well-meaning but weak-willed Shima hide behind the authority of the grand Administrator's desk.

"Now. Of course I'm aware that your research has entered a most critical phase. So naturally, what I'm about to ask will seem thoroughly unreasonable to you." Shima clawed the top of the desk with his bony fingertips as he spoke. "But in fact, I want you to call up Paprika."

"What?!" Atsuko all but fell off her chair. She'd been ready to accept almost any request, but this seemed a request too far. However jovially Shima tried to put it, calling up Paprika was surely out of the question at this time. "I'm sorry, but she doesn't do that work any more."

"Aha. I know. I know. What is it – five, six years since she quit? But this is a really important assignment. Can't you persuade her, just one more time? As a special favour? You see, it's not just *anyone* this time. Oh no. It's someone very important, someone with a very high standing in society. I'm not going to send him to any old clinic, am I."

"Psh. No one else seems to mind. They're all going for psycho-analysis these days."

"Yes, all very well, but this particular person is in a very delicate position, you see. Well, that's partly what triggered his neurosis in the first place. You see, a lot of people are just waiting for him to mess up and make a fool of himself. His name's Tatsuo Noda. He's the same age as me, fifty-four. We were good friends at school and university. He's still my closest friend, in fact. But now he's a senior executive in a motor company, and he's trying to produce a zero-emissions vehicle. A lot of people are against it, both inside and outside the company. So his every move is being watched, not only by rival firms but even by the government. If word got out that he was being treated for a neurotic disorder, his enemies would try to discredit everything about the vehicle, even though he didn't design it himself. That would cause his company untold damage. Of course, being an experienced businessman, he must often find himself in this kind of position. The cause of his neurosis must therefore lie elsewhere."

"Yes, I suppose it must." This Noda was Shima's friend and contemporary. He was trying to produce a zero-emissions vehicle. Before she knew it, those snippets of information had made Atsuko rather interested in this most important of clients. "The opposition from people around him probably takes the form of harassment. But that would only cause a typical nervous breakdown, at most. Not neurosis."

"That's right. That was my diagnosis too." Noting Atsuko's interest, the good and honest Shima felt instantly buoyed. "So the proper thing would be to psychoanalyse him, and that's something I can't do. In any case, whoever did it would need to spend a lot of time with him. Get into his dreams. That's why I want Paprika to do it. She's the very best dream detective."

"But it won't be easy to treat, even for the dream detective. It'll take time." Atsuko was in two minds. She felt she'd been jockeyed into a position of compliance and no longer had a choice. But if she agreed to Shima's request there and then, her research would be interrupted at a most critical phase. Being trial research, she wasn't certain exactly how long it would last, but it should be nearing completion now. "And anyway, Paprika hasn't worked as a dream detective for six years now. She's not so young any more. PT devices may no longer be taboo, but this therapy is still very risky. I'm not sure she can do it any more."

None of this came as much of a surprise to Shima. He said nothing but merely stared at Atsuko with slightly moistened eyes, waiting for her to empty her bag of troubles.

"Look, will you promise me something first?" Atsuko said at length.

The very question brought an expression of rapture to Shima's features. He puffed up his chest in anticipation. "But of course. If you'll help with Noda's treatment, ask anything you want." Shima wasn't the kind to evade an issue with a mere *"I'll see what I can do"* – he was far too pure for that.

"All right. I want you to accept that your own position right now is just as precarious as that of your friend Mr Noda." Shima stared at Atsuko with a look of wonderment – just what would she say next?! "First of all, you should speak to all the directors individually, once each at least. You've been ignoring them, can't you see? You're so preoccupied with your work that you've lost touch with them. Second, I want you to hold a Board Meeting, as soon as possible. You can think of the reason later, but first decide a date."

Shima had been bracing himself for something much worse. "All right," he replied with some relief. "I can do that."

It was just as Atsuko had expected – he was refusing to take her advice seriously. "So, where exactly do you want Paprika to go?" she asked with a little sigh, let down by his lukewarm nature once more.

Shima wrote the details on a memo pad, using his thickest-barrelled Meisterstück pen. "In Roppongi, there's a bar called Radio Club," he said jauntily. "Only men go there. It's always quiet, and it's a favourite haunt of Noda's. I'll call him now. Can Paprika meet him tonight?"

"Does he mind if it's late?" It would take time to call up the dream detective, and besides, Atsuko had so many other things to do.

"I think he'd prefer it that way."

"How about eleven o'clock?"

"Right. Eleven it is." Shima wrote two memos and passed one to Atsuko. Then he opened the drawer in his desk and took out a file containing some documents. "These'll bring you up to speed on Tatsuo Noda. His case records are in there too."

"Oh, and Doctor Chiba?" Shima called as Atsuko was about to leave the room. He'd already picked up the telephone and was dialling the number to Noda's office. "I've got to say I'm a bit jealous of Noda. Why can he have a drink with Paprika when I can't?!"

Eight years back, when Shima had only just been appointed President and Institute Administrator, Paprika had treated him for a neurotic disorder.

3

Roppongi was a lot quieter now than it had once been. It was all thanks to a change in municipal regulations, introduced to ease the atrocious congestion around the Ginza. What they did was to license late-night opening there, with the result that fewer customers were turned out onto the streets in the early evening hours. Another reason was that exorbitant prices for food, drink and entertainment had driven the younger revellers away from Roppongi.

Radio Club was in the basement of a thirty-four-storey building, amid a cluster of high-rise blocks. The rental premiums were preposterous, but Radio Club was nearly always empty. It didn't even have its own membership scheme. The customers were always the same, though; they were like members without a scheme.

Tatsuo Noda had arrived well before eleven and was sitting at the far end of the bar, in one of the booths lent a modicum of privacy by their high backs. The booths faced each other in pairs on one side of the room, overlooked by the counter on the other side. Noda's booth was at the very back of the bar, forming a little private room of his own. There were no other customers in the bar. Jinnai the bartender stood behind the counter wiping glasses with a tea towel, occasionally glancing over at Noda, smiling and performing a little bow if their eyes met. The solitary waiter Kuga,

21

a man of considerable girth, stood motionless beside the door and appeared to be deep in thought. The professional dedication of this middle-aged double act had probably dictated the profile of their clientele. *P.S. I Love You* played over the speakers.

Noda sat drinking whisky as he waited for Paprika. But not just any old whisky – this, according to Jinnai, was highest quality, twenty-seven-year-old Usquaebach, which he'd managed to get at a discount. *Paprika.* Now that was an odd name for a psychotherapist. But, as Shima had explained, it was just a throwback from the days when using PT devices was illegal and the therapists all had to use code names. Shima had also gone on at some length about how very beautiful this Paprika was.

Noda felt no anxiety at the prospect of being treated with PT devices. He had little faith in the latest fads of modern technology, but trusted Torataro Shima implicitly as a psychiatrist. Actually, he had little choice in the matter. For who else could he trust, if not the administrator of a psychiatric research institute?

Noda was about to order another measure of Usquaebach, which was really rather good, but caught himself in time. He was already beginning to feel pleasantly tipsy, buoyed by the prospect of meeting a woman of renowned beauty. He looked forward to the time he would soon be spending with her – not working time, but time in which he could just let himself go. He didn't know whether the treatment would start right away that night, but in any case sobriety was surely the best policy. Then again, as it was Shima who'd recommended this bar for the assignation with Paprika, it would have been rude *not* to have a drink or two. Drink would loosen the inhibitions, after all. If anything, Noda was grateful to Shima for choosing this location. No one from his office, none of his competitors would ever come here. Shima must have known that.

Noda somehow sensed that he wouldn't suffer an anxiety attack while he was in the bar. Of course, he couldn't afford to be complacent. An attack could occur at any time, and the knowledge of that merely added to the problem. Ironically, this was the only cause of his anxiety that could be identified with any certainty. That terrifying sensation of not knowing when an attack would occur was just as loathsome as the attacks themselves, events that would have brought the strongest of men to their knees.

The first occurrence had been about three months earlier, shortly after lunch one day. Noda had been sitting in a taxi on his way back to the office after a meeting. At first, he just felt dizzy. Then the back of his head began to feel heavy around the neck muscles, and his head started to spin. He'd previously suffered mild bouts of dizziness due to shoulder stiffness. Thinking it was one of those, he tried to ease his anxiety by massaging his shoulders. But then ominous words like apoplexy and stroke started popping up in his mind. A number of his contemporaries had been dying of such afflictions recently. He'd also heard that many people die of stroke after "selectively disregarding" precursor symptoms that must have been present beforehand – in other words, refusing to acknowledge the inevitability of ageing. He started to feel nauseous. It was a really terrible feeling. He imagined that he might collapse and die right there and then. The anxiety of that thought made him break into a cold sweat. His heart suddenly seemed to be beating faster. The sound of his pulse grew louder. Fear made his breathing shorter. His throat began to feel parched. To his credit, he summoned up enough will-power not to cry out to the taxi driver for help. On the contrary – he stiffened his limbs and made no sound at all, in an attempt to conceal the attack. He even surprised himself when he thought about that later. And when at last the attack had subsided, his concern shifted to when the next attack would occur. Perhaps it was a stroke of good fortune that the first one had happened in a taxi. But what if the next attack came while he was at work? The very idea sowed the seeds of a new anxiety. Something had to be done. And while he was still thinking about what that something might be, the second attack occurred while he was at work – the very thing he'd feared most of all.

Luckily, he was in his own office, which he'd earned as Director of Development. As he struggled to bear the anxiety and pain, Noda was struck by two conflicting desires – one, to cry out for help, and the other, not to be seen by anyone. The telephone didn't ring, and no one entered his office during the attack. But if it had rung, if someone had walked in, he would definitely have asked the other person for help, whoever it might have been. His fear of dying was far too great to do otherwise.

Noda knew it was considered bad for sufferers of mental disorders to read books about their condition. Even so, he bought several volumes on the subject and, while his wife and son were asleep, secretly took them out and read them. The first thing he discovered was that his symptoms resembled something called "anxiety neurosis". But he remained in the dark as to the cause, or whether there was any chance of self-treatment.

Noda also discovered that there were drugs called anxiolytics, which were often effective in treating his condition. He knew he would need to see a doctor to get them. But he vacillated, not wanting the world to know he was seeing a psychiatrist. For some reason, he didn't hit upon Torataro Shima right away. Then he discovered, in another book, that anxiety neurosis can sometimes progress to other mental illnesses like schizophrenia, temporarily at least, owing to diminishment of personality. It was then that he finally made up his mind to see a doctor. He thought long and hard; he had to find one who would respect his privacy, a clinic he could visit without the whole world knowing. Then he suddenly remembered his old friend. They still met once or twice a year; Shima would be the perfect person to consult on such a delicate matter.

"Frankly, the notion that most people live *without* anxiety is more of a mystery to me," Shima had declared with a laugh after hearing Noda's story. Noda reflected on his good fortune at having such a great friend, not to mention the burgeoning sense of well-being he now felt at the prospect of a cure. Shima, on the other hand, retained a modicum of concern, feeling that he'd perhaps overestimated Noda's intellect and the strength of his ego. After all, Shima was aware that anxiety neurosis could be resolved by elevating it to an "objective experience" through the strength of the ego; he also had no doubt that Noda's illness would cure itself. What's more, Noda himself had felt, after reading a book, that the cause of his anxiety was a psychological problem peculiar to middle age. It was not the same as that crisis of awareness when a son becomes a father for the first time, or when an ordinary employee rises to middle management. It was certainly not the same as an inability to absorb new technology. Those problems were all long past; for Noda, they'd already been solved ten or twenty years earlier. Even when it came to human relationships, he'd successfully seen off numerous challenges in the past. Noda should now be quite capable of overcoming such challenges with relative ease by drawing on his own experience.

Shima had given him some tablets. After their meeting, Noda had started taking them surreptitiously, mixed with vitamin pills to disguise them. For a while, the attacks had seemed a thing of the past. But two days after the tablets ran out, Noda suffered a third, more violent attack while on his way home late one night. This time he could bear it no longer, and asked the taxi driver to take him to the nearest hospital. The symptoms had subsided before the taxi could reach the hospital, so Noda diverted the driver to Shima's residence instead. Shima seemed to understand the gravity of Noda's condition, and promised to set up a course of treatment immediately. And now, about a week later, Noda was to meet the therapist called Paprika. Her name sounded like something out of a fairy tale, but, as Shima had assured him, she was "the very best dream detective".

At five past eleven, the music changed to *Satin Doll*.

The heavy oak door opened and a girl wearing a red shirt and jeans walked in. Naturally, she looked quite out of place in the bar. Kuga met her with a greeting that sounded more like a challenge. She whispered something to him. Kuga started to twitch nervously on realizing that she was Noda's assignation. Noda shared his surprise. Jinnai widened his eyes.

Kuga led the girl to Noda's booth, and there she stood with head tilted slightly to one side. "Hi," she said. "I'm Paprika."

Noda woke from his reverie and rose hurriedly. "Why... Hello!"

"And... You're Tatsuo Noda, right?"

"That's right. That's right." With growing surprise at the girl's helpless appearance, Noda pointed to the sofa opposite him. "Take a seat."

She was an attractive girl with a cutely shaped face and freckles around her eyes. In the dim half-light of the bar, Noda thought her skin looked quite tanned. Evidently feeling as incongruous as she looked, Paprika fidgeted restlessly for a while and cast uncertain glances around the bar.

Am I old enough to be her father? Noda wondered with some apprehension. Eventually he spoke: "Well... Miss..."

"Call me Paprika," she said coquettishly.

In fact, she was deliberately using that tone to help Noda feel more relaxed. Now the name slipped effortlessly from his lips. "All right – Paprika. What will you have to drink?"

"I'll have the same as you."

Noda nodded to Kuga, who still stood beside their table. Kuga cast a questioning look that only Noda could see – "*Surely you're not going to let her drink the very best whisky?!*" – then bowed in resignation and walked off.

Noda suddenly realized that Paprika had come empty-handed. Had Shima given her the case records? Would he have to explain his symptoms all over again?

It was as if Paprika had read Noda's thoughts. Until then she'd appeared tense, but now she suddenly smiled. "I hear you've developed a zero-emissions vehicle? That sounds cool."

She may speak plainly but at least she knows her manners, thought Noda. *She must be exceptionally clever*. Even her air of helplessness seemed designed to put him at his ease.

"Well, yes. Of course, there are already low-emission vehicles, like the LNG-powered ones." Now feeling more relaxed, Noda started to explain the project as if he was teaching a pupil about it. That seemed to be what Paprika wanted, anyway. "But even they emit nitrogen oxides and carbon monoxide in their exhaust fumes. So we're developing a zero-pollution vehicle that won't have any of those either. Well, I say developing. Actually, we've already made one."

"So you're actually producing them? Wow. I bet there are people who want to stop you."

"Ah yes, but of course. And it's not just the competitors. I even have opposition within my own company. They're all jealous, of course," Noda said with a laugh. "But naturally, that was no more than I'd expected," he added more seriously, lest it be considered the cause of his illness.

"Yeah, I bet they're just jealous," said Paprika. She spoke casually, suggesting not only that she understood Noda's concern but also that she wouldn't mention anything to do with his work again. She took a sip of the whisky brought by Kuga, who again stood beside their table. "Aah! Usquaebach!" she breathed quietly.

Kuga started to twitch again. At length he bowed solemnly. "Glad you like it."

4

From her hairstyle and dress sense, Paprika seemed a rather simple girl. But the more she spoke, the more her intelligence seemed to shine through, like the gleam in her eye.

"Um... Would you mind if I had another?" asked Noda.

"Sure. Go ahead," Paprika said at first, then suddenly added, donning her therapist's hat, "Wait a minute. How many have you had? This is your second, right? Well, OK. If it's only your second. Go ahead."

Paprika's funny little flurry made Noda feel even more relaxed. "Mind you, I'd better not, if you're going to start the treatment soon," he said. "They say it's best if you don't drink."

Paprika smiled precociously before looking hard at her client. "You're a gentleman, Mr Noda. I'll stop here too. Though I'd love to continue."

"I'll treat you some other time," Noda said, then lowered his voice. "Talking of which, where do you do the treatment? Shima didn't say…"

Paprika looked around the bar again. They were still the only customers. But even so, perhaps this wasn't quite the place to discuss the ins and outs of psychoanalysis. She emptied her glass in one gulp, then nodded. "I'll show you. Come on!"

P.S. I Love You was playing again as they got up to go. Paprika went straight outside, leaving Noda to settle up at the counter.

"Are you feeling all right, Mr Noda?" Jinnai asked in a tone of concern, having caught snatches of their conversation.

"Why?" asked Noda, taken aback.

"Well, the girl's a nurse, isn't she?"

Noda stepped outside to find Paprika sitting in a taxi by the kerbside. She must have stated her destination already, for the driver headed off towards Akasaka the moment Noda settled into his seat. The road was lined with high-rise buildings, most of which had apartments on their upper floors – investments for the filthy rich, or company housing for the top brass of large corporations.

"I'll scan your dreams in my apartment," said Paprika. "I've got all the equipment there." Her breath smelt sweet. It was the breath of a mature woman. Startled, Noda once again wondered how old she was.

"Do you think the treatment will take time, in my case?" he asked, raising the issue that concerned him most.

Paprika donned her therapist's hat again. "Anxiety is an integral part of being human. Heidegger saw it as a necessary evil. If you could tame your anxiety and find a way of living with it, or even make use of it, you would no longer need treatment. And then you could discover what caused your anxiety."

"I'm afraid I haven't got time for that."

"Sure, understood. You've got your work, after all. You've got your family. But you need to relax. Don't be so impatient. In principle, you'll definitely be cured, provided we can locate the cause. In a way, your condition is like a coin falling into a pocket. Pockets have bottoms, don't they. The coin will always be found. It's rare for the condition to get any worse than that."

Noda was relieved. Perhaps he could avoid going schizophrenic after all!

The taxi stopped in front of a multi-storey apartment block in Shinanomachi. It was where Shima lived, and the directors of the Institute for Psychiatric Research. The foundation owned rooms on several floors of the building. In that case, this "Paprika" must also be one the Institute's directors. The apartments were far too expensive to be owned by ordinary individuals, that was for sure. There was so much that Noda wanted to ask. But he held himself back, and concentrated instead on following Paprika's dance through the spacious lobby of the apartment building towards the lift. After all, Shima had strictly forbidden him to ask her true identity or her real name.

He was soon to discover her surname, though. As they reached the door to her apartment at the eastern end of the 16th floor, it was written in bold capitals on a metal nameplate fixed to the wall: Apt 1604 CHIBA.

The apartment was on a grand scale that could only have been designed for a senior executive. An eight-panelled glass door led out from a sumptuously furnished living room onto a veranda, with a panoramic night view of Shinjuku visible beyond.

"You must be some kind of VIP!" Noda exclaimed with unbridled admiration, but Paprika remained cool. Besides the kitchen and other facilities, this living room seemed to be where Paprika spent her time when not asleep. She beckoned Noda towards another room at the far end. It was dark and appeared to be a treatment room – the patient's bed suggested as much. The room also contained other furnishings, including another bed and a wardrobe that must have been Paprika's. Various devices lined the wall next to the crude pipe-assembled patient's bed. Monitor screens gleamed with motionless graphics. They were the only source of light, as the room had no windows.

"You don't suffer from claustrophobia, I hope?"

"No. Fear of heights, if anything."

"I'll remember that. Will you be able to sleep straight away?"

"I'm always tired. I never have any problem getting to sleep," said Noda, feeling at a loss in such unusual surroundings. "But I wonder whether I could fall asleep under the eye of one as pretty as you?"

"Just relax. Would you get undressed now?"

Noda first took off his jacket and handed it to Paprika. She placed it on a hanger, which she hung in the wardrobe. Next came the tie, then the shirt. Paprika tidied Noda's clothes with the dexterity and professional attention of a nurse. Reassured, Noda had no hesitation in taking off his trousers.

"What great dress sense you have. Such high quality," Paprika said, smiling at last, as Noda lay on the bed in his underwear. "Do you always sleep like that?"

"I can't stand pyjamas," he replied. "They make me sweat. I usually wear as little as possible."

"You could take your vest off as well, if you liked."

"No, thanks. This will do fine," Noda laughed. He put his feet under the cold, pure-white sheet at the foot of the bed. The room felt cool. The pillow was hard and smelt of starch.

As he watched Paprika busily moving about and preparing

something in the ghostly light of the monitor screens, Noda began to feel a sense of déjà vu. He could hear music. It was Rameau's *Sommeil de Dardanus*.

Paprika put what looked like a shower cap over Noda's head. It was transparent, but had an electronic circuit pattern resembling a street map printed on its surface. A single cable trailed away from the back of the cap. Noda felt rather relieved at that; he'd expected it to be more of a hard helmet-like contraption.

"Is this what you call the gorgon?"

"I can see you've done your homework. Yes, it's the gorgon, named of course after the Greek myth. But now, rather than having cables all over the place, it just has the one. Soon we won't even need the cap."

"Is it a kind of sensor?"

"You could say that. You could also see it as a combination of interfaces between a highly sensitive brainwave detector and the central processor. In the old days, they had to embed electrodes under the skull just to investigate brainwaves in the cerebral cortex. Now all you have to do is wear this. Aren't you lucky?!"

"And none of these devices have been commercialized yet?"

"No, they're still being developed. That's why it's so untidy in here..."

So who was developing them? If not Paprika herself, then whoever it was must have assembled the equipment there. In that case, since the devices were still being developed, it would have to be that scientist at the Institute for Psychiatric Research, the one who was up for the Nobel Prize or something. Would such a person really come all this way to a private residence, just to assemble the devices? Noda was beginning to feel anxious again. "So it's cutting-edge technology, you might say?" he asked with a hint of irony.

"Sure," Paprika replied as if "cutting edge" were perfectly normal. That at last put Noda's mind at ease. He allowed his head to sink back onto the pillow.

"Aaah… No electrodes embedded under my skull… I shouldn't have any trouble falling asleep at all."

"Good. And you've had a drink, so I hope you won't be needing any hypnosis or medication." Paprika sat on the chair next to Noda, then started talking to him in her relaxed bedside manner. "Do you often have dreams, Mr Noda?"

"Yes, strange dreams. Often."

"It's better to dream a lot, actually. It's good for the brain. Interesting people have interesting dreams. Dull people only have dull ones. I'm looking forward to seeing yours."

"And you actually appear in people's dreams?"

"Well, I won't tonight, as it's the first time. I'm not familiar with your dreams, and anyway we've only just met. It would be too much of a shock to your system."

"Oh well. But I must say, I never thought psychotherapy could be so enjoyable!"

"You say that because your condition is only mild. There are people who really hate seeing the dream detective. Right. I'd better not be here. You'll fall asleep more easily on your own, won't you."

"Probably, but I'd far rather you stayed." Yes, Paprika was young enough to be his own daughter, but Noda had started to feel as if he could indulge himself a little with her.

Paprika laughed and rose from her chair. "No, you should sleep now. And anyway, I'm famished. I'm going to get something from the kitchen." It sounded like a deliberate ploy to make him sleep. Paprika left the room.

What an excellent therapist – as I expected, thought Noda. She made him feel relaxed just by talking to him. They'd never met before, but her posture and expression made her seem somehow familiar, almost as if they were related. She made him feel it was all right to talk about anything he wanted. And while she tended to speak childishly, she never said anything that made Noda feel uncomfortable – *unlike most young women these days*. Yes, she was young and beautiful, but at the same time she had a motherly quality that served to restrain a man's baser urges, surrounding him instead with warm, reassuring sensations. Noda breathed a huge sigh of satisfaction. There would certainly be no anxiety attacks occurring here tonight.

Several times a month, Noda would arrive home at four or five in the morning. His wife, preoccupied as she was with their son's education, had never shown undue concern; Noda knew she wouldn't be particularly perturbed, even if he turned up at seven o'clock. And Noda's wife must have known, more perhaps than Noda himself, that having an affair was simply not in his nature.

"*Your condition is only mild*," Paprika had said. Maybe, to a therapist, his condition seemed unspectacular. But Noda himself found no comfort in that at all. It mattered little that the symptoms were not yet affecting his daily life. Now was the most crucial time. Above all, his enemies must never know of his illness; he had to be cured before they could hear about it.

In the old days, thinking about his enemies both inside and outside the company would have been enough to keep him awake until the small hours. But now he'd grown accustomed to the struggle. Now, planning cunning strategies in his head would send him off to the land of nod with a satisfying degree of mental fatigue; he almost enjoyed it. He felt sure he would fall asleep quickly tonight. As his consciousness started to fragment and crack, meaningless images started to cavort through the crevices of his mind.

5

Noda woke naturally. Or perhaps he only thought as much; perhaps Paprika had roused him with some kind of device. Paprika sat in a position where they could see each other if Noda turned his head slightly to the right. She was looking at the console monitor with a helmet-like apparatus on her head. Noda thought it must be the "collector" he'd heard about. The light from the monitor screen lent Paprika's face an ethereal glow.

"What time is it?" asked Noda.

Paprika removed the collector and smiled. "Not yet two o'clock. You've just finished your first REM sleep. Do you always wake up around this time?"

"No. I thought perhaps you'd woken me deliberately."

"No, I wouldn't do that. It must have been this dream that woke you. You remember it, of course?"

"Yes, I do." Noda sat up. "But how do you know that?"

"When we're woken during REM sleep, we usually remember what we were dreaming at the time. So, shall we just analyse this dream tonight?" Paprika took Noda's clothes from the wardrobe and placed them at the foot of the bed. "Although morning dreams are actually much more interesting."

"It was a very short dream. Can you really learn anything by analysing that?" Noda said as he dressed himself.

"Of course! Dreams in this phase of sleep are usually short, but the information they contain is condensed. It's like watching an experimental short film. Morning dreams can sometimes last an hour or so. They're more like epic feature films."

"Really? You have statistics of that sort? How interesting."

"Let's watch an experimental short then, shall we? Come on, sit here," Paprika said, patting the foot of the bed invitingly. Now fully dressed, Noda sat next to Paprika. He looked at the monitor. The screen was motionless for now, frozen in an alternating pattern of grey and black waves.

"Can dreams only be monitored in black and white?"

"There's not much point seeing them in colour, is there?" Paprika said as she pressed a button to start the picture.

It was a school classroom. In Noda's dream, he was looking towards the teacher's podium. On the podium stood a slender man of about sixty. He was talking, but his speech was so muffled that it was difficult to hear what he was saying.

"Where is this classroom?"

"My old junior high school." To Noda, it felt quite unnerving to be seeing the same dream twice. And with Paprika sitting there next to him, he also felt rather uneasy – as if a total stranger might be about to witness some past act of self-gratification… "But when I was having that dream, I didn't think it was a classroom. I thought I was at work."

"Why's that, I wonder?" Paprika paused the picture. "And who is that man?"

"Well, it's because of him that I thought I was at work. It's Sukenobu, one of our directors."

"Don't you get on with him?"

"You could say that. He's frightened that I'll rise too high in the company. He's also jealous of my success with the zero-emissions vehicle. He says we're rushing things too much. In fact, he's been colluding with a Ministry official to obstruct the development."

"Why would he do that?"

"He wants to be the next President. Well, it's a long way off yet, but that's why he's worried about my age. I'm ten years younger than him, you see."

"And why's he worried about that?"

"He thinks he'll be the first to die, or that he'll be forced to retire when he goes senile."

The picture started again. Sukenobu continued to talk while writing something on the blackboard. He could be heard mentioning the poet Basho and his book *Oku no Hosomichi*. The words *Hakutai no Kakyaku* appeared on the blackboard.

"It looks like a Japanese literature lesson."

"Classics. I hated those lessons. The teachers always had it in for me."

"And does your old teacher have something in common with this Sukenobu?" The picture was frozen again.

"No. The teacher was always changing – sometimes it was a man, sometimes a woman, now young, now old. I had so many teachers of Japanese literature that they couldn't possibly have anything in common with anyone. Except that they all had it in for me."

The picture started again. Sukenobu asked Noda something from the teacher's podium. Noda stood and was about to answer. Freeze-frame.

"This never actually happened in reality, but in the dream I mistakenly pronounced *Hakutai* as *Hyakudai*. I wonder why that was. I took the trouble to read *Oku no Hosomichi* recently, so I should know the correct reading is *Hakutai*."

On the screen, Sukenobu was facing Noda, scolding and chiding him.

"Now. The problem is this next bit," said Paprika.

"Yes."

Noda's classmates were laughing at him as he was being scolded. A low ripple of laughter could be heard, and as Noda's line of vision surveyed the classroom, his classmates all appeared to have the faces of wild animals. Bears, tigers, boars, wolves, hyenas – all mocking him. Freeze-frame.

"Why do they all look like wild animals?"

"I don't know."

"Do you recognize any of them?"

"No. I don't know any wild animals! One of the bears looks a bit like the senior executive of a rival company, though."

"What's his name?" Paprika was writing everything down on a memo pad.

"Segawa. I don't particularly see him as a problem, though."

"People who aren't a problem in our waking lives often appear in our dreams. If someone who really *was* a problem appeared in your dream, the shock would wake you, wouldn't it."

"I suppose so. As it happens, I don't see Sukenobu as much of a problem either. Though I hope you won't think me big-headed for saying that."

"You've every right to be big-headed. After all, you're a big player, aren't you?"

"Yes, but do big players suffer from anxiety neurosis?"

"Well, I don't know about that." Paprika restarted the picture.

The experimental short moved on to the next scene. It was a funeral. A photograph of a middle-aged man could be seen surrounded by flowers. A woman in mourning dress turned to face Noda's line of vision, and seemed to be pleading with him about something. The woman was young and beautiful; in a way, she resembled Paprika.

"Who's that woman?" Freeze-frame.

"The wife of one of our employees, a man called Namba. But I've never actually met her in the flesh."

"Well, does she look like someone else?"

"No one in particular. You, perhaps."

"And who's the man in the photo?"

"That's Namba."

"So Namba's dead."

"Yes, but in reality he's very much alive. I met him just this afternoon."

"Is he one of your enemies in the company?"

"Quite the opposite. He's very important to me – he manages the Development Office."

"So he's your junior?"

"Yes, but it doesn't feel like that. To me he's a colleague, a comrade in arms, an ally – someone I can talk to."

Paprika started the picture again. After showing mourners at the funeral for a few more moments, the picture suddenly broke off.

"Yes, that's when I woke up. When I saw the mourners, it came home to me that Namba really had died – in the dream, I mean. I think it was the shock that woke me."

Paprika played the same short dream back twice more.

"Fancy some coffee? We'll have it in the next room," she said as she got up, looking distinctly weary.

Noda was willing, and they moved to the living room. The bright night view of Shinjuku showed no sign of dimming, even after two in the morning.

"You seem to have a lot of residues," Paprika said as she arranged coffee cups on her glass table.

"Residues?"

"Residues from your day's activity. It's a Freudian term."

"You mean the office, Sukenobu, Namba, all that?"

Paprika poured the finest Blue Mountain coffee into Noda's cup, with the precision of a scientist transferring a solution from one flask to the other. "You said your Japanese literature teachers 'all had it in for you', didn't you."

"Did I?"

"You said it twice. But people don't usually use that phrase in that kind of situation."

"I suppose they don't. They'd normally say they were always being told off, or something like that. So it must have something to do with how I feel about Sukenobu."

"So you're saying this Sukenobu has got it in for you?"

Noda groaned as he picked up his cup. "Well, now I think about it, that's not really true either. 'Itching for a fight' might be a better phrase." The rich aroma of the coffee wafted into his nostrils. "Ah, that smells good."

Paprika said nothing but gazed out at the night sky, apparently lost in thought as she sipped her coffee.

"Could I venture my opinion as an amateur?" asked Noda.

"Go on."

"Why did I give the wrong answer to the teacher, even though I knew the right one in reality? Well, it's a strategy I sometimes use against Sukenobu at work. To deliberately let down my guard, you see, as a trap. So as well as being a 'residue', it could also stem from my superiority complex towards him."

"Was *that* what it was?!" Paprika laughed. "Is there anything else you can tell me?"

"I don't know why Namba died in the dream. And why did his wife appear, when I've never even met her?"

"An unknown woman who appears in a man's dream is what Jung calls the *anima*."

"What's that?"

"The feminine inner personality present in the subconscious of the male. And a man who appears in a woman's dream is her *animus*."

"But she looked like you."

Paprika blushed. "It was just your impression on meeting me for the first time. You imprinted that on your *anima*. It wasn't even a residue of your day!" She almost sounded angry.

"In that case," Noda said, calmly returning Paprika's glare, "if my *anima* is a representation of myself, or an idealized vision of the feminine inside me, would that dream just now express some feminine concern that Namba could die?"

"Hmm. What standing does Namba have in your company?"

"He's not popular, if that's what you mean. He's isolated, a loner. I can't decide whether the problem is his scientific aloofness or his artistic temperament. He's stubborn and won't listen to others. He understands nothing of strategy and even argues with me sometimes."

"But you feel protective towards him."

"Frankly, it's getting to be a bit of a pain. Though yes, he is a valuable person." Noda noticed how terribly tired Paprika looked. "Well, it's getting rather late, isn't it. Should we leave it there?"

"Thank you. And sorry. It's just that I've got an early start tomorrow, and there are still things I need to do."

"All right then, that's it for now," said Noda, getting up quickly. "I look forward to the next session."

"Right. I'll be in touch."

"By the way... Paprika?" Noda said as he made to leave. "That second part of the dream? Does it mean I should protect Namba more than ever, because he has so many enemies?"

Paprika opened her eyes wide and laughed. "That's maybe how Jung would have seen it! But I think something else caused your neurosis. Something to do with your school days, I'd say."

6

It was already past one in the afternoon when Atsuko finally arrived at her laboratory. She'd been up all night studying a memo of questions from the newspaper companies.

A press conference had been called for two o'clock. The memo contained a schedule of the questions to be asked; the newspaper companies always provided them in advance. Atsuko usually needed to prepare the answers beforehand, partly because Kosaku Tokita was such a blubberingly inept speaker. And since there were always bound to be some questions that weren't on the memo, Atsuko had to prepare answers for the hypothetical ones as well.

Atsuko ordered Nobue Kakimoto to make two copies of the answers and to take one each to Shima and Tokita. Then she made some coffee. She loathed press conferences. There would always be some jumped-up new science or academic correspondent who really thought he knew his stuff, but just asked the same old questions as everyone else. No matter that Atsuko had answered that very question ad nauseam in the past; they still expected her to provide a neat, easy answer every time. On this occasion, as it happened, the news that Tokita and Chiba were leading contenders for the Nobel Prize in Physiology or Medicine had started to circulate. There were bound to be a few social affairs correspondents who were itching to ask banal questions about that; it was Atsuko's job to protect her naive colleague from them.

Torataro Shima had always insisted that it was important to inform society of the Institute's achievements and enlighten the public as to the value of its research. But to Atsuko, attending a press conference simply meant being exposed to public view in a way that was barely welcome. In her view, the journalists weren't interested in noting some form of higher intelligence in the young, beautiful woman called Atsuko Chiba. They hated the idea that she was their intellectual superior, and merely seemed bent on finding something in her that would reinforce their preconceived image of Japanese femininity.

At five to two, an employee from the Secretariat came to call Atsuko. The Meeting Room reserved for the press conference was already humming with the chitter-chatter of more than two hundred journalists and photographers. The room was like a pressure cooker ready to blow.

The seating arrangement had been decided long ago by Torataro Shima. As always, Atsuko sat in the centre with Tokita to her right and Shima to her left. Behind them in the corner sat the Secretary-General Katsuragi, who acted as moderator. Once Atsuko had taken her seat, the party was complete. Some social affairs correspondents who were attending for the first time let out involuntary gasps of astonishment at her ravishing beauty, which even exceeded its reputation. Atsuko wore a navy-blue suit.

Katsuragi stood, declared the press conference open and introduced the trio. Then Shima himself stood and greeted the throng most genially. He stressed, somewhat patronizingly, that the press conference was being held at the urgent request of the media; he stopped short of mentioning that Tokita and Chiba had been shortlisted for the Nobel Prize. But no sooner had Katsuragi invited the journalists to ask questions than a man who was obviously a social affairs correspondent started grilling them on that very issue. What chance did they each have of actually winning the Prize, in terms of percentage? None of the three could find words to answer such a half-witted question. So then the journalist directed his question to Atsuko in person.

"I don't think that's a question I'm qualified to answer," she answered.

"Why is that?"

"Because I'm not qualified to answer it."

A modest round of laughter ensued. Then a science correspondent, a familiar face at the Institute, rephrased the question. He prefaced it with an apology that a social affairs correspondent who was attending his first press conference had been allowed to start proceedings with a question of the very lowest calibre. "This is a question for Doctor Tokita," he went on. "Doctor Tokita, your nomination for the Nobel Prize must of course be related to your achievement in developing PT devices. Now, I've heard it explained a number of times, but I still have a lot of trouble understanding the actual principle behind these devices. Do you think you could explain it to us once more, in words that we can actually understand?"

In fairness, the question *was* on the memo; Atsuko had no choice but to let Tokita provide the answer himself. The problem was that there were no more than three people in the whole world – including Tokita himself – who understood the principle behind the PT devices. And now Tokita, a bad speaker at the best of times, was going to explain it all in words that everyone could understand? The very thought made Atsuko squirm, and Shima must have felt the same. Nevertheless, Tokita began to reply. He normally spoke with a pronounced lisp, owing to his short tongue, but when he became agitated it developed into a veritable slobber. He always did his level best to speak intelligibly, in his own way. But it was always after the first few words that his intelligibility began to fall apart.

"Well... Um... Er... To explain it all from the beginning, er, when I was at primary school, and secondary school for that matter, I was known as a 'geek', you see, because I did nothing but play computer games, but then I gradually started programming games and messing about with semiconductors and making all kinds of things. You know. But then my late father said I should become a doctor, so I went to study psychopathology at a medical university, you follow, but even then I kept messing about with computers on the side, and apart from that I got quite interested in ECG, that's electrocardiograms, so then I thought, what if I were to put the two together, and then I suddenly hit on the idea of using fibre bundles to create a slit-no-check system for floating computer image processing, and when I did brain tests using this, all sorts of things started to appear on the images besides the brain waves—"

"Er, sorry, but that's where you always lose me," the science correspondent interjected hurriedly. "What exactly do you mean by a 'slit-no-check system', for example?"

"Ah. Yes. Well, how shall I put it. Er. A slit electron stream electro-transmission efficiency, by which I mean, the electrode in the slit through which the electrons pass, well, the ratio of the average rated current to the non-slit current injection, if we applied that directly to the fibre bundle designed to universalize the conversion code on the analogous mapping space using discrete fractal com-pression, we would no longer need a validity check, nor a slit, nor a floating core, and so—"

"Er – sorry," the science correspondent interrupted again, now growing quite impatient. "Could we possibly take these phrases one by one? First off, this 'fibre bundle' – is it the same as the ones they use in a gastrocamera? It's a bundle of fibres just like that, yes?"

Atsuko gave an involuntary sigh. It was quite a loud sigh. The journalists all turned to look at her.

"Oh. Sorry."

"The reason why Doctor Chiba sighed just now," Tokita laughed, gallantly trying to cover for his colleague, "is that I have only just started to explain the principle of PT devices, and if I were to explain all the concepts one by one, as you say, we would quite literally be here for hours! If I may just answer about the fibre bundle, though, you're quite right. Yes. So then we construct horizontal parallel buffers with these bundles of fibres, and then superimpose vertical parallel arrays over them. So then the field quite literally becomes infinite, and we no longer need to check the input data, or what have you. That means we don't need a floating core or anything like that, you see." In his own mind, Tokita felt sure he'd explained the principle in terms that any schoolboy could understand. He nodded in satisfaction at his feat. "Are you with me thus far?"

The room fell silent. None of the reporters had a single idea what he'd been talking about.

A middle-aged journalist stood up, his face contorted in an ironic smile at the sheer unintelligibility of it. "Sorry, but I'm not *with* you at all. And if *we* can't understand it, how are we to write articles that our readers will understand?"

"I see," replied Tokita, a look of discomfort on his face.

"So you see, Doctor Tokita, it's really up to you to help us understand, isn't it."

"Yes. I see."

"Doctor Chiba. Of course, you understand it all very well, don't you," the science correspondent said, now turning to Atsuko.

"Yes, I think I do."

"You think you do? What do you mean by that?"

"Most of these PT devices have only just been developed, including their components. Some of them don't even have names yet. Even the principles by which they work are new. So there are no existing scientific terms that can describe them."

"Well, that certainly is a problem." The journalist broadened his nostrils and changed his tone. "Sorry, I should have introduced myself. I'm the Senior Science Editor at the *Shinnichi*." And he paused as if to confirm the effect.

Atsuko now saw her chance for some retaliation. "And when did you start thinking *that*, exactly?"

The room erupted in laughter and the tension was dispelled. The Senior Science Editor raised his voice in irritation. "Excuse me, would you mind? I know you have your corporate secrets and all that, but I'd be grateful if you'd desist from these smokescreen tactics. They're very confusing."

"Yes, yes. Understood, understood," Shima said loudly, silencing the Senior Science Editor. "It has nothing at all to do with corporate secrets, I can assure you – Doctor Tokita has even published papers on the subject. Of course, they're all in English, so that foreign scientists can read them. Anyone who wants to use the research results is welcome to do so. I'll get these papers rewritten in simple, everyday Japanese and have them distributed to you all."

"Actually, I'd rather have heard it directly from Doctor Tokita," the science correspondent said glumly before moving on to the next question. "Incidentally, I understand that these PT devices aren't limited to accessing the subconscious of your patients. They could also be used – or misused – on ordinary citizens, for example. Did you not realize that? Of course, it would be fine if it was just for criminal investigation or the like, but what about a company trying to modify its employees' personalities? Or a government manipulating the minds of its subjects? This is a question for either Doctor Tokita or Doctor Chiba. In your own time."

Tokita hadn't fully read the model answers Atsuko had given him. Instead, he now started to regurgitate his usual grievance, like a toddler about to have a tantrum. "Why, oh why, oh why does it always have to go like this?! We're working at the forefront of science here! Why do you always have to trivialize things for the sake of the masses?!"

"What are you implying, exactly?" Atsuko interrupted quickly from the side. "That we'll just go around scanning people's minds willy-nilly? Utter nonsense. The public will of course have every right to refuse treatment. If done without permission it would be a criminal act. In any case, there are only a limited number of specialists authorized to access a patient's subconscious using the collector. The reflector can detect the user's intentions, and access may be denied if those intentions are deemed improper."

"And I've asked Doctor Tokita to ensure that all devices developed from now on are equipped with this kind of function," Shima said helpfully.

"A bit like Asimov's three laws of robotics."

No one reacted at all to Tokita's infantile muttering. The journalists had already despaired of hearing normal everyday speech from him.

"Doctor Chiba, it seems you've been collaborating with Doctor Tokita for some years now," said a bespectacled female reporter who looked about thirty. She was doing her best to conceal her burning curiosity under a contrived smile. "One thing I'd like to ask, out of interest as a woman, is whether there's been any hint of romance in the meantime?"

The journalists all grinned. Not only were they inwardly keen to mock Tokita's repulsive obesity, thereby absolving their sense of intellectual inferiority; they would also happily grasp any chance of belittling Atsuko Chiba, whose exasperating combination of beauty and genius made her a suitable target for their wrath. A scandalous affair with the unsightly Tokita would surely do the trick.

"The question received from the Press Club concerned only my involvement with Doctor Tokita's development work. So I shall answer that question." Atsuko managed to maintain her practised expression of affability. "It started when I was a student in the Medical Faculty. One day, Doctor Shima gave me the chance to collaborate with Doctor Tokita in his research. Well, I say Doctor, but he was just an assistant then."

"Doctor Chiba was already an outstanding therapist at the time," added Shima.

"Doctor Tokita's research was almost complete. I merely selected patients whose cerebral images were to be recorded. I then analysed and interpreted those images as a therapist. Sometimes we made ourselves human guinea pigs and recorded each other's cerebral images. As a result, we found that the devices developed by Doctor

Tokita could faithfully detect and record fields of consciousness. This meant that they could be applied very effectively as a means of psychotherapy."

The female reporter couldn't hold back any longer. "So if you did all that to each other, I mean peeping into each other's thoughts and that, your relationship must have been much closer than is normally the case between two professionals?"

7

"Aaaahhhh! Why is it, why oh why is it, that whenever people see an ugly man and a beautiful woman, they always start churning out all that Jean Cocteau rubbish?!" Tokita suddenly moaned aloud as he writhed in his seat. In their astonishment, the journalists all turned their attention to him. "Or was it Victor Hugo?! All my life, all my life I've had to put up with this! Even when I was a child, when I was already fat and ugly, the other children would shove me together with the prettiest girl in the class and stand around jeering. And it wasn't just me they were taunting, oh no, it was the girl too! They couldn't stand the thought that such a pretty girl was so much better then them!"

Tokita thrust out his fleshy red lips as he continued to whine like an infant. Stifled laughter started to spread among the massed ranks of journalists. It was a diabolical, insidious kind of mockery that they must all have observed, or even experienced, during their own childhoods.

"I mean, even *I* can like pretty girls, can't I? But they didn't care, oh no, they didn't care, they'd just stand around and jeer nastily, or they'd push me onto a girl and make me kiss her against my will. Whether I liked her or not, I'd always end up feeling sorry for her. But the girls all resented me for it, they hated me. So in the end I didn't want to be with other people any more and started to think of nothing but computers. Well, what else could I do?!"

Tokita's babyish wailing could almost have been an act designed to hoodwink the female reporter, but it was altogether too undignified for that. Out flowed the moans, on and on, until the journalists had simply had enough.

"All right. All right. I understand. I'm very sorry that we asked such an insensitive question." The science correspondent stood with a pained smile and bowed his head repeatedly until Tokita's whining had ceased.

The female reporter, mortified at such a put-down by a colleague, slapped the palm of her hand on the tabletop in frustration.

"Would you mind continuing?" the science correspondent entreated Atsuko. "I assume you went through a phase of trial and error before applying the devices to psychotherapy?"

"Well, first we recorded patients' dreams, purely to discover the abnormal way in which they associate *signifiant* with *signifié*. To me, for example, *you* look like a science correspondent from the *Mainichi Times*. But to a patient, you might look like a spy from some foreign country. Then the patient would always put those two concepts together as a kind of mental association – spy *equals* newspaper reporter. But this isn't like some word association game on TV, where you know the answer but it's hidden at first. The very fact that the concepts are associated is unknown to the patient. Using patients' dreams, we discover this kind of abnormal association on their behalf. In some cases, this alone has proved very useful in treating patients."

"In a single institution, twenty patients entered the recovery phase during the same period," Shima threw in with some pride. "Well, we call it the *remission* phase, but anyway. This was quite unheard of, and caused quite a stir in the psychiatric world at the time, I can tell you. Globally, that is. Perhaps some of you can remember it."

"Next, we discovered that we could access patients' dreams and treat those patients using the collector," Atsuko continued – only to be interrupted again, this time by the science correspondent.

"Sure, but as soon as it was reported in academic circles, it came out that the treatment was extremely dangerous, didn't it. Then you were forbidden to take the devices outside this Institute or use them for other purposes – weren't you?"

"That's it!" the Senior Science Editor from the *Shinnichi* suddenly exclaimed, making a crude scraping sound with his chair as he stood. "Now I remember! When the devices were banned, wasn't there a rumour that they'd been taken outside the Institute and used in experiments to treat mental illnesses other than schizophrenia?"

This new input caused quite a commotion. Some nodded. Atsuko instantly realized that the newspaper reporters had secretly been circulating such rumours for some time, but that, for whatever reason, they'd hesitated to come out with them until now.

Seeing that he'd properly set the cat among the pigeons, the Senior Science Editor now directed his chin towards Atsuko with a triumphant look of satisfaction. "Am I right? You secretly used the devices to experiment on patients other than schizophrenics outside the Institute. Experimenting on human beings." He suddenly stopped when he remembered that the devices could only be used on humans anyway; anything else would have been impossible. "Am I right or am I wrong?"

"I am aware that there were such rumours," Shima said casually. "But there was not one ounce of truth in them. Not one ounce. On the contrary, I heard that the rumours were spread by patients and their families who were already anticipating the huge benefits of the devices."

"Naturally you will deny it," said the Senior Science Editor, vexed by a lack of firm evidence with which to press his case. "It's just that there were rumours going around to that effect."

"On the subject of rumours," started a white-faced young reporter who looked like a man to be reckoned with. He even had the nerve to remain seated. "Five or six years ago, when PT devices were still banned, a certain rumour was doing the rounds. I say 'rumour' – it was more like a legend. According to this 'legend', a certain young woman would use PT devices to treat people in high positions who didn't want it known that they were suffering from mental problems. I heard the rumour again recently, so I decided to investigate it. Once the ban was lifted, people started revealing information that had been kept secret until then. All of them agreed on one thing. The main character in this legend was a young girl who went under the pseudonym of 'Paprika'. Now, this is something that I'm extremely interested to discover the truth of," he said with a meaningful look in Atsuko's direction.

"Rumours, rumours, nothing but rumours!" Shima repeatedly interrupted the journalists' claims with dismissive laughs, though his voice was beginning to falter now. Atsuko was only too aware of the heavy burden he felt, honest and well meaning as he was. He was being forced to tell untruths to cover up illegal acts committed in the past; that went against his better nature. "Rumours. No truth in them whatsoever."

"Come to think of it, I heard that rumour too," said the social affairs correspondent who'd asked the very first question. "Her name was Paprika, that's right. She called herself a 'dream detective'. She would get inside men's dreams, then engage in some kind of sex act and thereby cure them of their mental hang-ups."

"I heard it too," piped up the science correspondent. No one stood to speak any more; the place began to resemble a courtroom. "Paprika was some kind of code name. She was about eighteen, and quite a stunner, or so the story went."

"Only a moment ago, President Shima said that Doctor Chiba was already an excellent therapist when she was still a student in the Medical Facility," said the Senior Science Editor, peering diagonally across at Atsuko with a vulpine expression. "I also heard about the legend of Paprika. I'd always thought it was nothing but a fairy tale, a whimsical product of the ban on PT devices. But now I'm beginning to wonder if it really was true. Surely it can't have had anything to do with Doctor Chiba?"

"Could we have a clear answer from Doctor Chiba?" the female reporter now demanded loudly. "Would you please confirm that this young woman was not yourself?"

It was partly her anger at the female reporter's gall that made Atsuko feel the colour draining from her face. But even then, she still had confidence – just – that she could control her expression, and thereby prevent her inner turmoil from being exposed to all and sundry. "It's just as Doctor Shima said. This story of a young woman called Paprika is a complete fabrication."

"Really?" asked the female reporter. She was more than happy to follow the standard pattern of brainless questioning usually reserved for celebrity press conferences.

"There were only two people who could access the devices – me and Doctor Chiba. Honestly, I assure you. Nothing like that ever happened," Tokita said in his usual cack-handed way. "So do you want to keep asking about it? Even when no one else really knows what happened at all? How about asking the question in different words and just going round and round in circles ad infinitum? I really love that kind of argument! Come on then! Come on!" He assumed the challenging expression of a child and rolled his shoulders in excitement as he surveyed the journalists' faces.

"She was supposed to be about eighteen years old," Atsuko said with a snigger. "Five or six years ago I would have been twenty-four. And anyway, an eighteen-year-old would only just have started at university. How could she already have been a practising psychotherapist?"

"Well, of course, now that it's legal to use the devices, I guess we could overlook the fact that they were used illegally in the past," said the white-faced reporter, with disconcerting calm and an expression as inscrutable as a Noh mask. "But I think a more serious situation has arisen in this Institute recently, has it not? Being able to access a patient's dreams using PT devices is different to just observing them on a monitor, isn't it. It means actually *identifying* with the patient. So doesn't that mean the doctors themselves could become schizophrenic? In fact, I've heard that one of the therapists in this Institute has been infected with a patient's schizophrenia. Is that true?"

Atsuko was again shaken by an anger that made her vision blur. The news had obviously been leaked by Vice President Inui, or perhaps by Osanai and his gang.

"There is absolutely no truth in that either," she said. She would have to strike back and discover the source of the reporter's information. "I'm very concerned that you labour under such a misconception. Where exactly did you hear such nonsense?"

"I'm afraid I cannot reveal my source," the reporter replied defiantly, betraying no emotion. "But I repeat, I have heard that such a thing did actually happen."

Commotion descended on the room once more.

Atsuko decided to provoke her adversary. "I cannot believe that anyone in this Institute would say anything so utterly stupid. Moreover, I find it utterly incredible that someone who calls himself a journalist could swallow such nonsense from an outsider."

With the interrogator's thrust firmly turned on him, the young reporter at last showed some colour in his face. "What do you mean by that? You appear to be questioning my integrity."

"Well, I ask you!" Atsuko laughed, looking out over the roomful of journalists. "It's clearly nonsense! Can you all believe such rubbish? Infectious schizophrenia?! Whatever next!"

Several of the reporters laughed loudly. They were the ones who didn't know that people close to a schizophrenic *can* be affected by related delusions – even if not "infected".

"But I heard it from a very reliable source, one who knows everything that goes on in this Institute," the reporter shouted angrily.

"If your source 'knows everything that goes on in this Institute', it must be someone who works here."

"I didn't say that."

With the origin of the rumour gradually becoming clear, Atsuko chose to push the increasingly wretched reporter a little further.

"That's a special privilege of the press, I suppose. Claiming something to be fact without having to disclose the source."

"Now, wait a minute. I haven't claimed it to be fact. All I'm doing is checking out what I've heard."

"And now I want to check it out too. I want to know whether you heard it from the mouth of someone in this Institute or not."

"And as I've already said, I can't—"

"All right, all right!" For Torataro Shima, it was peace at any price. Now he spoke up to douse the heat of the contest, and not a moment too soon. "If I'm honest, it is possible for a therapist to be affected by a patient in certain ways. But that would only happen with an inexperienced therapist. We don't have any of those here, so it couldn't possibly happen. And the very idea that someone has been 'infected' by PT devices, well…"

"And I tell you that I have heard, from a reliable source, that that is exactly what happened!"

Just as the now crimson-faced reporter was about to kick off again, Tokita started to wail shamelessly in a manner that suggested he was sick and tired of the whole charade. "Oh for crying out loud!" he groaned. "Not this again, not *this*! Why can no one understand? This is cutting-edge science we're engaged in here! How can it possibly be understood in layman's terms? Whenever there's a problem, it's always some side issue that's nothing to do with the matter at hand! No one, not one of you, has asked about the most important thing! Even though, for me, PT devices will soon be a thing of the past! And I don't mean to sound arrogant by saying that – it's the normal speed of progress in machine technology! Why can't anyone see that?!"

As the journalists sat there in stunned silence, beaten into submission by Tokita's slobbering rant, Atsuko alone held back her anger. She was thinking of a way to flush out the traitor in the camp.

8

Atsuko removed the collector. She was already tired of wandering through the bizarre world of the schizophrenic, a sinister, metaphorical world that could have a direct impact on the subconscious of the observer. A world in which, for example, a patient's mother who was always having affairs and produced too many children appeared in the patient's dream as a dog. Atsuko discovered the link between the two when the patient dreamt of the dog cooking supper in his kitchen. But now this particular patient was well on the road to recovery. Through the glass wall, a man in his forties could be seen lying on a bed in the examination room next to Atsuko's laboratory.

"He says he often dreams of dogs talking to him outside the Inari Shrine," Nobue Kakimoto said, looking up from the reflector screen to smile at Atsuko.

"His dreams are more or less normal now, aren't they. Would you get some coffee?" Atsuko skipped back through some still images of the dream she'd just recorded. She started to write her thoughts on a memo pad as she looked across at the reflector screen. The reflector's memory device was programmed to automatically scan recorded images at intervals of one second. "All right, Nobue. You can go home now."

Nobue seemed unwilling to leave quite yet. "He's not identifying so much with other people or things now, is he," she said while pouring coffee for her superior.

"That's right." Atsuko watched the monitor as she drank the coffee. On the screen, a half-eaten grilled fish on a plate was calling out. Atsuko instantly thought of Tokita. He was quite partial to grilled fish. Suddenly, she wanted to see him. Atsuko cleared the screen.

"I'm going to Tokita's lab," she said as she got up.

Atsuko removed her lab coat to reveal the dark-blue suit she'd worn at the press conference. Now Nobue's eyes were filled with an expression of rapture. "My! Oh, my! How beautiful! How very, very beautiful you look! What have I done to deserve this?! Doctor Chiba, please! Won't you appear on television again, just for me?"

Feeling slightly embarrassed at such unfettered adoration by a member of her own sex, Atsuko hurried out into the corridor. The corridor was deserted. It was after nine o'clock.

From the corridor, Tokita's laboratory could only be reached by passing through a small anteroom occupied by his assistant, Kei Himuro. The gloomy anteroom was surrounded by shelves piled high with cases and boxes containing general purpose LSIs, custom chips sent in by manufacturers, prototype elements awaiting shipment as samples and various other components. Electronic parts and tools were scattered haphazardly all over the floor, not to mention the desks. Beneath the shelves, desks lined the walls on either side, allowing just enough room for a person to squeeze through to Tokita's laboratory. The desks were littered with naked Braun tubes and bright monitor screens displaying an array of graphs and diagrams. Himuro had been using an image scanner to input design drawings. He tensed and stood up when he saw Atsuko.

"Er, Doctor Chiba! He's in the middle of an experiment right now. I'm afraid I can't let you in."

Like Tokita, Himuro was fat, but marginally less so; when standing side by side, they resembled a pair of babushka dolls in descending order of size. Himuro, another computer geek, had taken it upon himself to act as Tokita's bodyguard, a role in which he was extremely resolute. He stood before his master's door to prevent Atsuko from getting through.

This was what always happened. But Atsuko knew how to handle him. She went close to him, so close as to frost up his glasses. "Come now," she breathed as she peered into his widening eyes. "Still so persistent? No one's going to take your precious master from you!" And she prodded the tip of his nose with her index finger.

Himuro instantly turned bright red, then cast his eyes down and started muttering indistinctly. "Well, I suppose... It's just the same old... You know, that bipolar IC... thingy... You know..." And with that he crept back to his seat.

Tokita's room was in the same state as the anteroom – only much darker, three times as large, and therefore three times as chaotic. But this was no ordinary chaos. The ends of spiral fibre bundles had been shoved into used pot noodle containers, ceramic elements torn to pieces, Braun tubes smashed. Testing monolithic semiconductor chips had been piled up inside coffee cups, while weird electronic components and tools designed by Tokita lay strewn all about. It was clearly the workplace of a genius, but then again, the endlessly bewildering appearance and juxtaposition of objects could equally have been the product of madness. Beads of perspiration glistened on Tokita's brow as he fabricated some infinitesimal thing using a compact laser processor. His face was bathed in the light emanating from countless display screens that projected design drawings, images and graphs in full colour, as well as CAD line drawings and fractal graphics in high definition mode.

As Atsuko walked in, Tokita threw his tools down onto the desk. The abruptness of his reaction made Atsuko regret having interrupted him.

"Oh. Hi there," said Tokita.

"Is it OK?"

"It's fine. I was just about to open the window anyway."

Tokita got up dozily, opened the thick curtain and pushed the double-leafed windows open. His research lab offered the same view as Atsuko's over the spacious gardens of the Institute, as well as the illuminated office buildings in the centre of the metropolis beyond. An evening breeze carried the smell of freshly cut grass into the room.

"I just came to thank you," Atsuko said, walking towards Tokita's back as he stood by the window.

"Thank me? For what?" Easily embarrassed at the best of times, Tokita did not turn to face her, but continued to stare into the distance.

"Hey, why don't you look at me? I won't bite! It's so dark in here you won't even see my face!" Atsuko laughed.

"True. True." Tokita slowly turned round, like a good boy. His face was barely visible in the gloom.

"Now I'll tell you," said Atsuko. "It's thanks to your fine performance today that we got through the press conference in one piece. I just wanted to thank you."

"Performance? Oh. That childish nonsense. I'm sorry, I can't help it." He turned to look outside again.

"Well, I'm glad you can't help it. It was really a great performance. Oh, come on! Why don't you just face this way?"

"Because I can see how beautiful you are, even in this darkness. And when it's dark, your beauty turns into something devilish. It scares me."

Atsuko went to embrace Tokita's massive back from behind, pressing her cheek into his shoulder. "I'll say it again. Thank you. If they'd kept questioning me like that, I would soon have been driven into a corner. Then they would all have believed that the rumours were true."

"That reminds me," Tokita said carefully after a short silence. "Who could it have been? Who leaked the story about Tsumura to the press?"

"Well, not Tsumura himself, that's for sure. How's he doing, by the way?"

"I heard he'd been sent home to rest."

Tsumura occupied one of the Institute's apartments, in the same building as Atsuko and Tokita. The building was out of bounds to unauthorized personnel and was under constant surveillance. And anyway, even if someone were to see Tsumura, they would discover nothing, as his appearance was perfectly normal.

57

"Tsumura was one of our best therapists. It doesn't make sense," said Atsuko.

"Did he have some kind of trauma?"

"Well, he's only human. We all have our psychological scars. That's why I suspect something untoward here. Actually, that's partly what I came to ask you about. Can you identify Tsumura's trauma from the collector he was using?"

"Sure. Easy. All you have to do is play back the recording of the patient's dream he was accessing."

"I thought so. But on the other hand, what if someone had done it deliberately while he was using the collector? I mean, fed his mind with images that spark his trauma, without him knowing it, as if they were part of a schizophrenic patient's dream?"

"They could do that. They'd just have to devise a program that let them search for some suitably intense images from the patient's dream, then project them intermittently into the collector Tsumura was using, below the threshold of consciousness. Easy."

"Everything's easy with you, isn't it!" Atsuko couldn't help but laugh. "But what I want to know is whether there's anyone in the Institute who can do that?"

"Well, if he could get hold of the images, my man Himuro could manage it. He could do the programming, no sweat. I wonder if someone's been leaning on him. I'll just ask him, shall I?"

Tokita started towards the door. "No – wait!" said Atsuko, quickly barring his path. "We need to keep this quiet, don't you see?"

"Ah. Really. All right, I'll look into it later. Everything he does is recorded in a log."

"Thanks."

"But anyway, what would be the point of doing that to Tsumura? Who would stand to gain from it?"

"Someone, I'm sure. There's someone who'd stand to gain if the Institute's reputation took a nosedive."

"And who would that be?"

"That's what I'm trying to find out."

"Exciting! So now you're a real detective?!"

"Silly!" Atsuko laughed again.

"But you know, on that subject, it'll be a lot easier if you use the unit I've just developed. Daedalus plus the collector." Daedalus was basically the gorgon without cables. Tokita had invented the next generation of devices before they could even be tested.

Atsuko stood open-mouthed. "What?" she said at length. "What did you invent that for? What will you do with it?"

"I thought it was your job to think of that. Look what we can do already! If it's used properly, it'll improve the treatment, won't it?"

"Just a minute. That's way too dangerous. It's too much."

"But see, it's been my ambition all along! To go into each other's dreams, you know…"

Atsuko's head started to reel. "A *unit*, you said? How big is it, then?"

"That's the point." Atsuko's surprise seemed to suddenly excite Tokita. "It's about the same size as a calculator. Once I've finalized the principle, I'll be able to make it infinitely compact. The other day I was hacking into computers to see what other people had invented, when I accidentally accessed the biology department of some university. There I pocketed some samples that were being researched by some bloke doing bionics. I was amazed to see all that stuff, so I applied it to make a basic element that can process practically anything! If we used it for our devices, we could make them as small as we liked!"

"By which I suppose you mean biological elements? The ones that permit self-assembly of proteins? And how much smaller are they than the silicon chips currently being used?"

"Well, they're a hundred ångström each, so, er, their memory capacity would be ten million times that of a silicon chip. I should think."

Atsuko gazed at Tokita. "You're a genius. That's what you are. Think of the stir this'll cause when it's announced!"

Bashful as ever, Tokita looked out at the gardens once more. "Actually, I hope it won't be announced. I mean, of course I'm glad you're surprised, but I'm not interested in what the rest of the world thinks. Some people yack on about nothing else once their work has been recognized. And usually that's the end of the road for them."

Atsuko went to hug Tokita from behind again. "That's exactly what a genius would say."

They remained in that pose for some time, until Atsuko could feel Tokita's body stiffen with tension through her breasts. He obviously wanted to say something but couldn't find the words to express it.

"What is it?" asked Atsuko.

"Well... You remember when I was just an assistant, when we were developing these things, and you came into my dream? And I thought, well, it's just a dream after all, so I could easily, you know, make love to you?"

Atsuko laughed. "I remember. But you only thought it, didn't you."

"I've often had that dream since then."

"And do you make love to me every time?"

"I can't. Even though I know it's a dream, I just can't. What's it called? That kind of resistance. 'Reason within a dream', wasn't it?"

"No. 'Reason within a dream' means thinking you can do something just because it's a dream. The inhibition that prevents you from doing it is what I call '*dreason*' – dream reason."

"Do you think it's because I love you?"

Atsuko embraced Tokita so firmly that her arms sank into the soft flesh of his belly. "Yes. So why don't you just come out and say it? Say you love me!"

"I can't. Whenever I try, all I can think of is Beauty and the Beast. Like earlier today."

"Well, we know each other's feelings. We don't have to say

anything. But if we did say it, would it have to come from me? It could, if you liked. On a rational level I want to deny you, despise you for your obesity, your lack of self-control. And your face is no oil painting. I often think that, if we were to marry, the incongruity of our looks would be just too awful. But I love you so much I can't help it. You know that, don't you?"

As Atsuko spoke, Tokita continued to moan feebly as if he were about to cry. Now, at last, he slowly turned to face her. "I know. But it's the first time you've said it."

Atsuko grasped his cheeks with both hands and brought her face close to his. Tokita timidly put his hands around her waist. And they kissed. Those thick lips of his, always glistening, always moist with dribble like those of a small child, yielded so softly to hers.

Tokita pulled himself away and turned to look out of the window once more, almost apologetically this time. "It's only because it's dark, isn't it. You could never have kissed me otherwise."

9

Tatsuo Noda managed to extricate himself from the party and find the toilet, where he splashed his face with cold water from the tap. That made him feel slightly better, but did nothing to improve the pallor of his face in the mirror.

The party was meant to mark the appointment of a new CEO by one of the company's parts manufacturers. Though held in a top-class hotel in the centre of Tokyo, it was not a particularly important event; Noda, together with his President and Sukenobu, the Managing Director for Sales, had planned to make a brief appearance and then leave. But many of their counterparts from the industry were also present, and the President had been pulled this way and that by people needing a moment of his time. As a result, neither Noda nor Sukenobu had been able to get away as planned. There were people they hadn't met in a while; there were even some that Noda needed to talk to.

It was just at this time that Noda had started to feel anxious. He'd started to imagine what would happen if he had an attack at the party, a gathering of all the main players in his trade. Suddenly a chill had gone down his spine and he'd broken out in a sweat. If he'd stayed where he was, he would definitely have had an attack. And with that certain knowledge in mind, he'd managed to pull himself away.

He hadn't suffered any further attacks since the session with Paprika. But a single treatment was never going to cure anxiety neurosis altogether. The awful knowledge that an attack could occur at any time – naturally, choosing the most inopportune time and place, like tonight – remained the same as ever. He'd already finished the anxiolytics Paprika had given him.

Noda decided not to return to the party venue. Instead, he made his way to the lobby. There, he announced his imminent departure to the reception desk staff, and graciously accepted his paper bag containing the customary party gift. Then he went to sit on a black leather sofa offering a view of the entrance to the party venue. There he rested while waiting for the President and Sukenobu to emerge. The lobby was well ventilated. Noda was feeling better already.

The President appeared, released at last by his petitioners. "Where's Sukenobu?" he asked.

"I saw him just now… He was nabbed by the President of Aoyama Seiki… Getting an earful of something or other…"

The President sat in the armchair opposite Noda. He was the second President in the company's history, and fifteen years older than Noda. But his healthy complexion gave him a rather youthful look.

"Now, what was his name? That Managing Director of Teisan."

"Segawa?"

"That's it. Segawa." The President smiled. "He was here, wasn't he."

"Yes. He was here."

The President seemed only too aware that Segawa was the chief opponent of the zero-emissions vehicle.

Segawa, fat and bull-necked, emerged from the party in conversation with Sukenobu. Sukenobu took his party gift. Segawa did not; that meant he was staying. Noda had heard that he was always one of the last to leave any party.

Sukenobu looked a little flustered when he saw Noda. The President didn't notice the pair, as he sat with his back to them. Not realizing who was sitting opposite Noda, Segawa moved towards him with a leer, fully intent on making his customary snide remark.

"Well hello there, Noda. Haven't seen you at the usual place recently? Kurokawa misses you so badly!" Kurokawa was a Ministry official.

The President turned to look. Segawa was taken aback. "Oh! Hello, Mr President. Leaving so soon? Really. Well, well."

Smiling inscrutably, the President watched Segawa walk off towards the toilet.

Sukenobu's head glistened with perspiration as he eased himself into an armchair. "Er, sorry to have kept you waiting," he said to Noda. "That man just now, what was his name, yes, Segawa, you seem to know him quite well?"

Noda gave a wry smile. *That's rich, when you've only just been talking to him yourself!* Sukenobu seemed unduly concerned that the President might have noticed him coming out of the party venue with the senior executive of a rival company. A petty concern, really, but typical of Sukenobu. The President also smiled wryly.

The three eventually agreed to have one last drink in one of the hotel's quieter bars before going home. They went down to an exclusive bar in the basement; Sukenobu was a member.

Noda, Sukenobu and the President sat and talked in the far corner of the bar, which was otherwise empty. First they discussed the plans for marketing the zero-emissions vehicle. Even Sukenobu was working on that now.

Suddenly, Sukenobu started to complain about Namba. He'd been subjected to another of Namba's selfish rants that afternoon, he said. But while he complained about Namba's infantile behaviour, it was also a roundabout dig at Noda for doing nothing about it. Noda just let Sukenobu have his say. He made no attempt at all to defend either Namba or himself. If he had done, he would certainly have fallen into Sukenobu's trap. Inwardly, Noda was laughing. This was the very situation where his skill would come to the fore – his skill in taking his opponent by surprise.

The President didn't exactly spring to Namba's defence either, but merely punctuated Sukenobu's complaints with the occasional "That's too bad". Of course, Sukenobu's strategy was based on the knowledge that even the President had started to dislike Namba.

Noda himself had had yet another argument with Namba that very day. Noda had suggested a minor compromise as a way of avoiding a larger one. Namba had rejected it, though well aware of the reasoning. The only possible explanation was that Namba had deliberately wanted to pick a quarrel. In the end, Noda felt utterly exasperated, as they just seemed to be arguing for argument's sake. He realized he'd been indulging Namba too much. In fact, Namba now seemed to be testing him, to see how far his insubordination would be tolerated.

Despite all this, Noda still refrained from adding his weight to the attack on Namba. In his view, a superior who criticized a subordinate behind his back was a man of questionable integrity. In any case, a superior had the power to make or break a subordinate's career; if there were accusations to be made, they should be made to the man's face.

"By the way, Mr President, how about young Kinichi as Manager of the Development Office?" Noda said, taking Sukenobu completely by surprise. Kinichi was the President's nephew. He'd graduated from the engineering faculty of a state university, but had worked in General Affairs since joining the company.

The President could barely conceal his delight. His nephew had been eyeing the post of Development Office Manager for some time, but Namba's presence had made it impossible.

"Oh, yes! That's right!" Sukenobu exclaimed loudly. Though momentarily thrown by Noda's suggestion, he now cast daggers at Noda, as if to accuse him of currying favour. "I'd forgotten about Kinichi." He suddenly seemed to realize how contrived his statement had sounded, and now tried to justify himself: "Of course, that doesn't mean I hadn't been thinking about Kinichi…"

In reality, of course, the President's nephew had been the furthest thing from his mind; he had never for a moment imagined that Noda would suggest him for the post.

"Nevertheless, Namba has really done very well, hasn't he," the President said in apparent modesty. Since the two directors had finally managed to agree on something, he seemed happy just to let them think it out from now on. He looked quite satisfied.

"Well, anyway, we'll talk about it some other day," Sukenobu said with a meaningful nod towards Noda.

Noda thought about Namba on his way home in the chauffeured limousine. Namba certainly had talent, but in the final analysis he was not suited to management. Was the man aware of that himself? Probably not. After all, he probably thought he could one day become President.

Noda realized that he had absolutely no wish to protect Namba, in contrast to his own analysis of the dream in Paprika's apartment. It had been bound to happen sooner or later, but he'd inadvertently used Namba to curry favour. It was now certain that he would ask him to step down as Manager of the Development Office. He didn't feel even slightly guilty about that, as he could happily explain that Namba's downfall was his own doing. After all, Noda had frequently made far more cold-hearted decisions during his time.

Namba was a proud man, not the kind to start yelling and screaming when transferred to another post. Nor should he become too despondent, if his ego really was that strong. Noda turned his thoughts to Sukenobu. Naturally, *his* take on things was that he'd been robbed of a trophy, the kudos of being first to recommend the President's nephew as Manager of the Development Office. So what would he do next? Noda remembered the meaningful look Sukenobu had given him at the end. Perhaps he was already planning something. He probably was, knowing him.

But what was this? Noda had just acknowledged that he felt no guilt towards Namba. So why the sudden feeling of anxiety? He'd been thinking about Sukenobu, admittedly, but he wouldn't normally feel anything like anxiety about his machinations. He'd never attached much significance to them before. As if to prove the point, Noda had never once felt the slightest concern about suffering an attack while he was talking to Sukenobu. So why this attack, now?

Noda started to perspire. His heartbeat quickened. He desperately tried to allay his fears, persuade, convince himself that it was just another panic attack. It would surely pass, in time. But reasoning had no effect. Above all, he felt a searing pain that made him think he was dying. That was enough to destroy all reason. He didn't exactly feel confident about the state of his heart. He might even suffer a stroke. He might die here in the company's hired limousine. The very thought struck Noda with intense fear. The scenery along the route home and the lights in the office buildings had become such a familiar sight that they normally filled him with ennui. But now they suddenly seemed like an old friend, dear and irreplaceable; after all, he might be seeing them for the last time. At the same time, it galled him to think that those sights would continue to exist as if nothing had happened, even after his death. He started to wax philosophical about the unfairness, the senselessness of death. It was then that he really began to panic. He couldn't breathe. It was too late to go to Paprika's apartment. The limousine was pulling up in front of his house.

With the greatest difficulty, Noda summoned up the energy to speak to the driver. "I don't... feel... so well," he managed to say. "Would you... call... one of... my family?"

"Certainly sir," the driver replied, tensing as he noted the tone of panic in Noda's voice.

"You must... tell... no one...." Noda felt that if he kept talking, he might be able to distract his mind from his anxiety. "Please... tell no one..."

"Yes, sir. I understand."

Until about ten years earlier, the part of Tokyo where Noda lived had been a high-class residential area. Now, his house was hemmed in by apartment buildings; now, ironically, a detached house of only modest proportions was seen as a sign of great social prestige in this area. The chauffeur got out and alerted Noda's family via the front-door intercom. Noda's wife Ito and his son Torao immediately came rushing out, ashen-faced.

"What on earth's the matter?" shrieked his wife. Slinging a shoulder under each of Noda's arms, Torao and the chauffeur helped him into the reception room next to the front hallway. Noda was unable to speak; the most he could manage was to keep breathing. Still his wife continued to question him.

"Can't you speak? What is it? Can't you breathe? You can't breathe, is that it?"

Torao loosened Noda's necktie as he lay sprawled on the sofa.

"I'll call Doctor Kuroi right away," said Noda's wife.

Noda simply had to speak out now. Not only was Kuroi openly envious of Noda's material opulence, but he was also a prattler. The truth would be sure to leak out.

"No... not Kuroi..."

"What?! But look at you!"

"I'm not... ill... It's... something else..."

"What then?"

"Neuro... neurosis..."

"You mean... you mean mental illness?!" Noda's wife had been bending over him, wiping the sweat off his brow, but now she stiffened and took a step back. "Why haven't you told us before?!"

Noda's son Tarao had been trying to persuade the chauffeur to stay behind a little longer. He turned to his father. "What do you want us to do then?"

Noda took a card out of his breast pocket. He'd put it there in readiness for this very eventuality. The card gave an "Emergency Contact Number"; it was Paprika's.

"You've even got an emergency contact number!" wailed the wife, now in tears.

Torao moved to a corner of the room to make the call. After giving directions to the house, he returned to his father. "It was a woman who answered. She said she'd arrange it right away."

"*Arrange it right away*"?! So it couldn't have been Paprika who'd answered the phone – could it? And did that mean the apartment wasn't Paprika's either? Noda's chest heaved violently as he considered the implications.

The chauffeur left the room, causing Noda to raise his voice once more. "Pay the... driver... pay the driver..."

"What's that? The driver? He's already gone, dear. Don't worry. The company always pays!"

"No... To... keep him... quiet..."

"I understand. Leave it to me," said Torao, following the driver out.

Paprika's taxi pulled up an hour later. Noda's attack had already subsided.

10

Noda was standing alone on a deserted country road. He seemed very familiar with his surroundings; it must have been a scene from his childhood home in the country. From the far end of the road, someone was riding towards him on a red bicycle. Noda began to feel anxious. Before Noda could deny the existence of the red bicycle or the person riding on it, Paprika entered his dream.

"Who is it?" she asked.

"Don't you know, Mari?" Noda replied in a boy's voice. "It's Sukenobu!"

Noda seemed to have mistaken Paprika for his childhood sweetheart Mari.

The person on the bike certainly looked like Sukenobu, as had the old literature teacher in the previous dream. But it couldn't have been Sukenobu riding towards Noda on that country road. He was merely a mask, a substitute for one of Noda's boyhood friends. One that Mari must also have known well.

"No, it's not Sukenobu!" Paprika said in the voice of a child. Noda started to feel agitated. "Look closer!" Paprika shouted, but it was too late. Noda had already changed the setting of his dream.

He had entered his final REM sleep in the morning hours. Paprika had sat with him all night trying to unravel the darkest secrets of his psyche.

When the call from the Noda household came through, Atsuko had only just returned from the Institute. She was tired, but agreed to go to Noda's house right away. Of course, she needed time to change into Paprika; she had to alter her hairstyle, change her make-up and, most troublesome of all, attach freckles under her eyes. They had to be positioned one by one with tweezers, stuck fast to ensure they wouldn't come off when she washed her face. These changes altered her appearance completely and made her look younger. At the same time, they gave Atsuko an opportunity to prepare herself mentally for the transformation into Paprika.

Atsuko had to be careful when leaving the apartment building. Ever since the press conference, a number of journalists had started to suspect that Paprika was in fact Atsuko Chiba. As a leading candidate for the Nobel Prize, Atsuko found herself caught in the media spotlight, though few suspected that she was still secretly working as a "dream detective". Caution was essential, nonetheless, as Atsuko had no way of knowing who was watching her, or from where.

Now metamorphosed into Paprika, Atsuko had left the apartment building through the garage door. She couldn't risk using her own car, so had decided to hail a taxi on the street.

On returning to the building later with Tatsuo Noda, she had come in through the back entrance using her security code and fingerprint. The caretaker who kept watch over the lobby knew Atsuko and had a good understanding of her relationship with Paprika. But if any newspaper journalists or media people had been lying in wait, they might even have inquired into the identity of Noda himself. That would certainly have been counter-productive.

After entering the apartment, Atsuko had first examined Noda, attached the gorgon to his head and waited for him to fall asleep. Then she'd programmed the PT devices to wake her later, and with that had entered a deep sleep. At five in the morning she'd been awoken by a barely detectable, momentary charge of static electricity. She had immediately put the collector on her head and entered Noda's dream.

Now Noda was walking along a beach at night. A bizarrely shaped speedboat was racing over the water.

"Get down, ******!"

Noda used some foreign-sounding name to call out to Paprika, who had just entered his dream and was holding his hand.

Desperate to avoid being spotted by the speedboat, he then threw himself onto the sand.

"What *is* that?!" asked Paprika.

"*****!" Noda replied with a word that even he didn't understand.

In her half-sleeping, half-waking state, Paprika was unable to distinguish the field of vision in Noda's dream from that on the monitor screen she was watching. In both, Noda seemed to equate her with his childhood friend Mari, now transformed into an adult, a preposterously tall foreign actress wearing a wetsuit. Paprika was not in the habit of watching such things, but even she recognized it as a scene from a Bond film.

Now the two set off on an insanely fantastic adventure. First they jumped into a river that continued from the sea, then headed off upstream, sometimes gliding underwater, sometimes bobbing on the surface. Something that could have been a boat, or possibly a dragon, started to approach them from further upstream. It projected beams of light from searchlights resembling eyeballs, and spewed flames from its mouth. Noda and Paprika had no choice but to return fire with their submachine guns.

"What ridiculous dreams you have!"

Appalled at the realization that she'd been completely transformed into Ursula Andress, Paprika turned her attention to Noda's thought patterns. He was enjoying this dream.

Next, Namba, the character whose death had been mourned in Noda's earlier dream, thrust his upper torso from the head of the boat-beast and started firing wildly towards them with his own submachine gun. Namba was Noda's junior, the maverick Manager of the Development Office; if anything, Noda should have been protecting him. But now they were engaged in a battle that felt more like a war game. Noda showed not the slightest concern that he might kill Namba, nor any fear that he could himself be killed. Perhaps Noda enjoyed having arguments with Namba.

"What film was this?" asked Paprika.

Paprika's question made Noda vaguely aware that it was only a dream. He started acting absurdly and yelling incomprehensible phrases as he crawled out of the river.

They stood on the bank of a small river next to a broad road. Beyond the river, farm fields stretched endlessly towards a range of mountains in the distance. A small number of rustic shops lined the road. The pair were standing behind one of them, an old tobacco store. Noda seemed to feel a strong anxiety about being there. Paprika followed him round to the front of the tobacco store, where there was a bus-stop sign.

"You used to catch the bus from here, didn't you," said Paprika. To Noda, she now appeared as the pretty, freckled Paprika.

"Yes. The bus to... junior high school..."

"In that case..." In her half-sleeping state, even Paprika had difficulty finding the right words.

Paprika wanted to go back behind the old tobacco store, as Noda seemed to have some kind of complex about it. But by now he'd already arrived in his old junior high classroom, the same one as in the previous dream. Standing on the teacher's podium this time was a thickset, bull-necked man. He appeared to be teaching maths.

"Who's that?" asked Paprika as she took her seat next to Noda.

"Segawa..."

As Paprika recalled, Segawa was a senior executive of one of Noda's rivals. He had appeared as Noda's bear-faced classmate in the previous dream.

"Wasn't he... a bear?"

"No... That's ********..."

The faces of Noda's classmates were blurred and difficult to tell apart.

Segawa now started spouting nonsense while madly scribbling numbers on the blackboard. "The sum of n non-negative integers that start from 1 in arithmetical progression haven't seen you at the usual place recently, and therefore the sum of odd numbers is $1 + 2 + 3 + \ldots\ldots + n =$ misses you so badly! And this means that, Oh! Hello, Mr President. Leaving so soon?"

The teacher must also have been someone else, hiding behind the mask of Segawa. Paprika decided to focus on Noda's emotions towards Segawa.

She stood up and started shouting. "Don't just sit there! Go and give him one!"

"Right!" Noda stood up.

On the podium, Segawa showed an expression of fear, whereupon his face changed. He now looked like an old man. The classroom had changed to what looked like a company meeting room.

The old man seemed to have been talking for some time. "... and that kind of thing just will not do. Office politics and other ******* simply cannot be tolerated. What if there were victims..."

"Who's he?"

Now completely unaware that he was dreaming, Noda remained transfixed with terror at the sight of the old man.

"*QUI EST-IL?*" Paprika said again in her best schoolgirl French.

"*IL EST...*" Noda started, but his schoolboy French failed him. Instead, he just muttered, "But he's dead... he's dead..."

According to Noda's *signifiant*, the old man who was so sternly criticizing office politics was the former President of his company.

"And, CUT!" a voice suddenly called. The meeting was being filmed as a scene in a movie. A man unknown to Paprika was the director. The cameraman was Namba. The male actors in the meeting room, their faces unclear, all now relaxed and came out of character. The room was filled with commotion and chatter. The set was a lavish banqueting room that could have been a scene from a film by Visconti, say. Judging by the scarcity of women and the way the guests were dressed, it was obviously a company party.

Baseball cap, sunglasses, moustache. He was every bit a film director, a stereotypical caricature of a film director. But he lacked the comical touch of parody. Paprika intuitively felt that this was a "shadow", one of Jung's archetypes. It was without a doubt the "potential self" of Noda, as the person who was having the dream. The film director must have been Noda himself; he had probably dreamt of being a film director when he was a boy.

"Did you want to be a film director?" asked Paprika, hoping to confirm her theory. The viewpoint of the dream instantly changed. Now it was seen through the director's eyes. Noda, the director, yelled at Paprika.

"Come on, it's ********! Ready! And—"

But before he could say "Action", Paprika yelled back at him. "Who's the cameraman?!" It could not have been Namba.

This appeared to come as a shock. Just as he was mouthing "********", Noda woke up. Paprika may have failed as a dream detective, but felt instinctively that she'd come close to the heart of the matter.

"Sorry. I didn't mean to wake you."

Noda was lying on his side and staring vacantly at Paprika.

"What do you want to do? Can you get back to sleep?" she asked.

"Ah, Paprika," Noda said in unconcealed admiration. "You appeared in my dream, didn't you. That was wonderful. Just wonderful."

It's therapy, thought Paprika. *You're not supposed to enjoy it.* "Well, all right. You just stay as you are and we'll have a look at it, OK?"

"OK." Noda's speech was unclear, as if he was still in his dream.

Paprika decided to go through the dream strictly according to theory. "You were the director, weren't you."

Noda looked embarrassed. "Well, it was nothing really. Just a childhood ambition – we all have them!"

Paprika decided not to mention Namba, but skipped back from the still picture on the screen to the previous scene. "This first President, did he value you highly?"

"Well... yes, I suppose he did. It must be about six years since he died. But you know, he wasn't really the type to gather all the employees and lecture them like that..."

"You respected him?"

"Well, yes. I wish I could have learnt a lot more from him. He despised internal politics, and quite rightly so."

"Aah. The Wise Old Man."

"Pardon?"

"One of Jung's archetypes. The Wise Old Man. An old man in a dream is someone who teaches us how to act appropriately. It's supposed to be a personification of the unconscious wisdom inside us."

"So he's telling me that internal politics aren't good?"

"No, it's something else. He mentioned victims, didn't he?"

"That's right." Noda's expression changed to a grimace as he tried to remember something. "But I don't understand what he meant."

Back-skip. "What about Segawa's nonsensical maths lesson?"

"Yes. I met Segawa last night, at the party," Noda laughed. "A residue of my day, I suppose?"

"Could be, but why maths?"

"Well, he is a very calculating individual..."

"Does he look like your old maths teacher?"

"No."

"So who is this then, really? Try to think of someone from your school days. Someone who was good at maths and looked like a bear?!"

"Well, there was one boy called Takao. He was sickeningly good at maths, and he was also quite thickset. But I hardly had anything to do with him."

If he was nothing more than a classmate of Noda's, this Takao should have appeared as himself in Noda's dream. But he was being camouflaged as Segawa; he had to be someone Noda didn't want to remember.

Back-skip. "And the scene before that was the old tobacco store."

"Ah. By the bus stop. It was about twelve minutes on foot from where I lived. Or thirteen. About that." Noda had suddenly found his tongue. It was almost as if he were trying to hide something.

"So we're behind this old tobacco store. By the stream. Did something happen there?"

Noda groaned. "Aha. That's where my classmates used to have fights."

"Who had fights there? Was it this Takao?"

"Yes. Takao had fights there too."

"And did you?"

"No. I never had fights." Beads of sweat appeared on Noda's brow.

11

"It must be painful for you," said Paprika. She was being careful not to push him too hard; if she did, his defence mechanisms might overreact and the treatment would then be delayed.

The vacant lot behind the old tobacco store had evoked a strong sense of anxiety in Noda. If Paprika hadn't been there with him, Noda would have woken and suppressed it, thereby wiping the scene from his memory.

"Look, your face is covered in sweat."

"It's not just my face," Noda said in embarrassment. "I'm sorry, but your sheets are soaking."

"Never mind. Want to have a shower?"

"Yes, maybe I will." Noda started to get up, then hesitated. After all, this was a young woman's apartment, not a hospital. "But no, it wouldn't be right…"

"Not that again!" Paprika said with a sardonic smile. "Always so considerate. A proper gentleman."

Paprika changed the sheets, then threw some breakfast together while Noda took his shower. Bacon and eggs, toast and coffee. She would have made a salad, but had run out of vegetables. So she opened a can of asparagus instead. Paprika was quite looking forward to having breakfast with Noda; she even started singing to herself. The song was *P.S. I Love You*. She'd started to like Noda's personality. She would probably get to like him even more as the treatment progressed.

"Let's eat here while we continue," Paprika said as Noda re-emerged in a bathrobe.

Gazing through the window of Paprika's living room, Noda gasped at the sight of the metropolis bathed in early morning sunlight. "Look at that. How utterly beautiful." He wondered again whether this was really where Paprika lived, but kept his question to himself.

"We're facing west," said Paprika. "Means the living room doesn't get any sun in the morning. Too bad."

Noda buttoned his shirt and sat opposite Paprika. This was just what he would have for breakfast at home, he commented. *So his wife doesn't make salad either*, thought Paprika.

"Do you remember our battle?" Paprika said with a little giggle.

"You mean the Bond film? Yes, I remember." Noda shifted bashfully in his seat. "It was a scene from *Doctor No*. The very first Bond film."

"When did you see it?"

"Well… That would have been when I was at junior high. I went to town to see it on my own. Liked it so much I saw it twice. Nearly missed the bus home."

Noda spoke at some length about his childhood home. He'd been brought up in a farming village near the mountains in Yamanashi Prefecture. He came from a respected family; his father was a doctor.

Paprika changed the subject back to the Bond film. "Namba was in it too, wasn't he."

"Yes, he was the enemy. Ha! Just a 'residue of my day', I suppose."

Paprika smiled wryly. Perhaps she shouldn't have taught him that phrase. She wouldn't be able to analyse anything if he was going to laugh it all off as a "residue of his day".

"But before that, Mari appeared, didn't she. Was that you as well?" asked Noda.

"Yep. Remember the red bicycle?"

"Vividly. The colour was so vivid."

"Maybe we should make the reflector show colours after all. If I'd just been watching the monitor, I wouldn't have known it was red at all."

"That's right. Mind if I have some more coffee?"

"Help yourself. Sukenobu was on the bike, wasn't he. Do you remember anyone at your school who rode a red bike?"

Noda straightened his back and stared out at the Shinjuku skyscrapers. "Yes! I remember now. There was a kid who never took the bus but always rode to school on a red bicycle. He was in my class. Now, what was his name. Akishige. That's right, it was Akishige."

"Were you friends?"

"Certainly not! He was the class bully. Leader of the pack. A nasty piece of work."

"That must be why you identify him with Sukenobu. You remember the previous dream, when he was your teacher? You said he 'had it in for you', didn't you."

Noda looked hard at Paprika. "Ah, I see. So that's how you analyse dreams."

"Well spotted."

"And just now you said Segawa was Takao."

"Correct."

"And therefore Namba isn't Namba, but someone else."

"Got to be."

Noda thought hard. "But who?"

"Was Takao bullied by this Akishige?"

"No. He was too clever for that. He was good at maths, which would normally have made him a prime target for Akishige. But he did a deal with Akishige and became his crony instead."

"Were you bullied?"

"Yes. But not that badly, not that I remember. Or was I?…" Noda looked distinctly uneasy. Beads of perspiration again began to glisten on his brow.

"When I analysed your last dream, I asked if Sukenobu also 'had it in for you'. You said 'itching for a fight' might be a better phrase. Did you have fights with this Akishige?"

"No. I don't remember that either. But wait… Maybe I did…" Noda's voice was starting to sound gravelly.

"Well, don't force yourself. You'll only invent a false memory. But never mind, I reckon we're getting closer now. More toast? This Fauchon jam's good, isn't it."

"No thanks. That's enough for me."

"I wonder when you'll be able to stay over again?"

Disarmed by the bluntness of the question, Noda couldn't help but show his delight. "What? Well, whenever you like. Tonight, say."

"Won't your wife mind?"

"I'll call her from work. After all, it's my treatment. How could she mind?"

"Cool. Come again tonight," Paprika said with some enthusiasm. "I think you're about to remember something, some old trauma. A mental scar, what we call a psychological trauma. But you're suppressing it very strongly. There's a battle going on inside your head. So then your anxiety builds up, and that could cause another attack. I think you're on the verge of remembering. Once you remember what it was, the attacks will stop. And anyway, you're used to seeing me as a dream detective now. If I enter your dreams again soon, say tonight, you won't be surprised to see me any more."

"Do you think so?" Noda's eyes were gleaming. "I'd certainly enjoy that."

"You'll enjoy it even more when you know you're dreaming. Like I do when I get into your dreams."

"So we'll be together again? In our dreams?"

"Yes."

"Can't wait!" Noda said, stirring in anticipation, then repeated: "Can't wait. Is it always like this, when your patients get used to your methods?"

"Yes, the strong-willed ones, when the condition is only mild. Then again, my patients were always strong-willed, and their condition was always mild…"

"You know, I was expecting the treatment to be a lot more taxing," Noda said, staring at Paprika. "Shima must be green with envy. I bet none of your patients can ever forget you."

"I wouldn't know about that. I have a policy of not seeing them after the treatment's over."

Noda looked seriously disappointed. "What, because they're all so-called celebrities?"

"Well, they don't want it known they've been seeing a shrink, anyway."

"But we can meet just once, can't we, to celebrate my recovery? After all, you promised. When we were in Radio Club, you promised you'd let me treat you."

"Did I?"

"You did," Noda said most earnestly.

Resisting the urge to laugh, Paprika got up and went over to the medicine cabinet. "You've run out, haven't you? I'll just give you enough for today." *One more day should do it*, she thought. She had confidence in the next night's session.

"By the way, what about that girl Mari? Were you friends?" Paprika said as Noda was preparing to leave. She'd remembered that she hadn't asked anything about the girl.

"Mari?" Noda looked off into the distance with a wistful eye.

"She lived in the next village. She was really pretty, you know. I adored her from afar. She was so pretty that I couldn't bring myself to talk to her. That was the first time we spoke, in that dream this morning." He turned to look at Paprika with a smile. "But it was you, wasn't it."

When Noda had left, Paprika took off her make-up and had a nap. She'd developed the knack of falling asleep instantly; she'd got it down to a fine art.

She woke at ten and made herself up as Atsuko Chiba. That was no trouble at all – disguising herself as Paprika took five times longer. She slipped into an apricot-coloured suit, the one she usually wore, then went down to the garage and got into her car. Atsuko's car was a moss-green Marginal.

On arriving at the Institute, she pulled into the covered car park. The figure of a man stood by the glass door at the entrance to the building, hiding his face in the shadows. It was the young reporter who'd asked such awkward questions at the press conference. As soon as he saw Atsuko, he forced a smile and bowed apologetically. "I'm really sorry for my rudeness the other day."

"Oh! Were you waiting for me?" Atsuko said with a smile that would have charmed the hardest of hearts. "Was there something you wanted to ask?"

"Er, well, no, something I wanted to tell you actually," he said, glancing around. "Well, you could see it as my way of apologizing…"

Atsuko knew instinctively that the young man's feelings towards her had changed, for whatever reason. Either that, or he was an exceptionally good actor for one so young.

"What is it then? You won't be allowed in. You'll have to tell me here. Sorry."

"You'll hear me out then?" The reporter had obviously expected to be treated more dismissively. He now produced his name card with a look of relief and gratitude. "Thank you so much. My name's Matsukane. I'm with the *Morning News*. Well, anyway, it's about this 'Paprika', you see..." Atsuko showed no reaction at all, but the young journalist added hurriedly: "No, I won't ask anything about her real identity, as I said before. But now journalists from certain newspapers, not just my own, have heard a rumour that Paprika was seen just recently in Roppongi. So then, well, I wanted to say you might like to be careful about that..."

"Well!" Atsuko said with a little laugh. "Why would I possibly be concerned with that?"

"Yes. Exactly. Absolutely. Why would you?" The young reporter smiled ambiguously and looked up at the roof of the car park. "But what I meant to say is that, well, if you *did* know Paprika, you might like to warn her to be more careful, that's all."

"Well, that's very kind of you. And why do you tell me this behind your colleagues' backs?"

The man suddenly looked serious. "To apologize for the other day, as I said just now. But also... Well, you know..." He trailed off into silence.

"No. I don't know. What?" Still smiling, Atsuko invited him to continue. "Are you going to say who told you all that nonsense?"

"Well, it's about that, yes." Matsukane looked down at his shoes, as if he was desperate to reveal the truth but couldn't quite bring himself to say it. "But I think we should talk about it some other time. After I've discovered more of the details. Anyway..." The young reporter was clearly driven by a strong sense of justice. He straightened his posture and looked Atsuko directly in the eye. "Please be careful."

"Careful of what?"

"Look... I'll be back. OK? I'll be back." Suddenly spotting another car, he crouched down and crept along the wall towards the exit.

What had the reporter discovered that would urge him to warn her? So many questions went through Atsuko's mind as she pushed the glass door open.

12

Atsuko went straight to her laboratory. There she found a swarthy young therapist called Hashimoto, a contemporary of both Osanai and Tsumura, sitting deep in conversation with Nobue Kakimoto. So much so that their knees were almost touching. The conversation obviously involved Atsuko, for no sooner had she entered than Hashimoto rose hurriedly – though, being a therapist, he was of course able to cloak his surprise behind a façade of nonchalance.

"Sorry. I'm in the way," he said disingenuously.

"Same as always, isn't it?" countered Atsuko. "No need to stand on ceremony, as they say."

"No, I'd better be on my rounds." Hashimoto even managed a glance at his watch as he left the room.

Nobue cast an unusually critical eye at Atsuko as she donned her lab coat. "Apparently Tsumura wasn't only looking at the reflector," Nobue said. "He was also using the collector. Wasn't he?"

"So it seems."

"So they're all using the collector for treatment in the other labs? In that case, why am I the only one who's not allowed to use it?"

"Hashimoto has put you up to this, hasn't he. Tsumura was affected because he used the collector without sufficient training. Why is everyone so keen to use it, anyway?"

"You just don't trust me, do you."

"It's not a question of trust."

Nobue said nothing for a moment, then changed the subject. "I read the article about the press conference the other day. Then I had the idea of going around disguised as Paprika."

Atsuko looked at Nobue as if something had just struck her. "What for?"

"To clear suspicion from you, of course. The media suspicion that you are Paprika."

This mere slip of a girl wanted to parade herself as Paprika. Atsuko restrained her laughter at the very thought of that. "So in fact, the real identity of Paprika was none other than *you* all along," she said. "And you really think they're going to fall for that?"

"Did you know I'm being followed? Ever since that press conference? They obviously think I could be Paprika. But maybe you're saying I'm not even good enough to do that…" Nobue stared hard at Atsuko, patently unaware of her own lack of logic.

Atsuko simply returned the stare. Perhaps Nobue really was being followed by some newspaper reporter who suspected all the Institute's female staff of being Paprika. But that was barely credible; Nobue was more likely suffering from some kind of persecution complex. She didn't seem her usual self. Both her words and her tone of voice were different today. Atsuko felt a shudder. Had someone been tampering with Nobue's reflector? In that case, the danger was drawing closer. Atsuko realized she would urgently need to check the memory and software programs of her own reflector and collector.

Not wishing to convey her suspicions but knowing that Nobue had to be distracted, Atsuko immediately ordered her to photocopy and bind a large pile of research papers. That would surely keep her busy for three or four hours…

Atsuko bought some coffee and sandwiches in the Institute shop and took them to the Senior Staff Room. Tokita had already finished his lunch and was drinking tea with a face that looked like a damp floor rag. "Tea here tastes like gnat's piss!"

Atsuko paid no attention. "There's something wrong with my assistant," she said in the hope of getting some advice from him.

"Her too?" Even the normally docile Tokita was surprised. "Tsumura was subjected to subliminal projections that caused his trauma to be released at the imperceptible rate of one-twentieth of a second every three minutes of real time. Truly ingenious."

"Who could have programmed the device? Was it Himuro?"

"Well, whoever it was, the program came from Himuro's partition. But what would Himuro gain by doing that? No, someone else must have made him do it. Don't worry. I'll wring it out of him."

"No, I'd rather you waited. We don't know what the enemy would do if they found out."

"Well, I can get it out of him any time you like." Tokita seemed inordinately keen to "get it out of" his almost equally obese junior. "He'll soon spit it out."

"Not yet, though. Please."

"Oh, that reminds me. You know that DC Mini thing? I cracked it late last night."

Tokita casually announced his breathtaking achievement with the same nonchalance as if he'd just scribbled off a short essay. D stood for Daedalus, C for Collector. Tokita took something out of his pocket and placed it on a corner of Atsuko's desk. It was a conical object about a centimetre high, with a base about seven or eight millimetres in diameter.

"This is the DC Mini? What about the cables?"

"No need for cables. Same as the Daedalus."

"Ah!" Atsuko sighed in admiration. "You've done it at last!"

"Yeah. It transmits the content of different people's dreams to each other's brains, so it doesn't need fibre bundles any more. After all, if we're going to use biochemical elements, we might as well let them communicate by synaptic transmission, using the natural transmission width at bioenergy level."

"Er, sorry to ask a stupid question, but does it use bioelectric current?"

"It does that. It applies nonlinear undulation using the conductive surge of bioelectric current. You see, bioelectric current allows us to produce a new type of communication based on synaptic transmission, by varying the BTU output."

"So at what distance will it still be effective without cables?"

"Ah well, that's something I don't know yet. I think certainly up

85

to a hundred metres, even with obstacles. But then again, I think anaphylaxis might occur with repeated use."

"You mean some kind of hypersensitivity, the opposite of immunity? In other words, the effective range will increase the more you use it? Priceless. And how do you fit it on the patient's head?"

"You just stick it on."

"What do you mean?"

"You just press it on, so the point sticks into the skin. Well, you don't have to go as far as that. Just bury it in their hair."

"What if they're bald?"

"Stick it on with tape."

"And you call it the DC Mini. Brilliant. Are you going to announce it at the Board Meeting?" A meeting was scheduled for one o'clock that afternoon.

"What? Don't you want me to?" Tokita looked unhappy.

"Well, no, actually. Best keep it under wraps for the time being."

Atsuko was about to explain the reason for that when the part-time director Owada walked in. Owada was Chairman of the National Association of Surgeons and Director of the Owada General Hospital. Without even a peremptory glance at his own desk, which he hardly ever used, he went straight to confront Atsuko. "How does Doctor Shima plan to deal with this Paprika business, I wonder?" he asked.

"By keeping it hidden from the media, of course."

"Of course. Otherwise we'd certainly be up a creek." Six years earlier, Owada had asked Paprika to treat the Minister of Agriculture for neurosis. Of all the directors, he was the one most firmly on Shima's side. "But Inui says if we're to keep it hidden from the media, you'll have to resign your post as director."

"It's a bit late for that now, isn't it?" Tokita weighed in with some indignation. "All the directors were queuing up to book Paprika for their friends when the treatment was illegal."

"And that's why you have to take a stand," Owada continued, ignoring Tokita. "Say you'll publicly reveal you were Paprika if you're asked to resign. The only one who won't be wetting himself is Inui. Since he never had anything to do with Paprika in the first place."

Atsuko shook her head. "I don't want to do that."

"Just think of the scandal!" Tokita seemed to revel in the idea. He thrust out his lower lip and grinned like a child.

Morio Osanai, trusty sidekick of the Vice President, entered with his pale forehead gleaming. "Ah, Doctor Owada. There you are. Doctor Inui wonders if you could meet him in the Vice President's Office."

"Right away."

"Don't let yourself be won over," Atsuko said as Owada made his way out.

Osanai had already stepped out into the corridor. He turned and smiled with a glint in his eye.

Just before one o'clock, the two other part-time directors arrived and joined the rest of the Board in the Meeting Room. The meeting was chaired by the President and Institute Administrator, Torataro Shima. Next to him sat the Secretary-General Katsuragi; everyone else just sat where they liked. As it happened, Owada, Tokita and Atsuko all took seats on one side and their three opponents on the other, with the unintended result that the two opposing factions sat glaring at each other across the table. Directly opposite Tokita was Seijiro Inui, Vice President of the Foundation and Chairman of the National Psychopathological Association. He was thin and sported a greying beard. His appearance betrayed a certain fastidiousness; like Abraham Lincoln, he seemed to possess an instinct for justice bordering on the fanatical.

"Well now, you'll note I didn't write a detailed agenda for this Meeting," started Secretary-General Katsuragi, who was also a Managing Director.

Whereupon the stern tones of Inui's voice, reminiscent of some dull metal being struck, sounded out across the room. "You mean you *couldn't* write it."

Aiwa Bank Chairman Hotta, sitting to Inui's right, smiled fawningly at the Vice President.

"Well, in any case," President Shima said with a smile of his own, "I think you'll all know why it wasn't possible to write an agenda. And anyway, since nearly all of you asked for this Board Meeting to be held, you all knew what would be discussed and so there was no need to write it down."

"But we need to report the agenda to the Ministry, don't we. We'll have to work out what to write later on. Heh heh," Katsuragi laughed feebly.

"It's not a laughing matter," said Inui, his stern expression unrelenting. "We should be ashamed of ourselves for discussing things so secretively."

"But back in the days when everyone was clamouring for Paprika, none of us thought it remotely shameful, did we," said Owada. "On the contrary, we were all very much in favour of it. We all wanted to know how effective the PT devices could be for actual treatment."

"That's in the past, it's nothing to do with it," Koji Ishinaka interjected grumpily. He was the Chairman of Ishinaka Real Estate, a company that had donated a huge sum of money to fund the Institute. It was thanks to Ishinaka that the Institute could own such impressive facilities and its senior executives could all live in high-class apartments. "Precisely because Doctor Chiba has now been shortlisted for the Nobel Prize in Physiology or Medicine, the Paprika episode is being bandied about as our skeleton in the cupboard."

"Are you saying you want us to reveal Paprika's identity?" Shima said with a puzzled look. "Even though it would tarnish Doctor Chiba's reputation as one of our directors? Not to mention that of the Institute itself?"

"Well, if you put it that way," Ishinaka said peevishly. "That would of course be undesirable."

"Mr President," said Inui, turning to face Shima. "This secretiveness will inevitably spread to other things; you'll just find yourself having to hide more and more unpalatable facts. Look at the incident with Tsumura. If there really is any danger in using the PT devices, it will reflect badly on you if you fail to disclose it now, while you still can."

"There is no danger in using the PT devices," Atsuko threw in hurriedly, before Tokita could say anything more damaging. "And I think we'll soon know what caused Tsumura's condition."

"On the issue of Paprika," Hotta said with some hesitation. "Well, Doctor Chiba was not a director at the time, so it was merely an illegal act committed by a member of staff..." Hotta halted in mid-sentence, as if to say *"Think the rest out for yourselves"*.

"Are you asking me to resign?" Atsuko challenged Hotta with a steady glare.

"Well, I mean, just until this fuss about Paprika has died down a bit." Hotta was unsettled all right. "Temporarily, I mean. Just temporarily. As long as Doctor Chiba is not a director, the Institute could not be harmed even if the true identity of Paprika were revealed. And after all, you're just coming up to the end of your three-year term, aren't you..."

"And what about all the benefits brought to this Institute by Paprika, then?" asked Tokita, unable to hold back any longer. "What about the generous endowments received from politicians and financiers who were cured by Paprika, for starters? If it weren't for them, we would never have made such progress with the PT devices! For behind such advances in science, you will always find adventures and experiments that go against the sentiment of the masses!"

"That old chestnut again, is it?" asked Inui, turning on Tokita with a look of rage in his eyes. "You always say that, don't you. But that and Doctor Chiba's unconditional faith in the safety of PT devices show that you have absolutely no self-awareness regarding the volatile nature of science and technology. You see yourselves as brave pioneers riding on the leading edge of discovery! Where's your sense of social responsibility? You should be ashamed to call yourselves scientists!"

13

"Now now, Doctor Inui," said President Shima, doing his best to force a smile. He was already up to here with Inui's fanatical view of scientific ethics. "I shall have to take some of the blame for that. It was after all me who encouraged our two friends to challenge ever greater developments in their research."

"What exactly does Doctor Inui mean by 'the volatile nature of science and technology'?" Owada suddenly demanded with some annoyance. "Is he suggesting that our two friends have ridden roughshod, as it were, on the wave of technological development? What they've done is to apply cutting-edge technology to the treatment of schizophrenia for the very first time. That's precisely why they've been shortlisted for the Nobel Prize in Physiology or Medicine."

"And that is precisely the problem," countered Inui. His expression was transformed at the merest mention of the Nobel Prize. The sides of his mouth became distorted and his nostrils broadened to quite grotesque effect. How he must have detested that prize! "As I said before, even schizophrenics are human, and technology that enters directly into their psyche to treat them – yes, technology that could even be applied to normal subjects – should have been discussed in the minutest detail beforehand, from the angle of medical ethics. But that not withstanding, Tokita tell us he's already developing the next generation of equipment based on the alleged therapeutic effect of these PT devices – even though not a single patient has been completely cured by them! We don't even know what after-effects they may have. And he's been spending colossal amounts in the process, I may add."

"Eh? Colossal amounts?" Tokita seemed utterly mortified; he certainly hadn't expected an attack on that level. "I haven't used any colossal amounts!"

"Surely you saw the financial statements at the last Board Meeting?" said Shima, eyeing Inui suspiciously. "All those amounts were checked by our auditors and duly approved by the Ministry."

"Yes, but unbeknown to us, LSIs and other things were subsequently purchased from Tokyo Electronics Giken. Yamabe tells me the cost was astronomical." Yamabe, an auditor in cahoots with Inui, also acted as a consultant for the Medical Appliances Union.

"I didn't use that many LSIs, did I?" Tokita muttered with head hung low, as if he wasn't quite sure. "Did the cost go up suddenly? If so, let's not buy them from Giken any more."

"Er, I'm not sure we can pull out now," said Secretary-General Katsuragi with a pained smile and a scratch of the head. "We have a good relationship with them…"

"I read the article about the recent press conference. What are these new devices you mention?" demanded Ishinaka. Unlike Inui, he and Hotta were completely in favour of developing the technology further. "Spare me the scientific jargon, but could you just tell me what purpose they'll serve?"

"We're not at the stage where we can discuss anything yet," Tokita replied curtly, irked that Atsuko had forbidden him to mention it. "And even if we could, the Vice President would only claim it was the work of the Devil or something."

"I'm sorry, but we're the directors and you have to tell us everything," said Hotta with an exaggerated expression of disapproval. "Doctor Shima. You must know. Details of research conducted by a research institute must surely be reported to its President?"

"Unfortunately not, in this case. Doctor Tokita produces better results if we just let him get on with it, as it were. Well, I hear he's trying to develop what he calls a 'Daedalus' by removing the cables from the gorgon. But in any case, you must know that a genius like Doctor Tokita will make amazing discoveries and inventions quite fortuitously, and that's not something you can tie down."

The gullible Shima was starting to expose his uncritical pride in Tokita. Inui pulled a sour face. "Whatever the case, I trust you won't forget our guiding principles as scientists. These devices must be designed with functions to prevent abuse by society."

That last phrase gave Atsuko a nasty start. Had Tokita designed the DC Mini with a function to prevent unauthorized access, a protective code? That seemed unlikely, given that Tokita was completely incapable of such meticulous aforethought. And judging by the way he stiffened momentarily at the very mention of it, Atsuko was sure he hadn't. She knew the errors he was likely to make even better than he did.

"By the way, Doctor Chiba isn't the only one whose term ends soon, is she," chirped Hotta, lightening his tone deliberately. "Of course, re-election isn't prohibited, but that's not the point. Doctor Inui's grievances with the Institute's management are quite clear from his statements here today. So how about asking Doctor Shima to stand down for a while and letting Doctor Inui take over as, you know, President of the Foundation? After all, it would help prevent undue bias in the Institute's work…" This was a carefully planned statement designed to take the enemy by surprise.

Atsuko had feared this very turn of events. "Only the Minister of Education is authorized to appoint the President," she said a little too sharply.

"Well, yes, but the President can also be co-opted from the directors before that," Ishinaka said darkly. "In that case, the decision would only have to be *vetted* by the Minister."

"Or else I could resign," laughed Shima, well meaning as ever.

"Is this the first time you've broached the issue with the President?" Atsuko asked with a stare fixed on Hotta. "If so, don't you think your approach is a little discourteous?"

"Ah. I suppose it was unduly hasty of me. Awfully sorry. As you say, I should have prepared the ground properly first. I was merely stating my impression in reaction to what Doctor Inui has said. I haven't even broached the issue with Doctor Inui himself, how very rude of me." It was a stereotypical display of mock concern. "So I wonder if we could consider the co-opting issue before the next Board Meeting?"

Owada remained silent, probably to protect his own skin.

"OK then. If Doctor Shima is going to resign as President, then I think I'll resign as director as well," Tokita said calmly.

Atsuko followed suit immediately: "And that goes for me too."

"Why would you resign?" Inui said with a quiet expression of alarm. "Can you give me one reason?" He turned to Shima. "This is nothing but self-indulgence. Now we can see how badly you've spoilt these two until now. After resigning as directors, I presume they would also leave their positions in the Institute. The young ones are all like that today. They fritter away the Institute's budget on research, and then, when things don't go their way, they say they want to leave and take their research results elsewhere."

Shima leant forwards in surprise. "I think you'll find that neither Doctor Tokita nor Doctor Chiba is that type of person."

"I'll leave it all here, everything I've developed. Including the PT devices," Tokita said with the faintest of smiles.

Inui appeared none too pleased with Tokita's sardonic manner. "You needn't put on airs. What you said is only to be expected. You seem to think you developed the devices all by yourself, but that's merely the product of vanity. You didn't. What about the investors who provided all the funds, the engineers who installed the equipment, the therapists who tested the devices, the assistants, even the cleaning ladies? They all played a part in developing those devices. Everyone in this Institute. You can't claim the invention as your own. It belongs to the Institute. If you go, you'll have to leave everything here, including your research on devices yet to be developed!" he raged.

"Come now," said a suitably astonished Ishinaka to halt Inui's tirade. "The point was merely hypothetical anyway!"

"If these two were to leave now, we'd be in real trouble," added Hotta earnestly, hoping to placate the now dispirited Tokita and Atsuko. "We haven't even decided to co-opt yet, so for pity's sake there's no need to precipitate things. Yes, the discussion was merely hypothetical, but now it's gone out of all proportion."

"As you say. I'm sorry I allowed my emotions to get the better of me," Inui said with a little bow to the pair, twisting a smile at the severity of his own outburst. "Sorry. I should be old enough to know better."

"But everything the Vice President said was in the interests of this Institute," Shima said in defence of Inui. "Nothing should be taken personally."

"How are we to proceed then, President?" asked Katsuragi, who only had thoughts for the documents to be submitted to the Ministry. He brought his face close to Shima's. "We need to decide some resolutions for this meeting."

All resolutions on matters discussed so far were shelved, including the issue of Paprika. The discussion proceeded to the election of a successor to the ageing auditor Yamabe, who had recently tendered his resignation. The matter was entrusted to Inui, who claimed to have "someone in mind". Ultimately, however, auditors could only be elected by a meeting attended by the foundation's seventy trustees.

"You know that auditor," Atsuko said as she and Tokita walked along the corridor after the Board Meeting. "He'd better not be another of Inui's cronies."

"Why not?"

"Didn't you think it odd? All those mysterious purchases from Tokyo Electronics Giken?"

"Yes, I did. That's why I said we shouldn't use them any more."

"Katsuragi nearly had a fit when he heard that, didn't he."

"Yes... Did he?"

"It made me think there's something untoward going on here. I think they've taken advantage of your openness to bump up the purchase volume. They could use it as a way of making a fool of you."

"Oh. Could they?"

"We need an auditor who'll do his job properly. I'll talk to Shima. Ask him to recommend someone he can trust."

"What I find odd is that, well, you know, all the other directors were in a panic when we threatened to resign, because they know the Institute's R&D would stop dead if we left. And yet I could swear the Vice President seemed very keen not only on Doctor Shima resigning but also us two as well. He says he wants us to consider the volatility of science and technology, but if he carries on like that, the Institute will surely go under."

"Wait a minute." Atsuko stopped at the corner of the corridor. They were in front of the Medical Office, where the corridor widened slightly. From there, they would go their separate ways to their labs. Atsuko lowered her voice in awareness of the listening ears of nurses, therapists and other employees who incessantly passed to and fro. "Wasn't Inui himself once shortlisted for the Nobel Prize?"

"That's it!" said Tokita, eyes widening as he looked up at the strip lights on the ceiling. "He was! A long time ago, when we were still at school."

"He told you to leave all your research results behind, didn't he. Including devices still under development."

"To take the credit for himself? Surely not?! It would be impossible!" Tokita inadvertently raised his voice, then looked around with a pained smile. "Well. Let's talk about it later."

"Yes. Later."

Atsuko returned to her laboratory, kicking herself for not asking Tokita whether he'd designed the DC Mini with a protective code. In Atsuko's lab, Nobue Kakimoto was playing back the dream of a severe schizophrenic who'd been treated the previous day. She hadn't even started photocopying the research papers as requested by Atsuko earlier.

"You're not to see this patient's dreams! It's too dangerous for you!" Atsuko yelled as she quickly switched off the monitor. "What about those research papers?! I need to distribute them urgently!"

Nobue cast her eyes down for a moment, then suddenly stood and slapped Atsuko's cheek hard, with the unfathomable strength of the half-crazed. Atsuko had taken Nobue's confidence for granted, and that had made her complacent. "No need to act so arrogant, just because you think you're good-looking!" Nobue screamed.

14

The caretaker allowed Noda to cross the lobby unchallenged; Paprika must have told him she was expecting a visitor. It was after eleven in the evening. Noda passed through the glass door from the lobby and stepped into the lift at the far end of the reception lounge.

No sooner had he pressed the button for the 16th floor than a giant of a man stepped in behind him. His body seemed to fill the whole of the lift. *This must surely be that genius scientist who developed the PT devices*, thought Noda. He couldn't quite remember the face he'd seen in the blurry newspaper photograph. But since the article had repeatedly described the man as "massive", "enormous" and "gigantic", that detail had remained in his memory. The giant pressed the button for the 15th floor before turning to eye Noda suspiciously.

Noda gave his travelling companion a nod and a smile of familiarity, enough to imply that he knew all about him. "The name's Noda," he said. "I'm here to be treated by Paprika."

The giant seemed surprised. "Paprika?! Has she started that again? Oh my golly." Then, for no apparent reason, he smiled inanely and started to sway his gargantuan frame.

This sloppily obese man spoke in such an infantile tone that he seemed incapable of engaging in any proper conversation. As Director of Development for a leading motor company, Noda wouldn't normally have given him a second glance. But he somehow felt a liking for this man. It certainly helped that Noda gave preferential treatment to genius. More than anything, however, the man's huge eyes were limpid and quite beautiful.

Noda didn't know why the man had smiled. The ballyhoo about Paprika, nothing more than a rumour anyway, hadn't been reported in any newspaper read by the likes of Noda. The story had been carried by weekly gossip magazines, but Noda was unlikely to give them a second of his time.

The lift arrived at the 15th floor. As the doors opened, the man stepped out without a word. He seemed lost in thought. *A pure man without a malicious bone in his body*. That was Noda's judgement as an expert in human observation.

At the far end of the 16th floor, Noda waited outside the door to Apartment 1604, which was fitted with a fish-eye lens. Paprika eventually opened the door. Noda gasped when he saw her face.

"What have you done to your eye?!" he asked, like a father scolding his daughter for loose conduct.

"It's nothing. Don't worry about it."

Noda supposed she'd been attacked by a patient. "It looks serious."

"Does it?" Her left eye was bloodshot, its socket bruised and swollen. "Never mind. Fancy some coffee?"

Noda followed Paprika into the living room, then hesitated. "No, wait a minute. I'll need to sleep, won't I?"

"All right, how about a drink then?" Paprika took a bottle of Jack Daniels from her trolley and started to fix a whiskey on the rocks as she spoke. "I'll access your early morning dreams again, so it's OK for you to drink. Tell you what – let's have one together. I want to get some sleep myself tonight."

"Excellent!" Noda felt elated as he gazed across at Paprika, uncharacteristically dressed in a loose gown. Paprika returned his gaze, inducing a faint-heartedness he hadn't felt in years. He cast his eyes down in embarrassment. He no longer saw her as a young girl.

"But you're in no mood to drink and make merry?" he ventured.

"It's cool. Let's make merry."

The two sat facing each other across Paprika's glass table while they drank Jack Daniels on the rocks. The night panorama was visible in the background. The room was filled with a homely smell, perhaps because of Paprika's gown; Noda began to feel pleasantly mellow. But Paprika was still downcast and conversation was sparse. She would start to mouth words, but none would come out. It was as if there were something she wanted to ask Noda, but was unsure whether she should say it.

In the end, Paprika decided to say nothing at all. Ice still nestled in her glass as she put it down and stood up. "You were up early this morning. You must be tired. Bed?"

Noda half-lifted himself, then slumped back in his chair, not knowing quite what to do.

"Mmm. That's right," he said, nodding ambiguously.

"OK. You know where the bathroom is. You don't like pyjamas, right? You'll find a bathrobe in there."

"Right. Thanks." As a gentleman, perhaps he should go to bed first. Noda gulped down the rest of his whiskey and stood up.

It felt odd. This confused tangle of paradoxical relationships – doctor with patient, father with daughter, husband with wife, lover with lover – had conjured up a strange atmosphere unlike that of any hospital, or any home, and certainly not any lover's tryst. Noda emerged from the bathroom and entered the bedroom, doffed his bathrobe in the ethereal glow of the monitor screens and slipped into the bed in his underwear. Paprika followed a few moments later, dressed in a pure-white negligee, to fit the gorgon cap on Noda's head.

Noda couldn't get to sleep that night. He wanted to see Paprika in her white negligee once more, even in the dim light of the room. He could faintly hear the sound of her splashing in the bath.

By the time Paprika returned, Noda's eyes were closed. He half-opened them to see her standing by his bed and smiling down at him. From below she looked huge. Bluish light shone through her negligee from behind and below, revealing the voluptuous outline of her breasts. The swelling around her eye was hidden by shade. In this light, she looked like Kwannon, the goddess of mercy, or Venus, or Hariti, the goddess of children. As Noda stared on, she momentarily revealed a shapely pair of calves as she slipped into the next bed, muttering something about being embarrassed. Then she inserted a program memory into the device at her bedside and wrapped something around her wrist, before half-covering her face with the sheet.

Maybe it was something to do with his age, but Noda felt strangely comforted by seeing a sight he'd so longed to see. Paprika once more in her white negligee. When he could hear the reassuring sound of her breathing as she slept, Noda also fell asleep. He had several short dreams. He woke just once, when he removed the gorgon to go to the bathroom. On returning, he gazed at Paprika's beautiful face for a few moments, before returning to sleep a happy man. This time, he entered a deep sleep.

Once again, he was in the middle of an absurdly fantastic adventure, half aware that he was dreaming. He often had dreams like this. He rarely went to the cinema these days, but he'd been amazed on seeing a video of *Super Sabre* his son had rented. It had revived a certain thrill he used to feel in the days of his youth, when he'd been an avid film-goer. That thrill was more than evident in this dream.

Noda was cutting his way through a jungle, the adventure still clearly in progress. He was wearing a tattered safari suit, as worn by Johnny Weissmuller in *Jungle Jim*. In the stifling heat of the jungle, humanoid creatures scuttled back and forth through the undergrowth ahead. They looked like beggars dressed in rags. Noda had to capture one of them quickly.

One of the creatures disappeared into a thicket of shrubs. Noda followed it, flying into the thicket with a loud rustling noise. They fought, but the fight was completely bereft of strength. It somehow felt empty. His adversary had the face of a wild boar, or perhaps a bear.

Ah – this one's Segawa, Noda thought as he wrestled the creature to the ground. His adversary's feeble resistance was quite at odds with the savage look on its face. "No – it's not Segawa, it's… It's…" *I should know this, after ******ing last night's dream.*

"That's right. It's Takao, isn't it," Paprika chimed in to offer support.

*That's right. Segawa stands for Takao. When I'm dreaming, I've got to find out who is someone else's ****** in the dream. Paprika told me that. That's why it's so urgent.* The face of his opponent pinned down beneath him started to change. It began to resemble his hazy recollection of Takao's face. "I'm Taka–o!" the boy chanted in a child's voice, as if to confirm the point.

Noda set off through the jungle again. This time Paprika was with him. As always, she wore a red shirt and jeans – the "Paprika costume", as Noda saw it. He wasn't sure whether this was the illusory Paprika of his dreams or the real Paprika, the one who had willingly stepped in to help him.

"Sorry. Mind if I join you?" Paprika said with a smile.

By all means. Come on in. It's a pleasure to have you in my dream. Noda muttered words to that effect. Or maybe he just thought them. In any case, they were relayed to Paprika in an instant. As the two walked on, they were being watched by creatures with the faces of bears, tigers, wild boars, wolves, hyenas and other animals, their heads peeping out of the undergrowth all around.

"What are these animals?" Paprika said with an air of disgust. "Are they from a Bond film too?"

"No. This isn't a Bond film. It's ****************." He knew the title. But because it was a dream, the words wouldn't come out properly.

"What did you say?" asked Paprika, sitting in the seat next to him. They were in a cinema, watching the film they'd just been appearing in.

"*The Island of Doctor Moreau*. It's the film I went to see on my own."

"So you've been confusing *Doctor No* with *The Island of Doctor Moreau*?"

Paprika's sharp insight attacked Noda's stomach like a pungent spice. Perhaps that explained her name.

"True. If this is the film I went to see on my own, then it couldn't have been *Doctor No*."

Noda groaned and turned towards the seat next to him. Something he didn't want to see would be sitting there, he knew. Just as he'd feared, Paprika had turned into a tiger.

Through the window, Noda could see farm fields stretching into the distance. He was now a guest in an old-style inn. The fields outside looked like the countryside near his childhood home. In one field, a man was selling vegetables to a crowd of customers.

"Who's that?"

Noda turned to see Paprika standing in the room. She was no longer a tiger. She approached Noda, then sat on a rattan chair by the window.

"It looks a lot like Namba." But Noda had no idea why Namba should be selling vegetables in the field.

A commotion could be heard in the corridor outside. Paprika

smiled wryly. "They're all in a tizz because they think a tiger's on the loose."

"So it seems." Noda noticed that he'd gone goggle-eyed. "It would be no joke if a tiger got loose in a place like this."

"I wonder if it'll come in here."

I'm sure it will. I don't want any more of that infantile fighting, thought Noda, quite fed up with it all.

"By the way, why was I a tiger?"

Noda couldn't answer. He felt as if his tongue was frozen fast.

The sliding door opened and in came his son, aged four or five. He was wearing a cotton summer kimono. It was a memory from when the family went to a spa town for a short break.

"Is that really your son?" Paprika said, standing in surprise. "The one who phoned me that time?"

"Yes. It's him, but more than ten years ago." Noda remembered something important. "His name's Torao. It's written differently, but *tora* still means tiger."

The boy disappeared immediately. The scene changed again, leaving Paprika sitting on the rattan chair, immersed in thought.

Now they were in the empty lobby of an office building. It was Noda's company building, with a glass front door that opened automatically. Paprika was still questioning Noda, standing beside him in the lobby. They were both staring at the automatic door.

"Can you remember why you called your son Torao?"

"Because I thought it was a good name. You see... well..."

The door opened. Sukenobu came riding into the lobby on a red bicycle.

"Now. That isn't Sukenobu, is it? It's not him but..."

"That's right," said Paprika. "It's Akishige. The leader of the pack, the class bully."

Sukenobu turned into Akishige, the boy Noda had been trying his hardest to forget. He stopped the bicycle in a corner of the lobby and started talking to another boy who was suddenly standing there.

"Who's the other one?"

"Shinohara. One of Akishige's cronies." Noda started to walk as he spoke. "But to answer your question just now. There was a friend I had, a long time ago. His name was Toratake. I think I named my son after him."

For some reason, Noda was in no small hurry to leave the lobby. He was pretending to have remembered some other important detail; there seemed to be something he didn't want Paprika to know. Paprika was well aware of his dissembling, but pretended not to have noticed. Now he spoke with ever increasing speed, as if he wasn't in the middle of a dream. As if he was trying to wake himself. In fact, he probably was beginning to wake up. That explained why he could talk so lucidly.

"I often saw films with Toratake. *Doctor No* was one of them. Toratake's parents owned a large inn. He was film mad. My dream was to be a film director and his was to be a cameraman. We used to talk about it. We said we'd make a film together one day."

Paprika seemed aware of these revelations already. She was looking around warily while walking next to Noda. They had left the building and were walking along the pavement. As they approached the crossroads at the corner, Paprika stopped and pointed back to the building. "There's a tobacco store there," she said loudly. "The place where Akishige and Shinohara were talking just now? It's behind it. You see? Behind the tobacco store."

The scene changed immediately to the banks of the stream they'd seen in the previous night's dream, the small plot of waste ground behind the tobacco store.

"********!" Noda shouted something that even he didn't understand, thereby changing the scene. It was the place where he felt most at ease, his favourite *okonomi-yaki* restaurant from university days. He felt a little ashamed at that, but was in no position to be fussy.

As a character who shared his dream, Paprika blocked the change of scene.

"I know it's cruel, but you can't."

In her half-sleeping, half-waking state, she must have pressed the back-skip key with her fingertip. The scene changed back to the vacant lot behind the tobacco store. Akishige, Takao and Shinohara were bullying Namba. Namba was rolling helplessly on the ground while the three bullies kicked him.

"It's not Namba. Who is it?"

With a cry of despair at Paprika's merciless questioning, Noda fled once more to the comfort of the *okonomi-yaki* restaurant.

Back-skip.

Behind the tobacco store. This time, it was Noda's son who was being bullied. He was four or five years old again. Shinohara was sitting astride Torao and strangling him.

"Stop it!" Noda screamed as he went to punch the bully. "It's not Torao, is it? It's Toratake!"

Noda woke with a start. He sat up in bed, his face drenched in sweat. Tears filled his eyes. "You see," he said to Paprika, who was facing the collector. "Toratake died. I killed him."

15

"Sorry to have forced that on you," Paprika said as she removed the gorgon. "I wanted you to remember as much as possible before you woke up. It wasn't you who killed Toratake. Was it?"

A sweet fragrance from Paprika's bosom invaded Noda's nostrils as he tried to catch his breath. Paprika supported him as he sat up. She was still wearing her negligee. The troubled wanderings of his mind now held in check, Noda gave a large sigh.

"He committed suicide. But it was my fault. I might just as well have killed him myself."

"You can't know that. You may only have convinced yourself of it." Paprika soothed Noda's fears in a tone that suggested she'd long realized the truth of the matter. "Well now. Have a shower first. Then I'll make us some breakfast. Let's analyse the dream while we eat."

Paprika spoke as if deliberately intending to satisfy a middle-aged man's need for a mother figure, or perhaps a nurse. She had a huge smile on her face; the previous night's mood was but a distant memory.

I remember. I remember everything. As the hot water of the shower rushed over his body, Noda began to immerse himself in a sense of comforting reassurance. He felt so relaxed that he could barely understand why he'd been unable to control his anxiety until now. He'd been so smugly sure of himself, especially when it came to the finer points of human relationships. He should have felt no anxiety at all. And yet, he'd felt so anxious that he thought he was going to die. The only explanation, he'd then feared, was that something was growing inside his brain. Now he could laugh it all off.

"So this Toratake was your best friend, yes?" Sitting opposite Noda, Paprika did her best to hide her swollen eye as she started the analysis.

"That's right. His parents owned an inn. That must be why I dreamt of one. They were saying a tiger was on the loose, weren't they." Paprika's salad tasted good, even without dressing. Noda thought that slightly odd; her salads had always been dressed.

"So whenever you dreamt of a tiger, it always represented Toratake. Even I looked like a tiger in the cinema, didn't I. The dream was trying to tell you that Toratake was the one you went to see films with."

"Yes. It's as if the dreams were trying to tell me about him all along…" Noda sensed a change in Paprika's approach; now it seemed she wanted him to analyse his own dreams. But he was happy to go along with that. "One of the animals in the classroom was a tiger, and Toratake's death was symbolized by Namba's funeral. And you remember the *Doctor No* scene? When me and Namba were happily firing at each other? That showed how well

I used to get on with Toratake. But the strange thing is that I couldn't remember him. Why would that be? I've no idea. After all, he was my best friend. Actually, I seem to remember dreaming about tigers before. That's right. I remember now. Whenever I dream about tigers, I'm always torn between feelings of fear and nostalgia."

"But you remembered Takao. The one who looked like a bear."

"Yes. But even Takao appeared as Segawa." Noda was getting quite carried away with his analysis now. "By showing me the present group, I mean Sukenobu, Segawa, me and Namba, the dream was reminding me of my bullying classmates from junior high school."

"Bingo. But that can't be all. Can you think of anything else? I think we can learn a lot from this." Paprika's cheeks were flushed with the thrill of the chase, as if she felt entertained by this quest for truth. To be sure, the challenge to unravel the mystery of dreams always came as a pleasure to her.

"The dream in the cinema, and the one when I was a film director, they were both hinting at Toratake, weren't they. The same goes for the scene behind the tobacco store. That was where Akishige did his bullying. Him and his cronies, Takao and Shinohara. If there was someone they didn't like, they would take them there and beat them. Akishige didn't like Toratake because he studied hard. So he told me to take Toratake behind the tobacco store. I knew that if I'd refused, they would only have beaten me instead of Toratake. So I took him there. I just stood to one side and watched as the three of them beat him up." Noda groaned in frustration. "Damn it! I used to make myself sick remembering that scene!"

"And you've suppressed it because of the Namba problem at work?"

"Of course – that must be it. The situations are just too similar." Noda glanced across as he brought the coffee cup to his lips. "So is that what caused my anxiety neurosis?"

"Yes. It won't be the only reason, of course. But did your friend Toratake commit suicide because of that?"

"I took him home after they'd finished beating him. He was covered in blood. He knew I'd betrayed him, but wouldn't utter a word of reproach. I couldn't say anything either. That's when it happened. We stopped being friends. My betrayal ruined our friendship, and his life." Noda looked out at the sky behind Paprika. "That's it! I must have called my son Torao in the hope of making up for my guilt."

"But would someone really commit suicide just because of that?" Paprika repeated. She peered at Noda with an expression made all the more intense by the swelling around her eye. "Have you ever thought about it as an adult? Knowing so much about human behaviour, as you do?"

"What?" Noda was stunned. "What do you mean?"

"Well, you know, sometimes we convince ourselves of certain things in childhood, and thereby create an illusion of truth that remains with us even as adults. However illogical it may seem."

"But they kept bullying him after that."

"Are you sure? Did you see it with your own eyes?"

"No. I never saw it…" Noda gradually started to doubt his own memory. He'd always considered his memory flawless, but his recollection of events had often been overturned by firm evidence to the contrary.

"All right, you say he committed suicide, but did you go to the funeral?"

"No. I have no memory of that." Noda let his gaze roam over the sky once more.

"See? If you look back from your present perspective, you start to realize there's something wrong with the way you remember things."

"But I heard it clearly from Shinohara. That's right. He said it on the telephone, when he called about the school reunion."

"Reunion?…"

107

"Ah... I see. That means Toratake couldn't have died when we were still at junior high," Noda mumbled in growing confusion. "It was the first reunion we'd had since leaving school. I was already at university. My whole family had moved to Tokyo, but most of my classmates had gone to senior high schools near the old village. So there hadn't been any call for a reunion until then."

"And what did Shinohara say on the phone?"

"He asked if I knew about Toratake's suicide."

"You sure? Is that what he really said?" Paprika pressed Noda further, her voice laden with doubt.

"Well, yes! It was such a shock. I remember it clearly."

"Why? After all, even if he did commit suicide, it had nothing to do with you, did it? It would have happened long after your school days."

Noda looked deflated. "You're right. Why have I convinced myself all this time that it was my fault?"

"Because you've been suppressing your feelings for Toratake," Paprika said as she stood and began to clear away the breakfast things. It was a deliberate ploy to make her words sound casual, thereby mitigating the shock Noda would surely feel. "And you had to do that, to suppress your feelings for Namba. When feelings are suppressed, their energy turns to anxiety."

"Feelings?..." Noda felt a brief sensation of dizziness. "You mean, homosexual feelings?"

"Don't sound so surprised! We all have them you know," Paprika said calmly. "More coffee?"

Noda was speechless. Paprika smiled like a mother telling her child about sex for the first time. "Well now. That seems to have come as quite a shock to you. But what I just said is a Freudian interpretation. It's not the only cause of anxiety neurosis. There are many different ways of analysing it. Ah yes..." Paprika toyed with her spoon as she pondered her point, then nodded and looked up at Noda. "In your case, maybe another explanation would be easier to understand. Anxiety is often discussed within a framework of theories on human relationships. In the early stages of life, by which I mean childhood rather than infancy, anxiety appears as a third unpleasant experience. Before that, there were only pain and fear. You were rejected by Toratake, an important character at an early stage of your life. The object of your fear of rejection shifted in adulthood. Now, it was no longer a person who was important in your childhood, but a successor to that important person. It didn't have to be a person at all; it could have been some kind of social convention, for example. In any case, anxiety is born of human relationships, and either evolves or disappears within that framework."

Noda thought for a moment before reacting. "You remember when I met Namba's wife in the dream about his funeral? You said she was my *anima*, didn't you."

"That's right."

"And so you're saying the woman was in fact me. Or at least, the part of me that has feelings for Namba."

"Yes. The female inside you."

"Could I have some more coffee? Thanks. Yes – maybe I should give more thought to Namba…"

"Hey! You're not coming out, are you?!" Paprika laughed as she refilled Noda's cup.

Noda grimaced. "I wouldn't go that far! But you know, Namba could find himself in real trouble thanks to Sukenobu." Noda mentioned his exchange with Sukenobu and the President in the hotel bar, and his own suspicion that Sukenobu was plotting something.

Paprika smiled meaningfully. "You'll probably find the answer to that in your dreams as well."

"So… Am I completely cured now?"

"Yes. The treatment's finished."

Noda couldn't help noticing that, as Paprika spoke, her eyes appeared to glisten wistfully. It would certainly not have been the first time a young woman had taken a shine to him. But he decided to write it off as nothing but vain delusion.

"It's all down to the strength of your will, and your intelligence. I mean, the fact that you've been cured so quickly," said Paprika. "But there's something else I want you to do. I want you to solve your problems with human relations in the here and now. Well, that goes without saying. And another thing. Find out what really happened to Toratake. How did he die? It's important. You mustn't leave things like that unresolved. You can do that, can't you?"

"Aha. I'll phone Shinohara. He seems to like me. He's called me about the reunions several times."

"Children who are bullied remember it for the rest of their lives. But the bullies forget all about it. I've witnessed that so many times."

As Noda prepared to leave, he could hardly bear his sadness at parting. He turned at the door and met Paprika's gaze.

"I don't think I'll ever be able to forget about you."

"I know. We call it *rapport*. A patient's feelings for a doctor," Paprika said as she removed a loose thread from Noda's lapel. "But sometimes it happens to the doctor as well. I won't ever forget you, either." Paprika's eye remained fixed on Noda's chest as she spoke. "You won't mind me looking like this, will you? I just want you to kiss me goodbye. Just once."

16

Torataro Shima was just putting the phone down when Atsuko walked into his office. "You know Tatsuo Noda?" he said, beaming. "He's only gone and donated ten million yen to the Institute!"

"Well, I never!"

"He's rolling in it, after all. I assume that means the treatment went well?" Shima got up and directed Atsuko towards an armchair in the reception area. He himself sat at one end of the sofa, diagonally to her right. As always.

"I'd say he's almost completely cured," Atsuko replied.

"He certainly sounded happy. But it's amazing that you managed to cure him so quickly! Er – of course, I mean *Paprika* managed to cure him so quickly!" Shima chuckled in self-amusement, before addressing the matter that really concerned him. "You know, I'd be awfully keen to hear what method of treatment Paprika used?…"

"Method of treatment?" Atsuko laughed, knowing the true motive behind Shima's interest. "There was a positive relationship between therapist and patient, if that's what you mean. But since the patient's problem was anxiety neurosis, all Paprika did was to analyse his dreams. She didn't go as far as she did with you. Don't worry. But she did let him kiss her at the end. Just to say goodbye."

"She let him kiss her? Ah." Shima groaned enviously. "You mean in his dream? As she did with me?"

"No. In reality. She found him rather attractive, and got caught up in a reverse rapport. Just a bit."

"That's inexcusable."

"Isn't it."

After a pretence of glaring at each other for a second, the two burst into laughter. But even as he laughed, Shima could not wipe the look of jealousy from his face.

"President Shima." Atsuko sat up. "About the Board Meeting the other day…"

"Ah." Shima's expression was instantly transformed into one of heaviness. He peered up at Atsuko's face with a look of apology in his eyes. "I understand how very unpleasant it must have been for you and Tokita. I never thought things would go that far. But as you said in the first place, it was definitely a good idea to call the meeting so quickly."

He didn't seem very keen to talk about it. Shima was a person who, deep down, found it hard to cope with the intricacies of human relationships.

"I know you don't like talking about this kind of thing," Atsuko said in a tone of regret. "But I have to ask your advice about remedial measures."

"Yes. Of course. First Tsumura was affected, then your assistant Kakimoto. Inui and the other directors must surely have heard about it."

"I'm really sorry."

Nobue Kakimoto had started to behave violently, and had been confined to an isolation unit in the hospital. Atsuko inevitably had to accept some of the responsibility, since Nobue was her assistant. She would almost certainly face charges of professional negligence at the next Board Meeting.

"Have you contacted her family?"

"Well…" Her conscience pricked, Atsuko cast her eyes down. "I didn't mention any illness, as I'm sure it's only temporary. I just told them she's suffering from fatigue and we're giving her time to recuperate."

Nobue lived alone in a sleepy Tokyo suburb; her family home was in Aomori, far to the north.

Atsuko lifted her head. "I'll treat her myself," she said. "I think she'll recover quickly."

"I'll leave it to you then," Shima said with an imploring look in his eyes. "I couldn't bear to think of them criticizing you like that."

"Don't worry. She'll be cured." Atsuko realized she would have to analyse the memory images accumulated in Nobue's reflector. She would ask Tokita to do it immediately. "And another thing, President Shima. About Yamabe's successor as auditor."

"Ah yes. The matter that was entrusted to Inui."

"I think auditors should be elected by the President. I just can't trust Inui."

"Hmm." Shima's forehead was etched with deep vertical lines. "Not only does he want me to resign as President, but he's even trying to hound you and Tokita out of the Institute. I just don't understand it. What could be his aim? And at this of all times – a critical time for the Institute, when you two have a chance of winning the Nobel Prize!"

"Doctor Shima." Atsuko leant towards Shima's face. "You know Inui was once shortlisted for the Nobel Prize?"

"I do. Though it was nearly twenty years ago. He'd discovered a very effective method of treating a certain psychosomatic disorder that had grown to pandemic proportions at the time. For that, he was apparently shortlisted for the Prize. But the medical world in those days had little understanding of psychiatry. In the end, the Prize went to a British surgeon who'd incorporated Inui's method into his theory..." Even as he spoke, the true purpose of Atsuko's enquiry started to dawn on him. "That's right! Ever since then, Inui has become increasingly stubborn. Unduly intolerant of others, in particular. Obsessive about justice, doctors' ethics, the virtues of science..." Shima had been almost recumbent on the sofa, but now sat bolt upright. "And this tendency has become all the more pronounced of late. Yes, it must have been sparked by the rumour that you and Tokita were up for the Prize!" Shima's eyes widened with astonishment at the import of his own words.

It was just as Atsuko had already imagined. She moved her face even closer to Shima's. "This fanatical sense of justice is very dangerous," she said, as if to sow the seeds of doubt in his mind. She was well aware of the effect her good looks and *Poison* perfume would have on him from close quarters. "What's worse, he's now suppressing his own jealousy. You must realize how warped his personality has become."

"I do. I do." Shima nodded twice, thrice as he replied, returning Atsuko's gaze with the hollow eyes of a hypnotee. "He's begun to look like the Devil recently, hasn't he?"

"Tokita only purchased a very small lot of LSIs from Giken. So why did Katsuragi refer to it as 'an abnormally large quantity'? There's something improper going on here."

"I see. I see." After nodding again with the same hollow look, Shima suddenly lifted his head. "So you mean... Katsuragi too?"

"It's a conspiracy, of course. The purpose being to ensnare Tokita. We need to have the books looked over by an auditor we can trust."

Shima was immersed in thought.

Atsuko felt a twinge of remorse for sowing suspicions that so greatly troubled her well-meaning boss, a man whose mind was usually so tranquil. She decided to introduce a note of positive enthusiasm. "It's clear there's a conspiracy. Both Tsumura and Kakimoto have fallen victim to it. I think someone's been tampering with the reflectors or collectors. Actually, I'm already looking into it." She placed her hand on Shima's thigh. "Doctor Shima. Will you fight this with me?"

"Yes. Of course. Of course." Shima stood and started walking uncertainly towards the window. His mind appeared to be elsewhere. "Let's think what we can do. Yes. Let's think what we can do."

Shima continued to repeat meaningless utterances as he gazed out of the window. Atsuko performed a bow towards his back. "Good. Then let's call it a day for now. I'll report anything as soon as I hear it."

"Right. Right."

Shima turned and nodded, smiling faintly, then started walking towards the small room at the back of his office. In the room was a little bed he used for naps. He would curl up on it for a snooze whenever he felt tired by his work, or when he wanted to escape from something unpleasant. It was an infantile habit, but at the same time a reliable method of tranquillization. And it seemed to suit his disposition perfectly, even on a logical level.

In Atsuko's opinion, Shima's meek personality made him less than reliable as an ally. She renewed her resolve to fight as she walked along the short connecting passage towards the hospital. She had merely succeeded in confirming that Shima would provide little in the way of firm support.

Atsuko went to the end of the passage and took the lift to the 5th floor. Before she could reach the nurses' station opposite the elevator hall, the senior nurse from the 5th floor approached her with a challenge.

"Doctor Chiba?"

"Ah. Senior Nurse Sayama. I've come to examine Nobue Kakimoto."

"Oh…" The slightly plump, pale-skinned senior nurse gave Atsuko a perplexed look. "But Doctor Osanai said I wasn't to let anyone see her…"

"Visitors, you mean?"

"No. Other doctors too."

Atsuko was stunned. "What's the meaning of this? Who decided that Osanai would be in charge of her?"

"Well… Doctor Osanai is responsible for this floor, after all."

In the confusion caused by Nobue's raving, Atsuko had carelessly admitted her to a ward on the 5th floor. That was obviously a mistake. The whole thing had obviously been planned that way from the beginning.

"Well, anyway, Kakimoto is my assistant, so it's my responsibility to examine her."

"Oh dear…" Sayama blushed and looked as though she were about to cry. She was a good-looking woman, about two or three years older than Atsuko. The motive for her resistance was not hard to discern; even Atsuko had heard rumours of a scandalously licentious relationship between Osanai and Sayama.

"Surely you must know? I'm authorized to examine all patients in this hospital."

"Yes, I do know that, but Doctor Osanai said this time was an exception. He said Kakimoto's symptoms would actually get worse if she saw you, in particular."

Ah. This was Osanai's ploy to convince the nurses that Atsuko was responsible for Nobue's derangement. Atsuko was overcome with a rage that made her head reel, but remained as composed as ever. "I think there's been a misunderstanding," she said with a smile. "Miss Kakimoto's condition has nothing at all to do with me. But never mind. I'll call Osanai directly. Let me use your phone."

Osanai was not in his research lab. *Good*, thought Atsuko as she replaced the receiver. Arguing with him over the phone in front of Sayama, not to mention the four other nurses who were willingly bending their ears, would only further compromise Atsuko's authority in the hospital.

Atsuko returned to the Institute building and went straight to Tokita's lab. As she walked, she started to entertain doubts about her own behaviour. She was beginning to neglect her research in pursuit of fame and honour, choosing to dabble in office politics instead of doing her job. Atsuko smiled grimly as she realized that Inui may have been right to criticize her. *At least I can still afford to smile*, she thought as she walked through the open door to Tokita's lab. There, she would meet a situation that would make a smile even harder to afford.

There was no sign of Himuro in the anteroom. Cases and boxes were scattered around the room; monitor screens continued to flicker. Custom chips of various types were strewn all over the floor. It looked as if someone had been frantically searching for something, or as if there had been some kind of fight. The internal door was also open. Atsuko entered to find Tokita slumped in a chair, breathing heavily with his hair madly dishevelled. His room was in the same chaotic state as the anteroom.

"What happened?" Atsuko asked with a sense of foreboding. She hardly dared hear the answer.

"The DC Minis. They've gone." Atsuko saw Tokita's bloodshot eyes for the first time. The terrible state of the room must have been his own doing.

"They've been stolen!" Atsuko cried. "They must have been. You won't find them here now. How many were there?"

"Five. No, six. One disappeared some time ago."

"You made six? And they've all gone?"

Tokita nodded weakly.

"What are we going to do?!" cried Atsuko. She heard herself using that clingy, whining tone that women often use when asking something of a man, a tone she abhorred more than anything. But she couldn't help it. "Where's Himuro?"

"Don't know. Haven't seen him since I arrived this morning. Can't find him anywhere." Tokita looked up at Atsuko with an expression suggesting that he'd more or less abandoned hope already. "He's disappeared."

17

At the Board Meeting that morning, Sukenobu had proposed that Namba be made Manager of the Third Sales Division, with responsibility for the zero-emissions vehicle. All the senior executives bar Noda had agreed, and Noda had returned to his office with a heavy heart. The President had instructed Noda, as Namba's direct superior, to deliver the bad news. Noda was sure Namba wouldn't take it lying down.

Ah, so this was Sukenobu's revenge, Noda thought as he looked out of his window onto the sun-drenched streets below. He gave a wry smile. It was certainly a token revenge, enough for Sukenobu to feel some self-satisfaction. At the Meeting, Sukenobu had cunningly presented the proposal to make the President's nephew Manager of the Development Office, *as if it had been his own idea*. All in attendance had summarily approved Sukenobu's next proposal to transfer Namba, a man whose nature made him utterly unsuited to sales. To Noda, the total acquiescence of the Board suggested that Sukenobu had been manoeuvring beforehand. The fact that Noda hadn't even been consulted was typical of Sukenobu. To his infantile mind, even taking a rival by surprise could constitute a sort of revenge.

117

Only Sukenobu knew that Noda could not oppose the transfer, for it was Noda himself who'd first suggested making Kinichi Manager of the Development Office. And the President would have remembered that very well. The President himself was only too delighted to let his nephew serve in that role, and didn't appear overly concerned with Noda's misgivings about how Namba would react.

Serves him right, thought Noda. Namba had brought it on himself. At the same time, Noda regretted having been so hasty in launching his counter-attack, without thought for the consequences, the sole purpose being to parry Sukenobu's offensive. But Noda had suggested the change in the sure knowledge that the President's nephew would sooner or later be sent to the front line of production, and that Namba would eventually lose his place in the Development Department. What's more, he firmly believed that it signalled positive progress for the company. There were several other departments where Namba could manifest his talents.

Even so, Noda hadn't thought of making him Manager of Sales! *Sukenobu must have hatched that one*, he thought. The Manager of the Development Office was equal in rank to a Deputy Manager, so it was actually a promotion for Namba. Sukenobu and the rest must have been saying, "*You've developed the zero-emissions vehicle, now go and sell it! And you've got your promotion, so what are you moaning about?!*" Brilliant! After all, Namba had already made quite a nuisance of himself with his ideas about selling the vehicle. As he looked down on the streets below, Noda smiled and shook his head a number of times.

Noda thought back to the dream he'd had a few days earlier. In the dream, Namba had been selling vegetables. That must have been a premonition that Namba would be transferred to sales. Noda had been concerned about how Sukenobu would strike back, and just as Paprika had said, the solution had appeared in the dream. If Namba had actually grown the vegetables he was selling in the dream, then the dream had even presented the

118

solution – that Namba should be put in charge of selling the zero-emissions vehicle.

Noda suddenly straightened his back and laughed aloud. The code name for the zero-emissions vehicle was "The Vegetable". He gasped in amazement and shook his head again. The strange power of dreams, the mysterious working of the subconscious had finally come home to him.

This was no time for mere wonderment, nevertheless. Noda had a duty to perform, one that might not be all that pleasant. Remembering Paprika's instruction to "*solve his problems with human relations*", Noda had his secretary call Namba.

However contentious, however stubborn Namba may have been, he would never have been appointed Manager of the Development Office without a basic grasp of business etiquette. He arrived neatly dressed, quite in contrast to his usual slipshod appearance; he'd even combed his hair.

"You wanted me?"

"Yes. Some staff transfers were decided at this morning's Board Meeting. You're the new Manager of the Third Sales Division. Take a seat."

Noda spoke quickly, casually. He avoided looking Namba in the eye until he'd shown him towards the lounge and sat facing him across the low table. When he finally glanced at him, he noticed that Namba's eyes were glistening and darting about madly. He appeared not quite sure how he should react to the news.

"Did you recommend the move?" Namba said in a stony voice.

"Well – somewhat against my better inclinations..." Noda fended off the question; he hated passing the buck.

"Thank you very much!" Namba lowered his head slightly as an eerie smile spread over his features. He was unusually calm, but it was quite unlike him to use sarcasm. Noda gazed steadily at Namba's angular face.

"That's exactly what I was hoping for! I asked you some time ago, in passing, and I was sure you'd forgotten all about it."

Suddenly, Namba started to sound excited. "If anything, I thought it would be better to transfer to sales straight after the vehicle was completed. But never mind. I'll be promoted anyway, to compensate for the time it took. Or perhaps it just took time to get promoted. In any case, I could wish for nothing better. Though of course, I understand it's all thanks to your kind consideration. But I really am so sorry. I thought you'd forgotten all about me asking you for this so long ago. I've been making a nuisance of myself lately, partly to get you to remember it. This is something that will affect my whole future, you see. But then I thought I couldn't keep bothering you about the same thing all the time. So that's why it all came out in that rather unfortunate way." Namba spoke with the fast delivery of a skilled tactician, yes, the loquacity of the self-satisfied.

Noda could no longer hold back a snigger. He'd remembered that, when the zero-emissions vehicle was first being developed, Namba had let it slip that he had a plan for marketing the vehicle. He said he wanted to be transferred to sales as soon as the vehicle was commercialized. At the time, Noda had thought it nonsense, assuming it to be nothing more than a momentary whim, and had proceeded to forget all about it. The fact that Namba now challenged virtually everything, and kept sticking his oar into the sales programme at every opportunity, obviously came from his dissatisfaction at not getting his own way.

"What's so funny?" Namba reacted to Noda's snigger with a laugh of his own. "You're imagining what kind of blunders I'll make as a Manager of Sales? Well, you may be right. To an experienced campaigner like yourself, it must seem dangerous to put me in that position."

"No, no. That's not true…"

"Yes, it is. I'm well aware of my own weaknesses. But even a fool like me will consider his future, won't he."

Not only was he a maverick, but he also had a sharper mind than Noda had previously given him credit for. He had ambition to get ahead in life. He must have realized that if he'd stayed on as Manager of the Development Office, he would never have made it to Senior Director. If a man like him were made Manager of Sales, he would learn the principles and techniques of sales with the same enthusiasm that he'd applied to research and development. He would convince himself that he was now a "sales professional". Using his loquacity, he would quickly learn the skills of personal relations and other things required of the Manager of Sales. As Namba continued to speak, his eyes glistening with joy and relief and hope, he started to resemble Toratake. He began to look like someone who was very dear to Noda.

"And will Kinichi be my successor?"

"You mean you'd already thought of that?"

"I'm not a complete idiot, you know." Namba grinned again. It seemed he'd long since foreseen that he would eventually lose his status as Manager of the Development Office to the President's nephew, and had mentally prepared himself for his new position.

Noda's dream had been trying to make him remember. It had been trying to remind him that Namba had expressed a wish to sell the zero-emissions vehicle ("vegetable") that he'd developed ("grown"). After Namba had left the room, Noda gasped in astonishment on realizing the true meaning of the dream for the first time. In the dream, everything had been resolved. Released from his sense of guilt, Noda felt his spirits lifted.

"Right!" he murmured quietly. This was the perfect time to call Shinohara. In spite of Paprika's advice, he'd hesitated to make the call, partly out of self-consciousness, partly because he was afraid to learn the awful truth about Toratake.

He'd copied Shinohara's telephone number into his diary from a list of junior-high-school alumni. He hadn't spoken to him for six months. That was when Shinohara had called to tell him about a reunion to be held in a restaurant in their old village, which had since been upgraded to a town.

Shinohara had inherited his father's hardware store. He appeared quite taken aback to actually hear from Noda. "What a surprise!" he said, his voice leaping with surprise. "How have you been? Everyone wants to see you again!"

"Yes, I'm sorry I can never make it." Noda had forgotten his preoccupation with Shinohara's role in the gang of bullies. "It's just, well, there's something I wanted to ask you."

"Oh yes? What is it?"

"How long is it since Toratake died?"

"Since Toratake *what*?"

Noda raised his voice. "You must know he was my best friend at school? I've been thinking about him a lot recently. So I wondered when—"

"Hold on, hold on! What are you talking about? Toratake isn't dead! He's as alive as you or I! He runs an inn now."

"What?…" Noda was stunned.

Shinohara laughed. "Who on earth told you he was dead? Someone's been winding you up!"

"What do you mean?! You called to tell me about it!"

"And why would I do that? Yes, I called while you were at university, to tell you about a class reunion. That's when I told you that Takao had died."

Noda was lost for words. He'd completely forgotten that Toratake's given name was "Takao". Noda and Toratake had been on first name terms. Yet it was not Takao Toratake but Akishige's crony Takao who had died. Noda had been labouring under a delusion for thirty years.

"I think you must have made some mistake," said Shinohara.

Noda moved the receiver from his mouth and sighed quietly.

"Yes. I must have done."

"Toratake would go mad if he heard that. He's always saying how much he wants to see you."

If that was so, Toratake must no longer have felt any resentment about Noda's betrayal. As the only one to leave the old village,

Noda had continued to harbour bad feelings that had long been forgotten amongst those who'd stayed. Those old complexes had all been dissolved and resolved as people forged new relationships in the new town.

"What did Takao die of?"

"Tetanus, poor bloke."

The idea that it was suicide must also have been a trick of Noda's memory. He probably hadn't even asked Shinohara what had caused Takao's death in the first place.

After promising to attend the next reunion without fail, Noda hung up. His dreams had been trying to tell him all along: Toratake's death had been nothing but an illusion. That was why Toratake had appeared in the old inn, disguised as a tiger. That was why he'd entered Noda's room, disguised as the boy Torao.

He would see Toratake again at that year's class reunion. For a moment, Noda smiled as memories of their boyhood friendship came flooding back. He wanted to share this joy with someone. The only possible candidate was Paprika. Ever since they'd parted, he'd longed to see her again, speak to her again. Though he felt a little ashamed of that sentiment, he convinced himself that he would, after all, merely be reporting something to her. He called her apartment. But of course. It was the middle of the day. She wasn't there.

18

This man's goody-goody nature is the source of all evil, thought Morio Osanai as he looked down at Shima's face, bathed in the yellow light of the standing lamp. He had crept into the room at the back of the Administrator's Office, knowing Shima to be sleeping there. Being of an easygoing disposition, Shima never locked the doors to his office or back room, even when he was taking a nap. Osanai had slipped in with ease.

To Osanai, there was nothing more despicable, no one less worthy of his service than a leader who had no policy. He hated this Administrator, this man whose only wish in life was to maintain the status quo and prevent anything untoward from happening. Osanai began to shake with rage at the sight of this man, snoozing there with that expression of utter complacency, so full of false assurance, surrounded by the sickly-sweet, lukewarm smell of his own breath, a smell that filled the room. What profound dullness of instinct! Was he really a psychiatrist?!

If Shima so openly flaunts his defencelessness, thought Osanai, *he deserves all the harm that befalls him. Then maybe he'll realize that he himself is the root of all evil.* Just because, by sheer coincidence, two of his pupils had turned out to be unnaturally clever, Shima had based his record as Institute Administrator solely on their achievements. Now that they were shortlisted for the Nobel Prize, he was bathing himself in the glory of being their mentor. He had happily given free rein to their demonic wilfulness and deviation from ethics. He was a disgrace to the profession, and so thick-headed with it! For he could never hope to understand the truth of this, never even try to understand, however directly it was said. No, there was nothing at all that Osanai could tolerate about this man, in soul or body. He deserved everything that came his way.

Osanai took the DC Mini out of his pocket. It was shaped rather like the seed of a loquat fruit. Shima himself should fall victim to this "seed of the Devil", as Inui had dubbed it, this device whose development Shima had encouraged without the faintest awareness of its diabolical potential. Taking his lead from Inui, Osanai felt no trace of conscience as he planted the DC Mini on the sleeping Administrator's head. Himuro had told him all there was to know about the device – how it worked, its functions, even the fact that it had no protective code. Everything, that is, except for its name. The DC Mini wobbled slightly, but still managed to attach itself to Shima's thinning hair. Shima remained in deepest sleep.

Osanai returned to the Administrator's Office, where he connected a portable collector to a PC that stood at one end of Shima's desk. Now he could access Shima's consciousness as he slept. If Shima had any history of neurosis, he would easily be affected by the delusions of a schizophrenic. But a lengthier strategy had to be planned, as with Tsumura and Kakimoto. Shima's abnormality must be allowed to seep out gradually, so that no one would suspect a thing. Osanai inserted a disk that would intermittently project the dreams of a mildly schizophrenic patient. Himuro had prepared the program specifically for Torataro Shima. Then he stepped into the corridor and locked the door to the Office. He'd found the key, covered in dust at the back of a drawer in Shima's desk. The Institute staff might think it odd that the door was locked when it was usually open, but no one would make a fuss about such a petty thing.

As he made his way back along the connecting passage towards the hospital, Osanai thought about Atsuko Chiba. He knew that she and Tokita were already searching for Himuro and the stolen DC Minis. Osanai felt a rising irritation every time he thought of the close spiritual bond between Chiba and Tokita. He remembered the passion he felt for her, a passion that had grown even stronger recently. He wanted her so much that it hurt, but he could never reveal it openly. For Atsuko, he was sure, regarded him merely as a co-conspirator of the enemy, a trusted ally of the Vice President. She would only misinterpret his love as a ruse to help Inui win the Nobel Prize.

He spotted Tokita in the Medical Office, but passed it without stopping. To him, Tokita was nothing more than a jumbled mass of inferiority complexes. Osanai regarded Tokita's development of devices as the warped product of his various complexes, including inferiority. These distorted stimuli allowed his energy to run wild, with no concern for ethics or morality. That was why he could develop devices that were increasingly bereft of humanity.

Like his mentor Seijiro Inui, Osanai fervently believed that technology had no place in the field of psychoanalysis. Many mental illnesses in the modern era had arisen from the rampant excesses of science and technology in the first place; the very idea of using science and technology to treat them was fundamentally wrong. It violated the principles of nature.

Of course, even Osanai recognized the utility value of PT devices, and had applied them to his treatment in line with the Institute's policy. But he felt that Atsuko's practice of indiscriminately accessing patients' dreams, violating their mental space for the sake of her treatment, ran counter to all accepted morality; it far exceeded the tolerable limits of psychotherapy. If such actions were to win her the Nobel Prize, it would mean that psychiatry for the sake of humanity had been reduced to science for the sake of technology. Patients would then start to be treated as objects. The warm, human psychoanalysis that Osanai and the others had expended so much effort to learn would become discarded as old-fashioned medicine, ungrounded in theory and no better than alchemy or witchcraft. Until PT devices could be properly evaluated and used correctly, Tokita and Chiba had to be prevented from winning the Nobel Prize, whatever it took. This was Osanai's firm conviction.

Even so, Osanai found himself better equipped to tolerate the role of Atsuko Chiba, compared to that of Tokita. After all, she was a just woman. As a woman, she had no ideology. So it stood to reason that the only thought in her mind was to faithfully, cheerfully pursue the utility value and application of the PT devices developed by Tokita. That was what all female scientists were like anyway; nothing more could be expected of them. This was not a question of looking down on women, but rather one of recognizing their natural disposition.

The more he thought about it, the less Osanai could resist Atsuko's allure as a woman. Ah! Her lightly tanned skin. Her body, so taut and healthy. He could imagine the pleasure of holding her. Given his rich self-awareness culled from past experience with women, he had no reason to doubt that, if he were to confront her directly, declare his love for her and ask her to sleep with him, she would be only too glad to oblige. After all, he had good looks that even men found attractive. Those good looks were supported by integrity and intelligence, not vacuous empty-headedness. There was nothing offensive or vulgar about him. Atsuko surely had the sexual appetite befitting a woman of twenty-nine years, and there could be no more suitable partner for her than Morio Osanai. Once he had declared his love for her, she would no doubt accede most willingly to his advances.

His infatuation with Atsuko merely increased at the thought that this situation could become reality at any time. He could bring himself to climax just by imagining the physical sensation of making love to her. Her eyes, normally shining with cool intelligence, would now be moistened with lust. Her usually pert lips would be distorted in ecstasy. Her self-restraint, the flag-bearer of her superior intellect, would crumble and dissolve through the sheer pleasure of sex. This would be a pleasure akin to madness, worlds apart from the risible sensations she shared with that idiot Tokita merely by using PT devices. In Osanai's imagination, making love to Atsuko Chiba would be an experience light years away from that of humping the pale, sagging body of Misako Sayama, Senior Nurse on the 5th floor.

Osanai could make love to Senior Nurse Sayama whenever he liked. He could even provide her for the titillation of the un-married, highly sexed Seijiro Inui – the master just had to say the word. In fact, Inui's sexual appetite was so voracious that Osanai, the real object of his desire, could never hope to satisfy it fully, however greatly he respected and revered his mentor. By providing his lover for Inui's gratification, he at least lightened the burden of expectation on himself. Not that this had any adverse impact on the deep affection shared by Inui and Osanai; their love for each other, which had originally started as a teacher-pupil affair, merely grew more intense as they shared more and more secrets.

Osanai entered the hospital building. After making sure he wasn't being followed, he took the staircase behind the kitchen down to the second basement. In the second basement were the detention rooms, now no longer in use, a throwback from the days when violent or abusive patients would be confined there. Most of the Institute staff didn't even know the rooms existed. Osanai used a key to open the massive iron door of the detention ward and walked to the end of its ice-cold corridor. He entered the last detention room, where he'd imprisoned Himuro. The prisoner was sleeping, in his lab coat, on an iron bedstead that didn't even have a mattress. A collector sat on the table next to him. Sent to the land of dreams by drugs and with a DC Mini implanted in his head, Himuro was having the nightmares of a schizophrenic intermittently fed into his mind. He was trying his hardest to resist them by settling into dreams that he found more comfortable.

Controlling the urge to throw up, Osanai stared for a moment at the ugly face and body of Himuro as he slept. Osanai felt sick at the thought that he'd yielded his body to this pig, introducing him to pleasures that were wasted on him. It had been a necessary price to pay for Himuro's betrayal of Tokita. Osanai would probably have nightmares about it for the rest of his life. *Damn you! May you now be driven mad by subliminal projections you programmed yourself! And with that, may you forget all about your sordid relationship with me! Yes, my friend, you will forget about everything!*

Osanai looked at the monitor. Himuro was having one of his own dreams, in which he was frolicking about with a cute bob-haired Japanese doll. The doll was alive, the size of a human. The images in the collector were a program for subliminal projection that had been previously used for Tsumura, or perhaps Kakimoto. Osanai had ordered Hashimoto to feed the images to Tsumura and Kakimoto while they used their collectors and reflectors.

"Much too mild," tutted Osanai.

It was Osanai who'd persuaded Himuro to steal the DC Minis and bring them to his room, expecting his usual reward in the form of gratification on the sofa. He had then tricked Himuro into drinking a sleeping drug. He'd called Hashimoto, and together they had dragged the sleeping Himuro down to the second basement. Osanai had then ordered Hashimoto to feed the subliminal projections to Himuro. But the projections used for Tsumura and Kakimoto lasted only one-twentieth of a second every three minutes. And they'd been programmed only to stimulate the traumas of Tsumura and Kakimoto. The worst effect these programs would have on Himuro would be to give him delusions of reference; they would not cause a complete disintegration of personality, the desired effect.

Tsumura and Kakimoto were the ones who were most infatuated with Atsuko Chiba. As such, it sufficed merely to give them delusions of reference and remove them from the front line of research and treatment. Then they could be turned into fodder for spreading bad rumours about the Institute to the outside world. But Himuro was different. Having been a willing participant in Osanai's machinations, he knew everything. There was nothing for it; his mind would have to be destroyed.

Osanai decided to feed Himuro's mind with the nightmares of a severe schizophrenic, having logged the images from the memory accumulated in his reflector. With this, Himuro would be driven to the very basement of his subconscious, whence never to return. The result would certainly be a complete destruction of his personality.

Before starting the projection, Osanai checked Himuro's pockets, just to be sure. There should have been six DC Minis, but Himuro had only brought five, saying they were all he could find. Osanai suspected Himuro of hiding one for his own use. But the missing DC Mini was not in any of Himuro's pockets – unless he'd buried it inside a half-eaten chocolate bar that Osanai found in the unfortunate man's lab coat.

Osanai started to project the nightmares directly into Himuro's conscious mind. The images were so horrifying that even Osanai found them difficult to watch on the monitor. Himuro's limbs instantly went rigid. His facial expression turned to one of heart-rending sorrow. He started to issue moans mixed with weak cries. This continued for about two minutes. Suddenly, Himuro opened his eyes wide, fixed a gaze on Osanai and howled in anguish. The shock was evidently immense. He had the terrified face, the terrified voice of a man who can see his killer in front of him, and realizes for the first time that he is going to die.

Osanai felt a little shiver as Himuro continued to contort his body and scream. Eventually he closed his eyes again. The sobbing continued, but his expression gradually changed to one of imbecility, as if he was being dragged to the very bottom of his subconscious. Even that expression gradually became deformed. Finally, Himuro smiled inanely, suggesting that he'd reached a fundamental state of animal pleasure. This was not a refined pleasure, one made uninteresting by civilization; it was the true, deep essence of pleasure. Reality would suddenly seem extremely boring for anyone who saw it, though it was the product of depravity. Himuro started to issue the low, insane laugh of a psychotic maniac.

19

"Toshimi. Toshimi!"

Noda had made his usual brief appearance at a business party and was heading towards the hotel lobby, firmly intending to make a swift exit, when he'd spotted Toshimi Konakawa stepping out of the hotel pharmacy. Konakawa was a friend from his university days. Tall and well built, he now sported a moustache and looked thinner than before. In fact, Noda was surprised that his friend looked even thinner than when they'd last met two years previously.

Konakawa reacted to Noda's call with a faint smile and a nod.

"What's up? Aren't you well?" asked Noda. There had never been any reserve between them, however exalted their careers.

Konakawa grimaced and looked up at the ceiling. "Is it that obvious?"

"Of course it is! You're too thin! What are you doing here, anyway?"

Toshimi Konakawa worked for the Metropolitan Police Department. He'd graduated in the same year as Noda, passed the Civil-Service exams, and started his career as a trainee detective constable. He'd then worked his way up through the ranks of detective sergeant and inspector before joining the Met. There, he'd risen to chief inspector and superintendent to cement his place as one of the elite members of the force.

"Well, it's the Chief Commissioner. He's retired now, you see, and…" Konakawa spoke diffidently with downcast eyes. For some reason, he seemed to be finding things difficult to express. "We've just had the… er… farewell party."

"Oh, I know. That guy who's standing for parliament or something. Is the party over, then?"

"Aha." Konakawa was still stuck for words. "I was invited to the, you know, second party, the informal one, but… Well, I didn't feel like it."

He seemed in very low spirits, unable even to look his friend in the face. Noda could see right away that he was ill.

"Let's go to Radio Club," Noda said in a tone that offered no room for refusal. "I've just come from a party myself."

This was too good a chance to pass up. Noda used to love cruising the nightlife scene with friends in his university days. Sometimes, made brave by drink, he'd pick fights with thugs and hoodlums. Konakawa, a martial arts expert, had saved him from certain injury on many an occasion. If it weren't for his good friend, Noda might easily have lost an arm, if not more. He still shuddered to think back on those days.

"But…" Konakawa was decidedly lukewarm to the idea. Normally, he would have accepted any invitation from Noda without question. But now he was reticent, even towards the friend who put him most at ease. Noda instinctively felt that something was wrong.

"Come on! Just a quick drink. Yes? I've got a car waiting outside. Let's use it. All right? Jinnai and Kuga have been asking after you…"

"Really? Well…"

As they made their way to Roppongi in the hired limousine, Noda managed to extract one piece of information from his oddly taciturn friend: Konakawa had been promoted to Chief Superintendent about six months earlier.

"Wow! So you're up to three stars now? Congratulations! And I suppose you'll be up for Chief Commissioner next?"

This man, once his best friend, had risen so high in society that there was hardly any higher he could climb. Noda was overcome with emotion – so much that he could hardly speak. So much that he could have wept.

Konakawa sighed. It was a dark, mysterious sigh, one that seemed to spring from the depths of his soul, one that spoke of sorrow and remorse, despair and rejection. Noda thought this must have something to do with his promotion. He had to find out about it. Do something to help this precious old friend who stood on the verge of greatness.

Radio Club was still playing old songs like 'My Generation' and 'Lola', amid the nostalgic wine-hued atmosphere produced by its teak-clad interior. It still retained its air of tranquillity, thanks largely to its customary absence of customers.

"My!" gushed Kuga, smiling like a Buddhist icon as he bowed solemnly. "Mr Konakawa! How delightful to see you again!"

"We've missed you," Jinnai called from behind the counter, his whitish teeth contrasted against his darkish skin.

Noda and Konakawa would normally have sat at the counter, to be joined by Jinnai for some light, congenial conversation. But tonight they would need a more select location. The intuitive Kuga instantly understood this from the air that hung about them. He led them to the booth at the back, the one that was like a private room of its own.

"So what's caused all this?" Noda started without further ado, as soon as their twelve-year-old Wild Turkey on the rocks had arrived.

"Well, you know. I can't sleep at night." Konakawa had kept up the same faint smile from the outset. Noda took it to indicate a lack of facial expression.

"Yes, but *why* can't you sleep at night?"

Konakawa gave his friend a slightly mysterious look. "No reason."

"Ah – I see. Cause unknown."

Konakawa said nothing for a moment, but seemed to be ruminating over what Noda had said. Then he straightened his back and slowly shook his head. "There is no 'cause', known or unknown. There's nothing that could be remotely described as a cause."

Noda had read books about psychopathology when looking for the cause of his own anxiety. From his knowledge of the subject, Konakawa's reply immediately suggested clinical depression. One particular characteristic of depression, the type most prevalent at the time, was that it occurred without reason. Of course, Noda couldn't suddenly tell his friend that he was suffering from depression. He remembered that, in the field of clinical psychiatry, it was considered taboo for a patient to be told the nature of his illness.

"Otherwise you're in good health, then?"

"Physically? Sure. We have a health check every year," Konakawa replied firmly. "There's nothing wrong with me."

"I'm sure there isn't…" Noda noted that Konakawa's thrift with words hadn't changed.

"Sounds as if you're interrogating me…"

Noda laughed out loud, but Konakawa still wore the same faint smile.

"But anyway, it can't be good for you to be losing sleep all the time…"

Even the expressionless Konakawa nodded sadly at this. "That's true. My sleeping and waking rhythms are all over the place. And I've lost my appetite."

"Your appetite too?" That explained why he was so thin. "So this must be getting in the way of your job?…"

"Right," Konakawa said, almost as if to mock his own predicament. "But you know… In the force, once you've got your qualifications, you just continue on your set path. Promotion, promotion, promotion. Unless you have to stand down because of some blunder."

"Really…" Noda stared vacantly at Konakawa's face. He'd never imagined that working for the Metropolitan Police Department could be so undemanding as Konakawa seemed to suggest. But now it sounded like the kind of place where "blunders" were committed all the time. By all except the most talented, that is.

They drank on in silence for a minute or two. Kuga served the next round of drinks without a word, a smile of great joy on his face.

"So your work's going well, then?"

"Well, you know…" Konakawa clearly didn't want to talk about it, but started to let his story out in morsels. "The Chief Commissioner is always meeting government officials, top people, you know. But the Deputy Chief Commissioner – I mean, the one who's just been promoted to Chief Commissioner – well, he not only lacks charm but he's also a poor talker. So, more and more, I'm being asked to attend functions in his place."

"You cut quite a commanding figure, that's for sure." Noda cast an eye over his friend's appearance – all proper and correct in a manly way, the very image of the classic Japanese male. "So is that a problem for you?"

"Well, it's getting in the way of my main job," said Konakawa. "And anyway, I'm not exactly a great speaker myself, am I."

"No, but I'd say that's your strong point," Noda laughed. "I mean the fact that you're not always yacking on about things. People may say you're the silent type, but surely that's desirable in your line of work?"

Konakawa declined to answer. He was clearly dissatisfied with himself.

Eventually he spoke again. "All I want is to be good at my job."

"And aren't you?" Noda decided to remind his friend of his past exploits. "What about the serial shootings in Kami Kitazawa?"

"That's the only case I ever solved," Konakawa said with a grimace. "Why do people keep going on about it?"

"Come on. You're being too hard on yourself, aren't you? After all, you just said you'd get promoted without doing anything."

Konakawa fell silent again. Noda felt there was nothing more he could do to help. "Of course, you do know that sleeplessness and loss of appetite can be caused by psychological factors?" he said slowly, choosing his words with care.

"Yes. I'm sure they are," Konakawa replied lifelessly.

"Right. And do you want to cure your condition?"

"I'll be in trouble if I don't." A look of scepticism started to appear in Konakawa's eyes.

"All right then. Would you let me arrange the treatment?"

"Treatment? You mean a psychiatrist?" Konakawa gave his friend a withering look and shook his head. "Or a psychoanalyst? Out of the question. I'd be finished if people knew I was seeing one of those."

"Yes. I know exactly what you mean," Noda said, nodding vigorously. "That's why I'm asking you to let me arrange it. Do you think I'd suggest such a thing without considering the delicacy of your situation? Of course not. But what if I could guarantee that no one would ever know about it? Come on. Let me introduce you to someone. What have you got to lose?"

"You seem very confident!" Konakawa laughed, letting down his guard. "Who, then?"

"A therapist," Noda replied as he leant across the table. "Have you ever heard of Paprika?"

"Paprika? The spice?"

"Paprika, the therapist."

"Strange name for a therapist. No, I haven't." Konakawa shook his head as if it were of no concern to him. That was his customary way. He appeared not to have heard the rumours about Paprika.

"All right, you must have heard of the Institute for Psychiatric Research?"

"Oh, I've heard of that." Konakawa showed a spark of interest this time. "It's got one of the best psychiatric hospitals in Japan. As a sister facility, that is. And two of its staff have been shortlisted for the Nobel Prize in Physiology and Medicine."

"Physiology *or* Medicine."

"Aha."

"And do you know the Administrator, Torataro Shima? He did medicine at our university. I've known him since senior high."

"I don't know anyone who did medicine."

"Well, there's this woman called Paprika who works for him. She's actually the best psychotherapist there is."

"Woman?" A bald expression of uncertainty suddenly appeared on Konakawa's face. Noda remembered that his friend had always held a certain mistrust of women.

"Shima introduced me to her. She cured me of a mental illness."

Even Konakawa had to be interested now. He cast a questioning look at Noda. "Mental illness?"

"Don't worry. It was only anxiety neurosis," Noda said, and proceeded to tell his friend the whole story.

20

Atsuko returned to her apartment in a state of fatigue. It was nearly midnight when she and Tokita had given up their search for Himuro and the DC Minis. Himuro lived with his parents in Saitama. Atsuko had phoned them, but he wasn't there. She had gradually become convinced that he'd been locked away somewhere. She'd slipped the master key from the nightwatchman's room and tried all the other rooms in the Institute, but Himuro was nowhere to be found.

Tokita had confirmed Atsuko's fear about the DC Mini – it didn't have a protective code to block unauthorized access. If word got out that they'd lost such a potentially dangerous device, there would be public outrage. For that reason, they could ill afford to take others into their confidence; their only option was to continue the search unaided.

Torataro Shima was their only conceivable ally. They decided to ask his advice the following morning. Unreliable as he was, he would surely understand the gravity of the situation once they'd explained it to him. He would surely keep it confidential. What's more, a word from him would authorize them to search the wards in the 5th floor of the hospital, which were closely guarded and had been inaccessible that evening. This was the conclusion the pair had reached on their way back to the Institute apartments in Atsuko's Marginal. Tokita lived with his mother on the 15th floor, in a large apartment with a fine view – the one directly below Atsuko's.

As she soaked in a hot bath, Atsuko started to wonder if Himuro might actually be somewhere in the same building. He could have been taken to Osanai's apartment, or Hashimoto's, or one belonging to some other lackey of Seijiro Inui. Both Osanai and Hashimoto were single; their apartments were on the 15th and 14th floors. The senior members of the Institute staff who lived in the building had a tacit understanding that they would respect each other's privacy. The unspoken rule was that they would keep away from each other's apartments. Atsuko only spoke to Shima when they met at the Institute; she had never once visited his apartment, even though it was on the same floor as hers.

In any case, Shima was not the man she desperately wanted to meet and ask for guidance. It was Tatsuo Noda. He was the only person who sprang to mind as someone she could really depend on at this time. She was not overestimating his qualities simply because she'd started to fall in love with him. She even thought he could serve as the Institute's next auditor. Atsuko didn't know what qualifications were needed to fill such a post, but he was the type who would instantly spot anything untoward in the accounts. In fact, Atsuko thought she might propose this to Shima the very next day.

Above all, she wanted to open her heart to Noda, share her bag of troubles with him, ask his advice, borrow some of his wisdom. He could guide her in the ways of dealing effortlessly with all the complex relationships and internal conflicts at the Institute. She knew he would listen to her plea and extend a helping hand. Because he loved her.

No! Atsuko shook her head in denial.

That was exactly why she *shouldn't* ask his advice. Had she not always depended on her own guile, her own wits, never those of others? Surely she could never do anything so pathetic as to ask the advice of a former patient. Noda had problems of his own. To take advantage of his feelings towards her and beg for his help, without a thought for those problems, would make her no better than those self-centred young women she observed all around her.

That notion acted like an alarm bell, set off by the realization that she would fall helplessly in love with Noda if she were to meet him again. She could ill afford that kind of entanglement in her current straits. Atsuko resolved to banish all thought of Noda from her mind forthwith.

The telephone rang in the living room. Phone calls at this hour were always from the media, or people related to the media. They were usually from people who'd called the Institute during the day and had been refused a connection, but knew that Atsuko would be home later that night. She wrapped herself in a bath towel and went to pick up the phone.

"Atsuko Chiba."

"Ah – this is Tatsuo Noda."

Unbelievable. The man she'd just banished from her mind was calling to say "*You can't do that!*" In her state of fatigue, Atsuko had answered the call with the gravelly voice of an old woman. Noda didn't seem to realize he was speaking to Paprika in person.

"You want Paprika? All right. She'll be with you in a moment." Now Atsuko was deliberately trying to sound old. She went back to the bathroom, dried herself properly and threw on her gown. If Noda didn't know he'd been speaking to Paprika, who did he think she was? He must have seen the name Chiba outside the door to her apartment, and must have assumed it to be Paprika's surname. Did he think the old woman was related to Nobel Prize candidate Atsuko Chiba? Did he know nothing about Atsuko at all? Or did he know the whole truth about everything?

Atsuko returned to the telephone, smiling to herself at the oddness of the situation and her undeniable feeling of joy.

"Hi there. Good to hear from you." By now it was second nature for Atsuko to raise her voice half a tone when transformed into Paprika. The joy she felt at this unexpected call from Noda raised it another half tone. She expected him to ask who had answered the phone. What would she say if he did? That her mother was visiting, or something? But it didn't matter. Noda was far too discreet to ask.

"Paprika – is it OK to talk? This might take a while…"

"It's cool. I'm not doing anything."

She wanted to ask where he was calling from, but followed his example and kept the thought to herself. She could hear no music or voices in the background; she thought he might be calling from his study at home.

"Good. It's just that... there's something I want to ask of you."

"Yeah? What is it?"

"Well, first, I want to thank you. My condition seems completely cured. The personnel problems at work have all been resolved, and my old friend Toratake wasn't dead after all."

"Result!" Some of Noda's exhilaration seemed to have rubbed off on Atsuko, or Paprika, as she now was. An almost dreamlike sensation of delight encircled her. "So you imagined the whole thing?"

"It seems so." Without going into detail about how he'd discovered the truth of it all, Noda immediately moved on to the matter at hand. "Now, as it happens, I have a good friend, someone with a very important standing in society... I wondered if you'd be prepared to treat him."

Noda had only known her as Paprika, and had clearly assumed that her job was to analyse people individually using PT devices. Atsuko could hardly blame him for that. Now she was caught in two minds. As Atsuko Chiba, she simply couldn't afford the time. But as Paprika the dream detective, her alter ego, she could find no excuse to refuse his request.

"What's wrong with him?" It would surely do no harm to ask. After all, his condition may have been so mild that a personal appearance from Paprika wasn't required.

"He says he can't sleep and has lost his appetite. But I think there's more to it than that. He seems terribly depressed. He won't speak and his expression never changes. It doesn't seem like a problem that'll just go away."

"Have you tried to cheer him up?"

"Well, I took him for a drink and got him to talk about it. But it was as if he was in a trance. And then he says there's nothing particularly wrong with him..."

These were classic symptoms of clinical depression. A person at this level of depression will rarely react to diversions, attempts to console or encourage, nor even to persuasion or threats.

"I suppose your friend has no idea what triggered his condition?"

"No. But in my view as a layman, I wonder if being promoted had anything to do with it."

"Promoted?"

"Yes. He was promoted to quite a high position recently."

Clinical depression is usually caused by nothing at all – or at least, by something that would seem utterly insignificant to the normal way of thinking. That could include promotion at work, career advancement, or other events normally seen as cause for celebration.

"So... Do you think it could be clinical depression?" asked Noda.

Paprika had thought Noda's explanation a little too technical for a layman. Now he revealed a more than competent grasp of the subject. "Sounds like it," she replied. "But you didn't tell him that, did you?"

"No."

"Good. Of course, I couldn't be sure without meeting him."

There had recently been a spate of depression among management personnel sent on job assignments away from their families. Atsuko thought that Noda could have arbitrarily pinned this label on his friend. He might have been focusing only on the symptoms that confirmed his suspicion.

"Very true. I'd certainly be glad if you could meet him. But haven't you got enough on your hands... Paprika?"

Atsuko said nothing. In her unusually vulnerable state, she felt like bursting into tears at Noda's kind concern.

"What's wrong?" he asked.

"I'm really glad you called. If it really is depression, there's no room for complacency. He could even try to kill himself."

141

Noda gasped.

"So – will you introduce him to me?" asked Atsuko.

Then she'd be able to meet Noda. Atsuko could hardly believe herself. Only a moment ago, she'd been deriding her own weakness in even thinking about asking for his help. But now, with the prospect of meeting him again, she suddenly felt like putting herself completely in his hands. She was happy to think that Noda had come to her for help. For then, her offer of advice didn't have to be for her own indulgence.

"How about tomorrow evening?" said Noda. "Eleven o'clock at Radio Club. The same as the first time. You remember?"

Atsuko remembered the relaxed atmosphere of Radio Club, and suddenly saw it as a rare sanctuary from her daily troubles. "Yes, good idea. What's your friend's name?"

"Konakawa. Toshimi Konakawa. He's a Chief Superintendent in the Metropolitan Police Department."

It was Atsuko's turn to gasp. "Superintendent?…"

"Chief Superintendent. One rank down from Chief Commissioner. In fact, he said he often deputizes for the Chief Commissioner these days."

"That's quite important…"

"As I said just now."

Atsuko felt as if her knees were about to give way. She could hardly ask Noda's advice about the Institute's problems in front of such a person – especially as those problems might involve acts of a criminal nature. She certainly couldn't mention the theft of the DC Minis, which could easily become a matter for the police. To make things worse, Paprika's own activities had once been illegal.

"There's something I ought to tell you," Atsuko started. "I'm… a director at the Institute for Psychiatric Research."

"Hmm. Thought so."

"…And I'm not actually allowed to treat patients individually."

Noda laughed. "Is that all you're worried about? Forget it. My

142

friend isn't as inflexible as you may think. After all, he's the one who'd have most to lose if this went public!"

"Yes, I can understand that. So you're saying he's not obsessed with procedure and loyalty to his profession?"

"He's a good man with plenty of common sense, and sensitive with it. He knows how to let his hair down, believe me. He's helped me a lot since university days. Even since he joined the police, he's given me a lot of advice about work-related problems. He's even solved some of them."

"A good man..."

Atsuko felt somewhat reassured, but couldn't rid herself of her misgivings. The loss of the DC Minis could have serious implications for public safety. This man worked for the police, and if he found out about it, he could hardly turn a blind eye. No matter how broad-minded he was.

21

Paprika reached Radio Club with time to spare. She'd been particularly careful this time; the journalist Matsukane had told her of rumours that had circulated after her previous visit to Roppongi. She didn't want that to happen again. Even so, she was loath to alter her usual outfit of red shirt and jeans. As Paprika, she somehow wouldn't feel the same without it. It didn't matter, anyway; unlike the previous occasion, she didn't have to wander around looking for the bar, and arrived in good time without appearing unduly conspicuous.

"My!" Kuga remembered Paprika. He thrust out his portly belly before bowing obsequiously. "A pleasure to see you again!"

"Come on in!" Jinnai called across with a smile.

A male customer was sitting alone at the counter. Though initially startled by Paprika's incongruous looks, he soon turned back to resume his conversation with Jinnai.

"Mr Konakawa has yet to arrive," Kuga said as he guided Paprika to the same booth as before. "Oh, and Mr Noda just called to say he's regrettably indisposed this evening. He said to give his regards to Mr Konakawa."

"Ah." Paprika was disappointed at first, but then saw it as an act of discretion on Noda's part. It was symptomatic of his perfectionist nature – he wouldn't use the association with Konakawa to engineer a meeting with Paprika. That was what she liked about Noda. And in any case, she could hardly ask his advice in front of a Chief Superintendent from the Metropolitan Police Department.

Kuga was standing next to Paprika's table, looking down at her with the genial smile of a Buddhist statue, eyes half-closed. Paprika returned the smile. She wondered why she was being treated like an old acquaintance when she'd only been there once before. They were playing *Satin Doll* again.

Paprika calmly asked Kuga if he had anything in particular to recommend. Kuga went back and forth to the counter, twice, to relay her questions and Jinnai's replies. Kuga seemed to relish his role as go-between, much to the amusement of the lone customer at the bar.

The arbitration process settled on an unusual seventeen-year-old Ballantine called Black Jack, served on the rocks. Paprika was taking a sip with eyes narrowed when the door opened and a man walked in. From Noda's description of his friend, she instantly recognized the man as Toshimi Konakawa. The reception he received from Jinnai and Kuga suggested he was a frequent visitor.

"I'm Paprika. Nice to meet you."

Paprika rose and greeted the man with a certain formality. For it was already obvious that, unlike Noda, he would not feel at ease with the laid-back style of a teenager.

"Konakawa," the man replied with equal formality. He lacked the usual expression of surprise whenever men first set eyes on

Paprika. She decided to continue with a formal style of speech. In any case, she found that more comfortable when speaking to an older man.

It was only when they sat facing each other that Paprika noticed Konakawa's manly demeanour. She'd heard from Noda that Konakawa often attended functions in place of the Chief Commissioner, and now she saw why. He was well built, his dark, taut face well proportioned; the moustache suited him well. Here was a man who could easily be mistaken for a hero in an American movie. Paprika had met a lot of men, but she felt a frisson of excitement at this man's appearance, enhanced by the sharp eye with which he observed her. It may have been the eye of a sick man, but it was still the eye of a high-ranking police officer.

"I hear Mr Noda won't be able to join us," said Paprika.

"Is that so." Konakawa remained expressionless. He eyed Paprika for another moment, but then seemed to lose interest, turning instead to the waiter Kuga who still stood beside him. He eventually ordered the same drink as Paprika.

"You must be a very busy man," Paprika started as soon as Kuga had left.

"Well... You know." Konakawa smiled unconvincingly.

"Yes, of course. It stands to reason. But please, don't think me foolish for asking. I need to ask all sorts of questions... Just as you do in your inquiries."

"I see. Yes. Of course." Konakawa corrected his posture, as if to signal that he might revise his view of Paprika.

"I know nothing about you, except what I've heard from Mr Noda."

Konakawa looked puzzled. The formality of Paprika's speech was so much at odds with her appearance; that made it difficult to guess her age. "Yes. By all means. Please ask whatever you like."

He sounded unnatural, as if he was forcing himself to speak when he didn't really want to. Paprika was merely applying a basic technique to make the patient feel relaxed, but it seemed irksome to Konakawa. Paprika found herself in two minds. After all, this was the first time she'd met a patient with such a high standing in society.

Paprika decided to treat Konakawa with unusual respect. If he really was suffering from depression, his innate self-esteem would have suffered a considerable blow; he would need more than the customary support from those around him.

"I must say it's quite an honour to meet a Chief Superintendent from the Metropolitan Police," she started. "And to be asked to diagnose such a person, well…"

Konakawa finally permitted himself the thinnest of smiles. "Really?"

"Absolutely. An honour."

Kuga arrived with Konakawa's drink. For a moment, the two drank in silence.

"But anyway," said Konakawa, initiating conversation for the first time, "you must find your own work motivating? As a therapist?"

Paprika thought it unusual for a man like Konakawa to show interest in the other person's work. Perhaps he'd said it to put her at ease. But to Paprika, it was a sign that he didn't find his own work "motivating" at all.

"And surely so must you?" she said. Konakawa forced another smile. Paprika had every confidence in the correctness of her judgement. She'd done her homework. Chief Superintendent was merely a rank; unlike Chief Commissioner, it was not a job description. That was why Konakawa had to perform other tasks that weren't really in his remit.

"I hear you're having trouble sleeping," Paprika said to broach the central issue. "That must be causing you problems."

"It certainly is."

"Is this the first time it's happened?"

"Yes."

"And you've lost your appetite, too?"

"Yes. My appetite as well."

"In what way are your insomnia, your lack of appetite affecting your work?"

Konakawa thought long and hard. Not that he was thinking what to say; he was thinking how to say it.

"Well," he replied at length, "I tend not to say much. I'm a poor speaker. But in my role as Deputy Chief Commissioner, I'm expected to talk in front of people. Now because of my insomnia, I can never find the right words to say. The ready wit or pithy remark that's required to suit the situation. It's quite pathetic. But that is what's expected of me..." And he trailed off in mid-sentence.

"So you dislike that kind of thing, in the first place?"

"Yes. But I have to do it." He flashed a sharp look at Paprika.

A perfectionist. The classic personality most easily prone to depression. Perfectionists make unreasonably high demands of themselves. They work towards unattainable goals and assume too much responsibility. They try to perform several tasks correctly and to the same high standard. When told that their expectations are too high, they reply that they wouldn't be doing their job properly if they didn't meet those expectations. And since they've convinced themselves that they should be able to meet them, their ears are closed to advice.

"Do you know why you can't sleep at night?"

"Yes. It's because I can't rid my mind of trivial thoughts."

"For example?"

"Really trivial things." He actually laughed. "So trivial I'd be ashamed to mention them."

It must have seemed perfectly natural, to a man like Konakawa, that he couldn't express such trivial things. Paprika knew about this from other cases of clinical depression. For example, the sufferer will hear some noise after going to bed, and will then lie awake wondering when the noise will be repeated, with resultant loss of sleep.

Paprika still knew nothing of Konakawa's private life. To get information of that kind from such a taciturn type would require repeated questioning. He was unlikely to proffer the information himself, and the discussion would turn into a kind of interrogation. She decided to ask just one thing for now, then play it by ear from there.

"Where do you live, Mr Konakawa?"

"In a police apartment near here." His reply was followed by a pause. Konakawa seemed to be expecting another question, but when none came, he continued: "I live there with my wife. My son lives in student digs near his university."

Children leaving the family nest. Depression often seemed to follow this kind of change in family circumstances, when parents were relieved of their obligations. Yes, Konakawa was almost certainly suffering from clinical depression. Now Paprika faced a dilemma. Clinical depression usually took time to treat, but she had all the problems at the Institute to deal with, not to mention her own work as Atsuko Chiba. How would she find the time to treat him? Then again, she knew she couldn't simply ignore Konakawa's condition.

"In cases like yours, the method that's usually most effective…" Paprika started, then stopped short.

"Yes?" Konakawa's eyes were full of expectation. He was about to hear an expert opinion at long last.

"…is recuperation for a period of several months."

"Ah." Konakawa's shifted his gaze to the space above Paprika's head, as if to say "*Out of the question*".

"But that's impossible, isn't it."

"Yes. Completely impossible."

"The best cure would be to take a complete break from everyday life, rather than vainly battling with sleeplessness or depression. But since you can't do that…" Paprika started to think again.

Konakawa was definitely not the kind of person to take time off work for recuperation. In fact, that attitude was probably the root cause of his condition. Paprika came to a decision: she would have to see him through it herself.

"All right. There's nothing for it – I'll have to analyse your dreams. I presume you've heard all about that from Mr Noda?"

"Oh yes." Konakawa spoke in a tone of resignation. He clearly had no faith whatsoever in the analysis of dreams.

"And to help you recover more quickly, I'll combine it with drug therapy."

"Drugs?" This also seemed to sit uneasily with Konakawa.

"You may feel uncomfortable about the idea of treating psychological symptoms with drugs. But in cases like yours, the conventional wisdom is that treatments based on psychoanalysis have no effect and are moreover unnecessary. So the treatment has relied wholly on drugs until now."

"You mean sleeping pills?"

"Anti-depressants."

"So you're saying it's depression, then?"

"Yes."

Konakawa looked crestfallen. Paprika wanted to avoid using trite platitudes merely to lift his spirits; her aim was rather to calm his anxiety over the treatment.

"I'll keep the drugs to a minimum, as I'll be analysing your dreams at the same time."

"But what sort of effect do the drugs have?"

Paprika gave him a smile of supreme confidence. She maintained that look as she started to explain things in a way that would appeal to his intelligence. This was an area in which she was particularly skilled.

"A number of drugs have been produced to date. And now we know precisely what effect each of them has." The development of PT devices made it possible to know the mental effect of a drug by scanning the patient's mind after administering it. "Drugs act on the synaptic clefts inside the brain. Substances called monoamines come into play when impulses are transmitted from one synapse to the other. Drugs control the effects of those monoamines…"

22

Clinical depression is one of the hardest conditions to treat in a short time without recuperation. Even psychoanalysis will not reveal the cause, and depression is naturally beyond the range of comprehension by modern medicine. There are various theories – Freud's oral fixation and Pierre Janet's exhaustion of mental energy, to name two – but none of these gives a satisfactory explanation of the condition.

Paprika had already enjoyed some success in treating depression using PT devices. Her method was first to identify, through psychoanalysis, the condition in which patients susceptible to depression had lived before the onset of clinical symptoms. Then she would calculate the point at which the "endon orientation condition" would cause endon fluctuation – in other words, the point of fluctuation that induced the condition – and would introduce endon-type energy at that point. Endons exist in a third dimension that is neither mental nor physical. For that reason, clinical depression is also called endon-derived melancholia. But since endons are merely the manifestation in the human body of genesis principles shared by humans and nature, it might better be called endon-cosmos-derived melancholia.

Konakawa couldn't go home that night, as he'd agreed to undergo dream analysis therapy in Paprika's apartment. He used the cordless phone at Radio Club to call home. "I won't be coming home tonight," was all he said to his wife in front of Paprika. The sound of his wife hanging up could be heard before Konakawa terminated the call. Even bearing his taciturn nature in mind, there was an exceptionally icy feeling to their exchange; Paprika could well imagine how chilly their relationship was. But Konakawa himself appeared completely unaware of this.

The lone customer at the counter had left. As Paprika and Konakawa got up to go, Jinnai came close to Paprika. "Take good care of him," he whispered. "Take care," Kuga echoed to Konakawa beneath his breath. Noda would surely not have divulged Paprika's profession to Jinnai and Kuga. They must have realized she was some kind of therapist, even if not a psychoanalyst, using their intuition alone. That came as quite a relief to Paprika; she was glad not to be seen as some kind of teenage prostitute for middle-aged men, being passed from one client to the next through personal introduction.

They hailed a taxi outside Radio Club to take them to Paprika's apartment. From the words Paprika used to address Konakawa, the driver knew they couldn't be father and daughter, and proceeded to tell Konakawa just what he thought of him. He was old enough to be her father and should be ashamed of himself. Had he tricked her or just bought her? Whatever. The driver cast all manner of slurs on Konakawa, in a circuitous way. But Konakawa reacted to none of them. He seemed utterly incapable of showing any expression, whether positive or negative. A characteristic of personalities susceptible to clinical depression is that they are obsessed with orderliness. This includes a certain weakness of spirit; they are reluctant to fight others, and should a personality collision appear on the cards, they will gladly yield. Paprika thought it unlikely that Konakawa could fulfil his duties as a senior police officer under such conditions. Or perhaps he was different when faced with an adversary of criminal disposition.

On their arrival at Paprika's apartment, Konakawa showed no particular surprise at the splendour of the place. He didn't react at all. In a way, his lack of expression, his lack of emotion could have been interpreted as a kind of defiance, as if he was saying "*Cure me if you can*". But in his condition, he wouldn't have been capable of such feelings of antagonism or animosity in the first place. Paprika knew he wouldn't be able to sleep straight away, but asked him to get into bed anyway.

Paprika suggested that Konakawa sleep almost naked for comfort's sake. Konakawa detested slovenliness, and appeared to hesitate a little. But when he saw Paprika handling things in a way that suggested familiarity with the procedure, he felt more reassured and took a shower, then got into bed in his underwear.

Paprika set the collector memory to eight hours. She wasn't going to hang around waiting for an insomniac to fall asleep. Besides, Konakawa was going to have even more trouble than usual tonight. He was in an unfamiliar place, and the apartment of a young woman to boot. Nevertheless, once he'd fallen asleep the memory device would be activated and the collector would record the content of his dreams. While the subject was still awake, resistance from the conscious mind was too strong and only meaningless images were recorded.

"I know it won't be easy, but please try to sleep," Paprika said before fitting the gorgon onto Konakawa's head. Konakawa just let her get on with it – unlike Noda, who had wanted to know how everything worked. Soporifics were out of the question, as merely sleeping would be meaningless without any dreams to record. *Please don't go the whole night without sleeping*, Paprika thought wishfully as she withdrew to the living room to sleep on the sofa.

In spite of her clever tricks designed to induce sleep, Paprika was unable to drop off. If anything, it was she who needed the soporifics. As Atsuko Chiba, she still hadn't discovered Himuro's whereabouts in the Institute, and there were papers she needed to write. The room where Konakawa lay was quiet. Paprika thought he must be keeping his body perfectly still to avoid making any noise, silently and stoically bearing the immense irritation of another sleepless night. Paprika felt touched by his impeccable behaviour. She started to think about Noda and Konakawa, comparing the relative merits of their manly attraction, and in the process eventually managed to fall asleep.

On waking the next morning, Paprika was surprised to see Konakawa sitting fully dressed at the dining table in the living room. Until that moment, he seemed to have been gazing at her face as she slept. Paprika blushed and felt a little flustered.

"Oh! Well! Good! Have you had a shower?" she said as she jumped up and started looking for her clothes.

It was half-past seven.

"Did you manage to sleep?"

"Aha."

"And did you have any dreams?"

"Well…" It was either that he had no interest in his dreams, or that he'd forgotten them immediately.

"You'll have some coffee?"

Paprika made a pot of coffee and took two cups to the side table in the bedroom. Konakawa helped by carrying the sugar bowl and cream jug.

"Now we'll replay your dreams," Paprika said as she called up the memory from the collector.

Numbers at the bottom of the screen revealed that Konakawa had started dreaming at 4.24 in the morning. He probably hadn't slept at all until then. As they drank coffee together, they watched the screen in silence for a few moments. Even Konakawa seemed interested.

He was inside an aeroplane, the large passenger compartment of what looked like a jumbo jet. The plane lurched first to one side, then to the other. None of the passengers looked at all surprised; they all sat calmly in their seats. Paprika remembered that passengers on a jumbo jet weren't normally too aware of the plane's motion, however greatly it lurched. The scene changed to a room, the dark interior of an old Japanese mansion. Konakawa was walking along a corridor towards a wooden-floored kitchen, where a middle-aged woman was washing dishes.

Paprika stopped the screen.

"Ah! You can even do that." Konakawa was mildly surprised.

"Whose house is this?"

"I don't know."

"And the woman?"

"Sorry."

"Do you know anyone who looks like her?"

"Well...."

"Can you remember anyone who cooked meals in a kitchen like this?"

"Well," Konakawa said after a pause, "that would have to be my mother."

He seemed to be saying *"But that woman is not my mother"*.

"She's quite beautiful," Paprika continued.

"Oh?"

The implication was that Konakawa didn't think her beautiful. The woman may have been his wife, appearing in the guise of another. Paprika decided not to ask whether the woman resembled his wife, and instead returned to the dream.

A garden. A dog appeared, but immediately disappeared again. Inside a western-style mansion. Someone was lying on the ground. A trail of blood flowed along a corridor. The exterior of what appeared to be the same mansion. It was on fire.

It looked like the scene of a crime. Konakawa gave no explanation at all. *That makes things difficult*, thought Paprika. But she'd experienced this level of difficulty many times.

The entrance to a stately building. A party was going on inside. Konakawa seemed to be trying to get in. A man who looked like a security guard was standing in front of him and blocking the way.

Freeze-frame. "Who's he?"

"I remember this bit. It's some embassy, and I'm saying, 'Let me in, there's a bomb inside,' but the guard won't believe me. He says I just want to gatecrash the party."

"Did something like this actually happen?"

"No." Konakawa seemed to have found his tongue. "And to make matters worse, I happened to be wearing party clothes at the time."

"Why?"

"Because I'd been invited to the party. Not only that, but I'd forgotten my formal invitation."

"So the security guard thought you were lying about the bomb as a pretext to get in without an invite."

"Yes. But there really was a bomb!" Konakawa said forlornly.

Next frame. The security guard's face was elongated in astonishment.

"What's wrong with him?"

Konakawa laughed. "I told him it was me who'd planted the bomb."

Next frame. Konakawa must have been allowed in, and was now at a party packed with people. Books were lined up on stalls, as if it were some kind of book fair.

Paprika suddenly gasped when she saw a face loom large on the screen. It was the face of Seijiro Inui.

"Who's that?" she yelled.

Konakawa looked at her in bemusement, little knowing why she'd raised her voice. "I don't know."

"Why is he in your dream?"

"I remember seeing the face in the dream, yes. But I've never seen him before. I suppose he does look a bit like my father, but my father didn't have a beard."

How had this image become mixed up in Konakawa's dream? Considering the structure of PT devices, it was unthinkable that part of a dream collected from another patient could appear. And there was no way that any thoughts in Paprika's mind could appear in Konakawa's dream without her deliberately accessing it.

"Is something the matter?" asked Konakawa, looking in bewilderment at the clearly shaken Paprika.

"Would you wait a minute?" Paprika skipped back to the frame that was filled with Inui's face, and printed it out.

"You can even do that?!" Konakawa was again impressed, though only mildly so.

"Let's continue," Paprika said as she restarted the picture.

155

Inui's face also appeared to have come as a shock to Konakawa. Perhaps it was because Inui resembled his father. The dream ended there; Konakawa seemed to have woken up. After a little while, dreams started to return, but only in fragmentary snatches.

"You hardly slept at all, did you." Paprika sighed. "This is serious. It's only your physical strength that keeps you going. A normal person would be on their knees right now."

Konakawa was immersed in thought as he stared at the printout of Inui's face.

"What is it?" asked Paprika.

"You were surprised when you saw this face," Konakawa replied. "You know him, don't you?"

23

Konakawa was as taciturn as ever, leaving Paprika to unravel the latent meanings behind his dreams over breakfast.

"The jumbo jet was swaying quite badly, wasn't it?"

"Yes." Konakawa had no appetite. He was forcing himself to eat the eggs and bacon Paprika had prepared, simply because it would have been bad manners not to. "I don't really travel in jumbo jets that much. But I know they don't sway that badly."

"I agree."

Paprika waited for Konakawa to continue, but he was too busy chewing on a piece of bacon.

"Could it indicate some problem in your workplace?" she asked.

He smiled faintly. He did appear to know the elementary basics of psychoanalysis. "You mean, the jumbo jet could represent the Metropolitan Police Department, for example?"

"Perhaps. And nobody seemed to notice it was swaying."

"No." Konakawa neither affirmed nor denied Paprika's interpretation, but fell into thought.

With no clues to assist her analysis, Paprika reluctantly moved to the next point.

"A dog appeared briefly, didn't it."

"We had a dog when I was a child. I mean, my father did."

"Was it the same dog as in the dream?"

"It was similar."

"Were you fond of it?"

"Yes. But one day I took him out without asking, and he was hit by a car."

"And died?"

Konakawa nodded.

"Oh dear." Paprika tried to read his expression, but couldn't tell whether he felt guilty about it or not. "Then we saw a scene related to some case you handled."

"That's right. I always forget about it when I wake up, but I do dream about that one," Konakawa said in surprise. He almost sounded enthusiastic. "It was an unsolved murder. A domestic employee was killed in that big mansion in Hachioji. I often dream about unsolved cases. But the funny thing is, I never dream about cases I've solved."

Paprika laughed. "You're so obsessed with your work, you even try to solve cases in your sleep!"

"Oh?" Konakawa looked at Paprika straight-faced. "Is that what dreams are all about?"

"But of course. Dreams often provide clues to solving criminal cases. There have been numerous examples in the past."

"Yes, I think I've heard of that." Konakawa grew pensive again. "But I dreamt of a fire, didn't I. There was no fire in that mansion."

"Does a fire remind you of anything else?"

"I've never handled a case involving fire as such." Naturally, he wanted to link everything to his work.

"It could have been a fire near your house. Any time in the past?"

"No. There's never been such a thing."

157

Konakawa was not one to volunteer information unless asked. The two drank coffee in silence for a few moments.

"You went to a party at an embassy, didn't you."

"Yes."

"I wonder if that embassy actually exists somewhere."

"No. I only thought so in the dream."

"You have no memory of a building like that?"

"Not in particular. I may have seen it somewhere. Buildings like that aren't uncommon."

Paprika was astonished to realize that it was she who remembered seeing the building somewhere. What building was it? She would have to print that scene out too.

"Do you often go to parties?"

"No. Rarely. Though I'm often invited." After a moment's hesitation, Konakawa started to talk again, though only in halting phrases. "My wife goes in my place. She meets other people there. Then she gets invited to more."

"You mean every night?"

"Well. Maybe not that often." Konakawa grimaced.

"Is this a recent thing?"

"No. It started six or seven years ago." Konakawa fixed Paprika with a look that said "*So that's not the cause of my insomnia*".

But Paprika wasn't ready to let the subject go quite yet – particularly as Konakawa himself had raised it. "Did your wife have a hobby before that?"

In the absence of an answer from Konakawa, Paprika ventured a guess. "Was it reading?"

Konakawa lifted his face. "I see. Yes, there were a lot of books at the party, weren't there. I wouldn't call it a hobby, but she certainly did like reading in the old days. So are you saying I want her to stop going to parties and stay at home with her books, like before?" He laughed for a change.

"Quite probably." Paprika shared his laughter. "By the way, what's your wife's family like?"

"Her father was a police officer," Konakawa said with a hint of pride. "Just like my own."

Paprika imagined how strict their upbringings must have been.

The conversation broke off again. Paprika was getting tired of reeling off questions; it was beginning to sound monotonous.

"Oh, I just remembered," she said to change the mood. "I've got some Italian ham. Would you care for some?"

Paprika couldn't fail to note the glint in Konakawa's eye. He obviously didn't lack a taste for good food. Perhaps the conversation had whetted his appetite.

Not only that, but eating seemed to enhance his interest in conversation. "Your dream analysis is quite fascinating," he said between mouthfuls.

"Well... This is only the beginning. It gets more interesting from here on."

"Noda says you can actually get into people's dreams?"

"That's right. Next time."

"You know that face you printed out?" Konakawa said as he wiped his mouth with a handkerchief. "I've no recollection at all of meeting that man. I'd really like to know why he appeared in my dream. Could you give me a copy? I'll have him checked out."

"By all means." Paprika supposed that he meant to search the criminal records. But it all seemed so unlikely. What – Inui had committed some crime in the past, his details had been kept by the police, and this had somehow remained in the Chief Superintendent's memory? Paprika stared long and hard at the printout of Inui's face, which still lay on a corner of the table. It was not his usual face. He was smiling; his eyes were soft and warm. They had the look of love about them. Paprika had never seen anything approaching this expression on Inui's face. The background couldn't be seen, as the image was framed by the top of his forehead and the bottom of his beard.

"This is not the face of a criminal," Konakawa declared after examining the printout.

Paprika held back a laugh. "Because he resembles your father?"

"Yes, that unforgiving look in his eye. And the mouth. "

"And did you notice that resemblance in the dream?"

"I can't say. But I'm sure I didn't think it was my father. The difference is too great."

"Then you woke up immediately, didn't you?"

Konakawa looked puzzled. "You're saying the face reminded me of my father and the shock woke me?"

"I think so."

"But why? I often dream of my father. It's never been a shock." Konakawa stared at the printout again.

"More coffee?"

"No, that's fine."

Paprika felt that was quite enough for the first session. "All right, I'll give you the medication now. You must take the first dose right away."

Paprika handed Konakawa one week's supply of antidepressants.

"And the next session?" Konakawa said after taking a tablet.

"When would be convenient?"

"For me, as soon as possible. The quicker I'm cured the better," Konakawa said sheepishly, as if suddenly ashamed of his earlier scepticism. As if he'd started to believe the effects of psychotherapy and was actually beginning to enjoy it.

"Let's take a break tomorrow. How about the day after that?"

"Excellent. Should I come straight here, same time as last night?"

"Please do. I'll notify security."

"So... Is that all for today?"

"Yes. Being the first time, I think it's a good place to stop."

Konakawa looked around the room as if something were missing.

Paprika stifled another laugh. "What is it?"

"Did you, well, *discover* anything during this session? I mean, something that could be of use in my treatment?"

"What?! The dream analysis itself is the treatment. Don't you feel better?"

"Oh, was that it?" Konakawa produced a bright, uncomplicated smile for the first time. "Yes, I feel much better. I was wondering why. I've never told anyone so much about myself."

No, I'm sure you haven't, thought Paprika. "Actually, I wanted to ask a lot more. If I'm to analyse your dreams, I need to know as much about you as I can. But if I pried too much into your private life at the beginning, it would seem like an interrogation. I don't think you'd feel comfortable with that."

"I see. So it isn't just criminals who feel better when they've confessed! Well, anyway, I'll tell you a lot more next time." Their eyes met; they smiled. Paprika felt herself being drawn to his personality.

"Do you have to be at work?" she asked as he rose.

"No. I'll go home first."

He might try to sleep again in his own bed. Perhaps he was feeling sleepy as a payback from last night, now that he'd found some peace of mind. Perhaps it was because of Paprika's unusually large breakfast. Or perhaps he just wanted to put his wife's mind at rest. Paprika's intuition as a therapist told her that Konakawa's wife treated him with some contempt. Paprika bridled with the righteous indignation that single women often feel against the wives of likeable married men.

Konakawa left Paprika's apartment, seen off by a gorgeous smile he'd probably find hard to forget. She said she would enter his dreams, but what would she do then? He thought about it as he walked along the corridor towards the elevator hall. Each word uttered by that sweet girl started to return to him. She suggested that the swaying jumbo jet represented the Metropolitan Police Department. She was right. The Department was veering out of control. It was only he, the only one who didn't belong to any clique, who could see that.

Paprika had said that dreams often provide clues to solving criminal cases. Maybe he'd received a clue to the Hachioji murder case in his dream that very morning. Yes, now he remembered – there *had* been a fire near the crime scene shortly after the murder, just when he was investigating it. Could the two perhaps have been connected? He would check it out.

As these and other thoughts flitted through Konakawa's mind, he stepped into the lift and pressed the button for the ground floor. The lift moved off, then stopped immediately at the 15th floor.

A young man stepped in. Konakawa was taken aback when he saw him. It had been a long time since he'd been overcome with such a nebulous feeling of guilt. The man had the classic good looks of a Grecian statue. The look in his eyes, the shape of his mouth reminded Konakawa uncannily of the man who'd appeared in his dream that night, the man whose picture he had in his jacket pocket – *what was his name, Inui or something* – except that he didn't have a beard. He must also be an employee at the Institute, thought Konakawa. He might even be the son of the man in the dream.

The young man gave him a dubious look. Perhaps this building was out of bounds to all but the senior executives of the Institute and their families. Konakawa was again overcome by pangs of guilt. Yet he felt no need to explain his business here, or his identity. And in any case, the young man looked decidedly nervous whenever their eyes met.

24

Osanai's first thought when he saw the man in the lift was that he must be a detective. He had that same look in his eyes as certain police officers who sometimes came to the Institute with neuroses caused by fatigue. But so much about this man suggested otherwise – his suit, with its fabric and cut of the very highest quality. His diffident manner. And his lack of expression, coupled with a certain nervousness when he saw Osanai.

He could have been a relative of someone on the 16th floor. Atsuko Chiba, perhaps, or Torataro Shima. No, no. More like Atsuko's secret lover, judging from his dress sense and virile good looks. Atsuko Chiba's secret lover, going home after a night of passion. Osanai wanted to ignore the man and stare resolutely at the floor indicator until he got out. But his interest was aroused. He turned to look at the man, who had retreated to the back of the lift.

The man was staring at Osanai with a look of interest. Osanai was struck by the piercing glint in the man's eye. Who was nervous now?

If he could confirm that the man really was Atsuko's lover, and if he could catch him entering the building again, he would phone Matsukane of the *Morning News* and get him to lurk around the main entrance with a photographer. So thought Osanai after the man had got out of the lift at the ground floor. It was his revenge for being made to feel so nervous.

Osanai went to fetch his car from the basement garage. As expected, Atsuko Chiba's Marginal was still squatting at the back of the garage, proof that she hadn't left for work yet. But then again, Osanai was on the early shift that day.

As he drove towards the Institute, Osanai started to feel just a little tired. He must have overdone things with Inui in his dreams that night.

The Inui Clinic faced onto a back road only four blocks from Osanai's apartment. Inui's bachelor pad was on the 4th and uppermost floor of the building, and Osanai was in the habit of visiting him there. Ever since they'd got their hands on the DC Mini – dubbed "the seed of the Devil" by Inui – the two of them had enjoyed attaching the device to their heads and falling asleep together after their lovemaking. The more they played with it, the more the functions of the device had become manifest. Tokita and Chiba must have developed the functions of other PT devices by playing erotic games with them, thought Osanai. As he drove on, he thought back over the unbelievable experience of the previous night. It didn't take too much to banish his fatigue.

Osanai braked hard.

Oy! Get out of the road! What do you think this is, a stroll in the park? You're in the city now, woman! Sad shabby trollop from the back of beyond! Moron! People like you aren't even worthy to lick my boots!

Oy, oy! You in the two-bit taxi, you think you can cut in front of me? How dare you! Don't you know who I am? I'm Morio Osanai, ten times your superior in status and intellect, that's who! Oh yes, don't look so surprised! I'm a leading Doctor of Psychiatry, winner of the Nobel Prize in the not-too-distant future! Kneel down before me! Cretin! Imbecile! The sun shines behind me, don't you know? And the sun's name is Doctor Seijiro Inui. He's a god! He's at the centre of the solar system, yes, he shines like the sun! Compared to him, who are Tokita and Chiba? Nothing but shooting stars that fly towards the sun and fizzle out as they burn! And me, I'm his right-hand man, his number one disciple. When he becomes President of the Institute for Psychiatric Research, and it won't be long now, he's going to make me a director! Oh yes he is!

Whenever Osanai used the DC Mini to enter Inui's dreams, his mentor gave him a new education in love. For these were no ordinary dreams. These were dreams that revealed the breadth of Inui's cultivation, exposed his deep aesthetic sentiment, underscored the sheer strength of his will. Osanai was simply overwhelmed by them. They brought him sheer unbounded rapture.

The power of Inui's massive intellect had led Osanai to a different world, an unknown world where he experienced wonders. And as they explored this new world together, they developed immune hypersensitivity to the DC Mini; the effective range of the device continued to expand. Osanai didn't even have to go to Inui's apartment any more. With the DC Mini, he could enter his master's dreams while sleeping in his own apartment only a few hundred metres away. And Inui could enter his.

Inui had warned that, if there were any PT devices in the vicinity, the images could be intercepted. But most of the PT devices were in the Institute five kilometres away, and anyway, no one would still be doing research at that late hour of the night. Even if Tokita or Chiba had the devices in their apartments, Inui and Osanai would be safe as long as they only used the DC Mini in the small hours of the morning.

On arriving at the Institute, Osanai paid a peremptory visit to his research lab, then went straight to the 5th floor of the hospital. There, he gathered up the students and nurses who waited in a gaggle by the nurses' station, and led them on his rounds of the wards. Nobue Kakimoto's condition had gradually grown worse, just as intended. Osanai still felt some fatigue, but while he was examining a schizophrenic patient, the patient's grotesque condition had the effect of stimulating his libido in a dark and menacing way. He gave a signal to Misako Sayama, who was staring at him wide-eyed over the heads of the student researchers. *Come to my lab at break this afternoon.*

During the lunch break, Osanai put in a rare appearance at the Junior Staff Room. It irritated him greatly that his desk had been placed there, not in the *Senior* Staff Room. That was why he handled most of his day-to-day work in his research lab. But now Inui had ordered him to spy on Tokita and Atsuko. Osanai's desk was closest to the Senior Staff Room, next to the glass door that was always left open. That gave him the perfect opportunity to watch the pair, since they usually had their lunch in the Senior Staff Room.

Tokita was sitting there alone, cramming food from a lunchbox into his mouth. Osanai exchanged a few words with Hashimoto, who sat opposite him, and was looking over the afternoon's work schedule when Atsuko Chiba came in with sandwiches and coffee clasped in her hands. She took them to her desk and sat there. Then she noticed Osanai and appeared unduly taken aback.

"Oh! You gave me a fright," she said, immediately adjusting her expression to a smile. "For a moment there, I thought you were Doctor Inui. You're beginning to look more and more like him."

"Surely not," Osanai quipped back. "I've heard of infective influence, but that would be ridiculous."

Though each perceived the other as an enemy, there was no need to draw swords in front of the other employees quite yet.

Perhaps I am beginning to look like him, thought Osanai. *They say couples start to look alike, after all.* It was indeed possible that his dream-world intimacy with Inui over the last few nights, a veritable honeymoon of passion, was having a profoundly infectious influence on him.

"What's that??" Atsuko suddenly shrieked. "A lunchbox from a lunchbox shop?!"

"My mum's away," Tokita explained mournfully. "A relative in the country has died. She's gone to the funeral and won't be back for a week."

"Poor thing!"

"Funerals in the country go on for ages."

"Where did you buy the lunchbox?"

"Yuraku-cho. They sell good ones there. But you have to queue for ages."

"Poor you."

They weren't speaking very loudly, but Osanai could hear every word without even straining his ears. The problem was that they spoke nothing but banalities. And since they hadn't yet mentioned the subject, Himuro's disappearance and the loss of the devices were not being discussed in the Junior Staff Room either.

I'll have to do something about those two, and quick, thought Osanai. Things couldn't be left as they were. Maybe it had been a mistake to start with small fry like Tsumura, Himuro and Kakimoto. That had merely succeeded in raising the alarm and unveiling their intentions. But no other opportunity had presented itself; the enemy had been too vigilant. There had been no choice but to deal with Tsumura, Himuro and Kakimoto first, especially as they'd been acting as shields. And now, Torataro Shima.

Osanai felt a smack on the top of his head. His ears whistled and his eyesight went fuzzy. Opposite him, Hashimoto was looking with some surprise at the space above Osanai's head.

Momentarily dazed, Osanai shook his head two or three times, then turned to see the Institute Administrator standing behind him. Shima had slapped the top of Osanai's head from behind with the palm of his hand. A slight expression of contrition played over Shima's features, but Osanai interpreted his faint smile as a look of self-satisfaction. As if he was saying "*Got you!*" As if he knew all about the subliminal projections and was now taking his revenge. But his grand gesture was surely too infantile for that. Perhaps he'd meant to perform his usual trick of going up to employees from behind and suddenly tapping them on the shoulder, but his hand had accidentally slapped the top of Osanai's head instead. Most of the staff evidently thought so; a few of them were laughing aloud.

Tokita and Chiba were not laughing. They were watching Shima with intense concern, as they could see that something was wrong. Osanai pulled a comic face and rubbed the top of his head.

"Ouch!" he joked.

Shima didn't appear amused. He did not mock Osanai, nor yet apologize, but simply turned and walked out of the Junior Staff Room while humming a little tune to himself.

Osanai was well aware that Shima had started to lose his mind. But the other employees didn't seem to have noticed, for as soon as Shima had left the room they burst into laughter and asked Osanai what he'd done to deserve such a fate. In the Senior Staff Room, meanwhile, Tokita and Atsuko exchanged glances. They were now sure that something was seriously amiss.

Had Shima been aware of Osanai's treachery, even though on the way to losing his sanity? Had he hit him over the head out of a hazy malevolence, a half-crazed sense of animosity? Osanai initially thought so, but immediately rejected the idea. No, no. Shima couldn't possibly have realized he'd been subliminally projected by the Devil's seed. Osanai had always attached the device just after Shima had fallen asleep, and he couldn't have noticed it then. If he had, he would obviously have removed it from his head. And as soon as the subliminal projection had started, he would have fallen into REM sleep and wouldn't have woken for some time. Osanai always went in and removed the device after an hour, but even then, Shima would still be sleeping like a baby.

Tokita and Atsuko were discussing something with voices lowered. It was too dangerous for Osanai to go to Shima's office that day. If they used the key to get in and discovered what was going on, all hell would break loose. Never mind. *Torataro Shima? I can make mincemeat of him, any time.* Osanai got up.

He remained in thought as he walked along the connecting passage. Did Tokita and Atsuko know that, because the device had no protective code, it could affect any PT collectors being used in the vicinity? Probably not. They surely hadn't found time to experiment on the functions of the device. But in fact, it had a lot of different functions. Undeveloped functions that even Kosaku Tokita, the device's creator, probably knew nothing about. The "Devil's seed" really had limitless potential. *The development of this potential will one day be attributed to me!* Osanai's heartbeat surged when he considered that possibility.

After eating a lunch of tasteless *soba* noodles in the staff canteen and briefly showing his face in the General Treatment Room, Osanai returned to his lab. He shared it with Tsumura and Hashimoto, but the former was "indisposed" and the latter was on afternoon duty in the General Treatment Room.

Osanai made some coffee and drank it while he waited for Misako Sayama to arrive. As he waited, his anticipation grew. He always felt immensely aroused after seeing Atsuko Chiba, particularly when he'd clapped eyes on her alluring figure from close quarters. It usually ended in an act of self-abuse, but today, as luck would have it, he was expecting a visit from Senior Nurse Sayama. He could use her body to relieve his physical arousal.

There was a knock on the door. Sayama walked in with a bashful grin on her face. She was not pushy like other women, but still retained an old-fashioned coyness. Osanai liked that. With her, sex was as easy as masturbating – no need for tiresome foreplay, certainly no bothersome conversation. Osanai locked the door and led her straight to the sofa. He always liked to have her in her lab coat.

"Oh!" she gasped.

Osanai lay the coyly hesitating Senior Nurse Sayama down on the sofa, gave her two or three peremptory kisses, then put his hand up her skirt and pulled down her tights.

"No, no, no!"

She was asking him to take all her clothes off first, but Osanai had no care for that. Little knowing that she was wearing several layers of unsightly old-fashioned underwear due to her hypersensitivity to cold, Osanai hitched up her skirt and had a look. Sayama groaned in despair and covered her face with her hands.

25

Konakawa had always hated his dreams. They caused a suffocating sensation that disturbed his sleep. The feeling of discomfort would remain for an hour or two after waking, enough to put him off his breakfast. He simply refused to believe that a dream could ever be pleasant.

But now he steeped himself in his dreams with a spirit free of cares. It may have been because he knew they were dreams, or because Paprika had explained their function. Tonight, he felt as though he'd been dreaming for quite a long time already, which was unusual in itself. Now he was in a place that seemed somehow familiar. The exact location wasn't clear, but he felt himself immersed in the dream like a foetus in amniotic fluid. For good measure, he was relaxing in a steaming-hot bath.

It looked like a public bathhouse. On the tiled wall was an advertisement for bath salts. A beautiful woman smiled down at him from the poster, a film star with the glamorous looks of a bygone age. Suddenly she turned into Paprika. *Well, well! There you are. I knew you'd be joining me, but not quite like that!*

"Be careful though!" warned the Paprika in the poster, winking cutely but raising a finger of admonition. She had evidently read the murmurings of his mind. "Dreams aren't always this much fun, you know. You do know that, don't you?"

"I do. Bad dreams are also important, yes?" said Konakawa, a little disappointed. "But anyway. I'll be all right with you here."

Konakawa remembered how he'd thought of nothing but Paprika while waiting impatiently for the second session. Was it all right for a patient to be so fond of his therapist? Of course, the reality was that he'd fallen in love with her. Was it all right for a patient to fall in love with his therapist? Was it all right for a therapist to be so attractive in the first place? To the extent that her patients fell madly in love with her? And if they did, could she still give them proper treatment? These and other thoughts coursed through Konakawa's mind in his dream.

"Maybe it's the other way round," said Paprika's voice.

The scene had changed; now it looked very much like a hotel room. Paprika was nowhere to be seen. *Where is she?*

"Actually, I'm not really that great a therapist. I just use my looks to help the treatment along. Maybe that's why I'm so successful. It shouldn't be allowed, should it."

Paprika's voice came from the radio next to the bed.

"So you even understand what I'm thinking?" said Konakawa. It didn't seem that surprising, actually. He was dreaming, after all.

A woman was sleeping next to him on the bed. He didn't know who it was. It wasn't Paprika; it certainly wasn't his wife.

He touched the woman with his hand. She turned to look at him. She was the man he'd seen in his previous dream. Seijiro Inui.

"What are you doing here?!" Paprika called out angrily. Inui looked genuinely shocked, then vanished.

Konakawa was similarly shocked, but Inui's appearance didn't mean enough to him. Not enough to wake him.

Inui's face did remind him of his father, nonetheless. But rather than his own father, it was his wife's father who appeared next. They were in some kind of temple. Hollow laughter rang out, echoing around the vaulted ceiling. Konakawa's father-in-law was sitting on a chair by the front entrance. Tourists were coming in and giving him money, which started to pile up in front of him.

He looked at Konakawa. "I brought her up like that. I brought her up like that." He seemed to be talking about his daughter. Brought her up like what? Konakawa felt an anger rise inside him.

The scene shifted to a stock exchange, a hall full of echoing voices. Now it changed again, to the inside of a stockbroker's office. Konakawa's wife was buying some shares. *Oh yes. Investing the money she got from her father. Oh no! She's buying nothing but worthless stock. Throwing the money away. Why's she doing that?*

"Wait! That's my money!"

Konakawa was often livid with anger in his dreams. The object of his anger was usually a person who, in reality, had done nothing to earn his wrath. This time, though, he really *was* angry with his wife. How sad that he could only express his anger in his dreams! Now he was lying in a field of scorched grass. A large dog slept next to him.

"Does your wife invest in shares?" said the dog, in Paprika's voice.

"Yes, but please don't appear as a dog!" Konakawa begged pitifully. "It's too much to take!"

Paprika's face appeared on the dog's head. The result was, needless to say, even more bizarre.

"You called up this dog," said Paprika.

"I've never seen it before." Konakawa felt pangs of guilt as he spoke.

"I said don't do it again, didn't I?!" Someone was yelling at him. He was in a room in the Metropolitan Police Department. The person yelling at him from the other side of the desk was none other than his subordinate, Superintendent Morita. "You only have to ***** the storeroom once!"

"Who does he think he is?!" Paprika shouted, standing next to Konakawa. "Go and sort him out!"

But Konakawa couldn't move. Paprika picked up a collapsible chair and went to attack Morita with it.

"Hey! Stop that!" Still half aware that it was a dream, Konakawa tried to hold Paprika back. Before he knew it, he had joined her and the two were laying into poor Morita for all they were worth.

"*****!!" Morita yelled with a look of astonishment. It was as though he'd never expected Konakawa to fight back.

Konakawa felt exhilarated. But at the same time, he felt guilty about attacking his subordinate. Morita was actually a good man and a trusted friend. Why did he beat him like that?

"I don't think it was Morita," said Paprika.

Unusually for him, Konakawa had fallen asleep at around two in the morning. Paprika had observed his dreams from the start. As day broke, she had at last discovered the underlying thread that ran through all his dreams. It was then that she'd decided to access the dream in the public bath, posing as the woman in the poster.

Unlike Tatsuo Noda, Konakawa had offered no hints to help her find that underlying meaning, nor made any attempt to analyse it with her. Paprika found that really annoying. On the other hand, merely identifying the cause through psychoanalysis would not in itself constitute treatment. And while a knowledge of phenomenological anthropology of course came in handy, seeking the transcendental structure behind empirical events wouldn't be of much use to the treatment either.

Konakawa was now standing in a cemetery. He was gazing at a gravestone. It was on fire. *There's nothing I can do about it*, he thought.

"Another fire?" Paprika said to nudge his memory. The image of fire had appeared in a number of his dreams that night already.

"Ah! It's the fire that *****!"

Paprika had a feeling that it wasn't just a residue of some police case. Her surmise was that, when Konakawa was a boy, he'd started a small fire in a storeroom. Just as when the dog had died, he was then severely scolded by his father. But Paprika couldn't confirm these facts conclusively with Konakawa. It wasn't enough just to rely on his own recognition of them. Her only option was to keep alluding to them subtly.

Paprika also knew that Konakawa was beginning to understand the meaning of these "rejection" experiences. He'd clearly felt a sense of exhilaration when he was beating Morita, alongside his pangs of guilt. Morita had been scolding him in his father's stead.

Paprika felt sure the treatment was progressing, albeit gradually.

Konakawa was kicking up a fuss in the lingerie section of a department store. He was ranting and raging, ripping skimpy underwear to shreds with his bare hands. Paprika went to stand in front of him.

"Don't be angry. Please don't be angry! I'll wear those."

In her half-sleeping, half-waking state, Paprika had every confidence that she was doing the right thing. In the dream, she was naked. But to Konakawa, her perfectly proportioned figure was overlapped with his mental image of his wife. *No! My body doesn't sag like that!* Paprika insisted. She made him see the image of her own naked body, the one she always saw in the mirror. Then she chose the most erotic piece of lingerie and put it on. It was pink. Not just any old pink; this was shocking pink, a colour she'd never worn in reality. One thing for sure was that Konakawa's wife liked to use this colour as a means of seduction.

Konakawa showed an emotion resembling fear when he saw the shocking pink. At the same time, his eyes were mesmerized by the sight of Paprika's half-naked body. Had his wife been standing there instead of Paprika, she would certainly have mocked his sexual inadequacy; his confidence would have been shot to pieces.

"Paprika, is that really you?" Konakawa felt increasingly aroused by the sight of her body. He already had an erection.

"Yes. It's really me."

They were in a tiny space that looked like a maid's room. A thin futon mattress lay spread out on a tatami floor, surrounded by rattan trunks, clothes baskets and other objects lying around higgledy-piggledy. If anything, the squalor of the location seemed to stimulate Konakawa's libido.

Konakawa's wife was taking revenge on him for the harsh education she'd received from her father, as well as the psychological cruelties he'd meted out to her mother. Her revenge took the form of affairs, in imitation of her father, and treating her husband like dirt. That was why Konakawa had lost his confidence, and Paprika knew it.

"Can I do it now?" Konakawa said with little emotion, clumsily voicing his desire for Paprika.

"Yes. You can."

Some male psychoanalysts had openly claimed that it was a good idea for them to have intercourse with a certain type of hysterical female patient. Some had even published scientific papers on the subject, citing successful cases of treatment. But they were still criticized on ethical grounds; their opponents claimed that they were simply abusing a position of trust.

Never mind – this was just a dream. It would simply be one more secret to be shared between therapist and patient. Paprika had always explained it to herself like that, thereby convincing herself that it was all right. She had also felt, conversely, that this virtual sex act might be more immoral than a real sex act between a therapist and a patient who really loved each other; she could never be equanimous about it. She wondered if she was actually no better than a woman in a massage parlour, relieving sexual frustration and restoring confidence. Such misgivings were an integral part of her unique treatment.

Nevertheless, Paprika could continue her treatment based on erotic experiences without feeling too guilty about it. That resulted from her affection towards her patients, an affection she called "reverse rapport". She always felt irresistibly attracted towards men of high social standing. Of course, some of them were clinically depressed and thoroughly repugnant. She certainly didn't feel like giving her body to all of them, even in their dreams. And yet the patients who missed out on this treatment were always the slowest to be cured.

If Konakawa felt guilty about this method, she thought, she could always have sex with him properly after he was cured, with real passion. No. Perhaps the excitement of having sex with her in his dream would be so great as to wake him. Then she could make love to him there and then.

In the end, like most other patients in this phase, Konakawa clung tightly to his sweet dream and did not wake up. He was about to make love to Paprika on the thin futon mattress spread out over the tatami floor. Yes, there was an awkwardness about him, and that would no doubt irritate a woman who felt no love for him. She would ridicule him for his clumsiness. His wife probably voiced her dissatisfaction with him even during intercourse, and this must have fuelled his loss of confidence. But Paprika found his clumsiness charming. She even saw it as part of his attraction – even wondered if it wasn't the true attraction of a man.

Konakawa started to move more vigorously as his carnal desire became inflamed. Now Paprika's self-awareness as a therapist disappeared from her half-waking consciousness, and her half-sleeping consciousness was transported by the throes of passion. There was no physical contact between them, but she was already moist.

"Paprika? Is it really you?"

Konakawa was worried that she would suddenly change into someone else, someone he found repulsive, as so often happened when he dreamt of having sex. Perhaps what worried him most was that she would turn into his wife.

"It's really me. You're really doing it with me."

As she finished speaking, Paprika let out an involuntary moan. Konakawa reacted to her voice with a violent surge of passion. For the first time in another person's dream, Paprika found herself washed in a baptism of orgasm.

Konakawa ejaculated in reality, as in the dream, and thereby woke himself up.

"Sorry."

"Why? It's all right. It's your treatment."

"I think I've messed up your sheets."

"It's OK."

Overcome with embarrassment, Konakawa made for the bathroom. Paprika stood up in front of the collector and called to stop him.

They kissed in the dim light of the room.

26

Osanai could enter any apartment he liked, having surreptitiously borrowed the master key about a week earlier to make a copy. But before visiting Atsuko's apartment that night, he took the trouble to phone in advance. He would say he had something to discuss, knowing she couldn't possibly refuse.

At ten that evening, he called from his own apartment to find Atsuko already at home. She agreed to his visit without question;

he imagined it was because she wasn't expecting anyone else that night. He immediately went up the single flight to her floor.

Three nights earlier, when he and Inui were using the DC Mini to share each other's dreams and search for the true essence of sex, they'd suddenly realized that Atsuko was using PT devices to treat someone in her apartment. At the frantic command of the startled Inui, Osanai had woken up immediately. But he'd left the DC Mini on his head, and had secretly continued to observe the "dream detective" at work. Inui had also continued to access the patient's dream, concealing his identity to ensure his presence went unnoticed.

"You must rape her," Inui had told Osanai at the Institute that day.

An order from Seijiro Inui was absolute. His commands always gave Osanai a perverse moral justification for acts he himself sought to commit; they converted his desires into firm action.

Osanai knew perfectly well that Atsuko and Paprika were one and the same. He also knew that the middle-aged man he'd seen in the lift was the patient she was currently treating. Osanai and Inui felt threatened, as the man appeared to be a high-ranking police officer. Both they and Atsuko were engaged in an activity that violated social mores and could be deemed illegal. But if their rivalry with Atsuko were to be made public, she would obviously hold the upper hand if she had an ally in the police.

Osanai had witnessed Atsuko having virtual sex with her patient in his dream, as part of his treatment. During the dream, the point of view kept shifting from the patient to Atsuko and back again. Both had been a big turn-on for Osanai, who so suffered with lust for Atsuko. Inui was aware of Osanai's burgeoning passion, and had judged that the time was right to execute his plan. Osanai would have his way with Atsuko, and violently. Inui's view, a product of empire mentality, was that a man only need rape a woman to put her under his dominion. This view was fully endorsed by Osanai, who had every confidence in his own desirability. His passion was now ignited and ready to burn. Its energy would lend force to the deed, give him unswerving resolve and help him to overpower Atsuko. In doing so, it would enslave her to him.

He stood at the door to Atsuko's apartment and rang the bell.

Atsuko had just come home.

"There's something we really need to discuss," Osanai had said on the phone. Atsuko hadn't understood Osanai's true intentions at the time. She'd been preoccupied with her concern for Tokita. He hadn't been seen at the Institute for the past two days, and Atsuko was thinking of calling him in his apartment that evening. Instinct told her that Osanai's call might have some connection with Tokita, and she therefore felt obliged to meet him.

At the same time, she'd already anticipated that Osanai, as Inui's mouthpiece, would have to contact her sooner or later. She had an inkling that Inui and Osanai had used the DC Mini while she was investigating Konakawa's dreams. They surely wouldn't want their theft of the DC Minis to be made public. Their ultimate objective, meanwhile, must have been to gain complete control of the Institute for Psychiatric Research. As such, Atsuko felt it conceivable that they would attempt to reach some kind of conciliation. She was still unaware that Himuro and Shima had suffered the same inhuman treatment as Tsumura and Kakimoto.

"Sorry it's so late," Osanai said as he walked in, bowing with a duplicitous smile.

He praised the interior of Atsuko's living room, gushed at the furnishings and swooned at the decor as she showed him through. Then he settled into an armchair with a swagger of supreme confidence. This was not the Osanai she knew at the Institute; this Osanai wore a loose sweater adorned with garish patterns. The atmosphere was mellow. It was enough to make Atsuko lower her guard.

"You'll have some coffee?"

"Don't mind if I do."

Osanai had been eyeing the drinks trolley, but Atsuko didn't consider him worth the alcohol.

"I've been thinking we need to talk," she ventured.

"Me too," he agreed.

They continued their pleasantries, she in the kitchen, he in the living room. For both of them, that was the best way of sounding the other out. The discussion would proceed more smoothly if they could agree on a subject before looking each other in the face.

"You're here at the Vice President's bidding?"

"Partly so."

While Atsuko wasn't looking, Osanai checked that the DC Mini was still embedded in his hair and attached to his scalp. He and Inui had contrived to remain in some form of contact by using the device. Its range had expanded so much that they could access each other's waking consciousness, albeit in fragmentary snatches. Inui lacked the physical strength to ravish Atsuko himself, but he could now enjoy Osanai's experience effortlessly, by remote control.

"And what," Atsuko asked as she made the coffee, "is this 'something' you need to discuss?"

"Well, it's about Doctor Tokita, naturally…"

Himuro's disappearance was starting to raise eyebrows at the Institute, and that would have seemed the more pressing issue. But Osanai evidently had bigger fish to fry. Atsuko brought coffee cups into the living room and placed them on the glass table, then sat in the middle of the sofa opposite her visitor.

"Are you saying all the Institute's problems are related to Tokita?"

"Cheers." Osanai took his coffee and supped a leisurely mouthful before fixing his eye on Atsuko. "Doctor Tokita is a genius. There's no doubt about that. But he's a very dangerous genius."

"I'd say there are others who are more dangerous."

Osanai decided to ignore Atsuko's irony. "The most dangerous thing about him is that he has no malice at all. He knows nothing of the world, he's naive, like a child. Unfortunately, when someone like that also happens to be a genius – well, it may be precisely *because* he's that kind of person – he keeps coming out with more and more crazy inventions. I'm sure you'll understand just how dangerous that can be."

"Now that's not quite true, is it. It's not Tokita himself who's dangerous, but the people around him who exploit his naivety and abuse his inventions."

"You're absolutely right," Osanai said, feigning wholehearted endorsement. He pretended to interpret *people around him* as *society in general*. "Tokita has no understanding of the society around him. His inventions will make a contribution to society, sure, but the larger reality is that they'll poison society. Anyone could abuse his inventions if they wanted to."

"There is that danger. It's a very big danger. That's why we need to protect him and his inventions."

"Good. So we're in agreement on that, at least." Osanai smiled in a way that he obviously thought terribly attractive. "But the thing that bothers me is that Doctor Shima doesn't seem to share our view. Don't you find it vexing that he, as Institute Administrator and President of the Foundation, is no less naive than our good friend Tokita?"

"At least he doesn't want to take advantage of Tokita. I find that quite reassuring." Atsuko smiled. "But I agree, we do need to be wary of Shima's naivety. That's why I haven't told him about the missing DC Minis. You know, the ones you stole from Tokita's research lab."

"Is that what you call them? DC Minis?" Osanai nodded calmly, making no attempt to dodge the sudden barb that flew his way. "To be exact, it was Himuro who 'stole' them, as you call it. I'm merely looking after them, since we can't trust Tokita with anything half so dangerous."

This was not the time to show anger. Atsuko smiled grimly. "But you're not 'merely looking after them', are you. You and the Vice President are using them every night. Aren't you?"

Osanai blushed and momentarily lost his composure. Atsuko knew her imagination was beginning to run away with her, but had no intention of being sidetracked now.

"Well, it doesn't matter," she continued. "Are you going to tell me your conditions for giving them back? That's why you're here, isn't it?"

"I'm sorry, but I'll need to look after them a little longer. If that's OK with you. You see, it would be unspeakably dangerous to let Tokita have them, not to mention yourself."

"No. The most dangerous thing would be for you and the Vice President to keep them," Atsuko said with a laugh. "What are you using them for, anyway? Games?"

Osanai mumbled something about developing functions, then fixed Atsuko with a stare. "They don't have a protective code, do they. There's no way of preventing unauthorized access." Mentioning Tokita's design fault was his way of regaining control.

"That's right. They're still being developed. That's why you must give them back quickly. Tokita will be the one to develop those functions. Not you. You wouldn't know how to begin."

Osanai started to look annoyed. He puffed out his cheeks like a sulking child. "All right. You just mentioned conditions. Let's put some on the table."

"Go ahead."

"First. When Doctor Inui is nominated for President, you will give him your unconditional support. Second. The functions of the DC Mini will be developed jointly, fairly, by all of us."

"All of us except Tokita, I suppose you mean. Totally unacceptable. Both proposals show your utter contempt for him."

Osanai narrowed his eyes and smiled faintly. "You love Tokita, don't you."

"Yes. I do."

The calm manner of Atsuko's reply fuelled Osanai's rising anger. He'd obviously expected her to be ashamed of her feelings for Tokita, to try to hide them. "What, that ugly lump of lard?

181

A man with the mind of a child? I just don't believe it. How can you say you love him and not die of embarrassment? You're Atsuko Chiba, for God's sake! Stop this nonsense! Even I'm embarrassed now!" Osanai had lost all semblance of self-control. He hammered on the arms of his chair with clenched fists.

"What are you getting so angry about?" Atsuko asked merrily.

Osanai's chest was heaving. He lowered his voice. "I'm getting angry for *you*!" He lifted his face and glared at Atsuko, then stood up. "Think about it for a minute! Do you really think Tokita is the man for you?" He walked around the table and went to sit next to her. "You probably haven't even noticed. I'm in love with you. Yes, me! I have been for a long time!"

"Stop it," said Atsuko, moving to the end of the sofa. "That's a brazen lie. You wouldn't have done all those awful things if you loved me."

"You're wrong. I do those things *because* I love you."

He put an arm around her shoulder. She tried to brush him off. But Osanai had the strength of a man who'd been restraining his lust for too long. He went to put both arms around her.

"Wait a minute! I don't want this. You can't force yourself on me!" Now Atsuko was getting annoyed.

"I will if I need to!"

"What do you mean, if you need to? Do you need to make me angry?!"

They struggled.

"Yes, to make you love me!" He tried to push her down onto the sofa while thrusting a hand under her skirt.

"Right! Now you have made me angry!" Atsuko yelled, using both arms and legs to hoist Osanai away.

Atsuko's rejection drove Osanai into a blind rage. A single blue vein stood throbbing on his forehead as he found himself dumped at the end of the sofa.

"I didn't want to do this!" he bellowed, then stood and punched

Atsuko hard on the jaw with his clenched fist. A mist descended before her eyes as she passed out.

27

Atsuko regained consciousness just a few seconds later. That was all the time Osanai had needed to pull her pants down to her ankles.

"Aren't you ashamed of yourself, doing this to a colleague?" Her anger had given way to despair and emptiness. "And you call yourself a therapist?!"

Atsuko tried to get up, but found herself forced back by the flat of Osanai's hand. Her bruised jaw ached, and the pressure of his hand on her chest made it difficult to breathe or speak. Osanai was trying to unzip his trousers with one hand while holding her down with the other. He said nothing either, but just kept breathing heavily through his nose. There was nothing he could have said anyway; no words could have justified his act of violence. Even if he had found any, they would have been the usual platitudes, the predictable excuses after the act. In any case, having brought his violent intentions thus far, his only remaining path was to execute his plan, whatever Atsuko did or said to stop him.

Atsuko continued her mute resistance for three or four minutes. In the meantime, Osanai had ripped the front of her dress and punched her around the mouth, which was now spattered with blood.

"Will you just keep still?!" Osanai suddenly started to plead pathetically. Perhaps he didn't like the sight of blood. "I don't want to hurt you any more. Because I love you. See? I love you!"

He sounded as if he was telling the truth. But his idea of love was the kind that could only be consummated by violating a woman. His pleading was no better a violent thug saying, "*Keep quiet if you don't want to get hurt!*"

Atsuko started to feel stupid. She realized that this man fully intended to force himself on her, to maintain his pride if nothing else. He didn't mind how badly he injured her, even if he had to half kill her in the process. Atsuko didn't care about the dress. She just didn't want to be hurt any more. She decided to let him rape her. She would think of him not as a vile beast, but as a man with the mind of a child. That would make it bearable. After all, she didn't necessarily dislike childish men. He probably didn't have any disease, his breath wasn't disgusting, he wasn't dirty. Yes, he was an enemy, and if she were a man she would have fought him until her dying breath. But she was a woman. She had no intention of aping a man's senseless insistence on fighting to the death.

"All right. All right!" She slapped Osanai's back as he lay sprawled on top of her. "I'll let you do it. You don't have to be so rough. I'll let you do it."

"Ah!" The look of desperation on Osanai's face changed to one of relief and tearful joy. "At last you understand!"

"Yes. But you'll have to do it properly. You'll have to satisfy me."

"No problem." Actually, Osanai looked less than willing.

Atsuko resisted the temptation to laugh. It surely wasn't that he lacked the confidence.

It had been some years since she'd had sex with a man. Having intercourse inside a patient's dream didn't count. She was of course preoccupied with her research and treatment, but even then, she'd occasionally noticed an unnatural flow in her libido and a sense of unfulfilled desire. Though not of her own choosing, this would be the perfect chance to satisfy that desire.

Atsuko stood up, stepped out of her ripped dress and stripped off her underwear. She was starting to feel as if it were she who'd taken the initiative, lured this man into her apartment and seduced him. Of course, it did help that Osanai was so absurdly handsome, a fine gigolo indeed. And he'd professed his love for her, notwithstanding the means he'd chosen to express it. In fact, Osanai seemed quite happy to let Atsuko take command.

In full compliance with Atsuko's demands, Osanai did his best to create the atmosphere of a wholly pleasurable sexual experience for her. Atsuko had no reason to doubt his sincerity, even if it was the kind of sincerity that would only last until he'd ejaculated.

But now, with Atsuko's submissive body awaiting his pleasure on the sofa, the reality of the situation hit home. Osanai had so often imagined the thrill of making love to her, and now those imaginings were about to be realized. His buttocks started to quiver with an expectation that felt like a chill running up his spine. He wanted to see himself as a warrior trembling with courage before the battle, but then he realized the ghastly truth. He was still limp. Those great white thighs of hers, yielding such a sense of coldness, were opened wide before him. *Oh no*, Osanai thought as he started to panic. He thrust himself up to her crotch. Perhaps some friction would do the trick. It didn't. Knowing the game was up, he embraced her. He didn't kiss her, as he thought his manhood would shrink even more if he saw her face. He even tried calling her name repeatedly. *Atsuko. Atsuko.* There was another voice, a voice he couldn't possibly have been hearing, but he heard it all the same. It was Inui's voice, berating him, encouraging him. Inui was probably using his DC Mini to capture the moment.

"What are you playing at?! Pull yourself together, man! Pull yourself together!"

Moments passed. Nothing worked. The only thing that flowed was his pre-ejaculate. Even that was going cold, matting their pubic hair together in a most distasteful way.

Atsuko was getting irritated. She knew exactly what had happened to her young beau. She'd heard that men sometimes become impotent on their first sexual encounter with a woman they adore too much, or when their partner is overpoweringly attractive. Osanai probably did adore her, but felt overawed by her as a person. That was ample proof that he recognized her as a human being, at least. On the other hand, Atsuko's libido had now been awoken. If Osanai couldn't do anything to satisfy her, it would be a disaster.

"What is this?!" she screamed. "Do it if you're going to do it! You could at least have prepared yourself!"

"I'm sorry," Osanai said feebly. "Your aura's too strong."

Atsuko pushed him to one side and started to put her clothes back on. She would shower later. "The only thing you can make love to is a doll. You're pathetic."

Osanai, momentarily crestfallen, soon recovered his vanity and angrily returned the jibe. "It's your fault. You're such a bossy cow. You think you can give instructions to me?!"

"You're useless. You couldn't even make one small part of your body bend to your will. You're useless as a therapist, and now as a man."

"Ha! You can talk!" Osanai shrieked wildly. "Call yourself a woman?! You may be beautiful, but you're no woman. The only men you can love are freaks and mental patients who let you do what you like! That's not what I call a woman!"

Atsuko was beginning to tire of trading childish insults. It was quite unbecoming of a psychotherapist. She started to clear away the cups and other things that lay scattered about. Osanai continued to hurl abuse even as she did, before eventually leaving.

Atsuko filled her bath deep and soaked her aching body in its steaming hot water. Now she could think coolly, calmly. As a psychotherapist, certainly, she had failed. She should have shown more sympathy with Osanai for his impotence. Not that it had anything to do with philanthropy. It was a question of interests. She could have made him her ally in the process. Even so, she refused to blame herself for giving way to her emotions and insulting him.

Atsuko was troubled by the thought that she couldn't satisfy her passion now that it was ignited. She could of course regulate her bodily functions with her mind, but all she wanted now was an outlet for her lust, as if a valve had been unblocked inside her. Her body felt like one of those exotic plants that explode with seeds when touched by human hand. The plant possessed an energy that could never be satisfied by the self-pleasuring of any woman – let alone an intelligent woman who was always denying or suppressing the calls of physical pleasure. Atsuko thought of Kosaku Tokita.

If she'd had sex with Osanai that evening, she would probably have felt bad that she'd never enjoyed such an experience with Tokita. She wanted to see him now. She wanted to see him, beg him to make love to her. She'd been sickened by the inner ugliness of Osanai, a man who looked like a Greek statue and was even beautiful when angry. Now, the pure simplicity of an ugly man suddenly felt very dear to her.

She would call him. If his mother still wasn't back from the funeral, she would go to his apartment. Or he could come to hers. And she would ask him to make love to her. He would have no doubts or misgivings about her sudden request, but would happily oblige. Residents of the building were not allowed to visit each other at this hour, but she wouldn't be the first to break that rule. Osanai was guilty of that charge. He was responsible for everything. Atsuko smiled on realizing that her anticipation of sex with Tokita was making her think so illogically. She was still smiling as she reached out of the bath to lift the telephone from the wall beside her.

"Yes? Hello? Who is it?" It was Tokita's mother who answered the call. She sounded extremely agitated.

Atsuko hid her disappointment. "This is Atsuko Chiba. Are you all right?"

"Oh! Doctor Chiba! Doctor Chiba!" The relief at hearing Atsuko's voice seemed to put the woman into even greater turmoil. "It's Kosaku! My little boy! Something's wrong with him, Doctor Chiba! He's not right!"

The woman was crying. Atsuko stood up in the bath. "What is it?"

"He's not right! He's not right, I say!"

It sounded much worse than an illness or an injury, but rather something that was impossible to explain.

"I'll be right there." A chill covered Atsuko's skin with goose pimples as she stepped out of the bath. She tried to remain realistic, but couldn't prevent a series of ghastly images from appearing in her mind's eye.

On entering Tokita's apartment, Atsuko found her worst fears realized. Tokita's mother Makiko was still in her travelling clothes, having just returned from the country. She led Atsuko to Tokita's room. It was in the same state of disarray as his room at the Institute, the only difference being a gigantic bed to fit his massive frame. Tokita was sitting on the bed in his pyjamas, staring blankly into space in front of him. He showed no reaction when Atsuko called his name.

Atsuko laid the expressionless Tokita down on the bed, then went into the living room to hear all about it from his mother.

"I only came back half an hour ago," the woman said, still crying. "He was sat there just as you saw him now. Who knows how long he's been like that? My poor little boy!" She wiped tears from her face. In stark contrast to her son, Makiko Tokita was unnaturally thin; the only feature they had in common was the kind, unaggressive look in their eyes.

"Was the door locked?"

"Yes. I rang the bell, but seeing as he didn't answer I used my own key to get in."

"So the door wasn't latched from the inside?"

"No. The door locks automatically, so we hardly ever use the latch, either of us."

So both mother and son were equally careless. When Tokita was alone there were even times when he didn't fully close his door. Someone had sneaked into his apartment, Atsuko was sure of it. But Tokita's mother had already jumped to her own, quite different conclusions.

"That research was too much for him," she wailed. "He was always thinking about difficult things. Who wouldn't go funny in the head, thinking about things like that all the time?! And he's so naive!"

Atsuko went back to Tokita's room. She couldn't examine him there, as there were no PT devices in the room. Or rather, there were no PT devices as Atsuko knew them, as another person might recognize them from their shape. The objects in the room may have been destined to become the very latest PT devices at some time in the future. But for now, they were nothing but tools and components of electronic devices in mid-assembly, together with design drawings and three-dimensional models projected on flickering screens of varying sizes; it was impossible to be certain what they were.

In that case, thought Atsuko, whoever had done this to Tokita had not used PT devices, at least not in this room. They had done it with a DC Mini. It had to be Osanai, whether or not at Inui's instigation. Atsuko checked Tokita's hair. There was no sign of the DC Mini; it had obviously been removed. Osanai must have entered the apartment at will, attached the DC Mini to Tokita's head as he slept, then removed it. Osanai could easily have put Tokita's mind into this vegetative state by accessing the DC Mini from PT devices in his own apartment.

What an unspeakably horrible thing to have done to the sweet, angelic Kosaku Tokita. Still burning with rage at Osanai, Atsuko checked Tokita's head more closely. A small quantity of congealed blood covered a wound on his crown. His scalp seemed to have been pierced by something. Atsuko's suspicions multiplied. Could the wound have been made by the tip of the DC Mini? The device would need to have been thrust into his scalp with considerable force to leave such a wound. In that case, he would surely have woken up, however deeply he'd been sleeping at the time. Wouldn't he?

189

28

Atsuko finished examining Tokita the following morning.

Atsuko had warned his mother to keep her front door locked at all times, and had then taken Tokita back to her own apartment. That was certainly no mean feat; despite his mental vacancy, it was still beyond the means of any woman to carry his gargantuan body. Instead, she'd led him along with a combination of gentle cajoling and crude persuasion. Once he was asleep, she had attached the gorgon to his head and started to analyse his dreams with the collector.

To Atsuko's immense relief, Tokita's personality hadn't completely disintegrated. His condition might have been best described as acute schizophrenia, but not that of the acute phase immediately after onset. Rather, Tokita's mind had been suddenly and violently fed with delusions that were quite unnatural for him, as a person not inherently of a schizoid disposition. His condition would definitely be cured in time, even if it seemed serious now. Atsuko was confident of that. She only needed to make sure there could be no recurrence, and that the condition would not become chronic once he'd entered the remission phase.

The images projected into Tokita's subconscious seemed to have been taken from Himuro's dreams after the onset of schizophrenia. That was perfectly clear from the images appearing in Tokita's dreams: a cute bob-haired Japanese doll, intensely sugary sweets and chocolate bars, infantile TV games. Somehow, somewhere, Himuro had already been infected with schizophrenia. His condition had been induced by having the dreams of a severely schizophrenic patient fed directly into his mind. Atsuko had come to know this particular patient's subconscious world in the process of her treatment. She recognized the patient because the doll kept saying things in German, like *"In den sechziger Jahren schien die Sonne auch nachts"*, *"Wegen des Vietnam-Kriegs wurde ich von meinem Vater in ein hochwertiges Restaurant gebracht, und habe da eine sexueller Atmosphäre erlebt"*, and *"Während des Ise-Buchts-Taifuns besuchte ich ein öffentliches Badehaus mit Premierminister Nakasone und konnte ganz einfach im Wasser schweben"*. Even when awake, Tokita seemed mesmerized by the doll's incoherent babbling.

The perpetrator of this obscenity had first driven Himuro mad by implanting the dreams of a severely schizophrenic patient into his mind. The content of Himuro's dreams had been recorded at some stage of this schizophrenia, and then projected into Tokita's subconscious. Though their intellectual levels were different, it must have been relatively simple to contaminate Tokita with the latent content of Himuro's dreams, since the two were both equally geekish in nature. Judging from the genius behind this act of cunning, Atsuko had no trouble in identifying the culprit as Seijiro Inui.

Even while Atsuko was examining Tokita, her monitor occasionally intercepted images suggesting that Inui and Osanai were still communicating via the DC Mini. Many of the images had the atmosphere of an occult or esoteric religion, giving the impression that Inui was passing down some kind of quasi-sexual, quasi-religious education to Osanai in his dreams. Nothing more certain than that could be known, however, owing to the fragmentary nature of the images. Atsuko couldn't use her collector to access their DC Minis, as they were wireless. To access their dreams in person, and to discover what form those dreams took, she needed to have a DC Mini herself. She badly wanted a DC Mini. Desperately so. If only she had a DC Mini, she might be able to glean their plans in advance, avoid falling into their traps and turn their own conspiracy into a counter-offensive.

Tokita had previously confessed his love for Atsuko. Yet he was now so distant that he couldn't even hear her voice, not even faintly. Atsuko was deeply saddened to realize that. She began to feel intense hatred for the people who'd done him such harm. They must have known she loved Tokita; they'd committed their loathsome deed in the full knowledge of that fact. Now the thought of revenge flashed through Atsuko's mind. *If only I had a DC Mini, I could avenge him*, she thought. It was the first time she'd ever had such thoughts. She was sure she could find it in herself to see it through, whoever the adversary was. Her mind was now bent solely on vengeance; Atsuko forgot that she too was likely to face some danger in the process.

Atsuko woke at nine after a short night's sleep. She immediately called the caretaker and asked him to change the lock on her apartment door. She could well imagine that the perpetrator had somehow obtained a master key allowing free access, not only to Tokita's apartment, but to any apartment in the building. She then called Tokita's mother Makiko and asked her to watch over Kosaku in her absence. She gave detailed instructions to ensure no further harm could befall him. She finally called Shima's apartment on the same floor, as she'd started to worry that he too could be in danger. All she heard was his answering message; he must already have left for the Institute.

Some days had passed since Atsuko had wanted to talk to Shima, to ask his advice on various issues. But an unforeseen series of emergencies had prevented them from meeting since then. As she drove through the congested city centre towards the Institute in her Marginal, Atsuko decided to go to Shima's office immediately after arriving at the Institute.

On checking in at her research lab, however, she heard the news that Himuro had been found. The call came from the hospital. A nurse had spotted him wandering aimlessly amongst a group of outpatients in the hospital waiting room about ten minutes earlier. Atsuko immediately made her way there.

In the hospital office on the ground floor, Himuro was surrounded by a mêlée of doctors, nurses and office staff, all yelling at once. He smelt awful. His hair was dishevelled, as if he'd just woken up, stubble stood on his chin and his body was covered in grime and dust. His lab coat, which he'd evidently worn since his disappearance, was dirty and crumpled. He wore no trousers, possibly because he'd fouled them. And he was barefoot. No one knew where he'd been before his appearance in the waiting room, or how he had got there.

Luckily, there was no sign of Osanai yet. Atsuko instructed two nurses to take Himuro to her own examination room in the Institute. Himuro remained expressionless throughout, showing no reaction to the commotion around him, and allowed himself to be led without any resistance. Though lacking expression, his face was deformed. It had always been fat and puffed up, but it was now transformed into something hideous – something that seemed not of this world...

Atsuko asked the nurses to lay Himuro's soft, round body on the bed in her examination room. Once they'd left, she let him fall asleep, then went to her research lab in the adjacent room, where she examined his field of consciousness with the scanner. In Nobue's absence, she had to enter all the settings herself.

Atsuko shuddered with horror when she looked at the monitor screen. Nothing remained but fragments of Himuro's mind, a desolate landscape of random images. A virtually blank screen was occasionally interrupted by images of decomposing almonds, crushed Braun tubes, small objects that looked like buttons, paper clips, bits of toys and sweet wrappers, a symbol for a ladies' WC, underground signs and other symbols scattered sporadically in time and space. Even more infrequently, a broadly grinning Japanese doll would appear in a corner of that field of consciousness, making a rocking noise as it nodded repeatedly.

Next, Atsuko used the reflector to extract more detailed images from Himuro's brain. As before, she found nothing but intermittent recollections of disjointed fragments, entirely devoid of rational connections. Seized with fear, Atsuko abandoned the idea of accessing Himuro's mind via the collector. Entering the consciousness of a person whose personality had been so utterly destroyed could easily have driven her mad as well.

Whoever had put Himuro in this state must have known that his personality would be completely annihilated in the process. The perpetrators must have been confident that his mind was quite beyond repair, and that he could no longer give testimony against them. With that reassurance, they had released him from confinement. Even so, it would have required very intense projections over a lengthy period of time to so thoroughly wipe all signs of humanity from the mind of a human being. The evil nature of the perpetrators now became clear; their identity was beyond doubt. Theirs was a crime on a par with murder. Atsuko knew there was only one way to stop this series of criminal acts, to foil a conspiracy that even threatened her own safety. She would have to fight the enemy on their own terms.

Atsuko bit her lip hard as she watched the sleeping Himuro through the reinforced glass window. After a while she opened the partition door and went to examine Himuro's head. The perpetrators would surely not have released him with the DC Mini still in place, but the device could have left the same wound as she'd found on Tokita's head.

Himuro's hair was unusually thin and soft for a man. Atsuko parted it to discover a tiny bald spot about seven or eight millimetres in diameter on his crown. The spot was lead-grey in colour, contrasting with the whiteness of his scalp. According to Tokita, the DC Mini used biological elements that permitted proteins to self-assemble, and bioelectric current was applied to facilitate mutual access. Atsuko thought back over what Tokita had said about the shape and colour of the DC Mini.

She let out a cry.

The patch on Himuro's scalp was not a bald spot, but the base of the DC Mini itself. The device had been attached for so long that it had been absorbed into Himuro's head. It could no longer be pulled out by hand. And since it was fused with his head at an atomic or molecular level, it would be impossible to remove even surgically. Atsuko now understood what had caused the wound on Tokita's head. It was left there when the DC Mini was forcibly pulled out after the tip had started to fuse with his head.

In the horror of her realization, Atsuko failed to notice that she'd been crying out, almost screaming for some time. She also failed to notice that the telephone in her lab had been ringing continuously.

29

After recovering from the shock and returning to her lab, Atsuko made some coffee and drank it as she planned her next move. She tried to think as calmly as she could. Finally, she telephoned the hospital and asked the duty nurse to arrange a vacant room for Himuro, then to bathe and feed him.

Next, she called the Administrator's Office. Shima wasn't there.

Or was he? Atsuko had a nasty premonition. She decided to go to his office anyway. As she stood to leave, the telephone rang.

"I think he's from the press," the switchboard operator said uneasily. "He's already called several times this morning."

"So why didn't you refuse as usual?"

"He says it's an emergency. Not an interview or anything like that. He said his name was Matsukane and you'd know what it was about."

"Ah. Him. All right, put him through."

"Doctor Chiba?" Matsukane of the *Morning News* said in a tone of great urgency as soon as the operator put him through. "Can I talk to you somewhere? I'm not far away."

"Where are you? What's it about?"

"I'm in the café near the front entrance. Corcovado. But I can't really say anything… Not on the phone… Has anything untoward happened?" he added hurriedly, as if he was worried Atsuko might hang up on him.

"What do you mean, untoward?" Atsuko returned his question warily, stiffly. She'd started to feel she could trust no one, but at the same time thought it an unwise policy. She risked losing an ally and turning him into an enemy for no good reason.

"Well, if nothing's happened, that's fine. One thing I can say is that, well, I'm a friend of Morio Osanai, you see. Well, no. I don't mean a friend as such, rather that we went to the same university." Matsukane paused for a moment, as if he expected Atsuko to draw her own conclusions.

"So is that who it was? Your informant at the Institute, Morio Osanai?"

"Yes."

It was Osanai who'd leaked the information to Matsukane about Paprika's identity, about Tsumura being infected with schizophrenia and everything else.

"And now he's told you something new? That's why you're calling?" Atsuko could imagine how Osanai saw Matsukane as a trusted ally. He'd won his confidence by leaking information, and was now boasting of the plot he'd set in motion.

"Er, is this telephone safe?"

"No." Atsuko couldn't be sure that the operator wasn't listening in. "And I don't have a direct line."

"I wouldn't be allowed in the building, would I. Can you come and meet me in the café?"

"I can't go there. The nurses from our hospital use it. Come to the car park in half an hour. I'll meet you where we spoke last time."

"All right."

Atsuko replaced the receiver and got up immediately. Matsukane's call had given her ample cause for worry about Shima, as she'd suddenly remembered his odd behaviour in the Junior Staff Room the other day. That was certainly what she'd call "untoward". She hurried to the Administrator's Office, hoping beyond hope that Matsukane's phrase didn't refer to Shima.

The door to Shima's office was slightly ajar, as always. *I wish he wouldn't do that*, Atsuko thought with a sigh. Only recently she'd seen an employee going into the office without knocking. Though most of the staff liked Shima's easygoing personality, others were happy to take advantage of it.

Atsuko knocked, then opened the door wide. There was no one in the office. Anyone else would have given up and walked out again, but not Atsuko. Not today. She closed the door firmly behind her and went towards the back room, where Shima took his naps.

There, Atsuko's fears took physical shape with the sight of Shima in his underwear. Just as Tokita the night before, Shima was sitting on the edge of the bed, deeply withdrawn and gazing vacantly into space. His right arm was raised diagonally in front of him. He showed no reaction when Atsuko called his name.

Judging from Shima's raised-arm posture, he must have been fed the same images as were implanted in Tsumura's mind. Atsuko felt reassured to recall that Tsumura's condition had only been mild. She searched Shima's head but found no sign of the DC Mini. It must have been attached and removed intermittently, as it had in Tokita's case. That meant his condition could definitely be treated.

Why had the perpetrators set out to drive Shima insane in stages? They could have destroyed his mind instantly by projecting intense images, as they had with Himuro. They must have wanted people to think that the timid Torataro Shima had lost his mind naturally, under the strain of internal disputes at the Institute. His eccentric behaviour in the Junior Staff Room, caused by the initial stages of image projection, had given that very impression. As such, the plot had been more than successful so far.

Shima couldn't be left as he was. Pandemonium would break out if it were known that the Institute Administrator had been infected with schizophrenia. Even the internal conflicts would then become public knowledge.

197

Atsuko thought things over for a few minutes before deciding to take Shima back to her apartment. What he needed above all, before any thought of treatment, was a refuge. This was a war. A filthy, nasty war in which, instead of actually killing each other, the combatants would destroy each other's personalities along with their human dignity. Atsuko urgently needed to foresee the enemy's movements, yes, but the need to secure Shima's safety took priority over that.

Using the outside line in Shima's office, she called directory enquiries to find Corcovado's number, then phoned the café in the hope that Matsukane would still be there. A waitress called him to the phone.

"Something terrible has happened," Atsuko explained. "I don't want anyone in the Institute to know about it. Will you help me?"

"By all means." It was an answer that encapsulated the pride and righteous enthusiasm of a major newspaper reporter.

"I need to take Doctor Shima from his office without anyone noticing."

"This is a direct line, isn't it. What's happened?"

"He's been infected."

"Ah." Matsukane groaned as if to say "*Just as I thought*". "Damn. Too late. What do you want me to do?"

"Can you drive?"

"Of course."

"You'll find my car in the car park. You know? The moss-green Marginal. Bring it to the goods-loading bay at the rear of the Institute."

"What about the key?"

"I'll take it to the car park entrance. But listen. I can't find the key to Shima's office. That means I can't lock it from outside. So I don't want to leave him on his own for a second more than I have to."

"Come down in ten minutes. I'll be there – count on it. Then give me the key and go straight back to Doctor Shima. What about this loading bay? How do I get in from there?"

"Go through the side door. That'll take you to the garden at the back of the Institute. Shima's window faces the garden. I'll be standing there. That's where we'll get him out."

"Understood. I'll see you in ten."

Atsuko replaced the phone and searched Shima's desk for the key. She couldn't find it. She pushed open the window that faced onto the back garden, checked the state of the side door some eight metres away, then looked under the window. There was a drop of about two metres from the window ledge to the ground. Atsuko took a spare chair that was normally used for visitors, and lowered it to the ground as a foothold for Matsukane.

Ten minutes later, Atsuko made her way to the car park. She hurried along the corridor, expecting to see Matsukane waiting on the other side of the glass door at the far end. But he wasn't there. Atsuko stopped by the door and peered through the glass into the covered car park.

Morio Osanai was getting out of his car. He looked as though he'd just arrived. Matsukane must have held back because he'd spotted Osanai.

30

"Have you heard? Shibamata finally cracked!" declared a beaming Superintendent Morita on entering Toshimi Konakawa's office that morning. He'd been itching to tell his superior the news.

In Konakawa's dream, Morita had screamed at him for making a mistake, just as his father had done in the past. Morita's reward was to be violently attacked by Konakawa at Paprika's behest. In reality, however, the two enjoyed a most amicable working relationship.

"So my hunch was right," smiled Konakawa. "He confessed to Kumai's murder?"

"That and the arson. And the insurance fraud." A genial smile spread over Morita's heavily tanned face, the face of a university athlete who'd merely grown middle-aged. He nodded at Konakawa. "Seems he was stupid enough to share his plan with Kumai. He was going to set fire to his house and then claim the insurance. At first, Kumai went along with it all, to keep the friendship going. But when he realized that Shibamata actually planned to go through with it, he got cold feet and wanted out. It often happens like that. Friends half-jokingly plan the perfect crime, but when it actually comes to doing the deed, the would-be accomplice chickens out. It was a bit like that."

"But Shibamata had to go ahead with it, didn't he. He was up to his neck in debt."

"That's right." Morita took the liberty of sitting on the sofa opposite Konakawa's desk. "We discovered he'd been heavily in debt before the fire, but then had managed to pay everything off after the fire. That was when we took him in for questioning. Kumai had told Shibamata that if he went through with it, he would go to the police. So Shibamata had to kill him."

"Why didn't we realize it at the time? We were still at the murder scene when the fire broke out."

Morita shook his head vigorously as if to deny Konakawa's self-reproach. "We were fooled by the relationships in that house. All of us were. Anyway, everyone's full of admiration for you. You were determined not to close the case. Of course, Yamaji and the others were over the moon that you'd handed them the credit. More than that, though, they thought it strange. They wanted to know how you managed to link the murder with a house fire in the vicinity. It certainly didn't click with me at first, even when you said we should investigate Kumai."

"I saw it all in a dream." Konakawa said with a sheepish smile. "Can you believe that?"

Morita suddenly looked serious and nodded earnestly. "Yes. Yes! That definitely happens. I believe it. Then again, the fact that you were dreaming about it in the first place shows how determined you were to solve the case!" He seemed to know a little of the subject. "What sort of dream was it?"

Konakawa hesitated. Should a senior police officer relate his dreams to a junior? He would surely be considered weak in the head if he did. But he decided to continue. "Well, it was a dream I had more than once. That murder scene in Hachioji. It would always be followed by a fire. When I was a boy, I started a small fire in a storeroom. I was only messing about. I thought the dreams were all about that. Then I suddenly remembered there'd been a fire nearby after the murder."

"What? It was that simple?" Morita seemed inordinately impressed. "And have you always used dreams to solve cases?"

"No. Not at all. The thought hadn't even crossed my mind. But something made me think that way... You know..." Konakawa blushed uncharacteristically. He was lost for words.

"Well, well." Morita remained full of admiration. "If only all the senior officers had your enthusiasm for solving cases." He must have been referring to the ones who wasted their time on petty politics.

As soon as Morita had left the room, Konakawa called Tatsuo Noda. He hadn't given his friend a single progress report since Paprika had started treating him. He began by apologizing for that.

"You sound so well," was Noda's riposte. "It's just like the old you."

"Well, thanks to you, I'm feeling much better now. And I'm sleeping better at night."

"Has the treatment finished?"

"Not yet."

"And what sort of treatment is she giving you?" Noda said in a tone that failed to conceal his curiosity.

Noda had only just arrived at work himself. So many times he'd wanted to call his friend, to find out how the sessions with Paprika were going. But he'd resisted each time, fearing that his affections for Paprika would be all too transparent. As would the twinge of jealousy he felt towards Konakawa.

"Well, nothing special," said Konakawa, reluctant to spell it out.

Damn, thought Noda. *It's definitely something special.* "Well, as long as you're enjoying it," he said, suppressing his feeling of envy.

"I am. I feel better each time," Konakawa said with deliberate vagueness, as if he'd seen right through Noda's pretence.

"Paprika's a wonderful woman, don't you think?" Noda fished.

"Yes, she is."

"A really mysterious woman. Who do you think she is, really?"

"What? Don't you know?" Konakawa's voice leapt with surprise. "She's Atsuko Chiba. You know, the scientist who invented those PT devices along with that other one, Kosaku Tokita. At the Institute for Psychiatric Research. They've been shortlisted for the Nobel Prize because of it."

Noda groaned silently. "Her? Atsuko Chiba? But Shima didn't say anything... I did know her surname was Chiba, but... How did you find out? Did you ask her?"

"I didn't have to. It was obvious."

"Well, you're the detective, I suppose. But don't you think she's a bit young for someone in that position?"

"Do you think a top psychotherapist would really look her age? She's actually twenty-nine. I've checked out her background. I've even seen her photograph. There's no doubt about it. Paprika is Atsuko Chiba."

It came as no great shock to Noda – he'd half-imagined this very scenario. *So how does that affect things*, he wondered. Had it destroyed the fairy tale he held in his heart? No, it had not. Fairy tales belonged to the realm of fantasy. The Paprika who was not Atsuko Chiba, or anyone else, the Paprika with the independent personality, still lived inside Tatsuo Noda.

"Sorry to shatter your dreams," said Konakawa, noting Noda's silence.

"Ha! Don't be silly," Noda replied, even then letting out a sigh. "So I suppose she was even disguising her voice? When I called her apartment, another woman answered, an older woman. But there was never any sign that anyone else lived there. I did find that strange."

"Actually, there's something I wanted to ask you," Konakawa said in a tone of concern. "Did she tell you about any trouble she was involved in?"

"Trouble? Has something happened? Well, now you mention it, she once had a black eye. It looked as if someone had punched her. I thought she'd been attacked by a patient..." Noda thought back and remembered how it had seemed, at times, that Paprika wanted to ask something of him, or how, at other times, she'd been strangely withdrawn.

Relenting under Noda's insistence, Konakawa related an episode from his treatment. "...And this Vice President actually appeared in my dream. His face, at least. Of course, I didn't recognize him. At first I thought it was because Paprika was somehow concerned about him."

"What, you mean Paprika's thoughts appeared in your dream as images? Even while she was investigating your dream? That never happened to me."

"So you're saying it's unnatural?"

"Too right I am."

"Anyway, it bothered me, so I got her to print out an image of the man's face. And then I had this Inui fellow checked out." Konakawa's reticence of just a week earlier was gone. Now, in complete contrast, he was talkative and full of enthusiasm. "He's the Director of the Inui Clinic, a private psychiatric hospital not far from where Paprika lives. I was in the area the other day, so I drove up to it. It's quite an impressive building, although it faces a back street. What amazed me was that I'd seen the building in my dream at Paprika's. In my dream it was an embassy, but anyway, the image of that building somehow found its way into my dream. One thing I can say for sure is that I've never been down that back street. But Paprika didn't recognize the embassy as Inui's clinic when she was investigating my dream."

"So it's even less likely that her thoughts were feeding into your dream?"

"Exactly. I think something's going on at that Institute. Don't you think something's troubling her?"

"Now you mention it, yes, I do."

"I've got an appointment with her tonight. I'll think I'll just ask her straight."

"I wonder," Noda groaned. "If it were something she could explain just like that, wouldn't she have asked our advice about it long ago?"

"You mean she never asked your advice about it?"

"I got the feeling she wanted to, but was caught in two minds. Sometimes she seemed to be hiding something. That's why I was concerned."

"Well, if she didn't ask *you* about it, she certainly wouldn't mention it to a police officer. I reckon it's something that can't be made public."

"That reminds me, actually. When I told her what you did for a living, she nearly jumped out of her skin. I think she wanted to refuse. You see, it's actually illegal to use PT devices for dream analysis outside the Institute."

"Well, look at her. She's a famous scientist, shortlisted for the Nobel Prize. It stands to reason she'll have her fair share of rivals setting traps for her, people trying to bring her down. I could get someone to check out the Institute, based on the idea that something funny's going on there. But what if it turned out to be nothing? And we've gone in there with our size-ten boots and only made Paprika's position worse?! No, I think it's best to ask her about it first."

Noda was about to suggest approaching Torataro Shima, when a blue lamp lit up on his telephone console. His secretary was calling him.

"Hold on a minute," he said to Konakawa before switching the line. "Yes, what is it?"

"Time to leave for Aoyama Seiki, sir."

"Ah. They want me to see their new product. But I don't have to go, do I?"

"You did give your word."

"So I did. Right. No problem." Noda had his secretary organize the hired limousine, then switched back to Konakawa. "Are you working tonight?"

"It's nothing that won't keep. Paprika takes priority."

Oh dear, thought Noda. *He's falling in love with her too. He might just as well have said "because I love her".*

"I'm sure there's something troubling her," said Noda. "I think she needs our help. Shall we meet somewhere and talk about it?"

"Good idea."

"How about nine o'clock at Radio Club? That'll give you time to make your session afterwards."

"I'll be there."

Noda replaced the receiver. He could hardly wait to see Paprika. He convinced himself that he wasn't fabricating a story out of nothing just to see her. No, he really was worried about her.

The driver of the limousine was the same as before, when Noda had suffered his attack. He'd driven Noda twice since then, but even when there were no other passengers, he had never made any mention of the attack. He hadn't even asked how Noda was. Noda saw him as someone he could trust implicitly.

Immediately after turning onto the main road, they found themselves in heavy traffic. They edged their way through a set of lights, but were still hardly moving at all. On the opposite side of the central reservation, a moss-green Marginal was waiting for the lights to change. Noda gasped when he saw the passenger in the rear seat.

Torataro Shima was sitting there, but he looked decidedly strange. His eyes were directed straight ahead in a hollow gaze and his body looked rigid. His right arm was raised diagonally as if in a Nazi salute.

"Would you mind sounding your horn?" Noda said to the driver as he let down the window.

"What – here?"

"Yes! There's someone I know in that car."

The driver sounded his horn. The cars were no more than three or four metres apart, yet Shima made no reaction at all.

Noda gasped a second time when he saw the woman in the driving seat. "Paprika! It's Paprika, isn't it?!"

It must have been Paprika when not disguised as Paprika – in other words, Atsuko Chiba. She wore a mature suit, her characteristic freckles were missing, her hairstyle was different, her image was not so much cute as elegant. But it was definitely Paprika; that air of intelligence, those dangerous good looks put it beyond doubt.

Noda tried calling louder. "Paprika!"

She didn't seem to hear. It was as if she were thinking so deeply about something that she was oblivious to everything else. She certainly didn't notice Noda. He found that more than strange. She was normally the kind of person who would notice things immediately.

The traffic in the opposite lane started moving off. The Marginal headed straight through the lights.

A little further ahead, there was a gap in the central reservation. A U-turn looked possible. Noda's limousine also started to move off.

Noda leant towards the driver. "Hey! Would you follow that car?" he shouted. "That moss-green Marginal?"

Part Two

1

In the fifteenth century, the post-Renaissance Catholic church fell into discord as the power of the Holy Roman Empire waned. This sparked vigorous reform movements all over Europe, producing a number of heretical beliefs. By the beginning of the sixteenth century, popular movements for religious reform had taken hold in German and Swiss lands. These eventually yielded the heresy known as Protestantism.

One of the heretical sects that emerged at this time was the Saxon Order of Brethren. Its purpose was to claim for itself the cultural and ideological power that the Roman Catholic church had lost. It soon succumbed to intolerance, however, owing to an overzealous pursuit of dogma. It came to be seen as a heresy within a heresy, and suffered repeated acts of suppression. It survived nonetheless, albeit with very few followers, as a powerful and fanatically religious secret society supported by theologians, artists and natural scientists who went unrecognized by society at large in their respective eras.

At the start of the twentieth century, an atmosphere of erotomania flooded the streets of Vienna. Freud's sexual emancipation and the ideology of Gustav Wyneken's *Jugendkultur* group mutually influenced each other, while homosexuality became fashionable among students and middle-class youth, mainly those of Jewish extraction. Scholars and artists, thus awakened, joined the Saxon Order to become its principal members, and the sect's rituals assumed an overtone of homosexuality. At this point the sect changed its name to "*Sezession*", mimicking an artistic movement that emerged in Munich at around the same time. In this guise, it could avoid the opprobrium of society and the church, which was particularly strict on homosexuality, and could thus continue its rituals unmolested.

It was in his early thirties, while he was studying at the University of Vienna, that Seijiro Inui first came to know of the sect. More than ten years had passed since the end of the war, and old-fashioned homosexuality had been quietly revived in parts of the university. The comely Seijiro Inui had soon received his "baptism" from a professor in the Medical Faculty. He had then joined *Sezession* at the professor's behest, and received true baptism as a religious sacrament.

Sezession was characterized by ancient mystical beliefs based on Greek culture and thought. It conducted clandestine Hellenistic rites, in which respect it resembled the eastern Orthodox Church. However, its services were accompanied by suggestive music from the final phase of the romantic school, as well as the burning of incense mixed with narcotic substances.

As many of the believers were controversialists, arguments over the interpretation of the Bible and articles of faith were permitted without restriction. Nevertheless, observance of the dogma decided at public meetings was enforced as a doctrine that carried absolute authority. Much debate was conducted over how the latest cultural and ideological trends should be incorporated in this doctrine. Since these included notions like Nietzsche's *Übermensch*, the doctrine became divorced from real life and increasingly intolerant.

The "establishment" was seen as the embodiment of evil in all epochs. As such, it was self-explanatory that the members of *Sezession*, considering themselves children of God and superior beings, were not accepted by the society around them. They therefore felt themselves entitled to use any means at their disposal to wage a holy war against the power and authority of the establishment. Any power or authority that was won back reverted to the sect, to be used in the service of its members. To them, even Jesus Christ was a comrade in arms who had fought

against the establishment; he was even, occasionally, fêted as an object of homosexual love.

For Seijiro Inui, being robbed of the Nobel Prize by another medical scholar was a kind of religious ordeal. Ever since that time, he'd vowed to defend scientific orthodoxy in observance of the doctrine, even if it meant transcending the ethics and morals of the establishment. To him, this mission was in itself a holy war.

During his time at Vienna, he had visited art museums all over Europe. There, he'd seen and admired numerous heretical or homosexual paintings, like Reni's *Martyrdom of St Sebastian* at the Musei Capitolini in Rome. Under their influence, he had developed a liking for beautiful youths with classical, Grecian looks. But after his return home, he was disappointed to find there were hardly any young men of that description in Japan.

Inui never married. Sex and marriage with women were grudgingly permitted as a way of deceiving the establishment, but for members to be led astray by the amorous charms of a woman meant to betray the doctrine, even to betray themselves as children of God and superior beings. Inui had always treated women as commodities, outlets for carnal desires; he recognized no spirituality in them whatsoever.

The only person he had ever loved was Morio Osanai, a young man he'd met when already on the cusp of middle age. It was thanks to westernization, Inui thought, that such good looks had also started to appear in Japan. He rejoiced at his good fortune in living long enough to see that day, but at the same time, felt saddened by his own advancing age. In spite of that, Osanai happened to respect Inui, and eventually came to return his affection in kind. Inui had an unquenchable love for Osanai, this youth so imbued with classical Grecian beauty.

Inui's success in treating psychosomatic maladies came from an idea he'd garnered from the secret rituals of the sect, particularly its practice of mystic meditation using narcotic substances. Thus it was that, even when shortlisted for the Nobel Prize, he humbly attributed his achievements to *Sezession*. But those achievements were then hijacked by a British surgeon who had merely taken Inui's methods and applied them to actual treatment. At this, Inui was transformed into a kind of ogre who devoted his life to cursing the establishment. He believed the true orthodoxy of psychiatry to lie in his methods alone, together with the classical theories of psychoanalysis on which they were founded. He fought against all other theories as heterodoxies, perversions. Needless to say, the present enemies in his holy war were Kosaku Tokita and Atsuko Chiba, who sought to use the PT devices they had developed solely for purposes of inhuman therapy.

It was not that Inui denied the validity of PT devices, and particularly their pièce de résistance, the DC Mini. He merely felt they should be put to better use in improving the human mind. In fact, he and Osanai had used DC Minis stolen from Tokita to steep themselves in occultic raptures based on their love for each other. There could be no more effective tool than the DC Mini for teaching the quintessence of the doctrine via mystic meditation, thus leading the user to ecstasy, as Inui had done with Osanai. For the sake of the sect, the DC Mini should be available for broader use among the public, the irredeemable contemporary man. For the time being, in particular, he urgently needed to open the eyes of the doctors and scientists around him. For they had sold themselves completely to the establishment and were now serving the false god of technology. Following a chance remark by Osanai, Inui had realized that, whenever he treated Osanai with tender affection, he himself had come to resemble Jesus. He had even started to see himself as the saviour of the psychiatric world.

Osanai used his skill as a psychotherapist to read deep into Inui's mind, and resonated with what he found there. It was about six months earlier that he'd started his plot to deliver control of the Institute to his beloved master. He'd succeeded in the first stage of his plan, namely to win over Himuro. He had successfully induced mental illness in Tsumura and Kakimoto, those blind worshippers of Tokita and Chiba, and had spread the terrifying rumour that schizophrenia was catching. Everything had gone according to plan, almost like clockwork; things had developed at a speed that even Osanai found surprising.

Having at last got their hands on the DC Mini, Osanai and Inui had decided that now was the time to settle the matter once and for all. Then they had acted on that decision. Depending on how it was used, the DC Mini could indeed become the "seed of the Devil". They'd used it to turn Shima and Tokita into mental cripples. The only one left was Atsuko Chiba. She had started to suspect Osanai, and it wouldn't be easy to deal her the same fate. She would have to be isolated within the Institute, before she could exact a vengeance that would surely be severe. She was, after all, an experienced therapist who had already treated a range of mental diseases and neuroses under the guise of "Paprika".

Inui was in his own clinic when Osanai called to inform him that Shima had disappeared. Inui knew instinctively that Atsuko had taken Shima under her wing. Though it was already in the afternoon, in fact closer to evening, Inui went straight to the Institute. There, he gathered most of the important employees, therapists and senior nurses of the Institute and its hospital in the Meeting Room. This was the room where they usually held press conferences; it had a capacity of more than two hundred. First, Inui allowed Osanai to explain the situation.

"Awfully sorry to call this meeting so suddenly. The fact is that a very serious state of affairs has arisen, one that could have a grave impact on both the Institute and the hospital. As you may already have noticed, all sorts of unpleasant rumours have been going round recently, and this has disturbed the peace we need to continue our work. We must take a serious view of this situation and make earnest efforts to improve it. The Vice President would now like to say a few words. I'm sure what he says will open your eyes to a serious problem that affects the whole of the medical world, a problem that lies behind the superficial situation we now face. I hope you'll all give some very careful thought to this."

Osanai then handed the baton to Inui, who took to the rostrum. More than a hundred mostly white-coated listeners looked up at the tall figure of Inui, as if appealing to him with eyes full of fear. *Poor things*, thought Inui. There had been no one they could depend on until now. Neither Shima nor Tokita were the kind of people who could be relied upon as leaders, and Atsuko Chiba was just a woman. Inui felt pity and contempt for the employees. They would be putty in his hands; he could frighten them, threaten them, cajole them, anger them, sadden them just as he pleased. He stood before them with a stern expression that could have been interpreted as cruel.

"As servants of the medical profession, we should all be thoroughly ashamed of ourselves. For we have disregarded human dignity and relied upon science and technology alone. Have the principles of this Institute really been correct until now? Given the situation that has now arisen, I can only conclude that they were wrong. We have strayed from the path of true medicine. As your Vice President, I must accept partial responsibility for this. I failed to voice my ongoing opposition, and as a result, this truly lamentable state of affairs has occurred. I refer of course to the outbreak of schizophrenic symptoms among our staff, some of whom have fallen into an irrevocable state of mental desolation. This is a calamity inflicted by the haphazard and immoderate development of PT devices by a few of our employees. Sadly, their disgraceful behaviour has now come to the attention of the media. It stimulates their prying tendencies, even to the point of exposing the Institute's past violations of law. And I refer finally to the disappearance of President Shima, a scandal that has come to light this very day."

Many of the staff members were hearing about Shima's disappearance for the first time. Some let out cries of dismay, others groaned in despair. The news caused a ripple of commotion that ruffled the air in the Meeting Room.

"For that reason I will be standing in as President for the time being. But in doing so, I have to make something very clear to you all. My aim in the short term is to eradicate the pernicious practice of unilaterally developing technology, which I would liken to a runaway train. I'm sure you've all felt the same about this. You haven't been happy about the inhumane technology developed for treatment in the past, and you've had very serious misgivings about the obscenely hurried nature and breathless speed of such development."

This assertion brought vigorous nods from Hashimoto and Senior Nurse Sayama, along with several others sitting in the front row, who'd been instructed by Osanai to voice their support for Inui.

"And all of this bad practice has come about because the sole purpose of our research has been to win the Nobel Prize for certain individuals," Inui declared with voice raised. "But now it has got to stop. From now on, we will return to the fundamental principle of medicine, namely, to serve our patients. I strongly urge you all to engage in humane psychiatric research. As for the future development of PT devices, we will reform personnel practices inside the Institute and its hospital, practices that were arbitrarily put in place by President Shima. We will of course wrest development from the monopolistic and tyrannical control of Tokita and Chiba, and turn it over to you all for proper, diligent research." Inui's impassioned delivery had reached its climax, but he continued in the same vein. "The Nobel Prize is not the only goal for a scientist; fame and glory are not the only honours for those of us involved in medicine. The time has come to ask ourselves what exactly is the true orthodoxy of medical treatment. And that's not all. We..."

2

Atsuko didn't have a bed to lie in. Her own bed was already occupied by Tokita, and now Shima had the patient's bed in the treatment room. It wasn't the first time she'd had to sleep on the sofa; it had been quite a common occurrence in her days as Paprika, when her male clients would stay over on a frequent basis. It was, however, the first time she'd had two patients in her apartment at the same time.

Atsuko had thought better of letting Shima sleep in his own apartment. Osanai probably had more mischief lined up for him, and if he did have the master key to all the apartments, Shima on his own would have been the easiest of prey.

Atsuko had placed the gorgon on Shima's head and examined him using the collector. The result was as expected: he'd been subliminally projected with the same program as Tsumura. Atsuko started treating him right away. Whenever she reached an impasse, she would move across to treat Tokita in the other bed. Patiently she spoke to them, repeating the same phrases, until at last, and to her considerable relief, they started to utter words. It mattered little, for the moment, that those words had only opaque meaning.

Atsuko left the bedroom to go and fix some coffee, and was surprised to see the night-view panorama spread out before her in the living room. It was already nine in the evening. She realized she'd had nothing to eat since her simple breakfast of toast and coffee that morning.

As she was defrosting a frozen steak, the telephone rang. It was Matsukane, social affairs correspondent of the *Morning News*.

"Oh, hello," said Atsuko. "Thanks for your help earlier. I really appreciated it."

"How is Doctor Shima?"

Atsuko felt a certain foreboding. From the urgency of his tone, the call seemed to be more than just to confirm Shima's condition.

"He's on the way to recovery. Has something happened?" she asked.

"I've heard from, you know, my friend at the Institute…" Matsukane said hesitantly. He seemed reluctant to voice Osanai's name. "He says Inui has gathered the Institute's employees and declared himself acting President."

"What?…" Atsuko felt struck by an unforeseen blow. Inui and Osanai had obviously anticipated that she would rescue Shima and take him under her wing. In fact, they'd been waiting for her to do just that. "That's unbelievable."

"He gave a speech in which he denounced both you and Tokita. He also talked about reforming the personnel system. You've got to do something quick. Otherwise you both risk losing your positions at the Institute. You might even be forced out altogether."

"I know that."

Atsuko knew that, but she didn't know what to do about it. Not only had she never experienced this kind of conflict, but she hadn't even read any books about it.

Still, there was no point in crying to Matsukane about it. "Thanks for letting me know," she said tersely. "I'd be glad of your advice again in future."

"Of course! Any time!" Matsukane spoke with some vehemence, as if to counter Atsuko's coolness. "Anything you want to ask! Any time!"

Atsuko replaced the receiver and stood rooted to the spot in the kitchen. Not a single person, it seemed, had expressed any opposition to Inui's dictatorial high-handedness. That itself was proof of her unpopularity at the Institute.

The battle had finally started in earnest. But could it really be called a battle? Was she not completely defeated already? Both Shima and Tokita were spent forces, and the DC Minis, her only remaining weapons, were in the hands of the enemy.

She wanted a DC Mini, now more fervently than ever. If only she had a DC Mini, victory could be hers. Enemy. Weapons. Victory.

Battle. Atsuko was already thinking the vocabulary of war. A war against an adversary fanatically driven by a warped ideology that Atsuko couldn't even begin to understand. An adversary that was trying to wrest power through inhumane means, by abusing the functions of the DC Mini. Atsuko felt inclined to see this war as something very real, not just the product of "empire mentality".

As she pondered over her immediate strategy, Atsuko suddenly remembered that Konakawa was due for another session that evening. In so many ways, she was in no fit state to treat him. The session would have to be cancelled. She was about to call him when the intercom buzzer sounded; she had a visitor in the lobby. Atsuko froze when she saw the intercom monitor. There in the lobby stood Tatsuo Noda and Toshimi Konakawa.

"Yes?" said Atsuko, trying to make herself sound older. She'd decided to pretend Paprika was out, at least until she could glean their intention in visiting her.

"It's Tatsuo Noda. And Mr Konakawa is here with me."

"Ah. I'm afraid Paprika isn't here at the moment."

Noda and Konakawa looked at each other. For some reason, they seemed to be smiling and shaking their heads.

Now Konakawa moved towards the microphone. "It's not Paprika we want. We've come to see Atsuko Chiba."

From the gravity of his tone, Atsuko sensed a sudden change in their perception of her. They seemed to know that Paprika and Atsuko Chiba were one and the same. When could they have discovered that? Their smiling head-shake suggested that they hadn't come to discuss psychiatric treatment. On the other hand, neither of them was childish enough, nor indeed had the time, to come all this way just to surprise her with their new-found knowledge.

"I see. You'd better come up."

With a sigh, Atsuko pressed the switch to open the glass door in the elevator hall. Noda and Konakawa both knew the entry code; they could have got through without Atsuko's help. They must have opted to press the door buzzer because they wanted to give her time to prepare herself mentally.

It was the first time she would meet them as Atsuko Chiba. She had no idea how she would handle the situation. On the other hand, they probably felt the same way.

Atsuko led her visitors into the living room. They dutifully sat beside each other on the sofa, like two schoolboys hauled up before the headmaster. Atsuko herself sat in the armchair opposite.

"Miss Chiba," started Noda, leaning forwards.

Atsuko hated undue formality, no matter what the subject. "It's all right. You can call me Paprika," she said with a laugh.

"Right. Paprika. This afternoon, I spotted your car and followed you. Shima was sitting in the car, but he didn't look right." An anxious look appeared in Noda's eyes.

Atsuko nodded in realization. "Ah. I thought I heard someone calling. At that intersection."

"I followed until I saw you entering the garage below this building," Noda continued. "Then I drove off. I was supposed to meet Toshimi at Radio Club at nine. I thought I'd ask his advice then come and see you. We'd already arranged to meet this evening anyway. We knew you were caught up in some kind of trouble, and wanted to see if there was anything we could do to help."

"That's so kind..." Atsuko was on the verge of tears; her voice may have trembled. But she wasn't ready yet to show any sign of weakness. She took a deep breath and straightened her back.

"At first I imagined you wouldn't be happy with us meddling in your affairs," Noda continued. "But then I thought, what harm could we do? What could you lose by putting your trust in us, confiding in us? So now I'm imploring you to do just that."

Atsuko was choking with emotion. Konakawa had been watching her closely as his friend spoke. "Where is Doctor Shima now?" he asked. His tone was far from interrogational; it was as if he were trying to coax information from her.

"*Over there,*" Atsuko mouthed silently, indicating the bedroom with a wave of the hand. Then she got up. It was time to tell them everything. Atsuko paced in front of the glass door that led out to the veranda. She was wondering where to start, how to tell them, how to help them understand. Noda and Konakawa gazed at her, as if spellbound, as if watching an actress on stage against a panoramic backdrop.

Atsuko stopped pacing and squared up to them. "All right. I'll tell you everything I know," she said. "I'll disregard the fact that one of you is a police officer. Otherwise I won't be able to tell it straight. But before that…" Atsuko twisted her body and shouted, almost screaming at the top of her voice. "…Let me have something to eat! I haven't had anything since breakfast! And that was only a slice of toast!"

The tension dispelled, Noda and Konakawa laughed aloud.

"Of course. Of course!" Noda got up. "Can I use your phone?"

He booked a table at a restaurant that had private rooms. He occasionally used it for confidential talks with clients. Atsuko got herself ready. She undressed in a corner of the living room, using the wardrobe door as a screen. From the wardrobe, she pulled out an apricot-coloured suit. It was the one she usually wore, but she hadn't had a chance to recently. She hadn't had it dry-cleaned since the last time she'd worn it, but there were no creases or stains on it.

As she was putting the jacket on, she felt something odd near her right hip. She put her hand in the pocket. Her fingers touched a small, hard object.

It was a grey conical object, about a centimetre high, with a base about seven or eight millimetres in diameter. The DC Mini. Atsuko exclaimed loudly.

"There it is! I must have put it there and forgotten all about it! I'd forgotten it was there!"

Noda and Konakawa stood up, wondering what the fuss was about.

Now Atsuko remembered. On the day of the Board Meeting, Tokita had been showing her the DC Mini in the Senior Staff Room. She'd hidden it in her pocket when Owada suddenly walked in, and had proceeded to forget all about it.

"*One disappeared some time ago*," she remembered Tokita saying after the five DC Minis had been stolen from his research lab.

3

Noda and Konakawa were still gazing at the DC Mini. It looked like nothing more than a little grey polka dot on the white tablecloth. They could hardly conceal their incredulity that something so small could house so much power.

The three had finished eating and were relaxing in a private dining room that resembled the parlour of some stately home. Oil paintings by Hitone Noma hung on walls covered with maroon wallpaper. The lighting was subdued. Atsuko had explained the whole story while eating a steak of finest Kobe beef, fresh, not frozen. The tension had lifted from her shoulders, her heart felt lighter, her stomach was full. Noda checked with Atsuko that it was all right to light a cigarette, an unusual act for him, and offered one to Konakawa. Atsuko knew the occasional cigarette would have a positive effect on their minds. The room gradually filled with an evocative masculine smell, until Atsuko couldn't resist asking for one herself.

The waiter brought coffee. Atsuko slipped the DC Mini back into her pocket.

"Internal conflicts," Noda said once the waiter had left the room, "are in themselves nothing unusual. Especially in a corporate environment."

"That's quite true," Konakawa said, nodding at Atsuko to console her.

But that did nothing to help her deal with the problem. "Yes, but what do you think should be done?"

"Well, the normal thing would be to explain all the facts to the other directors and bring them over to your side," Noda said as if it were nothing. "Don't do it in writing. You should phone them. Or better still, go and meet them."

Atsuko sighed deeply. Where was she going to find the time to do that?

"There seems to have been some collusion between your Secretary-General Katsuragi, the Vice President and this company Tokyo Electronics Giken," Konakawa commented. "And if the auditor Yamabe has been won over by Inui, I think it'll all come clear when you inspect the books."

"I'm sorry," Atsuko said dolefully, "but you're talking about things I can't possibly do."

"Of course, we'll help you!" Noda countered with a smile. He seemed to positively relish the prospect; that gave Atsuko courage.

"By the way, Miss Chiba – I mean, Paprika…" Serious as ever, Konakawa pulled a photograph from his wallet and showed it to Atsuko. "Take a look at this building."

"Hey! That's the building we saw in your dream. An embassy or something…" The photo tugged at an important part of Atsuko's memory. "So this building actually exists, as I thought?"

"Have you never seen it before?"

"I feel as if I have. But…" Atsuko was startled when she saw the sign in the photograph. "Inui Clinic! That's right. I drove past it once. But I didn't remember it clearly. Not as clearly as it appeared in your dream."

"I drove past the clinic myself for the first time yesterday. It all seemed so odd that I just had to stop and photograph it." Konakawa looked Atsuko in the eye and spoke slowly, trying to maintain the low-key atmosphere. "Well now. Paprika. If all this is true, what we saw was not in my dream. Nor was it your memory, nor the collector infiltrating my dream."

"No. It was Inui and Osanai playing with the DC Mini," Atsuko agreed. "But what would they have been doing at that hour? Why were they wearing DC Minis, when they should have been asleep?…"

"If images from their DC Minis can appear in your collector, the reverse could also be true. They could use their DC Minis to observe your treatment with the collector. Couldn't they?"

"Hmm. When Inui appeared in your dream, I instinctively shouted out at him, didn't I."

"That's right. And he looked very surprised."

"They must already have known that the DC Mini wasn't protected. Then they must have realized that, as well as accessing my collector and observing my patients' dreams, they could actually enter them. But to access a dream properly they would have to be asleep themselves, or at least in a hypnotic state, just as with the collector."

"That means they could interfere with your treatment in future," Noda said with his customary concern. "After all, they must also be quite skilled at accessing dreams."

"I'm sure of it. But that gives us the perfect opportunity for a counter-attack. Now I've got a DC Mini too. When it comes to accessing dreams in a hypnotic state, I'm the expert. But if I'm to attempt a counter-attack, I need to know what they're doing when they use the DC Mini."

"This Osanai character, does he live in the same apartment building as you? On the 15th floor?" Konakawa said, looking pensively at the ceiling.

"Yes…"

"In that case, I think I met him once. In the lift. A strikingly handsome young man."

"What about it?" Noda said, his curiosity pricked by Konakawa's interest in Osanai.

"During my first session, I was surprised to see Inui's face in my dream. His face was huge, and yet I'd never met him before."

"It surprised me too," agreed Atsuko. "I thought perhaps you knew him."

"He was smiling, wasn't he," Konakawa said with a meaningful look at Atsuko.

"Yes. I'd never seen that look on his face before. Kind of soft."

"Soft?" Konakawa tilted his head quizzically. "I would have called it lecherous."

"And what would that imply?" Atsuko hadn't quite gathered Konakawa's meaning.

"In the second session, I dreamt Inui was lying next to me in bed."

"In other words..." Atsuko was beginning to catch on. "You were seeing images from a DC Mini worn by someone who was sleeping with Seijiro Inui?"

"Judging from the evidence, I'd say Osanai and Inui are having a homosexual relationship," Konakawa replied calmly.

"What? No!" Noda opened his eyes wide in astonishment. He knew Konakawa was not the sort to joke about such things. "That's disgusting!"

Atsuko laughed. "Ah, but you've never met Morio Osanai!" she said, starting to believe Konakawa's premise. "That would make sense of a lot of things. You know Osanai has begun to resemble Inui recently? His facial expression, I mean."

"They say that happens when people are in love. So you're saying they put that, you know, DC Mini thing on when they sleep together?" Noda said with a pained expression.

Atsuko thought back over her experiences with Tokita while they were experimenting with the PT devices. She was sure that wearing the DC Mini could be enormously sensuous as an act shared by lovers. For Inui and Osanai, it would promote the inner affections of homosexual love and turn them into darker passions. It was clear from Noda's pained expression that he was thinking back to the erotic sensations he'd felt when Paprika had accessed his own dreams – the sensuality of lovers sharing the same dream, making love to each other in that dream.

Atsuko explained the principle of anaphylaxis, or immune hypersensitivity. "And so you see, with repeated use they can enter each other's dreams remotely, even when they're not actually sleeping together. That's what we call anaphylaxis."

"I see! It's a bit like my jellyfish allergy," said Noda. "I was stung by a jellyfish when I was a boy. Now I can't go anywhere near the things without coming up in a rash. I can't even look at them in Chinese restaurants!"

"That's it. Anaphylaxis."

"You said there were originally six DC Minis," Konakawa said to confirm his understanding of the facts. "You've got one of them. One was absorbed into Himuro's scalp. So they must have the remaining four."

"If only we had two more here," said Noda. "We could put them on at night, then enter your dreams and help you fight those two."

"I wouldn't think of asking anything so dangerous," Atsuko said in astonishment. "Though I do appreciate your offer."

"You're right – we're just amateurs. We wouldn't know where to begin," Konakawa said dejectedly.

"But Inui and Osanai must already have observed Paprika investigating your dreams, through their DC Minis."

"True..."

"So they must know you're a high-ranking police officer. If you accessed their dreams in counter-attack, you might be able to contain them."

"Momentary access wouldn't be dangerous. It might be an effective way of exposing their crimes, and whatever they're plotting next." Noda's idea had struck a chord with Atsuko. "You may be able to help me one day."

"Any time," said Konakawa. "Normally, of course, I would just say it was a police matter and seize the DC Minis. But it's not so simple in this case."

"There would be a public outcry," Noda said ruefully. "The impact on society would be devastating. I'd rather you kept this well clear of the police. Couldn't we do something by ourselves?"

"I know what you mean. But" – Konakawa looked hard at Atsuko – "at least let me mobilize my second-in-command, if nothing else. I'll get him to provide protection for Shima and Tokita."

"Well, I suppose that can't be avoided," Noda said with a nod to Atsuko. "Would you permit that? You can't keep them in your apartment for ever. If they had police protection, you could leave the apartment without worrying about them."

Atsuko knew Konakawa's real intention – to provide protection not just for Shima and Tokita but for herself as well. Noda must also have sensed that.

"Thank you. I'll be glad to accept your kindness." Atsuko gave a little bow, then, thinking that overly formal, immediately returned to a more relaxed manner. "But I'd prefer you to leave them for the next two or three days. I need to treat them."

"Wouldn't you rather get a good night's sleep first, Paprika?" said Noda. "You've got rings under your eyes."

"They're the least of my worries!" Atsuko laughed. "But I'll take your advice anyway. I'll treat them during the day tomorrow. Then there'll be no risk of the enemy interfering."

"Good." Konakawa looked relieved.

"By the way, Paprika. Do you have a list of all the Institute's trustees?" asked Noda. Konakawa nodded in agreement.

"Yes, in my apartment."

"Let's go back then," Noda said, standing impatiently. "I know the director Ishinaka, together with six of the trustees. If I see the list, I may know more. Same goes for you, Toshimi."

"Yes. There must be some," agreed Konakawa, standing to leave.

"We'll pick them out and start contacting them right away. Our work starts tonight!"

4

Atsuko slept late and started her treatment the following afternoon. Shima's condition improved dramatically in very little time.

Atsuko ate a light dinner and fed her two patients. Then, as Paprika, she accessed the dreams of the now slumbering Shima. Past memories of treatment by Paprika must have been etched deeply on Shima's mind, together with a sense of nostalgia.

In readiness for the expected intrusion by Inui and Osanai, Atsuko attached the DC Mini to her head by applying a bead of adhesive to the point and placing it on her scalp. Now the device could be used in parallel with her treatment using the collector.

Shima's subconscious was contaminated with the same schizophrenic dreams as had been used to infect Tsumura. The Nazi salute symbolized submission to a father figure, but as this particular complex had never been one of Shima's personality traits, it had quickly been destroyed. What Atsuko needed now was for Shima to talk as much as possible in his dreams. Even if his speech was full of nonsensical delusions, expressing those delusions would help him recover his own ego.

Shima dreamt he was in the student canteen of his old university. *The university canteen?!* thought Paprika. Not that the real Atsuko had turned into Paprika; she merely had to assume Paprika's personality for the dreamer to recognize her as Paprika.

In real life, the student canteen had been modernized, expanded and made brighter during Atsuko's time at the university. What appeared in Shima's dream was the old canteen, when it was still cramped and dingy. Shima was still a student. He was peering inside, timorously, through a gap in the partition separating the canteen from the corridor. He seemed hungry, perhaps because he hadn't eaten much dinner just now. Or was it a visceral memory of chronic starvation in his student days?

In the canteen, part-time director Owada was eating with the other students. He looked like a student, but Paprika knew for a fact that he hadn't studied at that university. Shima seemed to fear him; perhaps that was why he couldn't enter the canteen.

"I'm sorry! I'm sorry!" Shima called loudly. But Owada seemed not to hear him.

It would have been highly inconvenient were Shima to suffer a recurrence of anxiety neurosis. To make sure that couldn't happen, Paprika sat at one of the tables and beckoned him over. She would try to make him forget his feelings of guilt towards the other directors, symbolized by Owada.

"Hey, Shima! Over here! You don't have to apologize!"

"It's a quarrel between friends," Shima said to excuse himself as he went to sit opposite Paprika. "That shouldn't be possible. You seem to be a woman."

"That's right," Paprika replied, smiling agreeably. "We are not the same person."

Shima was beginning to recognize that he couldn't identify himself with Paprika, but he persisted in remaining on the boundary between the two personae. In his own words, it was as if Paprika was "quarrelling" with his obsession over "friends". A side effect of using the DC Mini was that she could read Shima's dreaming thoughts with absolute clarity. Visual clarity was also enhanced; her field of vision had widened to include blurred areas on the periphery.

Shima leant towards Paprika. "It started with someone putting on airs," he muttered timidly. "There's a demon in the kitchen." They were sitting in a theatre, in a corner of the dress circle.

"I said don't worry! Is there anyone else in the kitchen?" she asked.

"Paprika!" The provocative nature of her question seemed to stimulate his memory. He at last remembered Paprika's name, and his love for her. "Ah. Paprika. After you put the empty juice bottle down and went home, I shaved my head and you were angry. Because young Tokita fought and was courageous, you went away. But the house of Mejiro hasn't gone under yet."

As she observed Shima's speech patterns, Paprika felt something untoward in his oddly dreamlike mood. She turned her attention to the stage. Seijiro Inui was standing in the centre, wrapped in what looked like priestly vestments. An altar appeared, the only lighting provided by hundreds of candles flickering on candlesticks. The scene had changed to the inside of a chapel. The congregation all rose in unison.

Again Shima called out in a voice of fear. "I'm sorry! I'm sorry!"

The dreams of Inui and Shima had merged. Paprika guessed so. Either that, or Inui was deliberately interfering with the treatment. Whatever the case, Shima was frightened, and the two had to be separated. Paprika decided to leave herself in Inui's dream and confront him there. It was the moment she'd been waiting for.

Paprika remained in her half-sleeping state while her experienced fingers pressed the keys on the PT console, breaking the connection with Shima via the gorgon. Shima would have to dream on alone.

The chapel resounded with music that was not at all solemn, but more evocative of debauchery. Inui was continuing to incite his congregation with the oratory of one who railed against the world. Paprika issued a loud yell of opposition from the gallery above. Momentarily surprised as he looked up to see her there, Inui forced a derisory smile, then pointed straight at her and hurled words of abuse in her direction.

"There is a ***** of science, a brazen ****** who knows no shame!"

Paprika knew what Inui was trying to say, since she could read his dreaming thoughts. It was his usual dogma; that made her angry. Had it been her own dream, she would have soared through the air, down to where Inui stood before the altar, and laid into him there and then. But sadly, it wasn't her dream. It was Inui's dream, and his resistance would probably have rendered such an attack impossible. To make it her own dream she would have to enter a deeper sleep, but then she would lose all control over her actions. There was nothing for it. Paprika would have to use the stairs.

Paprika ran to the bottom of the bizarrely twisting, crazily winding staircase, but still couldn't reach the altar. She passed through a corridor, a hotel lobby and a shopping mall, then found herself inside a shop that looked like a beauty salon. Why the detour? It could have been because Inui was trying to prevent her from approaching him, she thought, or because she herself didn't want to approach him. But in this case, she concluded, there was another explanation.

It was because there was something she had to do before she could confront Inui directly. Facing the mirror, sitting in a chair with his hair in curlers, was Morio Osanai. He must have come to protect Inui. That's right. She needed to deal with this man first.

"It's Doctor Chiba... Isn't it?" Paprika's image was reflected in Osanai's eyes. He observed her warily. "As I thought. It's Doctor Chiba."

"How did you know?"

"*Poison*. Unmistakable. But why the little girl act? Oh, I know. You're Paprika. Right? You're Paprika... aren't you!"

Paprika wondered how he could smell her perfume when he wasn't sleeping with her. Perhaps people who used DC Minis to share the same dream could even smell each other's body odour, even when they weren't sleeping together. These were Paprika's half-sleeping thoughts. To her, the bizarre no longer seemed bizarre. She may have been falling into a deeper sleep, and that may have been Osanai's plan.

Sensing danger, Paprika laughed aloud and started to fight back. "Yes – I'm Paprika! I'm young and I'm coming to get you!"

Osanai analysed the shock he felt on hearing these words from Paprika. Why was he so startled? Because it meant danger. Yes, that's right. What was so dangerous? The woman was too confident. Access seemed to be working both ways. If she was only using the collector, she would merely have been observing, not taking part. In that case.... Surely not?!... *She must be using a DC Mini!*

"Oh? I thought you'd stolen them all?"

But of course, Osanai could also read Paprika's thoughts, since he was also using a DC Mini. This was an attack from someone unaccustomed to using the device. She hadn't had time to familiarize herself with it.

Osanai was visibly unsettled. He stood up and tried to run away. *Damn it! She's using a DC Mini! Where did she find it?*

"I won't let you get away," Paprika said with a suggestive laugh, designed to make him sleep more deeply. "Don't forget – I can always follow you, no matter where you run!"

Osanai picked up a plastic make-up bottle and hurled it at her. Reading his thoughts, Paprika knew his intention was to wake himself up. He would wake up and think out a new strategy. Paprika clung tightly to his will to prevent him from doing that. Now, if ever, was the time to deploy a woman's disregard of logic.

"I'm awake!" Osanai shouted, almost shrieking.

Osanai was in his apartment on the 15th floor. His bedroom was full of PT devices. On the bed, Paprika was grappling with him in his pyjamas.

"How can you be here?!" Osanai yelled in terror. "I'm awake! I'm not dreaming any more!"

He hadn't returned to reality. In reality, she was Atsuko, but in Osanai's dream she was still Paprika, clinging to him like a bad girl fooling around. Odd, she thought, that she could sense a smell exactly the same as his breath when he tried to rape her.

"You only think you've woken up," said Paprika, "but that's a dream too. You're dreaming that you've woken up."

Paprika laughed as she reached out towards Osanai's head. She knew perfectly well that she was in a dream, but she simply had to remove the DC Mini from Osanai's head. "Hand this over. I'm confiscating it."

231

She felt the sensation of something solid in the palm of her hand. The device was attached to Osanai's head with sticky tape. She pulled it off. She seemed to have grabbed some of his hair into the bargain, but what the heck – it was just a dream. She wrenched it out with all her might.

"OWWWW!" cried Osanai. "What are you doing? You said it was just a dream!"

In acute pain, Osanai pushed the dream detective away. She hit her hip on something hard and awoke as Atsuko.

She was sitting in front of her PT equipment. Shima was sleeping on the patient's bed to her right, and Tokita on Atsuko's own bed to her left. The room was dark, the only light issuing from the monitor screen.

Atsuko's hip hurt. She must have had an actual pain there, which had registered as pain in the dream when Osanai pushed her away. Atsuko looked down at her clenched right hand. Human hair was protruding from between her fingers.

Atsuko opened her fist and caught her breath. If her two patients hadn't been sleeping there beside her, she would have screamed aloud. She was holding a DC Mini, together with some sticky tape and a clump of hair. It was the one Osanai had been wearing. "I brought it back with me," she said to herself. A shudder went through her. "I brought it back." From the middle of a dream, to the waking world.

5

"Something unbelievable has happened," Atsuko told Noda when he called the following morning. She didn't even give him a chance to state his business.

Noda felt inclined to believe the notion, however incredible, that Atsuko had brought something back from Osanai's dream. But even he couldn't resist the urge to check the alternatives.

"Paprika," he said with a little groan, "are you sure it wasn't the one you had before? The DC Mini?"

"It was still on my head. Now I've got two of them."

"Wow. This is serious." Recognizing the gravity of the situation, Noda chose his words carefully. "Paprika. Is there any way you could see Osanai and confirm this? Make sure you got it from him?"

"I ought to," Atsuko agreed. "I'll go to the Institute today and see him there."

She had other things to attend to at the Institute anyway. There were bound copies of papers that needed sending, as well as an unfinished paper she'd left there, not to mention her private belongings.

"The Institute? Where your enemies surround you?" Noda lowered his voice grimly. "They'll slaughter you."

"I'm not a child," Atsuko laughed. "And in any case, I've got the upper hand now. I've got one of their DC Minis. They're the ones who'll be sweating now."

"Be careful."

"I'll be all right. Thanks. Anyway, what were you calling about?"

"I've contacted one of the directors. I already knew Ishinaka, so I asked him to meet you and hear your side of the story. I think you should tell him everything. Toshimi thinks so too. Ishinaka was reluctant at first, but eventually agreed. I got him to contact the other two, Owada and Hotta."

"Owada's on our side already."

"That's right. He also agreed."

"And Hotta?"

"Hotta refused, apparently. He says he wants to hear both sides of the argument first. That's fair enough, really."

"What's fair about it?" Atsuko countered with some annoyance, remembering the Board Meeting just two weeks earlier. "He's on their side."

"Anyway, will you meet the other two? How about this afternoon? Toshimi and I will join you."

The Chief Commissioner's presence would surely impress the enormity of the situation on Owada and Ishinaka.

"All right. Four o'clock this afternoon. We'll meet here."

"And how are your patients getting on?"

"Shima's making a good recovery. I'll make a proper start on Tokita tonight."

"In that case, let's take Shima back to his own apartment. I'll contact Toshimi and ask him to arrange protection. You can't do anything with Shima stuck at your place."

"All right. I'd appreciate that."

"We should also arrange a watch on your apartment, for Tokita's sake. I'd rather you didn't go to the Institute until that's been organized."

"Agreed."

Konakawa turned up an hour later, accompanied by Superintendent Morita, Chief Inspector Yamaji and two Inspectors. One of the Inspectors was a veteran called Saka, a dark-skinned middle-aged man who'd worked his way up through the ranks. Inspector Ube was considerably younger than Saka. He seemed possessed of an intelligence that would eventually place him among the elite ranks.

"These four," Konakawa said, pointing to his subordinates, "are my right-hand men. You can ask them about anything."

Atsuko spoke with the officers over coffee. It was decided that Yamaji and Saka would guard Shima while Morita and Ube would watch Atsuko's apartment. Yamaji and Morita would occasionally return to the Department to see to their normal business. It would be a kind of rotating watch.

Once Shima had been returned to his apartment, Atsuko was to be driven to the Institute in a Met car, accompanied by Konakawa and Morita. Atsuko was concerned that arriving in a police car would cause unnecessary commotion at the Institute. Fortunately, though, the car was unmarked.

Since visiting vehicles could go no further than the hospital's front entrance, Atsuko was obliged to pass through the hospital reception after getting out of the car. The doctors, nurses, medical office and administrative staff who happened to be in the vicinity looked on in stunned amazement, stared wide-eyed or stopped in their tracks when they saw Atsuko. She deliberately greeted them with a cheery smile or a glib wave of the hand as she made her way through to the Institute building and headed for her own lab.

There, she found Hashimoto in the process of taking documents from her drawers and piling them high on her desk, peeping at them whenever he thought it necessary.

"Hashimoto! What do think you're doing?" Atsuko demanded, glaring at him angrily.

"This is my lab now," he replied with a sardonic smile, as if he'd been ordered to taunt her as much as possible.

"That's the first I've heard of it," Atsuko said, snatching her papers from Hashimoto's hands. "What you're doing is criminal!"

"It's your own fault for going absent without leave. If you don't like it, go tell the Vice President." He started to pile Atsuko's personal belongings together on the desk. "Here, these are yours." He'd brought his own things in and had placed them on the chair.

"I think you'd better stop what you're doing right now."

"There's no place for you here any more. The system has changed." Hashimoto was enjoying his moment.

"Is that right. Well, shall we call the police then?" Atsuko picked up the telephone.

Hashimoto instantly reverted to his usual chicken-livered self. "OK, OK!" he whined. "I'm leaving. OK? I'm leaving." He grimaced and mockingly twisted his body like a girl. "Gee, you're so scary!"

"Ha! So you're saying the whole thing was a joke?" Atsuko laughed back. "In that case, I'm sorry!"

Atsuko picked up the heavy bundle of documents Hashimoto had brought with him, hurling it through the open door onto the floor of the corridor.

Half an hour later, while Atsuko was still clearing up her papers, Osanai walked in. Hashimoto must have told him of Atsuko's arrival.

"Doctor Chiba."

"Well! Doctor Osanai. So sorry about last night."

It was a line she'd prepared in anticipation of his visit. Stunned by her pre-emptive strike, Osanai rolled his eyes in bewilderment. Now Atsuko was sure she'd taken the DC Mini from him in the dream.

"And did you know the DC Mini had such dangerous functions?" Osanai regained his composure and glared menacingly at Atsuko.

Atsuko glared back at him. She pretended to know, to maintain the momentum of her offensive. "What dangerous functions? There are so many. Do you mean the one where the DC Mini can be moved from one real location to another through a person's dream?"

"From a dream. Not from a real location. From a *dream!*" Osanai screamed as if momentarily afflicted with madness.

"What? You were awake, weren't you?"

"No! I only thought I was awake. You said so yourself. After that, I woke up properly." His hand made an involuntary move towards his head, as if in search of the missing clump of hair. "When I woke up, the DC Mini was gone. You'd stolen it!"

So she hadn't brought it back from reality via her dream. She'd brought it back from reality via *both* of their dreams. That aside, Atsuko was bothered by Osanai's mention of danger. She wasn't sure what he meant by it.

"Are there any other functions we don't know about?" asked Osanai. "If there are, you'd better tell us quickly. This device is dangerous. We need to control it rigorously, under high-level

236

isolation and in all secrecy. Please return all DC Minis in your possession to us."

"Who's this 'we' you keep going on about? Would it be you and your gay lover?" Atsuko countered with a smile. "I wonder if he's at work yet. There's something I want to ask him."

Osanai blushed slightly, but seemed well prepared for the moment when his relationship with Inui would be revealed. He quickly returned to the offensive. "See? If you keep them, all you'll do is abuse them to pry into other people's private lives. The Vice President will not be coming in today. Anyway, please give them back to us. You don't have the faintest perception how dangerous they could be. What if they also had a function whereby not just the DC Minis themselves but other matter could also be brought back from a dream? That would be no joke at all."

Indeed not, thought Atsuko. In that case, even virtual constructs that only exist in dreams could be made to materialize. Atsuko said nothing. Osanai and Inui may have discovered something while at the experimental stage; he may have been testing her to see if she knew about it.

"There seems to be some mistake here. I'm the one who wants the DC Minis back," Atsuko said icily. "They're not playthings for gay sex games. Come on. If you're not going to give them back, please get out. I've got a lot to do."

But Osanai wasn't going to back down that easily. He turned at the door and grinned. "The Institute's policy has changed. You're no longer wanted here. I reckon you'll be getting your notice soon."

6

"So the DC Mini was temporarily reduced to the level of atoms or molecules or whatever, using a function built into the device itself, or possibly the latent psychic energy of the person wearing it, and was then resynthesized, more or less instantaneously, in another place, where someone else was wearing a DC Mini?" Noda said incredulously. "That's amazing. It's like something out of a science-fiction story. Teleportation, or whatever they call it."

"That's the only possible explanation." Atsuko felt compelled to agree, although her only knowledge of teleportation came from *The Fly*, the science-fiction film based on George Langelaan's story.

"I tell you, if PT devices hadn't already been developed, we'd be falling around laughing at the idea," Owada said with a groan. "I'm beginning to think we shouldn't be surprised at anything Tokita invents from now on."

"No, no. I think this function developed itself spontaneously, as a side effect," said Atsuko. "It has nothing to do with treating schizophrenics, after all."

"But anyway, it's just too incredible. It's quite literally unbelievable." Ishinaka wiped the sweat from his brow. "Still, I suppose we shall have to believe it. Because it has actually happened. In reality."

Chief Superintendent Konakawa, Superintendent Morita, Chief Inspector Yamaji and Inspector Ube were also present. Inspector Saka was guarding Shima's apartment. The presence of so many high-ranking police officers left the two directors in no doubt as to the gravity of the matter. Their hearts leapt with astonishment as they listened to Atsuko's lengthy explanation of the situation so far.

"In that case, this affair can no longer be confined to the Institute," said Owada, Chairman of the National Association of Surgeons and a man of eminently sound judgement. Now, at last, he understood the reason for the unduly large police presence.

"That's true, but neither is it a problem we can make public," said Konakawa. "The Vice President and his gang are banking on that."

"All right, what about at government level?..." Ishinaka ventured.

"Personally, I think this is a case we should handle by ourselves," Konakawa said decisively.

Ishinaka wasn't stupid; even he could appreciate that the matter should be resolved under the cloak of secrecy. But there was an unmistakable air of fear about him. "So, what, in fact, are you suggesting we should do?"

"That's what we need to talk about," said Noda.

The discussion moved to remedial measures. It continued for another four hours, until eight o'clock that evening. Not that they'd made any particularly important decisions in that time. They had merely decided some basic principles for the time being; after all, they had no way of knowing how things would develop from now on. Inui would almost certainly call an urgent Board Meeting to solidify his own position. All in attendance agreed that the meeting should be opposed on grounds of Shima's and Tokita's absence due to illness. They also considered explaining the situation to as many of the trustees as possible, thereby trying to win their support. Such an approach promised little, however, since they wouldn't be able to explain the whole truth to them.

Owada left for Shima's apartment on the same floor, guided by Chief Inspector Yamaji, to examine both Shima and Tokita there. Noda and Ishinaka went to have dinner in the restaurant. They had other business to discuss anyway. Konakawa and Morita returned to the Metropolitan Police Department. Ube went to grab a bite to eat, promising to return soon.

Atsuko cooked some spaghetti and opened a can of seafood, which she stir-fried in sesame oil while blending in the pasta. She made extra portions for Saka and Ube to eat later that night. Noda had brought several cans of the seafood with him, explaining that Atsuko would probably be eating at home more often from now on. He'd arranged for the cans to be prepared specially by a hotel chef he knew. Ube returned just as Atsuko had finished a simple meal of seafood spaghetti and potage soup.

"Will you be treating Mr Tokita now?" Ube asked as he joined Atsuko for coffee. He looked at her with the keen eye of a young man.

"Yes. I appreciate your being here. I have to go into semi-sleep to carry out the treatment, so I'll be completely defenceless then."

"Semi-sleep?" Ube looked puzzled. "Can you make yourself do that?"

"It comes with practice. And seeing another person's dream itself has a soporific effect."

"So you mean, you can go to sleep anywhere you like and wake up any time you like?" Ube said with some envy. "We could do with that in the force. Then we could take routine naps while keeping watch on someone."

Atsuko laughed. "It doesn't work like that. When it's just for myself, I have a lot of trouble getting to sleep sometimes."

"And isn't there a danger that, once you're inside someone else's dream, you could fall fast sleep?"

"That's a big danger. It takes a lot of skill. If my reason starts to feel hazy while I'm in a patient's dream, I have to wake up immediately. Then again, with the DC Mini…"

Atsuko stopped short. She'd suddenly remembered something that had bothered her during the conversation with Osanai earlier that day. Did the DC Mini have the effect of making the wearer sleep more deeply? The previous night, in her half-sleeping thoughts, she'd been briefly struck by a sense of danger, as if she was falling into a deeper sleep. Even Osanai had been unable to wake up when he wanted to, and he should have been quite adept at using the DC Mini. He thought he'd woken up, but in fact was only dreaming that he had. If this was a side effect caused by anaphylaxis, it would mean that using the DC Mini over the long term could be extremely dangerous. Were Inui and Osanai aware of that?

"Is something the matter?" Ube asked to interrupt Atsuko's thoughts.

240

"No," she replied quickly with a shake of the head. At the moment, it was nothing more than a suspicion. It would have to be confirmed before she could share it with anyone.

Atsuko went into the bedroom. Tokita was still sleeping like a baby. She had fed him some rice soup just before meeting the others. Eating only twice a day might help him lose some weight, but a lack of exercise could make him even fatter, since he was generally inclined towards obesity. Atsuko fitted the gorgon on Tokita's head. Without warning, the maternal affection she felt for him as a patient merged with her true love for him. She found herself kissing him on the cheek as she started the treatment, aided by the DC Mini.

Atsuko was well acquainted with Tokita's habitual dreams. But they were difficult to distinguish from those of the equally geekish Himuro, which had been projected into his unconscious mind. Atsuko had no choice but to carefully isolate, one by one, the fragments that could clearly be identified as Himuro's. If the Japanese doll appeared, she would replace it with machine tools, Tokita's obsession; if an infantile computer game, PT devices. Luckily, Tokita lacked Himuro's sweet tooth. Whenever candy or chocolate bars appeared, Atsuko replaced them with grilled aubergine in sweet *miso* paste, or grilled fish, or some other dish Tokita loved, and was thus able to remove the offending elements immediately. Atsuko started to feel as if she'd reached a turning point in Tokita's treatment. It was already past midnight.

Tokita seemed to have returned to his own dreams at last. From a window on the 3rd floor of a building, Tokita and Atsuko were looking down at a vast railway marshalling yard. In the yard were various locomotives, including a diesel engine with a particularly nasty face. Atsuko was familiar with it, as it appeared to have some antipathy towards Tokita. It always chased him obsessively in his dreams.

"Oh, look. There it is again. Over there!"

Atsuko giggled as she pointed at the engine. Tokita looked scared and made a pitiful whining noise. For him, that diesel locomotive was something deadly serious, something that stirred up a fear akin to madness in his dreams. But that fear was an integral part of Tokita himself; the more he could feel it, the stronger his self-awareness would become.

The locomotive glared at Tokita with eyes turned upwards, jumped the rails, cut diagonally across another set of rails that ran parallel to them, and came rushing towards the bottom of the building.

"It's all right," said Atsuko. "We're too high up for it to hurt us."

Tokita had thought the same thing. But he also suspected that things wouldn't turn out quite as he thought; Atsuko knew they wouldn't.

As expected, the diesel engine started clambering up the outer wall of the building.

Tokita groaned. He was screaming inside.

"Oh dear, here it comes. Let's run away!" Atsuko took Tokita's hand and ran with him towards the back of the building. "Don't look round!"

If he had looked round, he would have seen the locomotive coming in through the window.

"But I'm going to turn in the end." The extremity of the situation caused Tokita to utter his first words. The security of having Atsuko beside him must have helped. It was a good sign.

The two turned together. What they saw was a broad Alpine pasture. They were standing on the terrace of a mountain cabin, with a handrail separating them from the Alpine scene. Side by side on a bench in front of the handrail sat Seijiro Inui and Morio Osanai.

"Ah. Our good friend Mr Tokita," said Osanai, smiling as he rose. "So it's not Mr Shima tonight, then."

"So you've come to interfere again?" Atsuko was instantly transformed into Paprika, and stood in front of Tokita to protect

242

him. Paprika's character was more suited to aggression, it had to be said.

As she spoke, Paprika became aware, albeit momentarily, of something strange in the landscape behind Inui and Osanai. Black objects were dotted around the pastoral scene. They appeared to be ordinary, everyday objects, which seemed to be coming closer. What could they be? Atsuko remembered the scene from a patient's dream.

"Which of us is interfering here?!" Osanai replied with a wry smile, whereupon Inui stood up slowly. He was dressed in the ostentatious robes of a barrister, and looked down at Tokita and Paprika from a lecturer's podium. His appearance certainly had an overpowering effect on the two. After all, Inui had been a professor at the university where they'd both graduated. But the content of Inui's lecture was utterly banal – perhaps because he was more or less asleep.

"Isn't it a ****** that should be used for the good of all humanity? This is surely the perfect *****. We should strive to discover a method whereby we may all understand each other, using the collective subconscious of the whole human race, joined together through our dreams."

"Gosh. How very Jungian, Professor," Paprika mocked. "How very *last century.*"

Inui's face was contorted with rage. He even seemed close to waking up.

"Silence!" he roared. "Insolent girl! Delinquent trollop!"

The high ceiling of the vast lecture hall started to collapse with a puff, like a crumpled paper ball. Tokita cried out. Peering through a gaping hole in the ceiling was the face of a gigantic Japanese doll, the size of an advertising balloon. It had expressionless black eyes on an oddly featureless white face. Tokita started to wail like an infant.

But Atsuko had already removed the elements of Himuro's dreams. The appearance of this Japanese doll must have been a conspiracy by Inui and Osanai to make Tokita's condition regress. Atsuko's finger pressed the key to isolate Tokita's dream from the collector.

"So who's interfering now?!" Paprika shouted at the same time.

But Inui and Osanai were motionless, their expressions and movements fixed like frozen images. It was almost as if they were rigid with fear. Perhaps they'd been startled by the sudden change of scene. They were in a desperately bleak landscape, surrounded by a deserted housing estate. Plastic buckets full of rubbish lay scattered along a road. There was no sign of life. The air and colours were funereal. Most of the windows were broken, and from each broken window a Japanese doll showed its pale white face, smiling inanely with both arms held aloft. A huge image of Buddha, at least ten metres tall, sat in an open space in the middle of the estate. It too was smiling while nodding continuously.

"This isn't ours," said Osanai, squirming in discomfort. "Seijiro. Wake up!"

Paprika now realized the truth. Himuro's nightmares as he lay in the hospital were being transmitted directly into Atsuko's dream, and into the DC Minis worn by Inui and Osanai.

"We've got to wake up. If we don't, we'll all go insane!" Paprika yelled, shaking with terror.

Paprika tried to restore her waking awareness. It wasn't easy. She knew the horrors of Himuro's dreams after his personality had been laid waste, as she'd seen them when she examined him. If she continued to see them for any length of time, she was certain to become schizophrenic herself.

It was the anaphylaxis effect. The DC Mini embedded in Himuro's head was continuously transmitting the nightmares of a schizophrenic patient, replete with images powerful enough to destroy a person's mind. The transmission from Himuro may have been gradually growing stronger, or the range of reception by Paprika, Inui and Osanai may have been gradually expanding.

Whichever the case, those nightmare images had travelled through the ether to their DC Minis five kilometres away.

7

"Doctor Chiba! Doctor Chiba!"

Someone was shaking Atsuko in the gloomy half-light. Groaning, twisting and turning, she summoned up the strength to break through an unseen viscous membrane that confined her to sleep, until, finally, she awoke in her own bedroom.

"Sorry, but you seemed to be in distress," Ube said with some concern. "I didn't know whether I should wake you, but it was too much to ignore…"

Her cries must have carried as far as the living room, where Ube had been sleeping on the sofa next to the window. Atsuko found that particularly unfortunate, as she'd only just been boasting that she could wake herself from autohypnosis at any time. She lowered her head and thanked him meekly. "No, you were right. I appreciated it."

Atsuko suddenly remembered the urgency of the situation. "This is really serious. Himuro's dreams are coming this way from the hospital. His dreams aren't funny, I assure you. Everyone who uses a DC Mini will be affected."

Atsuko played back the scenes recorded from Himuro's dream to illustrate her point. Ube was shocked by the flood of destructive images and instantly realized the enormity of the matter.

"You say they still have three of these devices?" he asked.

"Yes. But I've no idea who else they're allowing to use them."

"Himuro must be moved to a remote location, before all else."

Yes, but however remote that location, anaphylaxis could expand the DC Mini's viable range infinitely. Atsuko felt overcome by helplessness and a mild bout of vertigo when she thought of that.

"Yes, we'd better move him. Otherwise, they might…" Atsuko stopped short of saying "kill him". But knowing them, they might do just that. They surely had no alternative if they wanted to keep using the DC Minis.

"Yes." Ube nodded, intuiting Atsuko's meaning. "Himuro is in very great danger."

He immediately called the Chief Superintendent to give his report. Konakawa instructed Ube to stake out Osanai's apartment on the 15th floor and prevent him from leaving the building that night. Atsuko then asked if Saka, who was guarding Shima's apartment, could keep a watch on Hashimoto as well. She could hope for no more assistance from the police than that. They couldn't just go marching into the hospital, as nothing demonstrable had happened there.

Atsuko wanted to go to the hospital herself. Ube firmly opposed such a plan, arguing that it would be too dangerous to go there so late at night, especially in her state of fatigue. Atsuko reluctantly agreed to get some sleep first.

Just before nine the next morning, while Atsuko was still eating breakfast, Ube returned from his watch to report that both Osanai and Hashimoto had left for work.

"I'll have to go too," Atsuko said as she stood up.

"Be careful," Ube warned, as if she were setting off on an undercover job in gangland.

The streets that day were oddly shrouded in hazy sunlight, the colours all subdued. This had an unsettling effect on Atsuko as she followed her usual route to the Institute in her Marginal. It was almost as if she hadn't fully shaken off the effects of Himuro's dream. She had experienced similar sensations, temporarily, when she'd first started observing the dreams of schizophrenic patients, but that was some years ago now. It was possible that, when using the DC Mini, abnormal sensations acquired from a patient while accessing a dream remained in the subconscious after waking.

That would be another dangerous side effect of the DC Mini. And perhaps those sensations would merely become magnified with frequent use of the device.

Even then, Atsuko wondered why she was driving with such feverish haste. It wasn't that she was really anxious about Himuro's well-being. But if the struggle over the DC Minis were to result in homicide, it would severely tarnish her reputation, and Tokita's. That was all. It was just as Inui had said; she was driven by nothing but a greed for fame. Atsuko did feel a twinge of remorse about that, but still wanted to convince herself it wasn't true. She wasn't doing it for herself. She was doing it for Kosaku Tokita, the man she loved. That was her excuse.

Atsuko ran to the hospital from the car park. Her flustered appearance again caused heads to turn in the waiting room by the hospital reception.

Atsuko was making for her own duty ward when Sugi, a middle-aged woman who'd previously been the senior nurse on Hashimoto's floor, came rushing out of the nurses' station to block her way.

"Where are you going? This is Doctor Hashimoto's ward now."

"Himuro is my patient. I'm worried about him. I want to see him."

"I'm sorry. I can't let you through."

"Senior Nurse Sugi." Atsuko deliberately adopted a conciliatory tone. "You would hate the police to be involved, would you not? This is an urgent matter, and I intend to pass you, by force if necessary. Do you want to see your name in the newspapers along with mine?"

Sugi cast a pleading glance at the nurses' station, then be-grudgingly pressed her slender form against the wall to let Atsuko through.

Atsuko entered Himuro's room to find her worst fears realized, just like a nightmare where the worst fears always come true. Himuro was curled up on the bed. He was dead. He'd obviously been poisoned; his whole body was blue. His already grotesque facial features were even more distorted than usual. His expression seemed to suggest that he'd thought back over the events leading to his murder and couldn't help but find them amusing. Atsuko hurried out of the room, not wishing to be blamed for his murder.

"Don't you know he's dead?!" she shouted loudly as she ran back to the nurses' station and picked up the telephone, shouting again at the nurses who ran horrified to the scene. "I'll phone the police. Someone call Hashimoto!"

Of course, Atsuko didn't call the usual number for emergency services, but dialled the direct number to Konakawa's office in the Metropolitan Police Department.

"Dead?" Konakawa sounded strangely lethargic.

"He's been murdered," Atsuko confirmed, wondering how she could have known that.

"And by whom has he been murdered?" asked Konakawa coolly. He didn't seem terribly interested.

"Osanai... Hashimoto... Sayama..." There were so many candidates.

Atsuko ran to her lab. She felt sure she would find Hashimoto there. She did find him there, dead. He was lying face down on the desk that was once her own. He'd been strangled with an object that anyone would recognize – Shima's yellow necktie with black polka dots. Atsuko removed the tie and ran to Osanai's lab, clutching it in one hand. As she climbed the stairs, her head started to reel. The stairs were swaying.

Misako Sayama lay on the floor of Osanai's research lab. Atsuko knew that, and wondered why. She could see Sayama drinking poison and killing herself just moments before she opened the door to the lab. *She's in there, I know she's in there*, she thought, *and then... and then...* Atsuko ran to the Vice President's office. The door was open, but as soon as Atsuko entered the room, it closed behind her with a bang. Atsuko dropped the necktie. It was

Osanai who'd closed the door. He was standing right behind her. And sitting at the desk was Seijiro Inui. He was laughing.

"Hello? Is this a good time to be laughing?" asked Atsuko.

"Miss Chiba. Calm down. It may be impossible for you, but please calm down." Inui spoke as if in song. Then he jiggled his shoulders and laughed again.

Osanai also burst into laughter behind Atsuko.

"Himuro's dream did not travel all the way from the hospital to your apartment," Inui continued. "My good friend here was playing it back in the same building, so that it would appear in all our dreams."

"As I thought. A trick. And you even acted so surprised! But why? Why did you do something so obviously dangerous? When you knew we could all have lost our minds?"

"Ha! Didn't you know? We both woke straight after that, momentarily!" Inui flashed a look at Osanai, who was still standing behind Atsuko. They seemed to be smiling at each other. "You were the one who didn't wake up."

Atsuko felt somehow troubled by the word *momentarily*. "Yes," she said. "I had a lot of trouble waking up."

Inui and Osanai bellowed with laughter. It was a coarse laugh, the type a woman would never have produced.

"Yes, I'm sure. I'm sure you did." Inui nodded in hearty agreement. "In other words, it was the same as when you stole the DC Mini from Morio. He thought he'd woken up momentarily, as it were, when in fact he was still dreaming. You see, the DC Mini has the function of repeated effect and side effect, effect and side effect. Yes it does. It makes you dream, then dream of waking, and your waking dream is so very true to reality that you think it is reality, then you fall into an even deeper sleep, dream even deeper dreams, and so on. You see?"

Atsuko understood very well what Inui was saying. Almost too well. Even more so because of his faltering speech, which was quite unlike him. She felt she could even read his thoughts, just as

249

she could when she accessed a patient's dream. The things he was saying seemed altogether too preposterous, but that might just have been a misapprehension on her part.

"So you researched those functions, those effects and side effects, and then you... Yes! Then you tried them out on me? You experimented on me!" Atsuko exclaimed.

Inui declined to answer but stood up. He almost appeared to be floating on air. "It seems you are at last trying to understand. After all, have you not already written, in an unpublished paper, that if you access the dreams of a schizophrenic patient for too long you will become trapped in his subconscious and unable to wake up?..."

"Who said you could read that?!"

"It doesn't matter," Inui spat out irritably. "I've got more important... What?! That's why a woman!..."

"By *more important*," Osanai interjected, though still remaining behind Atsuko, "he means that, well, I think you've already started to realize that now, right now, right here and now, this *trying out* on you, this experimenting on you that you mention... Those functions, well... You know..."

Osanai's thoughts were also being relayed to her. In a flash, Atsuko thought back with horror over events up to that point. Inui's tongue-tied manner, not unlike the speech heard in a dream. Konakawa's oddly disinterested tone on the telephone, which was quite uncharacteristic of him. The series of improbable murders at the Institute. The grim appearance of the streets as she drove through them. Before she knew it, Hashimoto was standing next to Osanai, smiling weakly.

Atsuko cried out and leapt to the wall, bracing herself in combat position. "It's a dream, isn't it!"

"My, aren't you quick." Osanai smiled wryly as he approached her. He clearly intended to steal the DC Mini from her head.

"You're quite right, Paprika," said Inui, staring at Atsuko.

Paprika?!

Atsuko looked down. She was wearing a red shirt and jeans. At the very moment she'd realized that it was a dream and that her DC Mini could be stolen, she had automatically turned into Paprika.

8

Atsuko was dreaming. It did seem a surprisingly realistic dream, though parts of it were typically outlandish. She'd gone back to sleep after Ube had woken her. Or had she? Had even that been part of the dream? According to Inui, he and Osanai had woken "momentarily" before that. Then Atsuko, alone of the three, must have remained asleep. In that case, it must all have been a dream. She had dreamt of going back to sleep and waking the next day. Her discussion with Ube about Himuro's well-being, and the detailed arrangements with Konakawa over the telephone, must also have been a dream. A dream that was impossible to distinguish from reality.

But then that realistic dream had started to lose its realism. Perhaps it was because Atsuko had succumbed to a deeper sleep. She had fallen into their trap. As she stood there in combat-ready position, Atsuko, now transformed into Paprika, observed the three men and wondered how she could regain the upper hand. She had to find an effective way of waking herself, and soon. Otherwise she would fall into a sleep that grew ever deeper – and the ultimate conclusion of that could only be death.

"Ah, so now Master Hashimoto has joined us," Paprika said, eyeing him sternly. It wasn't easy to judge whose thoughts were behind the images. Now even Atsuko's dream had become confused with the others. "Are you dreaming this too?"

"I'm taking part in the DC Mini experiment, yes," Hashimoto said casually. He raised a hand to his head, as if to check that the DC Mini was still there.

Hashimoto's casual reply seemed to annoy Inui. "Not another word!" he barked.

Paprika instantly realized that Hashimoto was not yet familiar with the DC Mini. She decided to recover the next one from him.

"Run!" shouted Osanai.

Hashimoto also seemed to have read Paprika's thoughts. But he couldn't move. He was still looking dozily at Paprika, apparently unable to control his own dream.

They were in the cosmetics section of a department store. Now, at last, Hashimoto started to run. Paprika chased him as he beat a retreat, weaving his way through showcases and customers who stood there like statues. She could smell Osanai's hair lotion, which brought back unpleasant memories. Judging from the department-store setting – and men's cosmetics, to boot – this must have been Osanai's dream.

Paprika envisioned a lift with its doors open, directly ahead of Hashimoto as he ran. The lift appeared on cue. Hashimoto, now enclosed on both sides by grey prison-like walls, had no choice but to run straight into it. *Got you*, thought Paprika. She would pursue him into the sealed chamber of the elevator cage, close the door and rip the DC Mini from his head. She would certainly be in danger if she couldn't find a way of waking up quickly. She had yet to hit upon a good method, but in any case, she needed to recover one more DC Mini before she awoke.

The elevator cage was spacious inside; the back of it seemed to go on for ever. Along the sides stood a number of male and female figures with ill-defined features. They looked like stuffed dolls. The door closed behind Paprika. She ran but still couldn't catch Hashimoto, who fled further and further into the depths of the elevator cage. The lift started to rise with a great rattling sound. There was suddenly another door at the far end of the cage; Hashimoto seemed intent on escaping through it. Paprika continued to chase him, knowing she would have to catch him before the lift came to a halt.

The lift came to a halt. Hashimoto opened the door manually. But because Paprika willed it to be, there was a gap of more than two metres between the door of the lift and the opening. Below the gap was nothing but a dark chasm. Hashimoto rattled the elevator cage to bring it closer to the opening. The cage started to shake. The opening came closer. Paprika leapt onto Hashimoto just as he prepared to jump across.

As they plummeted into the void together, Paprika tried to confirm something that was troubling her. "You'd better not have killed Himuro?!"

"If we'd let that cretin live…" Hashimoto blurted out incoherently, unable to control his consciousness with its diminished sense of morality. His mind started to recreate an image of the truth.

"Don't think about it!" screamed Osanai.

But Hashimoto had lost sight of the consequences. He thought about it. They were in a broad, enclosed space reminiscent of a baseball stadium, surrounded by walls that sloped inwards. It was a waste-processing site at the dead of night. Paprika and Hashimoto were grappling in the middle of it, illuminated by floodlights.

"You've killed him, haven't you!" Paprika yelled. "And this is where you brought his body! Where is this place? What's it called? Tell me!"

"Wake up! Wake up, you fool!" Osanai continued to scream in desperation.

The ground parted. Himuro's body rose to the surface with a ghastly squelching, slithering sound, his face almost decomposed and his torso covered in garbage. At last Hashimoto reacted. Himuro was probably Osanai, trying to wake Hashimoto by scaring him.

But Hashimoto couldn't wake up. The stimulus of his involuntary embrace with Paprika had aroused his libido. He had an erection. Suddenly he was lying naked on a bed surrounded by white walls. It looked like a hotel room, the kind of place where he'd enjoyed numerous assignations in the past. He had flipped Paprika over and now lay sprawled on top of her in a coital position. His breath smelt fishy. Something hard pressed against the crotch of Paprika's jeans. Hashimoto had a faraway look in his eyes and started to make thrusting movements. Paprika grabbed the top of his head with a yell of triumph.

"Ouch! What was that for?!"

Paprika had no intention of taking this man's seed, or anything else of that kind, back from the land of her dreams. The very thought disgusted her. All she took from the head of Hashimoto, now defenceless in the throes of erotic delight, was his DC Mini.

"Where was it?" Paprika demanded. "Where was that rubbish dump?"

"The *****!" Hashimoto's thoughts were vague, impossible to read.

Hashimoto turned into Osanai. But his nakedness and coital position remained the same.

"Where's Hashimoto?" asked Paprika.

"He's woken up," Osanai answered with a snigger, leering at Paprika from above as he pinned her down. "But of course, you must know that. Having his libido aroused was too much for him. Poor chap had a nocturnal emission."

Paprika thought it was more likely due to "*dreason*" – dream reason. The act of raping her in his dream had stimulated his sense of guilt, and that was what had woken him. She preferred to think that he'd ejaculated *after* waking up.

Osanai was trying to open the fingers of Paprika's right hand, where she held the DC Mini. In a desperate attempt to stop him, Paprika reached out with her left hand and grabbed his limp member.

"Same as ever!" she laughed.

Osanai was livid. "What do you expect? I wouldn't want to do it with a tart like you!"

"I'll crush these if you like!" Paprika had already shifted her grip to his scrotum.

Osanai was duly scared, but then realized that she couldn't really do him any harm. After all, it was just a dream. He laughed it off and continued to prise her fingers open one by one.

Paprika couldn't bring herself to squash a man's testicles, even in a dream. It would just have been too ghastly. Instead, she put her left hand to his head. She wanted to take his DC Mini, but all she managed was to ruffle up his hair.

The DC Mini wasn't there.

Atsuko heard Inui's laughter close to her ear. He was sitting on a chair next to the bed. Like Osanai, he was naked. His pale, scrawny body, complete with limply hanging penis, was a seriously unattractive sight.

"Have you heard of anaphylaxis? Well done. It seems you have. We don't even have to wear the DC Minis now." He started to ogle her with a lecherous smile on his face. "How about stripping this young lady naked?" he said to Osanai. "Also, no need to waste your time with the one in her hand. Just take the one from her head! That'll be much quicker."

Osanai reached out to Paprika's head with a cunning smile, as if to say "*Why of course!*" She cursed her carelessness. No one was more surprised than Paprika to find she wasn't wearing a DC Mini either.

"Eh?! It's not there! She got into the dream without it!" Osanai yelled. Inui looked puzzled. He also stretched out a hand and groped around in Paprika's hair.

Paprika thought back. Maybe when she dreamt she was woken by Ube, she really did remove the DC Mini. It would have been the same as pressing a key on the console while accessing a patient's dream – a semi-conscious, semi-automatic act.

All right then! Inui stepped up to the bed with a defiant smile and grabbed Paprika from the opposite side. She was seized with fear. With enemies quite literally on both sides, she was unable to move. The two men busily started to remove her shirt and jeans.

She decided to let them do as they wished for a moment, to put them off their guard. But Paprika's special skill was in changing scenes. It was a skill she'd acquired from her need to manipulate her clients' dreams.

They were in a large café. Around them sat a number of young men and women, mostly in couples. Paprika was drinking coffee at a table in the middle. Inui and Osanai had moved their chairs towards hers and were fondling her from both sides, naked as the day they were born.

Having their nakedness subjected to public scrutiny seemed to come as quite a shock to them, even in a dream. The pair moaned and instantly vanished.

Paprika took a look around. She needed to wake up fast, as her reason was growing increasingly vague. But how? She knew many ways of withdrawing from the dreams of her patients and returning to reality, but she was too deeply immersed for such simple remedies. She needed help from the real world; how could she go about getting it? In any case, what time was it now? Outside the window of the café, she could see a busy thoroughfare in the middle of the day. But had the day already dawned in the world outside dreams?

Paprika corrected her slumped posture and stood up. She would seek the help of Tatsuo Noda. Until just recently, she'd been using the direct line to his office to discuss the schedule for his dream treatment. She had memorized his number. But could she get through to him – in a dream? If it really was the middle of the day, he might well be in his office.

Inui and Osanai had disappeared. But they were surely watching her, from somewhere. *Oh no*. The woman in that picture on the wall was Inui. Paprika was sure of it. Those incisive eyes. They were his eyes. They were laughing, mocking her, saying "*So you think you'll get through? Ha!*"

Paprika picked up the receiver of a push-button telephone next to the till. The numbers on the buttons were all jumbled up, like a table of random digits. The arrangement of the buttons was irregular, too. Some of them displayed letters of the alphabet. To make matters worse, the buttons kept moving when Paprika tried to press them. Then they began to proliferate and shrank in size. Paprika shoved the unwanted numbers and letters to the corner, leaving just the ones she needed in the centre. She dialled the direct line to Noda's office.

"Hello?... Hello?... Who is it?"

A connection?! She could just make out Noda's voice at the other end. But she was inside Shinjuku Station. The noise was so deafening that she could hardly hear what he was saying.

"Tatsuo! Tatsuo!" she called in desperation.

"Who is it? Hello? Who is it?" Noda's distant voice sounded from his distant office in some distant world.

"It's Paprika! Help me! Help me, please!"

"Paprika?! Ah! I do love you so! Where are you?"

"I'm in a dream. I'm calling from a dream. I can't get out of it. Get me out of it, will you? Please help me!"

"Ah. I do love you, Paprika. You're suffering now, aren't you."

"I'm suffering terribly."

"I'm on my way. I'm on my way. Where are you?"

"Shinjuku Station, in my dream. Please come quickly!"

"I'll be there right away. I'll come to help you. Ah. Paprika. I do love you so. I do love you."

9

Atsuko had fallen asleep while operating her PT equipment, and no manner of shaking could wake her. There was definitely something wrong with her. Hearing this news from Inspector Ube, Konakawa hurried to Atsuko's apartment, accompanied by Superintendent Morita. On arrival, he found Tokita already awake and sitting at the dining table, where he was enjoying some toast and coffee. Ube must have made it for him. Tokita seemed a lot better now, but still barely responded when spoken to.

In the bedroom, Atsuko was slumped face down on the keyboard of her console. In front of her, a monitor glowed hazily in the dimly lit room. Atsuko was moaning, murmuring as if in delirium, speaking in a quiet tearful voice, sometimes shifting in her seat. Her condition was quite clearly abnormal; Konakawa had certainly never seen anything like this.

"If this is the dream she's having right now," Ube said as he pointed to the screen, "she must be having a pretty horrendous time. It's been like this for a while now."

On the screen, a rope suspension bridge was swaying wildly over a deep ravine. Up ahead, some of the stepping boards were falling into the ravine, and the hand rope was beginning to fray. The river flowing below was the colour of blood.

"It's like an image of hell," said Konakawa, distressed to think of Atsuko's suffering. "We must wake her quickly."

"I tried splashing cold water on her face, but it didn't work."

"No, that's far too mild."

"A good way of waking someone is to hold their nose and interrupt their breathing," said Morita.

"Idiot. She would just dream she was suffocating. It might not kill her, but what if it did lasting damage?" Konakawa shook his head firmly. "No. The only way she'll wake up is by doing it herself."

Morita opened his eyes wide. "What? You mean there's no other way? So what are we supposed to do, then?"

Konakawa parted Atsuko's hair. The DC Mini wasn't there. "Did you take the device from her head?" he asked Ube.

"I did, sir. It was about seven o'clock this morning. I thought it might have been why she couldn't wake up." Ube put his hand in his pocket and produced the DC Mini he'd removed from Atsuko's head.

"What made you think that?" Konakawa mused as Ube passed him the small, grey conical object.

"Last night, Miss Chiba was telling me how dangerous it would be if she fell into a deep sleep while inside a patient's dream. Especially when she mentioned the DC Mini, she looked very worried and went quiet. She seemed to suspect that it could make the wearer sleep more deeply. Anaphylaxis, I think she called it."

"That would seem the correct conclusion," Konakawa said, impressed by the memory and sharp insight of the young inspector. "And even if that weren't the case, as long as she's wearing the DC Mini, the enemy can access her dreams and project offensive images into them."

Of course, neither Konakawa nor Ube knew the real truth – that Osanai had been prevented from taking Paprika's DC Mini when they were fighting because Ube had already removed it.

"By the way," said Ube, taking another DC Mini from his pocket. "Miss Chiba was holding another device in her hand. I took it from her, as I thought she could be affected by this one as well."

"That's funny." Konakawa took the device from Ube's palm and scrutinized it. "Was she holding another DC Mini when she started Tokita's treatment?"

"She had it in her drawer as a spare." Ube opened the drawer beneath Atsuko's console and exclaimed loudly. "It's still there! Chief Superintendent! She didn't have the third DC Mini before! She must have taken it from someone in her dream!"

10

The morning sales meeting ended, and Noda returned to his office.

He'd been up early, and as he cast an eye over the sales plan, he started to feel drowsy. He'd had some coffee, both at home and during the meeting, but he still felt sleepy. It often happened that way. This time was different, though; the lure of sleep was strangely seductive, strangely insistent.

Being aware of his own fatigue was nothing particularly unpleasant for someone of Noda's age or status. It wasn't a fatigue based on worry, and anyway, the sales plan wasn't particularly urgent. As he sat at his desk in his comfortable office armchair, he allowed his body to sink into a creeping state of drowsiness, and for a few moments enjoyed the sensation of dozing off. It was a sensation akin to numbness, as if his hands and feet were melting away. This was not the same as sleeping late, nor was it time for a midday nap. Noda liked to call it a catch-up snooze.

The telephone was ringing. Somewhere between waking and sleep, Noda stretched out his hand to pick up the receiver. He may only have been doing it in a dream; the telephone may not actually have been ringing in the first place. It was no longer even clear that he was in his own office.

Tatsuo. Tatsuo.

Someone was calling him. A distant voice began to seep into his mind. A woman's voice. Not his secretary's voice, nor that of any female employee.

Who is it? Who is it? asked Noda. *Hello? Hello? Who is it?*

Had his voice reached the other person? It seemed to have drifted off emptily into space. The woman at the other end was calling him again, more urgently now. Pitifully so.

Who is it? Who are you?

But Noda knew who it was. *Ah. Such a familiar voice. Yes, it's her voice. That girl. What was her name again?*

It's Paprika! Help me! Help me, please!

That's it. Paprika! The girl I adore. She must be in my dreams again. It sounds as if she's suffering because she can't wake up. I'll have to go and help her.

Where are you, asked Noda. *Shinjuku Station, in my dream*, answered Paprika.

Shinjuku Station, in her dream. How can I get there? If only I could think of a way, I think I could go there immediately. How can I get there, he asked. *How can I get there.*

260

Don't wake me. Don't force me to wake up. Come and join me inside my dream. With a DC Mini. Please. Please.

Please. Please. Noda woke with Paprika's words still echoing dreamily in his ears. He was sitting at his desk and had his phone pressed against his ear. All he could hear was the distant, continuous tone of a disconnected call. She must have hung up. Or perhaps there had been no phone call in the first place. It had been a dream. The whole conversation had taken place in a dream.

But Noda knew enough about the DC Mini and its functions to realize that he couldn't ignore his conversation with Paprika, just because it had been in a dream. It had been so clear: Paprika was really asking for his help. Perhaps, due to some foul trickery, she really was unable to wake up, she really was in trouble. What should he do? Shinjuku Station, she'd said. But there would be no point in actually going there. He would have to use a DC Mini and go to help her in her dream. Something he'd previously mentioned in jest was now coming true. The DC Minis were in her apartment. He had to get there. Noda stood up.

11

"So there's really no other way, is there? We have to put the DC Minis on, go to sleep and help Paprika in her dream," Noda concluded after hearing all about it from the police officers and discussing things briefly with Konakawa.

Noda had come to Atsuko's apartment saying he'd felt a vague premonition. He didn't mention that Paprika had communicated with him in a dream. Konakawa might have believed it, but the other two would surely have questioned his sanity. He would tell his friend about it later.

"But this is psychotherapy, specialist work. And highly technical too. We haven't got the skills!" Konakawa protested. "What would happen if we all fell asleep?!"

"That's why we have to join Paprika, to find a way of waking up together."

"In a dream?"

"In a dream."

Morita and Ube looked on open-mouthed.

"You're saying we can only help her by getting inside her head? Then so be it," Konakawa said resolutely. "Shall I go first? If she still doesn't wake up, you come after me."

"No. I think we should both go at the same time," argued Noda. "We don't know which of us will be more useful to her."

"Once we're asleep, be sure to remove the devices from our heads quickly," Konakawa instructed his juniors. "If the DC Mini has the effect of deepening sleep, it must be dangerous to keep it on after entering a dream."

"Er, you keep talking about going to sleep," Morita said with some misgiving, "but can you really go to sleep right here, just like that? And anyway, where will you do it? There are only two beds. If you put Miss Chiba on one of them, that leaves only one. Someone is going to have to sleep on the sofa. That's not going to be easy."

"We'd better sleep close together," Noda said, as if to banish Morita's fears. "We don't know what might happen as a side effect of the DC Mini. We'd better forget about distinguishing dream and reality from now on." Noda blushed under the astonished glare of the officers. Yes, what he'd just said must have sounded utterly bizarre. "Anyway, we can't leave Paprika in this pitiful state for ever. Let's move her to the bed. She's moving, yes, but it's not like during her treatment, when she needs to operate the PT devices. I'll sleep in the chair instead of her. I know a bit about computers. If Paprika gives me instructions in the dream, I might be able to operate the devices somehow."

"Can you really get to sleep in that chair?" Konakawa, himself a poor sleeper, said with a dubious look at Noda.

"Don't worry about me. I can take naps during meetings while

I'm pretending to think about something," Noda replied. "And anyway, I was up early today. I feel quite sleepy already."

Morita and Ube lifted Atsuko and placed her on her own bed. Konakawa lay fully clothed on the patient's bed, while Noda sat facing the PT equipment. Atsuko started to moan quietly, making occasional movements. Her face was virtually expressionless, but faint echoes of sorrow or suffering would occasionally flit across her features. Her appearance was at once childlike and alluring. As Noda put the DC Mini on his head, he was sure she'd been transformed into Paprika in her dream.

Konakawa was convinced that he would soon be making those muffled "can't get to sleep" noises, but tried to force himself to sleep anyway. He groped at the DC Mini on his head to check that it was still there. All he could do now was to rely on the soporific effect of the device.

"I can't sleep with you two standing there," Konakawa barked at his two subordinates, who hovered anxiously near the door. "Go in the next room, will you?"

There was nothing for them to do at that point anyway.

"All right. We'll wait till you're asleep, then come and remove the devices."

Morita and Ube transferred to the living room, leaving the three in the gloomy half-light of the bedroom, accompanied only by the quiet sound of their own breathing.

"She seems to be in some kind of park with a fountain," Noda said as he watched the monitor screen. Judging by the tone of his voice, he was already beginning to feel drowsy. Or perhaps he was deliberately using that tone to help Konakawa get to sleep, aware of the soporific effect it would have on him. "She's waiting for us there. I'm sure of it."

"We need to get there quick."

"Paprika telephoned me in a dream to ask for help."

"Really? I did wonder… How you knew she was in danger… Coming so suddenly like that."

"Well... That's how I knew."

Their conversation broke off.

In no time at all, Noda's head was starting to drop. *Hello – I'm feeling sleepy now...* Konakawa thought as his awareness grew increasingly opaque. A telephone call from a dream? He found that notion perfectly acceptable, proof indeed that he was slipping into the realm of dreams. If possible, he wanted to maintain the proper attitude of a police officer, even in his dream. Was he really capable of that?

They were in the living room of a small house that looked new. The living room was one of only two downstairs rooms. *Ah. It's the house where I was born, when my parents were still young.* Paprika started looking for her parents. They weren't there. The front door had been left open. It was dark outside. What if some bad person were to come in? It was a memory of her parents and their frequent absences, when she would have to look after the house again. *There! Someone's got in!* But it wasn't that scary man who always came peddling his wares, always aggressively, sometimes to the point of violence. No. This time it was a woman. She wore a flimsy yellow dress and her hair was all over the place.

"Hey, you! Think you're good-looking, don't you!" the woman shouted at the child Paprika. The woman stood with legs astride in the hallway. It was Nobue Kakimoto with her hair turned reddish-brown, eyes slanting upwards. "And I suppose you think you're clever, too. Well, you've no need to act so arrogant. In fact you're not clever at all. All you've done is learnt things from books, because you think men won't take you seriously if you're good-looking but stupid. You're only being stubborn, just to save face as a good-looking woman. But hey, it's not fashionable any more! It's the age of feminism, you don't have to be good-looking! And you know, you really are quite stupid. You want proof? You deliberately side with that gargoyle Tokita, as if to say that other men are inferior and they're not good enough for you, but then you go and fall in love with him and in the end you can't tell the difference between good and evil…"

Stop it! Please stop it! the child Paprika wanted to wail. But the words wouldn't come out. Of course they wouldn't. Because this memory of Nobue, who continued to hurl abuse at her, may actually have been a "shadow" of Atsuko Chiba. She was, in a way, hurling abuse at herself.

"Stop that!" shouted her father as he came in from outside. "You're a bad maid! Came after seeing the direct mail, did you?!"

No. It wasn't her father.

"Tatsuo!" Paprika gasped through her sobs.

"Goodness!" As Noda entered, Nobue momentarily changed into Paprika's mother when she was younger, flashed a coquettish glance at him, then disappeared into the understairs cupboard.

"Paprika! I've come to wake you up!"

"Tatsuo. Will you have some tea?" Paprika stood and started to go to the kitchen. Having been asleep so long, she didn't really understand what Noda meant.

"Paprika! Paprika! You called me!" Noda said impatiently as he grabbed her arm.

She could smell Noda's fragrance. *That's right. I must wake up.* "Ah. You're sleeping right next to me, aren't you."

"I'm sleeping in front of the monitor. You're on the bed. What should we do? Should I press one of the keys? I don't know if I can. But if you tell me how, I'll try and wave my arms about."

"There is no such key," said Paprika, shaking her head. "We'll have to find some other way."

It was the middle of the day. They were walking arm in arm along a road in a residential area, towards a main road that ran alongside a railway line. A dog was sprawled lazily at the side of the road. A big dog with rough black hair.

Ah. That's the one that always tries to bite me in my dreams. Paprika transmitted her fear to Noda, clinging tightly to his arm.

The dog slowly got to its feet.

"It's not that Osanai, is it? Or Inui?"

"I don't think so. What time is it now?"

"Just coming up to noon."

"Have I been asleep all that time?!" Paprika said in a tone of lament. Her thoughts were conveyed to Noda, who was using the same PT circuit. *Oh no. I'm just going to stay like this for ever, never waking up. My brain is just going to vegetate.*

No it isn't, thought Noda, turning to Paprika to deny her fears.

"If that's the time, those two won't be disturbing us," said Paprika. *Of course. They'll be in the Institute.*

Are you sure? I think they can access the dream from anywhere they like, as long as there are PT devices. "After all, isn't this dog..." *thinking vile things like it wants to rape you?*

"So it is." *We don't need DC Minis to access your dreams any more.* That sounded like Inui.

The dog came running towards Paprika.

"Stop! Or you're under arrest!"

Toshimi Konakawa, dressed immaculately in police uniform, appeared like a puff of smoke from the middle of a stone wall. He roared at the dog as he materialized.

Yes, the dog was Osanai. He looked stunned. *A p-p-policeman as I thought as I thought what's what's going on with a DC Mini that officer I met in the lift interfering police interfering this woman in her dream damn it!...*

The dog suddenly vanished, as if someone had switched off a monitor. They now seemed able to access Paprika's dreams at will, without wearing the DC Mini, just by monitoring her dreams on PT devices.

"The vile brute has disappeared, leaving only your spirits behind. I can see that clearly. Will you know who they are, whoever they come as?" Konakawa had just fallen asleep and accessed Paprika's dream. Paprika and Noda could also read his thoughts. The meaning of words, so unclear in a dream, became crystal clear with the direct transmission of thoughts.

They'd turned onto the main road, but could still see no way of escaping to reality. Paprika was hunting around a railway station. She couldn't be sure whether it was crowded with people or not. No clues could be seen. Then with tears of laughter Atsuko pointed to a large rectangular clock resembling a monitor screen, hanging from the front of the station building. Osanai's face appeared on the clock.

"Look! There he is! He's still monitoring us!"

Konakawa glared at the clock and thrust a finger towards its face. Osanai looked startled and disappeared. The clock went back to its normal face.

There was a red advertising tower in the middle of the station plaza. Paprika looked at a number of posters that were pasted on it, desperately seeking a way of waking up.

SECTIONALISM IS MATERNITY

NOW ON SALE – ENCYCLOPEDIA OF RAGE – ENCYCLOPEDIA OF ENCYCLOPEDIAS

A TASTE OF SADNESS – PATHOS CHOUX CRÈME MADE SIMPLY ON THE RADIATOR

"If it bothers you," said Noda, "there's a door over there." *Shall we open it?*

I will. Konakawa opened the rusty iron door and peered inside the advertising tower. It was empty.

"It's empty," said Konakawa. "No, not in that sense," he added hurriedly, knowing that Paprika would think it referred to herself. *The advertising tower is not you.*

They went inside the station building. It was the lobby of a hotel where Atsuko often stayed to complete research papers. They could see the front desk. Several guests were milling about there. A number of porters stood motionless like broom handles. Paprika remembered how Inui and Osanai had tried to rape her from both sides in the hotel room. *Did that really happen, or was it just a dream?*

It was just a dream, of course, Noda and Konakawa replied as one. *Ah. Wait a minute. I'm about to remember something. I think I'm about to remember something.* Paprika stopped in her tracks. She looked at a sofa in the corner of the lobby.

All right, let's go to the sofa. Noda started walking towards it, as if to encourage Paprika. *Shall we take a rest there?*

Who takes a rest in a dream?! Ah. That's right. Something flashed across Paprika's mind. But rather than explaining the reason, she quickly told them what must be done.

"Tatsuo. Please rape me, over there." *On the sofa. With all the guests and porters looking on.*

Noda and Konakawa were speechless. But Paprika's thoughts had assumed a kind of logic. She convinced them of it, at least in logical terms.

"*Dreason*" – dream reason. Having sex in a dream stimulates feelings of guilt, causing the dreamer to wake. *And having sex in a public place like this should wake us even more quickly, from the sheer embarrassment of it.*

"It's too absurd." *You can't do a thing like that. Impossible.*

Noda laughed at Konakawa's caution. *Of course it's absurd. It's a dream! Lighten up!* Noda now saw the truth – Paprika and Konakawa had made love in a dream during his treatment. *Well, then. You've already had your turn. You hid it from me! Look, you're both going red!*

It wasn't like that. It was for treatment.

That's right. It was for treatment.

But Noda wasn't fooled. Paprika and Konakawa had made love in his dream because they loved each other.

Even so, Noda doubted whether he could really do it right now. *See? Even thinking about sex with Paprika is threatening to wake me up.*

"Don't wake up!" Paprika cried. "You mustn't! Please! Rape me, here and now!" *Or if you feel bad about raping me, it doesn't have to be like that. Please make love to me! Tatsuo. I love you! I loved you long before I loved Toshimi!*

12

"You do? Even if I ***** you in a place like this?" Noda looked around him. "Well, it's a dream and it probably won't matter anyway… But what will you do if Inui and Osanai start ***** and interfering? Even during the day, they sometimes ***** you with their PT equipment."

"In that case I'll stand guard," Konakawa said decisively. *If I see so much as a shadow of those two, I'll threaten them, make them switch off.*

Forgive me, Toshimi. Noda knew all about Konakawa's burning desire for Paprika; he felt sincerely sorry. Paprika likewise. *Please forgive us. Right in front of you like this. Especially when we've ***** once before.*

*Hey, come on. It's OK. We sleep together, we share the same dreams, we feel everything as one. Our thoughts, emotions, sensations. Our ***. Don't worry. I'm sure to feel your *** too.*

It was no longer a hotel lobby, but a tatami-floored room with no furniture. *It's the room we used for sewing classes in my old high school. A boy called ***** attacked me here after school one day. I often dream about it*, thought Paprika. Konakawa opened the door and went out into the corridor. There, he stood guard outside the sewing classroom, where a highly inappropriate after-school activity was getting underway. Paprika lay on the floor and embraced Noda from below. The heat that lingered over the tatami mats was the moist warmth of suppressed adolescence. A grove of trees blocked the window. *Now you know why I'm trying to look as cheap as possible.* So thought Paprika. *Yes. As shameful as possible.* They were already naked. Foreplay. Paprika deliberately raised her voice in a wholly unbecoming way. She felt ashamed of that in front of Noda and Konakawa. *This isn't the real me.*

It's all right. I understand. That's why I'm feeling, so aroused.

Honestly, I'm not really, this cheap. I'm only doing it to make you, more excited.

I know. I am already. I'm excited. Suddenly, thrusting more rapidly in straight lines. Rising passion. *Ah. Paprika. I can't, hold it back, any more. I can't, hold it, back.* Noda moaned in distress and ejaculated. The three awoke more or less simultaneously, Konakawa last of all.

Atsuko must have shouted something in her sleep. She sat bolt upright in bed, under the astonished gaze of Morita and Ube. They'd already removed the DC Minis from Noda and Konakawa.

"Oh dear," said Atsuko, blushing to think that her behaviour in the dream might have been visible on the monitor.

"Ah. Excellent!" exclaimed Ube. "You all woke up together."

Morita too displayed nothing but relief that the three had all woken safely. "How did you manage it?"

Morita and Ube had no idea what sort of dream they'd had, since all three of their viewpoints had been jumbled up together on the screen. Atsuko was mightily relieved to know that. Noda did his best to maintain his dignity in front of the officers; there was nothing in his demeanour to suggest he'd woken by climaxing just a few seconds earlier. If anything, it was Konakawa who was unable to look his subordinates in the face. He himself had reached a considerable state of excitement, and this appeared to have woken him.

"Well, let's just say it was an emergency measure," said Noda with a laugh, meaning *a measure you could barely dream of.* "It's nothing we could explain really. Better not to ask."

"Actually, there were several calls from the Institute while you were asleep," Morita started, keen to get a worrying subject off his chest. "Apparently Mr Himuro's parents have come looking for him, being concerned over his whereabouts. And Miss Kakimoto's family are coming to Tokyo for the same reason. Doctor Osanai had to invite them to the hospital, since he's in charge of her case and he could hardly just ignore them. But Himuro's parents were told to meet Doctor Tokita and talk to him about it. Himuro's mother has called here twice already. What would you advise?"

"I'll talk to them," said Konakawa. "First, I think Doctor Chiba needs something to eat."

Both he and Noda had been almost painfully aware of Atsuko's hunger in the dream.

13

The restaurant was as massive as a bathhouse, with a high glass ceiling over its eastern half. Himuro's parents sat at a table by the window. Having already met Tokita many times, they stood and bowed deeply across the cavernous dining area as soon as they saw him enter with Atsuko and Konakawa. It was difficult to see how many other diners were in the restaurant; the tables were screened off into separate booths, untouched by direct sunlight due to the height of the ceiling. Whether there were many diners or few, the ceaselessly reverberating murmur of conversation made it impossible to hear what was being said, even at the next table. This made it the perfect place for Atsuko and the others to meet Himuro's parents. Superintendent Morita had suggested it, as he himself had used it on occasion.

Himuro's parents, a good-natured couple in their sixties, had travelled to Tokyo from Kisarazu in the neighbouring prefecture. Their expressions of uncontained bewilderment spoke volumes about their relationship with their unfathomable son; he had always walked all over them, and was continuing to do so, apparently. When Konakawa introduced himself as a Chief Superintendent in the Metropolitan Police Department, they seemed about to burst into tears at any moment.

"Has Kei been involved in some kind of incident?" asked Himuro's father, who had the face of a fisherman but in fact owned a clothes shop.

"We don't know yet," Konakawa replied, shaking his head. "Doctor Tokita informed us he was missing, and I thought it

271

possible he could be mixed up in something. I wondered if you could shed some light on things. That's why I've joined you here."

"I see. But we can't shed light on anything," said Himuro's mother, sending glances of desperation around the table. "You see, our son, well, all he's done is made fools of us, and you know, he's never even phoned us once?"

"Your son was involved in some very serious research," Atsuko intervened on Himuro's behalf. "I was a member of the research team. The nature of that research caused some internal friction at the Institute. You can see for yourselves how depressed Doctor Tokita is about it."

They were sitting around a family table, with Tokita's massive frame hunched between Atsuko and Konakawa. He merely groaned as Atsuko spoke, shifting in his seat as if he'd remembered something unpleasant. "I'm sorry," he said. "I'm responsible for what happened to your son. I didn't protect him enough."

"By which... surely you don't mean... he's been murdered?!" Himuro's father said darkly, placing his fists on the table top.

Himuro's mother moaned in distress and shook her head.

Tokita and Atsuko lowered their faces in the dismal realization that they couldn't reveal the truth. Konakawa was thinking how he could prevent Himuro's parents from filing a missing person's report. He alone was left to swallow his compunction and answer the couple's misgivings.

"We're doing everything in our power to investigate your son's disappearance. Please rest assured about that. I'm sure we'll find him. Just a little more patience, please."

In that case, their patience would have to be endless. Even if Himuro were found alive, he wouldn't be the son they'd once known. Atsuko felt saddened to think of that.

In her dream, she'd seen a waste-processing site at the dead of night. Could Himuro's body really have been dumped there? She had no idea where it was, but she'd played the scene from the reflector's memory device and given a printout to Konakawa.

Even now, one of his subordinates was secretly investigating the location of the site. Judging from Osanai's panic when Hashimoto had inadvertently revealed the site in his dream, Atsuko felt fairly sure that Himuro had indeed been murdered.

"Well, of course, we can't hope to understand anything about your research... But what is this internal friction you speak of?" asked Himuro's father.

Atsuko flashed a look at Konakawa, judging from his expression that he felt it safe to reveal something of the truth. They'd already discussed exactly how much of that truth they were prepared to reveal.

"To put it briefly, it's a struggle for control of the Institute. Others are envious of our research. They've even tried to steal it from us. Your son was in a position to know certain details of that research—"

The haze of dull reverberating voices inside the restaurant, like the nebulous echoing of a large bathhouse, was suddenly shattered by a sharp scream. It seemed to come from a young woman who sat at a nearby table. Next came the sound of a metal tray clattering to the floor, followed almost immediately by the sound of smashing crockery, no doubt the result of a waiter's carelessness. The sounds resonated through the restaurant at a level of decibels probably not factored in by its designer.

Diners started to stand and cry out in shock as they pointed up at the glass ceiling. Far beyond the ceiling, against the clear blue sky, a gigantic Japanese doll was looking down through the glass into the restaurant. The bob-haired doll had liquid black eyes and an eerie smile playing on its pale face. Its red lips should have been pursed but were wide open. It uttered an inaudible laugh.

"What?!..."

"What is it?"

"It's an apparition!"

Atsuko was unable to stand. This was surely Himuro's dream. Himuro's dream had merged with reality. Or was it her own dream again? Could it be that she was still asleep, under the side effects of the DC Mini, and Inui and Osanai were showing her Himuro's dreams again?

"It's Himuro," groaned Tokita.

"What's going on?" Himuro's father yelled in astonishment.

Konakawa slowly rose to his feet with a steady glare fixed on the doll. Then he looked around him. Tokita had buried his face in his hands. "It's Himuro," he repeated. "It's Himuro."

Himuro's mother leant across the table. "Why?" she asked loudly through the din. "Why do you say that's our son? What *is* that doll?"

Atsuko was more concerned with Tokita's state of mind than her own. Whether this was a dream or reality, the last thing she wanted was for his mental state to regress. "It's all right," she said to encourage him. "Pull yourself together. Please pull yourself together. You must remain in control. Please!"

Konakawa went through the motions of punching himself two or three times, then turned to Atsuko. "This may be a side effect of the DC Mini, but one thing I can say for certain is that this is no dream. I'm not saying, in a dream, that this is not a dream. This is reality. *This is reality!*"

He repeated it as if to convince himself. Side effects of the DC Mini... Perhaps one of them was that it made dreams appear indistinguishable from reality. Perhaps they were in the middle of one of those dreams right now. To Atsuko, Konakawa's statement could only mean that he suspected the same thing.

"It's a show. A PR stunt!"

The initial tumult having died down, a dull reverberating hubbub of confused voices had started to take its place. Now a number of diners stood and shouted to the others around them, pointing at the doll with outstretched arms, as if to reassure others as well as themselves.

"It's some kind of campaign."

"Who do they think they are?!"

"Something for TV."

"That's it!"

"Got to be."

Some were booing.

"This is stupid!"

"Stop!"

The doll spread its fingers wide and turned its palms downwards, the dark crease lines on its whitewashed hands looking like palm prints. Dressed in a trailing-sleeve kimono, it then raised its outstretched arms to around shoulder height before bringing its palms down onto the glass of the ceiling.

The glass shattered and fell to the middle of the floor. Now the diners knew this was no joke. They all stood up at once, revealing for the first time that the restaurant was almost full. Some seemed to have been injured. Cries and shrieks of panic were amplified by the reverberation. Most saw the doll as something not of this world. In their sheer terror, they had forfeited all common sense and rational thought. Some fainted, others made a mad dash for the doors.

The glass from the ceiling hadn't reached the table where Atsuko and the others sat by the window. Nevertheless, Konakawa seemed to agree that making a swift exit was imperative.

"Right. Let's go that way first."

Led by Konakawa, the five skirted the wall towards the exit. If the police were to arrive, Konakawa would have to explain his presence with Atsuko and Tokita. The most prudent course was obviously to leave. Atsuko wondered if they really would be able to escape. If this wasn't a dream, if the doll was merely a symbol from Himuro's dream, it would surely keep chasing them for ever.

"It's true that Kei had a doll like that, it was very precious to him," said Himuro's mother, shaking in bewilderment. Still concerned over the safety and whereabouts of her son, she called out to Tokita, who was walking ahead of her. "But why did you say it was Kei? I want to know why you thought that. Will you please tell me?"

"Never mind that," said her husband, taking her by the shoulders. His voice was shaking. "We've got to get out. We can ask about it later."

The doll's hand again broke through the ceiling. Atsuko looked up. Just as she'd feared, the doll's round eyes were clearly trained on them. Even if they left the restaurant, the apparition was bound to keep chasing them. That would be quite awkward for Konakawa, considering his role as supreme guardian of public order. For in chasing them through the streets, the doll would surely cause many more casualties.

If it wasn't a dream, there was no way of fighting the apparition. Or was there? Atsuko may also have retained the after-effects of using the DC Mini. But how should she go about fighting it? Should she act as if she were in a dream? Would that even be possible?

The five stepped out onto the street and looked back at the restaurant. The doll should have been towering over them at a height of ten metres or more, but it was nowhere to be seen. Traffic was travelling calmly along the road; the only commotion came from the diners, who still poured out of the restaurant. The glass roof on the east side had collapsed, along with its steel frame. It was clear that some considerable force had been brought to bear on it.

"What's got into them?!"

Passers-by joked at the sight of diners rushing out of the restaurant. But it was no joking matter; several men and women were huddled at the roadside with blood flowing from head wounds. However ridiculous it seemed, the high casualty count made it certain that police cars and ambulances would soon be arriving.

"We'd better not be here. Let's go," Konakawa said to hurry the group along.

Himuro's parents eyed him with suspicion. If he was a police officer, wasn't it his duty to stay behind and investigate the incident?

276

"For you, what happened just now must have seemed like a nightmare," Konakawa explained as they reached the nearest station. "And for us too, this really is a nightmare, though with slightly different implications. We must now investigate, calmly and scientifically, whether what happened just now had anything at all to do with your son. That's why, as Chief Superintendent of the Metropolitan Police Department, it was important for me not to get caught up in the confusion at the scene, but to evacuate to where we are now. It may be impossible for you to understand, but I need a little more time before I can ascertain the truth of this incident."

"But that doll!" Himuro's mother argued madly. "Was it our son? Was that doll really him? Why did he look like that?"

Holding back her surprise at the mother's intuition, Atsuko attempted to pacify her. "It was just that the doll reminded Doctor Tokita of your son. He's been worried about Kei's whereabouts, and only said that because he was confused. After all, how on earth could that thing be your son?!"

"I had a rush of blood to the head," Tokita said, now somewhat calmer. "I didn't know what I was saying. I'm sorry if I upset you."

After somehow managing to convince Himuro's parents and seeing them off at the station, the three decided to go back to Atsuko's apartment. There they would discuss their plan of action.

They picked up a taxi that took them back past the restaurant. As well as police cars and ambulances, several vehicles belonging to newspaper and television companies were already at the scene.

14

The inn at Hata Spa was an old building. It jutted out over the river from one side of the gorge, offering little scope for expansion even if guest numbers were to increase dramatically. In fact, the inn was so cramped that it had no banqueting room, and larger parties had to be held in three adjoining rooms with the sliding partitions removed. As one of the rooms protruded over the river from the end of the building, the party venue was inevitably L-shaped.

It was five o'clock in the afternoon. All the sliding screens along the veranda had been left open to let the cool river air flow in. Guests with cheeks reddened after a dip in the spa bath, and all dressed in matching cotton kimonos, filed in to take their places at the party; food already awaited them on low tables in front of their floor cushions. The seat of honour was near the tokonoma alcove in the corner of the L-shaped room.

Hata Spa in the Gorai mountains, part of the Echigo mountain chain, was about four hours by bus from the centre of Niigata. Tatsuo Noda had left Tokyo that morning with a group of five men. One of them was Namba, Manager of the Third Sales Division. He was responsible for sales of the "Vegetable", the new eco-friendly vehicle that was about to be put on the market. Besides Namba, Noda was also accompanied by sales staff and two section managers in charge of technology and parts.

The launch party was hosted by the owners of exclusive dealerships in Niigata. The following day, everyone except Noda and Namba would stay behind in the city, their brief being to tour the dealerships and explain maintenance matters to their sales personnel, mechanics and office staff.

The two section managers were last to appear at the party venue. They'd forgotten to empty their bowels before leaving home that morning, and had suffered stoically through the jolting four-hour ride in the bus. On their arrival at the inn, they had immediately rushed to the toilets, there to remain for an inordinately long time. That had made them late in taking their bath. To make matters worse, they'd had to wash their hair, as the windows on the bus had been left open and their heads had been coated in sand. All of which further delayed their appearance at the party.

"Sorry! Sorry!" they called as they finally entered the party room, their freshly washed hair gleaming with caked-on pomade supplied by the inn. And so the party could begin.

After a quick soak in the spa bath, Noda had taken a nap in his room until it was time for the party. He was suffering from fatigue. Out of concern for Paprika, he hadn't really wanted to come. But the President had asked him to make a special effort for Niigata, and there had been no way out of it.

With the party in full swing, the sliding doors between the room and the veranda were all closed. The night breeze was bad for the health, came the explanation. As fluorescent strips shone brightly in the ceiling, the informal party entertainment started in the wide area by the tokonoma, near Noda's seat. Several of the Head Office sales staff had eccentric and bizarre talents, but the Niigata dealers were men of diverse accomplishments too. In the end it was impossible to tell which was the host and which the guest. Some of those present would grow quite morose if they weren't allowed to perform; letting them perform was almost part of the service.

One middle-aged dealer transformed himself into a Chinaman, with an upturned bowl on his head, a long pipe in his hand and his jacket worn back to front. The party guests were all clutching their stomachs and helplessly rolling around with laughter at his antics, when a serving girl came stumbling in from the corridor. With hair wildly dishevelled and the hem of her kimono hitched up to her thighs, she ran though the party room as if something were chasing her.

"R-Run! Run for your lives!!" she screamed as she clung to the Chinaman's legs.

The party guests whooped and laughed raucously. They assumed it was part of the entertainment.

"Attagirl!"

"Very convincing!"

At first, Noda too thought the girl's entrance was part of the show. But when he saw her close at hand, her appearance was far too convincing for it to be an act. Her face and lips had turned mauve and her whole body was shaking. She seemed dumbstruck with terror.

"What's the matter?" Noda shouted as if scolding her.

She turned her strained face towards him. "It's a t-t-tiger!" she shrieked. "A tiger's on the loose!!"

A tiger in a Japanese inn. Everyone fell about laughing again.

But Noda wasn't laughing. He knew this was no joke. For a tiger had appeared in his dream a little while earlier. Coming to an old-style inn had reminded him of Toratake, and as he took his after-bath snooze, he had dreamt of a tiger. And now that tiger had become real, due to the residual side effects of the DC Mini.

Surely not?! he thought. Yes, he'd advised the others to "forget about distinguishing dream and reality", but he'd only meant that in reference to Paprika's world.

Noda shook his head. He'd read a newspaper article about a man who kept a pet tiger. Maybe the tiger had escaped.

The laughter subsided somewhat. The guests had started to realize that the girl's terrified appearance was not an act. Noda exchanged looks with Namba. "Where is this tiger?" asked Namba.

"At the foot of the stairs, c-c-coming this way!" the girl stammered in terror.

"Oh, pack it in!"

A man sitting near the corridor stuck his head out and peered into the darkness. He said nothing but turned back into the room, shoved his food table to one side and hopped forwards on all fours like a frog. While the others were still recovering from the sudden violence of his movement, a tiger leapt into the room from the corridor, as if the man's hopping had sparked its momentum. It was not a domestic cat, nor a stuffed toy. It was a huge, adult tiger. Unlike the tigers seen on TV or in cages at the zoo, this one was so big that all the guests firmly believed they were looking at a real, live tiger.

Its excitement and hunting instincts stirred by the panicking party guests, the tiger bounded over to the nearest man and duly sank its teeth into his neck, as if to prove its prowess.

Guests started shrieking and yelling as they pushed open the sliding doors, scrambling to vault over the railings onto the riverbed. Those in the room jutting out over the river fought with each other to tumble into the waters below. Some were so rigid with terror that they couldn't move. One clung fast to the alcove post and tried desperately to stand, another sat on the tatami floor and twisted his body effeminately as he tried to shuffle out on his backside. Some fled at the last minute, some clung to the feet of others who were escaping, some rested their backs against the wall and did nothing but spasmodically flex their outstretched legs.

A young sales employee from Head Office sat there staring blankly as blood spurted from the neck of the tiger's first victim. The tiger left its immobilized prey and came for more, making the sales employee its second meal.

The serving girl clung to the legs of the Chinaman as he fled, dragging her all the way out onto the veranda. Noda and Namba looked on from their seats with dazed expressions. They were by now the only ones left.

"Sh-shall we get out?" Namba suggested, placing a hand on Noda's shoulder and rising on legs that shook to the point of convulsion.

The tiger, its mouth covered in fresh blood, had ripped a chunk of flesh from the unfortunate employee's windpipe. Reacting to Namba's movement, it turned to glare at them.

15

Sleeping was too scary. Morio Osanai was in bits.

If he slept, someone else's dream would come flying at him, as a residual effect of the DC Mini. It wouldn't matter if it was Inui's dream, but sometimes others, like those hellish visions from Himuro's nightmares, would come to life in Osanai's dreams and scare the wits out of him. Himuro was dead, but in those dreams he was still very much alive.

Inui had admitted to Osanai that he shared the same ordeal.

"But listen," he'd said. "It must be the same for the woman. When night falls, she must also dread going to sleep."

That didn't make the dreams any less terrifying, though. Far from it; whenever Osanai met Atsuko in his dreams, a battle royale would ensue. For she, at the same time, was having a dream in which she was fighting with him. Yes, they shared dreams from different beds, but there was nothing romantic about it at all; these were always epic battles that frayed his nerves. First of all, he had to work out whether he was in his own dream or someone else's. If the latter, he had to ascertain whose dream it was. It may have belonged to Torataro Shima or Kosaku Tokita, men whose minds he'd tried to destroy with the DC Mini, just as he'd done with Himuro. The ability to intrude into other people's dreams may even have been acquired with just a single use of the DC Mini. In that case, even those former clients of Paprika's might appear in Osanai's dreams without actually intending to. That senior company executive, for example, or that senior police officer.

Osanai was particularly scared when the policeman made an appearance. Konakawa had the keen eye and sharp mind of a detective. If he were to chance upon the dreams of the weak-willed Hashimoto, he would sniff out Himuro's murder in no time at all.

Osanai could hardly go without sleeping, on the other hand. He also had to work, and so couldn't sleep in the daytime, when everyone else was awake. To protect themselves from the enemy, the only possible strategy for Osanai, Inui and Hashimoto was to make sure they all slept at the same time.

Hell. How long will these residual effects last? Or will they last for ever? Osanai had stashed his DC Mini in a lead storage box normally used for dangerous chemicals. Would the nightmares continue as long as the device still existed, however he tried to block its power? Atsuko Chiba had probably realized the dangers of the

DC Mini already and was no longer using it. But with or without the device, they were still accessing each other's dreams through its residual effects alone, since, as luck would have it, Osanai's apartment was directly below Atsuko's in the same building.

Osanai was trying to sleep lightly, so that he could wake at any time. It wasn't easy, but that was the only way. He fell asleep at two in the morning.

It looked like the Outer Garden of Meiji Shrine. Osanai seemed to be jogging. He had never jogged in his life, though he'd occasionally felt he ought to. That probably explained why he was dreaming about it. Another man in jogging gear approached him from afar. A man who looked too old to jog. *Idiot. Take up jogging that late in life, you'll only end up destroying yourself. Wait a minute. It's Torataro Shima!*

As expected, Shima recognized him and came towards him. *Is he back to normal now? He must remember me doing those terrible things to him. Oh no. He's coming to give me an earful!*

Shima and Osanai stopped and faced each other. Shima smiled. His good-heartedness irritated Osanai; he found it faintly spooky.

"Are you completely recovered now?" Osanai asked, speaking politely out of habit.

"Oh yes. Oh yes," Shima replied, still smiling. "That ****** ***** you gave me was cured by Paprika. She's a genius, you see. Not mediocre, like you."

Osanai saw red. *This isn't Shima manifesting in my dream. This is Shima in person. I'm mixed up in his dream. Now he can say things he's too scared to say in real life!* "Shut your mouth, you decrepit old fool. Old fuddy duddy wool-for-brains. I'm the genius round here! Get it? Go to hell, you useless old git. Why don't you just crawl under a stone and die?!"

As if startled by this unexpected abuse from an inferior, Shima's face suddenly grew longer. At the same time, his body sank into the ground up to his neck. With only his head showing, he started tunnelling through the earth like a mole, leaving trails snaking around the park. When he collided with a tree root and could go no further, he looked up and started wailing.

"Serves you right!" yelled Osanai.

Osanai was smothered by a vaguely pleasant sensation, as if he were about to give his bullying father some of his own medicine. He started walking towards Shima's head with the intention of kicking it away. Then a dangerous voice, taut and metallic like a piano wire, flew at him from behind.

"Stop that!"

It was Paprika. She was a small child, but her red shirt and jeans instantly identified her. Osanai seemed to have regressed to his boyhood. Paprika held a catapult with its rubber sling extended, ready to release, and aimed it at him. He knew through bitter experience just how dangerous this could be. A friend had once hit him in the eye that way. If he hadn't instinctively closed his eyelid, he would have been blinded. To this day he could still feel the violent pain it had caused.

"Don't!" Osanai pleaded.

They were on a gently sloping road with grand houses on either side, but Osanai had no time to flee into any of them. Instead, he covered his head with his hands and cowered down at the roadside. "Don't! It's dangerous! Don't shoot! Please don't!"

"Tee hee!" the bad girl Paprika chuckled triumphantly. "I knew it! Boys always hate this!"

Even with hands held over his face, Osanai knew that Paprika was standing right next to him, aiming the slingshot at the crown of his head.

"Oy! Look out, Morio! Here it comes!"

"No!!"

He couldn't stand it any longer. It may well have been a dream, but he was in danger of taking a serious injury back to the waking world with him. He stood up, waved his arms madly to avoid the oncoming shot, and ran all the way back to his boyhood home on New Year's Eve.

On New Year's Eve, the adults in Osanai's family had a habit of staying up late to prepare for the following day's festivities. They usually went to sleep at three or four in the morning. The children couldn't get to sleep for all the excitement, and would stay up with the grown-ups as they busily went about their work. They would eventually fall asleep in the living room, where their grandfather would be sitting grim-faced, a large bottle of sake at his side and a sake cup in his hand, firing off instructions to the womenfolk. But now, as Morio raced into the living room, he found there not his grandfather but Seijiro Inui, dressed in a man's kimono and sitting cross-legged on the floor. He glared up at little Morio with a look of immense displeasure.

"I took great pains to prepare a delicate draught of butarylonal and sulphonal, to help me sleep so deeply that I would not dream. I had only just fallen asleep, and what do you go and do? Dah!"

"I'm sorry!" young Morio whined. "But I was scared! I was so scared!"

"This must be your dream," Inui said as he looked around the room. "You must be sleeping more deeply than the rest of us. You've let someone else invade your dream."

"This is a nostalgic memory, but it's frightening," Osanai cried. "Maybe it never really existed. Maybe it's an after-memory, because I've seen it so many times in my dreams."

"What used to happen here?" Inui asked, every bit the psychiatrist.

Osanai turned towards the hallway. The front door had been left open. Because family members were constantly going to and fro, the door was usually left open most of the night. Sometimes vagabonds would take the opportunity to get inside the house. It always happened that way in his dreams, and maybe it really did happen that way, every year on New Year's Eve. Or maybe it only happened once. Or never at all.

Sometimes the uninvited guest was a delinquent youth who would smirk while filching things from the room. Sometimes it was a *yakuza* thug with dark menacing eyes, who would pick a fight about nothing and extort money and goods from the house. Sometimes it would be an enormous drunk who looked like a vagrant and would try to rape Morio's mother and sisters. The unwanted visitor would invariably be thick-skinned and brazen-faced, unfazed by the stout resistance from Morio and his family, and would keep reappearing when he seemed to have gone. One of these visitors would always appear once this New Year's Eve dream had started.

"I see. So who'll be coming tonight?" Inui groaned gloomily after tracing back through Osanai's memory. "This is part of your ego, a weakness you're desperate to protect. They'll prey on that, for sure."

A woman screamed in the hallway. "Who is it? Who's there?" It was the terrified voice of his mother. *They're here!* Osanai yelled, already on the verge of tears. *Go away! Get out!* "You have no right to come here!" *We're higher in status than you. This is a proud and noble family. We have nothing to do with poor uneducated people like you.* "We have nothing to do with you." "Penniless scum!" "Get out!"

"Ah. You must be Morio Osanai."

It was Chief Superintendent Konakawa who stood there in the doorway with the dark of night behind him. He was neither uneducated nor poor, but an elite member of society whom, if anything, Osanai should have looked up to with respect. His stern countenance betrayed no sign of sentimentality. He wore a newly tailored suit, like the one he was wearing in the lift that time. He wore it with impeccable style, as if it were perfectly normal, as if he hated looking slovenly, even in a dream. This was the type of adult Osanai had hated most of all when he was a boy. But suddenly Osanai wasn't a boy any more. Perhaps he'd been forced to change, against his will, by Konakawa's intrusion into his dream.

"Who is it?" Osanai was aware that both the question and the voice he used to ask it were those of an imbecile, but he was powerless to prevent his regression. The most he could manage was to keep standing upright, when his body wanted to slump down on the edge of the hallway step.

"You know who it is," Konakawa replied without a hint of a smile. He'd already started probing Osanai's consciousness. Chief Superintendent. Chief Superintendent. The sound of his rank alone was enough to turn Osanai into a whimpering heap.

At the same time, Konakawa's dreaming thoughts also flowed through to Osanai's mind. *So that's what she meant by "side effects". Good. It's the perfect opportunity. And it'll help Paprika. I'll use it to discover the truth and fight the enemy.*

"What have you done with Himuro's body?" he demanded.

Osanai screamed inside. *Must get away. Must get away. No energy left to fight.*

Luckily for him, the shock of confrontation altered the depth of his sleep, and that also changed his dream. He was in an old-style inn. No, not an inn, more like an old post station from Edo days. A throng of travellers filled the public vestibule. Osanai himself was a young samurai. *Must be careful*, he was thinking. His knowledge of period novels told him that places like this were crawling with sneak thieves, cutpurses, crooks, pickpockets, pilferers, luggage thieves and other such miscreants. This was where he now found himself. His dream must have been warning him: *"Be on your guard"*. Though dressed as a samurai, he was scared. *Who's here?* An itinerant merchant. A mother and daughter on a pilgrimage. A sumo wrestler. A young married couple. A monkey showman. All representatives of the squalid lower classes he so despised. *Ah! There he is.* That man peering at him from afar, through the crowd of human heads. It was the grey-haired, pipe-smoking master carpenter Torataro Shima. And there was Atsuko Chiba, dressed as a strolling musician. Osanai stood up. He'd had enough. *Hell, I can't get away from them. They won't leave me alone. Damn them! All right. I'll have to slice them up.* He drew his sword.

16

I'm still dreaming, Osanai thought in his dream. But that was no reason to make light of things. Osanai's subconscious mind demanded that he now be more serious than ever, suppress his will to just let things happen.

But was he alone in the dream? It certainly felt that way. He knew he was dreaming, as he was still dressed as a young samurai. He still held the sword in his hand. What had happened after he'd drawn it from the scabbard? There was no blood on the blade. In a way, it felt as if a lot of time had passed since then, but there were gaps in Osanai's memory. He could have been having a dream in which he'd just woken from a dream.

The young samurai sat up in bed. There were two beds, side by side. PT equipment next to them. A dimly lit room. Yes, perhaps a treatment room, but he only knew of the room from seeing it in someone else's dream. Paprika's dream. It was the bedroom in Atsuko Chiba's apartment. The room where she treated her clients.

Osanai existed in his own dream and had no substance in reality. Yet there was a sense of reality around him, the very palpable presence of someone instrumental nearby. Could such a thing happen? Since he was only dreaming, he couldn't think more deeply about it than that. Osanai crawled out of bed with a lethargy hardly becoming a young samurai.

A voice could be heard coming from the next room. A man's voice. The next room must have been the living room. Had Atsuko invited a man to her apartment, where they were enjoying a cosy chat? Osanai shook with jealousy. The young samurai suddenly tilted his body and leant against the wall beside the door. He opened the door a fraction, peered into the living room and strained his ears.

"But the tiger didn't come to attack me. Far from it. It sidled up to me and pressed its body against mine, as if we were old friends, affectionately. Purring, even."

It was that man. That senior company executive, Tatsuo Noda. He continued to talk as he looked around wide-eyed at the other people in the room – Atsuko Chiba, Kosaku Tokita, Torataro Shima and two unknown men. How could their presence be so clear and their speech so distinct, compared to Osanai's own vague existence? They were like reality itself.

"Apparently, that kind of thing couldn't usually happen. I mean, a rogue tiger sidling up to a person after going berserk in a place like that. And then, as I gently stroked the tiger's wiry hair, I realized the truth. It was either a dream, or if not a dream, at least the tiger had come out of a dream. To be more exact, it was my old friend Takao Toratake in the guise of a tiger."

Atsuko, Tokita and Shima were sitting around Noda, who had rushed straight over after returning from his business trip. Konakawa was absent, having an important function to perform as Deputy Chief Commissioner. Instead, he was represented by Chief Inspector Yamaji and Inspector Ube. Tokita and Shima had made a full recovery and now could look after themselves; Morita and Saka had been relieved of their posts.

"The tiger disappeared in front of my eyes. I kept shouting 'Disappear! Disappear! Please disappear! Go back to the land of dreams', probably in a dream myself. Or perhaps I was actually calling out in reality. Namba was next to me, and he also saw the tiger vanish, but like me, he didn't fancy exposing himself to ridicule by telling such a fantastic story to the police. And you know all about the ensuing uproar from the media. The police, fire service and Hunting Association made a search of the mountains, but of course they found no sign of any tiger. The trouble was that two men were dead and many more injured. It couldn't be dismissed as a collective hallucination. So now, they're keeping a close watch on the area in the belief that there's a real tiger out there."

"So it's the same as the Japanese doll in that restaurant," said Yamaji, his eyes gleaming as he struggled to comprehend the absurdity of it all. It was as if he were trying to retain the modicum of logicality befitting a police officer. "It came out of a dream, then disappeared because it didn't really exist, but still left people dead and injured. What can this all mean?"

Atsuko had no answer. Even if she could begin to reply, the best she could achieve would be an abstract hypothesis that would reaffirm the unfathomed power of dreams. For although they were merely messengers from the realm of dreams, these apparitions had the power to cause death or leave lasting scars in the real world.

"It's all my fault." Tokita had covered his face with his hands a number of times already, but now groaned loudly as though he could bear it no longer. "I should never have invented such a stupid thing. I was too careless. I should have given it a protective code. I'm a failure. A failure as a scientist."

They all fell silent. None could find the words to comfort or excuse him. His sense of guilt thus reconfirmed, Tokita squirmed in his chair as he continued to release little explosions of self-reproach.

"I didn't think of the consequences. I was drowning in a sea of my own invention. That's right." He turned to Atsuko beside him and slowly extended his fat palms. "I will dismantle the DC Minis. Give them all to me. At least the ones you've got. I'll dismantle them immediately."

"W-w-wait a minute!" Yamaji was on the edge of his seat. "I understand how you feel, but the enemy also has DC Minis. I'm not going to sit here and let you dismantle ours! It would be me who'd take the rap if we had reason to regret it later."

"That's right," agreed Noda. "At least discuss with it the Chief Superintendent first."

"All right. Just as long as the very existence of the DC Mini doesn't increase the residual effects," Tokita moaned on.

"But even if we disposed of all the DC Minis we have," Shima said weakly, showing signs of fatigue in his eyes, "as long as *they* still have them, they'll keep invading our dreams night after night. I can't take much more of this. Last night Osanai made a complete fool of me again."

He must have been talking about the way he'd been verbally abused, buried in the ground with only his head showing and made to scuttle about like a mole.

"Our only chance of getting the devices back from them is in our dreams. I don't think they're wearing them any more. But even so," Atsuko said to encourage the weak-willed Shima, "please be patient for a little longer. I'll always protect you, just as I did last night."

"Oh, yes! You did, didn't you. And you were still fighting..." Shima said dolefully. He seemed to have aged noticeably.

Noda and Tokita nodded towards Atsuko with the empathy of comrades who share the same dreams. Whether or not they'd actually appeared in those dreams, they had witnessed Atsuko's nightly battles.

"The Chief Superintendent was saying he'd had a fair old ding-dong with Inui last night," Yamaji said with a wry smile. "Ah, but of course it's nothing to jest about."

"You mean after *that*," Atsuko said, glancing across at Shima.

"It was like a scene from New Year's Eve. Osanai escaped from the Chief, but then Inui must have appeared in the hallway instead of him," Shima said with a worried look. "But of course! That hallway must have been part of Osanai's dream, so naturally the scene would have changed."

"I didn't see that bit," Tokita said nervously. "I wonder if he was all right, fighting with Inui?"

"Don't worry, he can look after himself," said Noda, as if to banish the notion that he himself might *not* have been "all right". "We're on the offensive, after all."

"After that, Osanai appeared as a young samurai in an old post house," Shima continued. "Even we were dressed in period costume. I was shocked when the samurai drew his sword, but around that time Inui and the Chief Superintendent would have been fighting in their own dreams, I suppose."

"Oh yes. He drew his sword," echoed a hollow voice from somewhere else. Everyone froze and stiffened with fear. Inspector Ube alone rose and stared at the bedroom door.

"Someone's in there!"

"Who is it?" Yamaji also stood. "Who's in there? Come out now!" he demanded, already bracing himself with a sense of foreboding.

The door opened slowly. The six in the living room gasped. There in the doorway, leaning on the doorpost, stood Morio Osanai. He was dressed as a young samurai and held a naked sword in his hand, his indistinct outline merging with the glimmering light behind him. His lifeless eyes of gloom and darkness glowered at them under heavy lids, casting a look that carried a vague threat of malice. Though his visual appearance was incomplete, he carried an evil presence that pierced the subconscious of the six. He was beautiful – so beautiful, indeed, that he could have stepped out of a *sashie* illustration from an Edo-period novel. But that merely enhanced the sense of danger.

"He's from last night's dream," Atsuko said as she retreated towards the kitchen. Her seat had been closest to the door.

"Disappear! Disappear!" Tokita incanted loudly while protecting Atsuko with his massive frame, mindful of the tale he'd just heard from Noda. "You don't exist. Disappear! Disappear!"

The young samurai smiled thinly, then started to murmur words that were clearly those of a man talking in his sleep. "What happened after I drew the sword. In my hand, it's in my hand. When I wake up, there's old Tokita. Ticky tocky tacky too. There's me. Adultery, is it. Devil of the white chair, devil of the gold chair. Wretch. Cur."

Ube aimed his pistol at the young samurai, who was approaching Tokita with sword poised at eye level. Unwilling to shoot, Ube turned to Chief Inspector Yamaji. "Er – what do you want me to do?"

"If you shoot him, he surely won't die in real life," Yamaji said in confusion. "But what effect will it have on him?"

The young samurai made for Tokita, wielding the blade above his head.

"Get him off me!" Tokita yelled as he cowered before the samurai.

"Shoot him!" screamed Atsuko. "It'll have no effect in reality!"

"Shoot!"

Ube sensed that the samurai was about to bring his sword down. He pulled the trigger.

The samurai's body jerked as a spray of red spattered his chest. His sword sliced aimlessly through the air. The sight of his Adonisian face distorted with pain, his hair all dishevelled, was not without its sordid side, as if painted with distemper. But at the same time it shone with a perverse beauty that seemed not of this world. His staggering lurch was a dance of death in full technicolour. Those faltering cries of anguish, the fresh blood that trickled from the corner of his mouth, those dying eyes staring fixedly into space – these were truly the aesthetics of death. And in the very instant before he fell face down on the floor, he vanished.

"Wha—?!"

A dizzy, falling sensation made Osanai sit up with a jolt. He was in the Vice President's office at the Institute for Psychiatric Research, sitting opposite Inui's desk. They had just been discussing the Board of Directors. Inui was staring at Osanai with a look of astonishment.

"Sorry. I just felt a bit dizzy," said Osanai. "Trouble is, I'm not getting enough sleep these days. Especially last night, as you know…" They'd both shared the same dream. It didn't need to be discussed. Osanai's speech trailed off.

"Are you all right?" asked Inui.

"I'm all right," answered Osanai.

But was he? He'd felt a certain emptiness since the morning; now he wondered if he could have lost part of his ego during that dizzy spell just now. *What's going on?* he wanted to ask himself. A void had formed in his senses. He shook his head vigorously to regain some vitality.

"What was that just now?" Inui asked, still staring at Osanai with his head tilted questioningly.

"What was what?"

Inui removed his glasses, put them on the desk and rubbed his eyes. "For a fraction of a second there, you seemed to disappear from your chair. Then you reappeared as a samurai warrior holding a sword. Your chest was stained with blood – you looked as though you were in your death throes. It was so unspeakably heart-rending, yet so indescribably beautiful. What on earth *was* that?" A gleam of eroticism hovered faintly over Inui's eyes. He got up slowly. His face softened into a look of lechery. "It was so very attractive. As if the dream you had last night had become manifest in reality for a moment, through the power of the Devil's seed. But who could it have been that killed you?" Inui walked behind Osanai's back and gently placed both hands on his shoulders. "My, but you were beautiful. I fell in love with you again."

17

Sleeping scared Atsuko as much as it did Osanai. The difference was that Atsuko had a mission: she had to get the DC Minis back. That fully justified the aggression she meted out to Inui, Osanai and Hashimoto in the dreams she shared with them. What did it mean to have the upper hand in those dreams? It meant she was free to dictate the setting and progression of the dreams to her own advantage, and to invade her opponents' dreams at will.

What scared Atsuko was the possibility that, while she continued to dream, she could fall into an even deeper sleep, become trapped in her unconscious and eventually be unable to escape from her dreams. To prevent this, Atsuko devised ways of sleeping lightly, disregarding the adverse effects on health over the long term. Among others, these involved using drugs or self-waking devices, or sleeping on her chair in front of the PT devices.

That night, she had decided to use a self-waking device. She'd set it to ensure that she would remain in shallow sleep without fully waking. She had also placed her telephone near her pillow. She had an arrangement with Tokita and Shima that they would phone each other every few hours, in case the device failed to work properly.

Despite the shallowness of her sleep, there were times when her body slept deeply and only her brainwaves followed waking patterns. This was during REM sleep. It was quite impossible to operate PT devices while dreaming at such times; usually, she wasn't even aware that she was dreaming then.

It may have been during her first REM sleep that night. Atsuko was dreaming but unaware that it was a dream. She was in a laboratory with Hashimoto, back in the days when they were still on amicable terms. It looked like a biology lab, or perhaps chemistry. In front of them were a number of test tubes containing what seemed to be bacteria; they may have been experimenting on bacteriophages. Atsuko felt unbearably thirsty, and went to drink from a bottle of mineral water. On closer inspection, the bottle was full of tiny, wriggling green things.

"Bacteria!"

"You need to boil that," advised Hashimoto, standing next to her.

Atsuko transferred the water to a flask and went to light a bunsen burner.

"Wait a minute!" Atsuko stopped the gas and held the flask up to the light.

The bacteria were growing.

"Not bacteria – fungi!"

Hashimoto nodded. "Mmm. Incomplete fungi, more like myxo-mycetes. Probably some kind of mutabile-type mutation."

There were three fungi, coloured in malignant shades of dark green, dark red and dark yellow. Due to contact with air, they'd already grown to a length of about three centimetres. They were like gigantic larvae, their bodies shaped like spindles with something resembling a face at the top. Traces of eyes and noses could even be seen on those faces.

"I can't drink this," declared Atsuko, her thirst more intense still.

"These are carbohydrates," said Hashimoto. He poked a chopstick into the flask, snared the yellow larva, took it out and bit its head off.

Yeurghhh! Almost retching, Atsuko peered into the flask to see her own face on the red larva.

"Wahahahahahahaha!" Hashimoto laughed loudly beside her. He was the green larva, which now bore Inui's face. He proceeded to coil his spindle-like lower body around Atsuko's larval form.

"It's a dream!" The shock of Inui's appearance made her realize that. She instantly changed her red body to a red shirt and turned into Paprika. She had fallen asleep unusually early; it was only seven o'clock in the evening. Like her, Inui must also have wanted to enjoy a nice, relaxing sleep without meeting anyone in his dreams. But Inui concealed his true intentions. He was exercising supreme self-control and restraint.

Hashimoto! Help! Help me! Paprika tried to call out. Perhaps it really had been Hashimoto just now. Perhaps he too was sleeping early, and had been dreaming of that experiment with Atsuko. In that case, Inui and Osanai must also have taken to sleeping early, hoping to prevent the weak-willed Hashimoto from revealing their secrets under pressure from Paprika.

They were in Hashimoto's favourite noodle bar. Hashimoto was reaching across from the other side of the table, trying to wrench the larval Inui from his coiled embrace of Paprika. Hashimoto's subconscious was preoccupied with that past time when he was on amicable terms with Atsuko. Paprika realized that Hashimoto had been in love with Atsuko, though fully aware that she was out of his reach.

"Ah, so you're sleeping after all!" said Paprika.

You idiot! Inui sneered as he lunged at Hashimoto. Paprika could read Inui's cruel intention: even if he didn't actually kill this bothersome traitor, this former ally who'd been nothing but a liability all long, he would at least drive him insane. *Hashimoto, run! No – wake up!* Paprika shouted. Flames shot up from a frying pan in the kitchen.

Inui turned into the devil Amon, a serpent's tail entwined around his body. Fire spewed from his mouth. Lord Amon, a Marquis of Hell with the face of an owl. The terrifyingly vivid presence of this occultic apparition was enough to scare Hashimoto out of his wits. He screamed. He'd suddenly seen his conciliatory gesture to Paprika as an act of betrayal, and could read the terrible punishment now being planned in his master's mind. The terror of induced madness or gruesome death at the hands of Lord Amon made Hashimoto urinate long and hard in his sleep. Whether he was in a dream or not, he knew there was no way of escaping his fate.

Both Hashimoto and Amon vanished from Paprika's dream. She knew, even before the warm sensation and smell from Hashimoto's nether regions reached her senses, that he had wet himself. That meant he'd woken up, but why had Lord Amon, the incarnation of Seijiro Inui, disappeared with him? Paprika shuddered with horror. She felt as though she could hear, from the distant reaches of the waking world, the sound of Hashimoto's dying cries. It sounded as if Amon had appeared in reality at the moment Hashimoto awoke, and was in the process of strangling him on his own bed.

But Hashimoto was not sleeping on his own bed, in his own apartment. He'd been taking a nap on the sofa in his research lab. He'd brought the torment of death back from his dream to the real world, and had awoken together with that torment. What a hideous reality, that even after waking from a dream to escape its torments, those torments still remain! What a heartless, cruel reality that, with no means of escape, the only possible conclusion was death! Hashimoto's chest was tightly bound by the demon's serpentine tail, its sharp claws clutching his scrotum, the flames that spewed from its beak-like mouth burning his face. Asphyxiated by fire, his testicles burst and his ribs broken simultaneously, Hashimoto suffered three deaths at once. A red death, a yellow death and a purple death. Having savoured Hashimoto's three-fold agony to its fullest possible extent, the Marquis of Hell moaned in satisfaction and disappeared.

Choosing to kill a disobedient underling for the slightest act of betrayal, even before pursuing the enemy, was an act truly befitting Lord Amon, a demon who commands forty legions in the realm of hell. Or perhaps, since Amon can discern the past and foretell the future, it was a deed done in the foreknowledge that Hashimoto would oppose him in future. After completing his butchery, Lord Amon hurried back to the dream where he'd left his real enemy, his reason restored as that of Seijiro Inui.

Left alone in her dream, Paprika finally remembered her original mission there. She was near the exit on the quieter side of a station in central Tokyo. As she walked out of the station building she saw a vast swamp spread out before her, a stark contrast to the high-rise buildings and bustling city centre she'd left behind. There she roamed about in the mud, seeking the atmosphere of Morio Osanai.

"Osanai? Morio? Where are you?!" she called. There was no reaction. He obviously wasn't asleep yet, and Paprika would be unable to locate his DC Mini this time. Even then, there was no room for complacency; it would still be too dangerous for her to fall into a sound sleep, believing herself to be alone. Inui seemed to have woken up with Hashimoto while still in the guise of Amon, but would almost certainly return. Paprika's only option was to challenge Inui, force him to reveal the location of the DC Mini. But how could she overcome his will, his conscious mind, thickly coated as it was with stubborn occultism? It might be a better idea to wake up first.

A number of men who looked like vagrants or labourers were wandering around in the mud. They seemed to be stealing glances at Paprika. A woman's sense of danger welled up inside her. The men could have been agents of Inui's dream; the swamp could have been an image inside Inui's mind. Paprika hurriedly changed the scene. She was in a library, a reading room where the air was cold and dry. It was a broad, clean space with a high ceiling. No one else was there; it seemed safe enough. Paprika opened out a large pictorial encyclopedia on the table in front of her. The title was *Bertuch's Picture Book for Children*.

Oh no. He's back! Paprika moaned. One of the plates in the encyclopedia was a picture of a griffin. This was a hideous creature with the head and wings of a bird and the body of a lion. The griffin was shown in profile, but as soon as Paprika made the connection with Inui, it stirred and turned to look at her. It had Inui's face and the smile of a cat.

"The DC Mini," Paprika said, to strike the first blow. "The DC Mini. Where have you hidden it?"

Violent emotion made the griffin Inui shake its body and flutter its wings.

"*Nuh!*"

Inui was desperately trying to suppress his consciousness, but through a chink in that consciousness, Paprika could see the inside of someone's laboratory. In a corner of the lab was a box containing dangerous chemicals.

"Inside that box, is it?" Paprika shouted. *Yes. The box is made of lead. There's no doubt. They've put the device in there to block its effects.* "Whose lab is it?"

"*Gaa!*"

Inui realized that his mind had been read, and his griffin went berserk. Inui lost his self-control into the bargain. *This young trollop. Must she keep peering in?! Wherever I go!* The griffin flapped its wings. It flew up from the pages of the encyclopedia, which were unfurled by the wind from its wings. The spectre flew up towards the transparent domed roof of the reading room. There it hovered as it changed direction, opened its claws wide in anger, and took aim at Paprika below.

Paprika had to avoid being attacked. Her only option was to continue her counter-offensive.

"Whose lab is it?" she shouted loudly. "Whose lab? Tell me. Tell me!"

The griffin vanished. Inui must have chosen to wake up rather than answer Atsuko's question.

Right. Let's go there. It's probably Osanai's. All I have to do is go to his lab, take the DC Mini out of the chemical box, hold it tightly in my hand and return to reality. That's all. Paprika changed the scene of her dream to the Institute. She appeared at the corner of the corridor in front of the Medical Office, where the corridor widened slightly.

18

Noda and Konakawa had delayed their arrival at the Institute until most of the staff had gone home. A few would still have been engaged in hospital-related work, but that couldn't be helped.

Finding the front doors closed, they walked round to the side of the building and went in through the staff entrance. There they were challenged by an elderly security guard, who poked his head through the window of the security booth. He had the look of a former worker who had been re-employed.

"What you two after?" he demanded haughtily.

"Where's the Secretariat?" Konakawa demanded with equal arrogance, brandishing his ID.

The guard barely glanced at it. "We're closed! Don't care what it is. Come back tomorrow!" he barked.

"What it is, is a police investigation," Konakawa replied with a calmness that was almost menacing. Noda was impressed.

The guard took a proper look at the ID and was seized with panic. "What?!... But!... This sudden?! A raid?! You got a search warrant, then?"

"Take another look, my friend," said Konakawa. "See there? Where it says 'Chief Superintendent'? I don't need a search warrant. I'm the one who issues them. See me as a walking search warrant, if you like."

The suitably humbled guard told them where they could find the Secretariat and the Secretary-General's office, which was next to the Secretariat. They walked to the end of the corridor as instructed.

"Is that really true?" Noda mused as he tried to keep pace with his friend's broad strides. "You don't need a search warrant? I thought they could only be issued by a court of law."

Konakawa smiled but gave no reply. Noda supposed he'd been bending the truth.

A telephone was ringing. It seemed to come from the Secretary-General's office ahead of them.

"Sounds like the guard's called to announce us!"

"Hmm."

They hastened their steps and entered the office without knocking.

Inside, they saw Katsuragi's desk with the window wide open behind it. In a blind panic, Katsuragi was desperately stashing accounts books into a safe in the corner.

"Freeze!" roared Konakawa.

Startled by the volume of his voice, Katsuragi turned and dropped the books onto the floor. His hair was dishevelled with fright, even though he'd made no particularly violent movement.

"What do you want?!" he shouted, clinging to a corner of his desk. "Coming in unannounced like that! And without knocking! Have you no manners?!"

"You know why we're here," said Konakawa. He strode towards Katsuragi's desk, took the accounts books that Katsuragi had clutched to his chest, and shoved them along the desktop towards Noda. "Check these, would you."

Noda opened the books and started to check through them.

"My card," Konakawa said, thrusting a name card at Katsuragi. "I think we'll be seeing more of each other from now on."

Katsuragi gasped when he saw the card, his eyeballs practically popping as spittle flew from his mouth. He reached for the telephone without a word.

Konakawa left Katsuragi to his devices and went to peer through the open door of the safe.

This is the "second journal", thought Noda. He knew it as soon as he'd opened the first accounts book. In that case, there should also be paperwork related to it. "Toshimi," he called. "Is there a bundle of accounting chits in the safe, or some other collection of papers? I think you'll find something like that. Will you have a look?"

"There's a bundle of chits."

"Have they been stamped?"

"Yes. All stamped with Inui's seal."

"That's it. Confiscate them!"

"Doctor Inui?" Katsuragi called into the mouthpiece. Inui had taken so long to answer the phone that the Secretary-General was stamping his feet in irritation. "I've got the Chief Superintendent from the Metropolitan Police Department with me here. A certain Mr Konakawa," Katsuragi started, and proceeded to give his report.

Konakawa and Noda quickly gathered together the accounts books, chits, related paperwork and other documents to be confiscated.

"I've just spoken to the President," Katsuragi said angrily after putting the phone down.

"President?" Konakawa quibbled. "You were talking to Inui,

weren't you? He's the Vice President. Why didn't you call the real President, Doctor Shima?"

At a loss for an answer, Katsuragi shuffled awkwardly around the desk to stand in front of them. He looked up with hangdog eyes and appeared to be pleading with them. "Could you possibly wait a few minutes? I mean, will you please meet the Vice President? He'll be here right away. That is… Otherwise… You see, I…"

Noda smiled wryly. "Of course we could wait, but what's with this 'Vice President'?" he said, repeating Konakawa's sentiment. "Does he scare you more than the President? Ah, but I should have introduced myself. How rude of me. Noda's the name."

The door suddenly opened. The security guard entered in a state of frenzy, closed the door behind him, then stood motionless in front of it, casting bewildered looks at the men in the room as he spread his arms out wide. The three had absolutely no idea what he was trying to say.

"What?" Katsuragi yelled in irritation.

"A b-bird… In the c-corridor…"

"A bird? Chase it away then!"

Katsuragi stopped short when he realized that, by spreading his arms out, the guard was trying to show them how big the bird was. Now he spread them wider still; the bird was even bigger than that.

"What sort of bird?" asked Noda.

Faced with the notion of describing the bird in words, the guard succumbed to paroxysms of panic. "It had the body of an animal," was all he could squeeze out at first. Then he bawled loudly in exasperation: "*IT WAS BREATHING FIRE!*"

Noda and Konakawa exchanged glances. Yes – this was just the kind of place, just the kind of situation where an apparition from a dream might appear.

"Idiot! You're half asleep! Get out of here!" barked Katsuragi. At that moment, the sound of roughly flapping wings could be heard in the corridor. Something heavy collided with the other side of the door. The guard had been standing with his back against it. Now he straightened his body in shock. Katsuragi's eyeballs almost popped out again.

"Got your pistol?" Noda whispered. Konakawa shook his head.

The flapping sound moved away. Konakawa went to the door and opened it a crack. After looking out into the corridor, he turned back to Noda. "Looks like it's gone."

Konakawa hurried back to the desk, took a large buff envelope containing important documents from Noda's hand, and clasped it firmly in his arms.

"Do not leave this room until further notice," he warned Katsuragi and the security guard. "There is very grave danger outside. Shall we go?" he said, urging Noda on.

"W-what was that just now?" a visibly shaken Katsuragi asked as they were about to leave.

"You called him, didn't you. I'd say it was the Vice President," Noda replied before stepping out into the corridor behind Konakawa.

The corridor was quiet. Some employees should still have been in the building, but there was no sign of them. Perhaps they'd been frightened off by the security guard's "bird". The lights in the corridor ceiling were broken, walls and doors on both sides scorched. They seemed to have been burnt at a temperature of several hundred degrees.

"I wonder if the bird, or whatever it was, has vanished? Like that doll, or the tiger I saw?" said Noda.

"I wonder." Konakawa picked up a single brown feather from the floor.

Noda looked to the end of the corridor and froze. There, where the corridor widened slightly and became brighter, something red had appeared out of nowhere, accompanied by a sparkle like the flickering of a TV screen.

"Paprika."

Konakawa looked up, and was amazed to see her there. "When did she arrive?"

Paprika seemed to be checking out the vicinity, but noticed the pair as they started off towards her. "Well!" she called. "You two asleep already?"

Konakawa didn't know what she was talking about. But Noda felt a shudder. He could sense a bizarre phenomenon in the making. Worried that their presence might have an adverse effect on her, Noda grabbed Konakawa's arm to stop him advancing further. They remained at a distance of four or five metres from where Paprika stood in front of the Medical Office. "So you're asleep now, are you?" Noda called loudly to confirm his fears.

"This is my dream. And you've come to join me. I've just been fighting them."

It was just as Noda had thought. Paprika spoke as though she was murmuring in her sleep.

"Paprika. We're actually here, in reality. We're actually standing here now. You've come here in a dream, and now we've met you here." Noda took a step towards her in the excitement of the moment. "Do you remember, earlier today? We said we'd come here unannounced, to investigate impropriety in the accounts."

"Ah." Paprika's eyes shone with an intelligence that seemed hardly possible for someone in a dream. As she stood there in the corridor, her sleek, slim figure a classic image from a bygone era, her whole being seemed to emit a faint brownish light. Noda and Konakawa were overcome with a great feeling of nostalgia. She was beautiful.

"This is no joke," Konakawa said with a groan of dismay. "I could never have imagined this. It's no joke at all."

"Dreams have merged with reality. Paprika, were you being chased by some kind of bird?"

"Bird? You mean the griffin? Yes. That was the Vice President." Without warning, Paprika floated up into the air. "I mustn't

305

wake up. Not yet. I've come to get the DC Minis back." Floating about a metre above the floor with her body tilted slightly downwards, Paprika seemed to be murmuring to remind herself of her mission.

"You mean, because we approached you?" asked Noda. "You think you might wake up if we approach you?"

"Not really, but please don't touch me. I think I'd wake up if someone touched me with a real hand."

Paprika was like the touch-me-not, *impatiens*, the busy lizzie – a plant whose seed pods explode when touched. The slightest indiscretion could have destroyed the delicate balance of this extraordinary phenomenon. Paprika, now floating in the air with her body tilted at around forty-five degrees, moved along the corridor towards the stairs.

"We've already found proof of impropriety in the accounts," Konakawa said as he followed her along. "Now we want to help you. I think you need help from real people here. You said you were looking for the DC Minis. Are you saying they're here, in this building?"

Konakawa's style of questioning made Noda nervous. Speaking so rationally might stimulate Paprika's logical thought patterns and wake her.

As a method of going from A to B in a dream, Paprika's movement was incredibly fast. Like a fish swimming against the flow, she floated along the ceiling of the stairway to the 1st floor, nimbly moving in little diagonal darts to right and left. Noda and Konakawa followed while watching her from below. Konakawa ran two steps at a time without breaking stride; Noda started panting immediately.

"The DC Minis must be in Osanai's lab… Judging by Inui's…" Paprika mumbled as she reached the 1st-floor corridor and leapt down to the ground, then slid along the corridor as if gliding on air. The first door on the right was the research lab newly assigned to Hashimoto. As the three passed along the corridor outside, little did they know that his bloody, lifeless corpse lay sprawled on a sofa inside the room.

A door on the left bore Osanai's nameplate. The door was locked; Konakawa broke it down with his shoulder.

As she entered the room, Paprika nodded in recognition. "That griffin. I only caught a glimpse through a gap in its consciousness, but... There's no doubt. This is the room. In there..." and she pointed to a chemical storage box in a corner of the room.

The box was made of lead and solid as a safe. It was also firmly locked. In her dream, Paprika's mind started to wander as she watched Konakawa and Noda struggling to open the box. This place was real, not a place in her dream. Maybe she could continue to exist in this real place, but with actions and abilities that could only be possible in a dream. In that case, there would be two of her in reality at the same time – Atsuko, now sleeping, and Paprika, a character in a dream.

Suddenly, the alarm bell rang. It was so loud that Paprika had to cover her ears. But Konakawa and Noda didn't seem to hear it at all; they merely continued their despairing attempts to open the chemical box. Only Paprika could hear the bell, it seemed. The noise was deafening, even with hands planted firmly over her ears. So it wasn't the Institute's alarm bell. It was a telephone ringing. The telephone next to the bed where she slept. As Atsuko Chiba.

Leaving her two comrades in Osanai's lab, Paprika woke in reality as Atsuko. Her telephone was ringing in the gloomy half-light of the bedroom. Even in the waking world, the noise was so loud as to become distorted. Atsuko picked up the receiver.

"Hello?..."

"Hello? Hello? Is that Atsuko Chiba? It is, isn't it?" The caller ignored Atsuko's sleepy tone; it was too early for anyone to go to bed, and he had no idea that he'd woken her.

"Who is it?..."

"It's Matsukane, social affairs correspondent for the *Morning News*. We've just heard from Sweden. Doctor Chiba, you and Doctor Tokita have won the Nobel Prize in Physiology or Medicine! Many congratulations!"

Atsuko wondered if she'd merely left one dream and entered another, as before. "But I haven't heard anything... Not from the Swedish Embassy..."

Atsuko's cool response seemed to irk Matsukane. He let out a little hysterical laugh; he was the one who was excited. "We heard it directly from a news agency that monitors the headquarters in Stockholm. They're always quicker than the Swedish Embassy."

"And what about Doctor Tokita? Does he know?"

"I haven't called him yet. I hope you won't think me rude, but I actually wanted to talk about holding an emergency press conference. I thought you'd be better equipped to discuss it than Doctor Tokita. But I could call him now, if you like?"

"No," Atsuko said sharply. "I'll call him."

Now the excitement started to build up inside her. She wanted to be the first to share this joy with Tokita. She was the only one who could really share any joy with him. Atsuko replaced the receiver and got up purposefully.

19

Atsuko arrived at the Institute for Psychiatric Research in her Marginal, with Shima and Tokita in the passenger seats. The entrance to the Institute was jammed with a large throng of media reporters, who were haggling with the night-duty staff, doctors and security guards. The entrance was bathed in bright light, despite the midnight hour, as the lights from television cameras illuminated the entire vicinity.

"A press conference at this hour? I never heard of such a thing!"

"Surely Doctor Chiba has called to tell you?" protested one of the journalists.

"Chiba doesn't work here any more!" said a middle-aged employee, obviously one from the Vice President's camp.

"She hasn't told *us* that!" Matsukane called loudly, glaring at the employee. "In that case, would you tell us about the conspiracy by the Vice President or whoever it was that forced her out?"

"Eh? What's that about a conspiracy?"

The other journalists started to make noises. The employee screwed up his face in a grimace. "We can't talk about it here. Are you mad?! You'll have to make an appointment."

"Out of the way, pompous git!" hooted a particularly short-tempered reporter. "We've no time for this crap! Two of your scientists have won the Nobel Prize. *The Nobel Prize in Physiology or Medicine!* What do you mean by obstructing the press conference? You jealous of them, or something?!"

Dazzled by the glare of the TV-camera lights, the chubby little security guard quickly raised his hands to cover his face.

"Let us through! Just let us through! We'll tell you all about it!"

Kosaku Tokita forged a path through the media scrum towards the entrance. Realizing that the Nobel prizewinners themselves had arrived, the battery of television cameras all turned as one and the surrounding clamour grew louder still.

"I can't let you through without the permission of President Inui," said the security guard, standing in their way.

"I am the President," said Torataro Shima. "I don't recall promoting Doctor Inui."

"I'm sorry, I don't understand any of that. I've just been ordered not to let you in."

Tokita casually brushed the still-arguing security guard to one side. "Well, that's him out of the way. And in we all go."

Still wrangling and quarrelling, the gathered throng surged through the automatic glass doors into the central lobby. Following

Tokita's lead, they headed for the Meeting Room usually reserved for press conferences.

"Wait! You may not enter!"

The middle-aged Senior Nurse Sugi glared at them as she blocked their path. Atsuko pushed her aside and, breaking free from the human tide, raced up the central staircase to the 1st floor. She was worried about Noda and Konakawa, having left them there on waking from her dream. Could they still be in Osanai's lab, where she'd left them in the dream – which, for them, was reality? Could they still be trying to open the lead storage box with the DC Minis inside? Atsuko held herself responsible for them, as if they were her own sons. She felt a harrowing sense of shame and regret that they, as upstanding members of society, had gone to such undignified lengths to help her.

Osanai's lab was deserted, the chemical storage box gone. They must have taken it away to open it. Atsuko felt relieved, but at the same time gripped by another nagging worry, something she hadn't considered in her dream. Hashimoto had escaped to the waking world while pursued by the grotesque Lord Amon. She had definitely heard his dying cries. Her fear that he might actually be dead was no longer unrealistic. In fact, it was more or less certain, and for that reason, it had to be confirmed.

The research lab newly assigned to Hashimoto was across the corridor from Osanai's and a little further towards the stairs. On its door was a plate bearing Hashimoto's name. Atsuko had no idea whether he was inside. Judging from the time of his appearance in her dream, he was more likely to be snoozing in this lab than sleeping in his apartment.

Atsuko overcame her fear and resolutely opened the door. Inside, her eyes met a sight that turned her stomach. An indeterminate mass of flesh was heaped there on the sofa, and it was definitely real. Her numbed mind gradually registered a pile of entrails spilling out of a lower abdomen, cascading down to the floor, a gaping red hole in a crotch with the genitals ripped out, a line of white ribs jutting from a bloody chest, an expressionless face so scorched by fire that it resembled a black mask. It was the pile of Hashimoto's remains after the butchery meted out by Lord Amon. An ashen-grey languor started to swirl loosely inside Atsuko. She closed the door, overwhelmed by her own powerlessness.

Of course, Konakawa should be the first to hear of it. He was probably with Noda, but where were they? Atsuko wanted to keep the door locked until Konakawa had arrived, but lacked the brute courage to go back into the room and search that lurid bag of dripping guts, that glistening heap of barbecued mincemeat for the key, which Hashimoto must have had on his person. Atsuko headed back to the Meeting Room, convincing herself that it was all right. Nobody would enter Hashimoto's room until the following morning.

By intentionally withholding the discovery of a murder, Atsuko knew she was sinking even deeper into guilt as a co-conspirator in evil. Even winning the Nobel Prize might have been part of that evil. Fortunately, though, she felt no such guilt about winning the Prize itself. She could therefore put on a brave face, drawing on her feminine ability to become impervious to evil as necessity demanded.

Atsuko waltzed into the Meeting Room as if nothing had happened. While expressing dissatisfaction at her absence, the reporters had reluctantly started questioning Tokita and Shima. Now they started to remonstrate and call out loudly to Atsuko, without even waiting for her to settle in her usual seat.

"Doctor Chiba. Doctor Chiba. If I might ask right away, could you explain why we were given that reception at the entrance just now?"

"What's been going on here?"

"Did the Institute oppose your winning the prize? Why did they try to block the press conference?"

"No, no, no. First of all, your reaction on winning the prize."

Employees in the Vice President's faction had joined the journalists in the Meeting Room. They now stood in a line beside the podium, glaring at Atsuko and the others with looks of suppressed spite. Secretary-General Katsuragi sat impudently in his usual moderator's chair, though no one had asked him to moderate anything.

Atsuko stood up. "I find this kind of attention most regrettable. It puts the spotlight only on myself and Doctor Tokita, and that goes entirely against my better wishes," she started, then turned to face the group that stood beside the podium. "In fact, it goes without saying that our great honour in winning this prize could only have been achieved with the fullest cooperation of all our colleagues here in the Institute and the hospital. Though not all of them are here with us tonight, may I take this opportunity to extend my sincerest thanks to them."

Atsuko bowed deeply; the group of six or seven shifted uneasily and pulled sour faces. Aware of the cameras trained on them, some grudgingly returned the bow.

"What were you doing when you heard news of the award?"

The question showed that the speaker had no interest in courtesies or niceties, but wanted only to drag a matter of lofty importance down to her own mundane level. It was the bespectacled female reporter in her thirties.

That's right. It was when I was looking for the DC Minis. Before that I'd been fighting the griffin. So Inui must also have been asleep then. Is he still asleep now? Has he heard about the Prize in his dream? Was he dreaming when he gave the order not to let the journalists in?

"What were you doing when you heard news of the award?" As she repeated the question, the female reporter's face began to look increasingly inane.

"I think Inui's sleeping now," Atsuko said to Tokita and Shima on either side of her, ignoring the gathered journalists.

"I know," Tokita replied, thrusting out his bottom lip and on the verge of tears. "We're in terrible danger. He appeared in my dream again, just now. It was a one-legged medieval creature called a sciapod, but its face was definitely Inui's."

"I saw something like that in my dream too," Shima sighed. "A dwarf-like thing the size of a child, with legs growing straight out of its head."

"Ah, that would be a glyro," said Tokita. A monster suggested by some to be a demonic manifestation of the child Jesus.

"What were you doing – when you heard news – of the award?" the female reporter repeated once more with an indignant sneer, almost singing the words.

The lighting in the room started to grow red. The photographers tutted, more concerned with the loss of precious light than the advancing redness. The reporters started murmuring and looking around them.

"I SAID NO!" came a coarse, boorish voice that seemed to be screaming over a cheap loudhailer. The voice came from far beyond the ceiling, way above the heads of those present, yea, even from the lofty heights of heaven. "I SAID, NO PRESS CON-FERENCE!"

"It's the Vice President," Atsuko breathed as she stood again.

Many of the reporters also stood in astonishment at the sheer volume of the voice.

"Who is it?"

"Such a loud voice! How rude can you get?!"

"Where's it coming from?"

Everyone in the room felt a dull, heavy crash. Those who were standing started to stagger. The wall between the room and the corridor vibrated under a force suddenly and violently exerted from the other side, causing the air and floor inside the room to shake.

There was a second crash, then a third. The reddish light in the room was emanating from this wall, made incandescent with heat. The ferocity of the heat started to melt the wall. The wall cracked, and there, in the centre of the white heat on the other side, something like a sunspot appeared. It expanded into a massive bull's head, causing dizziness in those who saw it and giddiness in those who tried to stand. The long claws of a gigantic beast appeared through cracks in the wall. A hairy black arm smashed through the wall and into the room.

Now two more heads appeared on the monster. One was the head of a ram, the other the purple head of a man. He had the face of a demon and was boiling with rage.

"GRRRROARRRRRGGGGHHHH!!!" roared the monster in a voice that covered the entire range of frequencies, including falsetto. The bespectacled female reporter gave out a lengthy and very bizarre scream as she rose to her feet, tried to run away, kept changing direction, then fainted, hitting her head heavily on the corner of a table as she fell rigid to the ground.

"It's Asmodai!" screamed Atsuko.

Asmodai, the demon of wrath and destruction. Master of all malevolent deities and governor of hellish legions, a monster with the three heads of a bull, a ram and a man, the tail of a serpent and the webbed feet of a goose. The monster sat astride an infernal dragon and held a lance bearing the war standard of hell. The three heads simultaneously breathed fire from their mouths while they surveyed the room. A television cameraman engulfed in flames ran screaming towards the window.

Tokita grabbed the microphone and shouted loudly above the tumult of confused screams inside the room. "Everyone, listen! This is a creature called Asmodai! Stand firmly where you are and face it! To exorcise this demon, we must call its name loudly and clearly! Don't be scared! Call its name!"

Tokita and Atsuko faced the monster and started chanting its name.

"Asmodai!"

"Asmodai!"

Shima joined them.

"Asmodai!"

"Asmodai!"

The monster's human head started to distort as if in torment. The white-hot wall gradually cooled to grey. The monster stopped moving, its further advance into the room halted by the voices chanting its name.

"It's in torment!"

"It doesn't know what to do!"

The reporters also started chanting, the tempo of incantation gradually increasing under Tokita's guidance.

"Asmodai!"

"Asmodai!"

Eventually, enclosed by the hardening wall, Asmodai turned to stone, his front half still protruding into the room. Bull, ram and human were all transfixed in expressions of spite, mouths wide open with rage but quite bereft of life.

20

At about the same time, spectres released from the realm of dreams started to appear all over the capital, wreaking havoc in the waking world. They caused real deaths, not fictional or dream deaths, and drove many more insane.

In various places around Shinanomachi, home to the Institute's staff apartments and the Inui Clinic, tens, hundreds or even thousands of Japanese dolls about a metre tall started walking towards every intersection from the darkness of every street corner. They quickly filled roads and pavements in the busy evening hour. The dolls all wore the same smile and the same clothes. They all walked in quick, short steps as if gliding along the ground, all in the same pose with arms outstretched on both sides, all issuing the same hollow chuckle.

"Ho ho ho. Ho ho ho."

"Ho ho ho. Ho ho ho."

It was this bizarre happening that caused many people to go mad. The dolls were typical examples of the "spooks" deeply rooted in the Japanese sentiment. In them resided a primordial fear that penetrates the subconscious with prickliness, a fear well known to all Japanese. The dolls formed an army that filled the roads and marched forwards en masse. A woman who caught them in her headlights couldn't stop laughing at the sight of them, causing an accident that killed two pedestrians.

Asmodai eventually disappeared, leaving the remains of the destroyed wall as his calling card. But then a gigantic Buddha tens of metres tall appeared in the garden in front of the Institute. With the merciful compassion of the enlightened one, it started to trample down the media personnel who came tumbling out of the Institute buildings. Several of them died the absurd death of being crushed by a nightmare. Then the Great Buddha began to chase their fleeing cars. From the main thoroughfare outside the Institute's gates, it walked off in search of the nightlife district, where it started indiscriminately attacking any passers-by and cars it found. As it continued on its trail of death and destruction, the Buddha emitted a vulgar laugh from the back of its throat, exposing the crimson lining of its mouth.

A flock of akbabas soared through the night sky. Akbabas are vultures that feed on the carcasses of the dead and are said to live for a thousand years. From time to time, these phantom birds of the night would swoop down to attack passers-by in the nightlife district, or peck out the eyeballs of the Great Buddha's trampled victims.

Sakurada-cho, seat of the Metropolitan Police Department, was visited by a variety of creatures diabolically converted from Christian-inspired constructs. One of them was the water-beast Hydra, which had a crown on each of its seven heads. Another was the buer; with five legs radiating from its head, it moved by rolling like a wheel. Then there was the fire demon Haborym, a monster with the three heads of a serpent, a cat and a man. It was running around the centre of Tokyo holding a firebrand and setting fire to everything it found. Fires started burning in wooden buildings, as well as parks and gardens where trees stood closely together. It was no coincidence that these phantoms all started appearing after Konakawa and Noda had taken the storage box containing the DC Minis back to the Department.

On arriving there, Konakawa had received reports of calamitous events occurring elsewhere in the capital, and had immediately sent Yamaji, Saka and Ube to the Inui Clinic. He suspected that Inui was still sleeping there, sending phantoms from his dreams to the waking world as surrogates of himself. The three officers were joined by Tatsuo Noda, who would serve as a civilian adviser. This was an exceptional measure; Konakawa knew that the officers, equipped only with their waking awareness, wouldn't be able to cope with Inui's unpredictable attacks.

As the four drove up to the Inui Clinic, they found the place unlit and deserted. Doctors, nurses and patients had probably fled in fright at the monstrous happenings, especially as the Clinic was at the centre of them all. But now the Clinic itself seemed to house a spirit, an energy, like an organic being crouching quietly in the darkness. It even seemed to be breathing.

"It's alive!" exclaimed Saka.

"It might attack us if we go in!" Even Ube was scared.

Yamaji turned to Noda with a questioning look.

"Let's push on," Noda said resolutely. "We've got to wake Inui. If we can do that, we'll only need to deal with the remaining creatures."

They'd started to suspect that the Clinic itself was Seijiro Inui, the entire building transformed into a living thing. They had found only a solitary DC Mini in the chemical storage box after wrenching it open at the Department. That left one more still in the possession of Inui; he was probably wearing it. In view of that, and the fact that the device made it harder for the wearer to wake up, this case wouldn't be closed until they'd captured Inui and woken him.

The officers entered the Clinic with Noda. Passing through the mouth-like lobby, they proceeded along endlessly winding corridors and stairways lit only by red night lights, like a journey through the innards of a body, before at last finding themselves on the 4th floor. Yamaji's research had already told them that Inui lived on the 4th floor, but it would have been too dangerous to use the lift. Lifts commonly appear in dreams as symbols of sexual desires. As such, they thought it highly probable that the lift would be used for an attack from the subconscious.

They broke down the door to Inui's apartment and made their way to the bedroom. The bed emitted a continuous moan, yet Inui was not there. There was a lingering warmth in his bedding, as if he'd just got up. The four searched the spacious study and library, the not-so-spacious other rooms, and even the wards and examination rooms downstairs. But there was no sign of Inui anywhere.

"He could have burrowed through his dreams like a tunnel and escaped to a different place in reality," said Noda. "I know that's possible."

"You're kidding?!" Yamaji stared in disbelief. "In that case, it's futile to search. He could be anywhere."

"No. There's one place we could look," Noda countered.

At around the same time, just before eleven o'clock that night, Atsuko was running along Gaien Higashi Avenue towards Roppongi, chased by phantoms. She'd been travelling with Tokita and Shima in her moss-green Marginal, but it had been crushed underfoot by the Great Buddha. The three had jumped clear moments before the giant foot descended. They'd quickly agreed that it would be best to run in separate directions, for it was patently obvious that the phantoms were targeting the three of them in particular. Tokita and Shima were rescued by separate media vehicles and driven off in different directions. Atsuko alone escaped on foot, deliberately moving away from the Institute's apartments.

But phantoms from the realm of dreams don't give up that easily. Wherever Atsuko went, wherever she ran, her relief at making a momentary escape would dissolve when they reappeared from the brightness of the nightlife district or the darkness of the night. Just as in a nightmare. These were spectres and hobgoblins driven by subconscious energy. As such, they would attack haphazardly, to the detriment of passers-by. As in a nightmare, they would change the scenery ahead to obstruct Atsuko's progress. The roadside trees would wriggle and squirm, the road would bend and twist. An akbaba flew down and crashed into the window of a coffee shop in front of her.

Near the Roppongi crossing, a wheel came to attack her from the road. It was about a metre in diameter, and in its middle was an old man's face leering at Atsuko. It was a buer. Atsuko had changed into Paprika without knowing it. She adopted a martial arts pose, poised to kick in self-defence. The buer passed beside her and disappeared into the wall of a building, leaving behind a laugh that sounded like coarse sand being rubbed together. Most of the nightlife revellers and passers-by were blissfully unaware of the crazy things happening elsewhere that night. These people had nothing to do with Paprika in the first place, but were merely human-interest items who would get caught up in things and be haplessly killed or injured.

The akbaba came to attack again. Seeing the ghoulish bird descending diagonally from high above the crossing, a young couple on a date commented disinterestedly:

"What's that? A vulture?"

"There's a few. Been flying round a while now."

"Gross."

Paprika escaped into a building. Inside the main entrance, to the right, were stairs leading down to the basement. She ran down the stairs and pushed open the heavy oak door. Paprika was relieved to feel the warm air and sense the soft, nostalgic smell of Radio Club.

"My!" gushed Kuga, smiling radiantly and bowing. But then he read from Paprika's expression that all was not well. "Is something the matter?" he asked, narrowing his eyes more than they were already.

"H-help. Help me." Paprika could barely speak.

Keeping a steady eye on her, Jinnai emerged from behind the counter. "As I thought. There's something going on outside, isn't there."

There were no customers in the bar, but any person of keen perception could detect abnormal events going on above ground, even from down here in the basement. Jinnai and Kuga supported Paprika's weary body from both sides as they led her to a sofa in one of the booths. There, she started to explain the whole story.

"A new device we developed for treating mental illness has turned out to have unexpected effects," she said, virtually recumbent on the sofa.

Jinnai sat opposite the sofa, looked Paprika in the eye and nodded in response to her every word. He seemed to be showing her that he understood, or perhaps rewarding her for attempting to explain a complex tale in simple terms. Kuga sat at Paprika's feet, closed his eyes and listened, a faint smile playing on his features. Perhaps her voice sounded like soothing music to him. Perhaps she was telling him his favourite story.

"Dreams have started to merge with reality. But it's not just that Inui's dreams have begun to infiltrate reality. What we're seeing now is the collective subconscious of everyone who's been exposed to the side effects of the DC Mini."

"So you're saying all these weird things were originally in someone's dream but are now real beings, real things that have an impact on reality?" Jinnai asked once Paprika had finished her tale.

"That's what I'm saying." Paprika had forgotten to mention something, and now made a point of emphasizing it. "To be killed by them means to actually die in reality. Please be careful. But by the same token, they can also be killed. The difference is that, when they die, their physical form also ceases to exist in reality."

Jinnai immediately stood and returned to his position behind the counter. "All right. We'll have to fight them."

Kuga half-opened his eyes. He rarely opened them more than that anyway. "So they take their strength from dreams, do they?"

"Yes."

"Right." Kuga stood up. The look on his face seemed to suggest that his whole life had been leading to the decision he was now about to make. He went straight to the sofa in the next booth and lay down on it.

"Oy, Kuga! What are you doing? This is no time for snoozing!"

"I'm going to sleep first," he said in a voice that was already sleepy, settled in a supine position and placed both hands over his midriff. "Then I'm going to fight these demons, using the power of the inner mind."

To Paprika's amazement, Kuga had already understood that the boundary between dreams and reality no longer existed.

The solid oak door was struck violently, as if something heavy had hit it from the other side. The sound of a living thing hitting the door was repeated a second and then a third time, accompanied by a vulgar cry of "*Gwaa! Gwaa!*" and the rough flapping of wings. A loud, high-pitched squawk seemed to come from the tip of the creature's beak.

"It's an akbaba!" Paprika shouted, edging into a corner of the sofa. Jinnai gathered together anything that could be used as a weapon – cutlery, sharp-edged tableware – and emerged again from the counter holding a thin knife. Timing his movement to the repeated banging against the door, he wrenched the door open.

A single akbaba whistled through the air, narrowly missing the top of the door frame. It flew to the back of the bar and turned near the ceiling.

"*Gwaa!*"

As the akbaba set its sights on Paprika and prepared to swoop down on her, the knife hurled by Jinnai sank deep into its right eye.

"*Gweeeeerghh!*"

The creature threw back its bald head at the end of its thin neck, then plummeted down to the table below, scattering black and white feathers everywhere. It writhed violently for a moment, then vanished.

Indifferent to the commotion as he slept on the sofa, Kuga was already starting to snore.

21

"Our enemies are phantoms from the realm of dreams."

Chief Superintendent Konakawa was appealing to the heads of the Riot Squad, the Traffic Riot Squad, the Special Task Force, the Mobile Patrol Force and the Police Aviation Unit. They had all gathered at the Incident Headquarters hastily set up in the Metropolitan Police Department. The time had come to reveal the ghastly truth, but there was no need to explain all the details.

"To overcome the enemy, the first thing we must have is will-power. We must remain steadfast to ourselves and impervious to the enemy's tricks. Our weapons will destroy the enemy, but we have no room for complacency, for they will keep reappearing. This is a battle that will seem to have no end. But weak-heartedness is as much our enemy as they are. I strongly expect the most strenuous efforts from all units. That's all. Now please go and mobilize your men."

22

Kuga had learnt how to regulate his sleep as part of daily life; he could drop off anywhere. He now stood up, empowered by his dream, and set off to fight the phantoms.

As if to symbolize his spiritual self-enhancement, Kuga climbed an imaginary staircase and reached the heavens above the metropolis. From the lofty heights of the starlit sky, he looked down at the nightlife district. It was in utter chaos. Having passed through the realm of dreams, Kuga had gained full control of his body and freedom of movement. Now he turned to confront the malignant spirits with a smile acquired by purifying the inside of his psyche. His body was several times bigger than normal.

A busy intersection was awash with the wailing of police sirens. There, one-legged sciapods and glyros with legs growing out of their heads were terrorizing passers-by, while the star-shaped demon Haborym harried drivers in their cars. Kuga made mystic signs with his fingers and chanted the Buddhist mantra of Acala the immovable one, the incantation of the fire-realm. The phantoms hurled looks of bitter reproach at Kuga as they burned up and disappeared.

The scene was like a pastel painting with uncertain depth or perspective, emphasizing the lack of boundaries between dream and reality. Light and dark that resembled neither night nor day alternated like the flickering of a cine projector. Buildings swayed and roads undulated as if they were playing a game. Vehicles and people, phantoms, policemen and police cars passed to and fro like coloured shadows cast on the glass window of a projection room. Paprika and Jinnai were running to find a more certain reality, but they knew, in themselves, that they wouldn't find it anywhere. How very unsettling! Perhaps that was what caused all kinds of uncertainty. Perhaps it was a world in which the winners would be those who could move freely across boundaries.

Still wondering how he'd got hold of it, Jinnai was openly brandishing and continuously firing a pistol. That made him wonder if he had some alter ego, or a secret past. He stuck his knife into the neck of a glyro that was clinging to Paprika. He and she were heading towards her apartment together. There they hoped to find the path to a kind of reality.

A large church appeared before them. They both knew it was a trap. But they would have to enter that trap and fight the subconscious of the abnormal, not to mention their own subconscious. They ran up the church steps without a moment's hesitation. The entrance opened wide and contorted itself, as if to say "*Enter!*"

"Swine!"

Jinnai took aim at the entrance and fired several shots at it. The steps started frantically shaking up and down, from side to side. The church vanished, and before she knew it Paprika was running up the stairs to her apartment. Alone.

Paprika was concerned over Osanai's safety. There had been no sign of him, in dream or reality, since his appearance as that perversely beautiful samurai, shot by Ube's gun. That tragic image of the dying young samurai had remained in her memory like a *sashie* illustration. She may even have started to feel love for him, coupled with a modicum of pity.

She reached a landing where the floor sloped slightly. The floor indicator was distorted and seemed about to melt and flow away. But Paprika knew she was on the landing between the 15th and 16th floors. Perhaps she was near the 15th floor because she'd thought of Osanai. She walked along the corridor towards his apartment. She could see him in his bedroom. He was lying on his bed naked, looking up at the ceiling with a lifeless expression. He had lost a significant part of his personality.

"But it's all right. You can get it back," she said to console him as she leant over his face from above. She had reverted to the form of Atsuko Chiba. "Your own personality, you know. After all. You are so very beautiful."

Osanai looked up at Atsuko from below. His eyes were like black obsidian holes that threatened to suck everything in. Hypnotized, Atsuko couldn't help being drawn down to his face. "Ah. You poor thing. You poor thing."

"Doctor Chiba. I have no sense of reality," Osanai said in the delirious tone of a man with no soul. "You can only love me in this state."

Wasn't that precisely why she *could* love him? Maybe not. Maybe it was because she had been an accomplice to evil. It was perfectly natural for them, as two individuals who'd fallen from grace together, to have their hearts so violently moved by each other's beauty. An embrace. An act of mutual seduction that could only occur within a framework of guilt. Atsuko was already naked. The whole room turned dark blue, dark as the bottom of the sea. Atsuko draped herself over Osanai, like a starfish trapping a mollusc. Her hands and feet felt numb. She could even anticipate her convulsions at the point of climax. *A devil, a devil has got in. It's inside me now. Inside my mind, inside my body. If not, what is this sublime sensation of pleasure?*

"No," said Seijiro Inui. "You think of God and the Devil as being two principles, good and evil as conflicting concepts, humans as unstable beings that exist between the two."

Where's he looking from, where's he talking from? Is he somewhere in this room? In the TV screen? Atsuko was so carried away by the surge of sexual desire that she couldn't even look around her.

"But you're wrong," he continued. "Good and evil are a single entity in conflict with humans. God and the Devil, as religious principles, are in conflict with worthless, banal conscience, morals, petty bourgeoisie, reason."

Inui appeared right next to them. He was lying on the bed naked, resting one hand on Osanai's shoulder as he spoke. Atsuko no longer felt it unnatural, as she would normally have done. Inui's words should have sounded like unclear utterances of opaque meaning. But his words resonated in Atsuko's ear and reached deep into her mind; they were clear in both meaning and language. Atsuko could no longer doubt the truth of his words.

"Yes, you should have known from the beginning. We share good and evil through our dreams. That's why you feel nostalgic about evil. That's precisely why all sorts of evil are as familiar to humans as God is. It's because there's evil that good exists, because of the Devil that God exists!"

The door burst open with a crash. Tatsuo Noda stumbled into the room, followed by Yamaji and the two inspectors.

"So this is where you are. Inui!" bellowed Yamaji. Inui responded by standing and roaring violently. Paprika was instantly transformed; she was no longer naked, no longer Atsuko Chiba. It was as if her personality had been reversed. As if she had, at that very moment, acquired the ability to cast aside her sensuality and the logic of dreams.

"Arrest him!" she shouted. "I mean Inui, the real Inui! He's got a DC Mini on his head. I saw it!"

Still completely naked, Inui's body expanded until it filled the room. "Go back!" he called down from the ceiling. "Go back to your own dreams! To your own subconscious! To your own fears!"

"Don't think about it!" shouted Paprika. "Don't let him kindle your fear!"

But it was too late. Before her warning could sink in, Noda's fear had already been kindled. *Oh no!* He was on the steel frame of a multi-storey building under construction. The very place he feared more than any other. *Damn! Damn that Seijiro Inui! How did he know about my fear of heights?!*

The reality was that Noda had taken himself there. He could see the city and houses spread out far below the swaying steel frame. The frame began to twist beneath his feet, snaking back and forth, trying to make him fall. Noda cried out. He tried to hold tight, but at the moment his hand reached a steel column, it slid away from him. This terrifying scene was being created inside Noda's mind.

"Help! Somebody! Paprika! Paprika!" he called, lurching violently.

He was crying. If he fell, he would die. He would die in reality. For although he was in a dream, it was also reality for him. A hideous reality that should never be allowed to exist.

Paprika didn't come to help.

23

Tokita was back in his apartment. He was completely unaware that, only a few moments earlier, Atsuko and Inui had appeared in Osanai's apartment on the same floor. He was equally unaware that Noda had then burst in with the officers to confront Inui. Those events might just as well not have happened.

Shima was also in Tokita's apartment, along with Matsukane from the *Morning News*. Matsukane had rescued Shima in his car, then driven him to the Metropolitan Police Department. Once the appearances by phantoms and hobgoblins seemed to have died down, they had returned to the apartment building together.

"I wonder what it means that they've died down," Matsukane mused as he accepted a cup of coffee from Tokita's mother.

"And can we be certain?" Tokita chipped in. Racing around for so long had made him hungry; he'd asked his mother to prepare some food, and was perfectly happy to scoff it in front of his guests.

"The Chief Superintendent said so," added Shima, lounging on a sofa in the living room.

"What? Has there been a press conference?" Tokita put his chopsticks down in surprise.

"No, no. That's tomorrow. He just said it to us."

"The fact that the appearances have died down," Tokita said, sounding relaxed again, "must mean that Inui has woken up. Either that, or he's entered non-REM sleep and isn't dreaming. One of those. I've a feeling he's been wearing the DC Mini all along. In that case, as Atsuko says, he'll find it harder to wake up. Yes. I reckon he's entered non-REM sleep."

"Non-REM sleep? But where?" Matsukane asked impatiently. "If only we could find out where he's sleeping."

"Well, he can travel through space at will," Tokita said ruefully. "What if he's in a hotel room where he used to stay when he was in Europe, for example? Some place like that from his memory? It would be hopeless. And seeing as he's getting there through the dream world, he could even go back into the past."

"Into the past?!" Matsukane gasped. "Travelling through space *and* time?!"

"It's all too horrid," Tokita's mother said with a shudder. "You're saying this man, whoever he is, can make all these terrible things happen, far worse than earthquakes or floods, and remain perfectly safe himself?!"

"Actually, these weird happenings may not all be coming from Inui's dreams," Shima said languidly. "Different people's dreams seem to be merging with each other. People who've only used the DC Mini once. People like you or I, who had the dreams of schizophrenics fed into our subconscious. Those schizophrenics themselves. People who come into contact with someone wearing a DC Mini. And so on. I'm sure you'll agree."

"Well, that parade of dolls and the giant Buddha, for a start. Those things were obviously not from Inui's dreams." Tokita picked up his chopsticks to continue his meal, but stopped when he saw the grilled fish on his plate. It was his favourite. "I mean, look at this," he said in dismay. "This is one of mine."

The fish, tail end already stripped to the bone, opened its mouth wide and started to talk in a loud, piercing voice. "What's the matter? What's the matter? I'm a clever boy. A clever boy. Why did you throw me in the waste-paper basket? Next year's conference will be held in Brussels. So be sure to eat two rice dumplings. Ah. Here's a pun for you. *Sayuri Yamaoka, the girl next door.* Ahahaha."

"It's got mixed up with some schizophrenic's dreams," Tokita muttered.

Tokita's mother had been standing next to him, watching it all with her mouth as wide open as the fish. She cried out in horror and fainted. Tokita caught her as she fell. He and Matsukane carried her to the living room, where they laid her on the sofa now vacated by Shima.

After returning to the table, Matsukane stared vacantly at Tokita's plate for a while. The grilled fish was now just food again. Suddenly, Matsukane said something that seemed quite unbecoming for a serious newspaper reporter. "Maybe the DC Mini could provide links with the spirit world. Channelling, you know." He stood up, evidently shocked by the stupidity of his own statement, and hurried towards the television to change the subject. "I know it's late, but there must be some news on?"

"*...chaos around the Metropolitan Police Department at the moment. The Department had earlier announced a press conference to explain the cause of these happenings, and measures to be taken against them. It's now thought highly likely that the conference will be attacked, just as the earlier conference to announce the Nobel Prize...*" The face of a breathless correspondent appeared in the centre of the thirty-seven-inch flat TV screen. "*The Department has therefore announced that it will cancel or indefinitely postpone tomorrow's press conference. And I've just been told that a TV studio was suddenly attacked about twenty minutes ago, at around four minutes past one this morning. The station was airing a special programme about this incident, which of course has been postponed...*"

The transmission was interrupted by unfamiliar patterns and flickering. It didn't seem like a faulty signal. The patterns and flickering gave way to reveal an aerial night view of the metropolis. The camera seemed to be on the construction site of a high-rise office building, pointing downwards through its bare steel frame. A man could be heard shouting desperately.

"Help! Paprika! Paprika!!"

"Did he say Paprika?" Tokita stood up.

"Wait a minute. That's Noda!" Shima muttered to himself.

Tokita walked to the television and stood staring at it with arms crossed, as if to demand an explanation from the TV set itself. The viewpoint of the camera seemed to have changed – the camera was now Tokita's eye. Perched precariously on a thin steel girder high in the night sky, swaying in the wind with nothing to hold on to, was a life-sized Tatsuo Noda.

"Noda!" Shima rose in alarm. "He can't stand heights! He'll be terrified! Something must have sparked his fear to make him go there! We've got to help him, or he'll fall to his death!"

"Where is this place?" asked Tokita.

Matsukane came to stand next to him. After surveying the whole screen as if searching for something, he thrust a finger towards the bottom of the picture.

"This is the Palace Side Building. Here's the Meteorological Agency. It must be that office building that's going up in Takehira-cho." He looked around the room. "Where's the telephone? I'll call the police right away."

"He's going to fall!" Shima shrieked. "They'll never make it!"

"That's right. They'll never make it," Tokita repeated calmly. "He appeared on this television, and that means he's asking for our help. All right!" He suddenly raised his voice. "Mr Noda! Can you hear me?"

Noda turned towards the screen, his hair ruffled by the wind. The movement made his body lurch again. From his reaction, it was clear that he'd heard Tokita's voice but couldn't see his face.

"No!" Shima howled as he covered both eyes with his hands.

At the same moment, Tokita thrust his arms into the television screen. The screen dissolved, and the scene inside it became a real space that was an extension of the room. The wind blowing high in the night sky started to bluster inside the apartment. Tokita gripped the arms of the life-size Tatsuo Noda. After a momentary expression of surprise, Noda clung tightly to Tokita's stout arms. With a great heave of strength, Tokita pulled Noda's body out of the television onto the floor of his living room.

24

Two weeks passed, then a third.

Inui continued to elude his pursuers.

Appearances of phantoms and other strange sights had decreased in frequency. But there was still no way of preventing them; bizarre happenings would occur whenever there was a press conference involving Atsuko and Tokita, or an announcement by the Metropolitan Police Department.

Real calamities would descend on reporters trying to cover these events. But Matsukane alone had courage. He alone refused to fear the evil intentions, the spiteful malevolence of dreams. Ignoring the fear that pierced his heart with the prickly sting of a thistle or a nettle, the fear that lurked in his subconscious like a skin rash caused by lacquer, he was actively gathering material and taking comments from Atsuko and Tokita. These he circulated among the newspapers as special correspondence. Luckily, the mischief of dreams couldn't change the content of newspaper articles, which demanded a waking consciousness. The most they could achieve was to make the letters on the page appear more blurry and harder to read.

Something was happening. People were suspicious and wanted to know, but, at the same time, had a vague intuition that wanting to know was in itself taboo. They'd grown used to reacting with more or less the same state of agitation, making no distinction between petty cases and major ones, confronted by a taboo presence that directly threatened their well-being.

The public had no means of resisting the seeping spread of madness. When people suddenly started laughing in the street, it was difficult to judge whether their insanity was caused by a bizarre happening in the vicinity, or by their suppression of their fear until that point. This was because some of these happenings took a form that could only be perceived by individuals. The digits on a watch might suddenly become jumbled, for example, or a mother's face might momentarily change to that of a seal. People only had to experience a single such happening for their own complexes, traumas and fears to be activated; they would be at their mercy thereafter. This most commonly took the form of an inferiority complex, or an Oedipus complex, sexual perversions or phobias.

The sufferers would make their own nightmares appear in reality, and the ensuing bizarre happenings would then swallow up other people around them as well. It was like a monstrous chain letter born of nightmares. That was why, when Atsuko's image on the front cover of a weekly magazine turned into the Devil, spoke or laughed aloud, some people would notice it every time while others failed to. That was why, on suddenly hearing some foul abuse about Kosaku Tokita or the Nobel Prize bellowed loudly in their ears, the only ones to flinch were those who were listening to radio-cassette players at the time.

These monstrous happenings had first occurred in central Tokyo, later spreading to three or four outlying prefectures. This made it easy to pinpoint the whereabouts of Seijiro Inui, their "epicentre", in the centre of the metropolis. But his malevolent intentions could now transcend time and space. Wherever Atsuko and Tokita went, those intentions were bound to pursue them in the form of nightmares.

The day of the Nobel Prize Award Ceremony was fast approaching. Although Atsuko's nightly dreams were still frightening, they were gradually softening in tone. Elements that seemed to come from Inui's dreams had started to appear only in fragments. Even they were no longer so aggressive, but appeared little more than fleeting reminiscences in which the atmosphere of his debauched paganism could still be felt. Atsuko couldn't know for sure whether he was sleeping in the day and rarely dreamt at night. Perhaps he could no longer wake up, due to the effects of the DC Mini, and was gradually wasting away in his sleep somewhere. Or perhaps he was keeping his malevolent ambitions warm somewhere, waiting for the perfect moment to strike.

Instead, the dreams of Tokita, Noda, Konakawa, Shima and even Osanai had started to merge with Atsuko's dreams. Being the dreams of men who loved her, they smothered her softly, as if to protect her from Inui's dreams. Sometimes she would yield her body to the pleasure of sleeping between Tokita and Osanai; at other times, the pair caressing her on the bed would be Noda and Konakawa. Since the men were in the majority, their dreams overwhelmed Atsuko's. She had no idea where her own dreams had gone, but she was by no means unhappy to consort with them in their dreams. The divine sensations of pleasure she found there, almost as if her body could melt, were not to be found in the real world; in many ways, they felt even more vivid than reality. Sometimes neither Atsuko nor the men could tell whether they were dreaming or not. For when they awoke, Atsuko would often find herself embracing one of them on her bed, or cavorting with any two at the same time.

When they saw her in the daytime, the men would remember the previous night's dream and look embarrassed. Then again, so would she. In any case, being perfect gentlemen, they declined to talk about it amongst themselves; they chose not to succumb to vulgarity, beyond the occasional witty comment.

The day of the departure for Sweden had arrived. The only reporters who made it to Narita International Airport at ten-thirty that morning were Matsukane of the *Morning News* and crews from three or four TV companies. The other companies had clearly been frightened off, thinking it inevitable that the event would be visited by outlandish phenomena. If nothing happened, ironically, it would be because they'd failed to anger Inui with their overzealous coverage.

At the request of the prizewinners, few came to the airport to see them off; the only people in attendance were two representatives from the Swedish Embassy, three or four members of the Agency for Cultural Affairs and other government bodies, and Torataro Shima. No one else came from the Institute for Psychiatric

Research. Police officers Morita and Ube were present, but that was obviously for security reasons. It was a lonely departure. Even the media coverage was nothing more than a brief interview with the pair as they stood in the lobby.

"Now that you're at last preparing to leave for the, er, Nobel Prize Awards Ceremony," started a female reporter, casting anxious glances around for fear of strange happenings, "how do you feel? In a word?"

"Er… In a word, at last preparing to leave… Awards ceremony… How do I feel, in a word." Atsuko was trying hard to vanquish the demons of sleep. "It's just like a dream. A dream. No. This *is* a dream."

"Yes, I'm sure it is." The reporter suddenly sprouted a cow's head, which flopped down low in front of her. The weight brought her to her senses with a sharp intake of breath, but the cow's slobber still hung from her mouth. "Do excuse me. I've only eaten one helping of rice porridge this morning." And she slurped the slobber back into her mouth.

"Have a safe journey," said Matsukane with tears in his eyes, seemingly trapped in the emotional incontinence of dreams. "You see, I also love you, so very acutely, I love you so very acutely. Because look here. It's so hard, so hard my trousers are about to split."

"Ah! Matsukane-san!" Atsuko kissed him passionately.

"And what about all those unearthly apparitions? Is there any chance they could…" A male reporter was interviewing Tokita. As he spoke, the reporter flinched at his own words and peered around nervously. "…any foreseeable apparitions at the awards ceremony… Is it not necessarily the kind of work where you mainly replace things at home, er?"

"You're right, you're not wrong. Yes. Apparitions appear because it's a dream, you see." Tokita was slobbering even more than usual. "Elbowing your way through a dream looking for reality, elbowing through, just like it's reality itself, all the way to Stockholm, all the way there…"

As the pair started off towards the departure gate, snapped by some but pursued only by a solitary television camera, there was a minor happening. The surroundings grew dim, as if bathed in a dark-purple light. The flight announcements were interrupted by Inui's voice, obnoxiously ingratiating as if he harboured some secret design, sounding over the speakers with a low menacing laugh.

"The host of Christ, assembled on the plain of Jerusalem, declares war on the host of Lucifer on the plain of Babylon..."

It was a line from the spiritual training of the Jesuits, well known for their militarism. Hardly any of the smallish number of passengers awaiting flights in the departure lounge seemed to have heard it. It was almost certainly a declaration of war on Atsuko and Tokita, and was sufficient to produce a chill in those who saw them off, causing them to hurriedly depart the scene.

The Scandinavian Airlines direct flight to Stockholm, a jumbo jet, took off from Narita at eleven-fifteen that morning. The scheduled time of arrival was just past two in the afternoon, but taking the time difference into account, the flight actually lasted more than ten hours. Atsuko took the window seat next to Tokita in the First-Class section. They were treated as privileged guests of the Swedish state; the cabin crew knew all about them.

About two hours after take-off, the plane lurched violently. *Hello?* thought Atsuko, and looked around the cabin. It was just as she'd thought. Sitting at the rear with his anxious face half-hidden, keeping watch over Atsuko and Tokita with worried looks, was Chief Superintendent Toshimi Konakawa of the Metropolitan Police Department. He had evidently appointed himself their escort to protect them during the awards ceremony, but had followed them secretly to avoid angering Inui. That almost made Atsuko smile. The lurch just now had been the thumping of Konakawa's heart under the tension of his mission.

In any case, there was nothing to smile about. Inui had obviously chosen the Nobel Prize Awards Ceremony, that occasion of great dignity and tradition, for the ultimate battle between heaven and hell. He was planning to plunge the ceremony into turmoil.

25

Standing on a podium surrounded by flowers and microphones, Professor Karl Krantz was giving a speech in Swedish to introduce the prizewinners in Physiology or Medicine. His Majesty the King of Sweden sat to his left on the stage, surrounded by members of the royal household, with formally dressed laureates and Nobel Prize committee members to right and left of centre. An invited audience of more than two thousand filled the spacious concert hall, sitting in hushed reverence as they followed the proceedings. An hour had already passed since the start of the ceremony at five o'clock. So far, nothing unusual seemed to have happened at all. But Atsuko could feel the faint tingle of electricity agitating the air inside the building.

He's here.

Inui was palpably present, but *fearing* his presence would only make that fear incarnate. On the other hand, Atsuko had half resigned herself to that already. Whether sooner or later, this ceremony would surely be reduced to chaos and confusion.

Very few of the assembled guests, including those invited from Japan, harboured any fear that the calamitous events in that strange, far-off land would reverberate as far as Sweden. Most of them had never heard of those events in the first place. Even if they had, they simply laughed them off as daft rumours.

"Er, the King's face just changed to Inui's," Tokita whispered to Atsuko in the seat next to him.

"Don't be afraid," Atsuko whispered back. "He wants you to be afraid."

Atsuko didn't understand a word of Swedish. Neither, surely, did Inui. Otherwise he would already have blown his top at the glowing praise that was being heaped on Atsuko and Tokita. Having finished his speech in Swedish, Professor Krantz raised his voice slightly and began to state the reason for the award in English. Atsuko tensed herself. With this part safely over, she and Tokita would then step forwards to receive their Nobel Prize Diplomas, together with a gold medal and an envelope containing a cheque, handed over by His Majesty the King.

"Doctor Kosaku Tokita and Doctor Atsuko Chiba," Krantz intoned, "for your invention of psychotherapy devices in the treatment of mental illness, and your considerable achievements in their clinical application, it is an honour and a privilege to convey to you, on behalf of the Royal Swedish Academy of Sciences, our most heartfelt wish to soak your sickening romanticism in blood on this altar of death. It is in blood that the power of atonement lies. There can be no life without blood, and with this life, with this blood, we must atone for our life on the other side."

Atsuko gripped Tokita's hand. "He's off."

Professor Krantz's voice cracked coarsely. His body started to distort grotesquely.

"Bastard. He's trying to stop us getting the prize," Tokita muttered.

"Ahahahahahahaha!" With an insane laugh, Krantz turned into a hideous, blood-soaked griffin. The griffin leant forwards on the lectern, turned its head to Atsuko and bellowed. "Woman! I shall offer up your blood on the altar of death! Woman, source of unrighteousness and sin, repository of misfortune and shame!"

The creature's repugnant voice was instantly drowned out by the screams, shouts and anguished cries that now filled the hall. The first to flee was the conductor of the orchestra. Next, the King and his retinue stood as one and made to escape. Foreign dignitaries either fell together with their chairs or just fainted. The laureates and committee members who sat close by, and the laureates' families further off in the dress circle, simply stood with mouths agape, as if they could hardly believe their eyes.

If Atsuko and Tokita were to succumb to their fear, they would be driven to a world where fear took physical shape; they would have nowhere left to run. "Be firm," Atsuko said, to give herself courage. "We'll have to fight him here."

"But how?" Tokita countered between panting breaths. "There's no way of fighting him."

How could Atsuko summon up the strength from her dreams, here and now? Where was Konakawa when she needed him? He hadn't been invited, so he shouldn't be in the hall. *Where is he?*

The griffin looked towards the high ceiling of the hall and roared at empty space. A violet light shone around the VIP seats in the dress circle. There, a massive being appeared and started to float through the air towards the stage.

It was Vairocana, the physical incarnation of the Buddha.

Moving along the central aisle through the stalls, meanwhile, came another one who bore arms and seemed to shine gold. It was Acala, the immovable one, destroyer of delusion and protector of Buddhism. A closer look at their faces revealed Vairocana to be none other than Kuga; Acala was Jinnai. The griffin roared in dread at these greats of the Buddhist pantheon, but was yet undeterred from its course. The creature changed its position, leapt up, and prepared to swoop down on Atsuko and Tokita.

A shot rang out. The griffin halted before the petrified pair, then disappeared. Toshimi Konakawa ran onto the stage through a door at the back. His pistol had saved the lives of the two laureates, just as the griffin was preparing to rip out their windpipes. Others around them were rushing in all directions, screaming and shouting in sheer panic. Fresh screams could be heard here and there; new phantoms were appearing everywhere.

"Come on!" shouted Noda, who also appeared before them. But Atsuko and Tokita were unable to stand. They knew there was no escape. "Come on! Come into my dream!"

Oh yes! It was night-time in Japan. The time when Noda, Jinnai and Kuga would all be sleeping, dreaming. Atsuko realized that instantly. The three had intercepted Inui's dream, using it to appear in reality and rescue them from his attack.

"Do as he says," urged Konakawa, breathing heavily as he battled against the tide of fleeing humanity to reach them.

Noda used the surreal power of a dream character to change reality. He, Atsuko and Tokita now stood beside a road, surrounded by farm fields that stretched to a line of mountains in the distance. They were standing at a bus stop in front of an old tobacco store; the scene was very familiar to Paprika.

"This is the start of my childhood home," Noda said in a dream-like tone. "So many of my dreams start here…" and the rest was no more than inaudible mumbling.

"Are we just going to stand around talking?" Tokita said disinterestedly. "Is there nowhere better we can go? Somewhere we can talk calmly about how to defeat the Vice President?"

"All right then…" said Noda, and with that, instantly transported them to a corner of his favourite *okonomi-yaki* restaurant from university days.

They sat around a table with a metal hot plate in its middle. Other customers nearby gave them curious looks. Many were student couples. *This place has changed*, thought Noda. *Does history work in dreams? Maybe this restaurant still exists. Maybe we're here in reality!*

"Do you think Jinnai and Kuga could still be fighting?" pondered Atsuko. "Toshimi's still there too…"

"No. The phantom disappeared." Jinnai turned to face them from his seat at the counter. He was no longer Acala the immovable one, yet had lost none of his fearlessness. "That Vice President, or whatever he's called. D'you reckon he'll be appearing here? Eh?"

The customer sitting next to him also turned to face them, bowing silently. It was Kuga, now back in his tuxedo.

"The ceremony hall must be in total chaos now," Atsuko lamented. "No more Nobel Prize for us."

"It's OK. Using the power of dreams, we'll go back in time, back to before the ceremony started," Kuga said with a confident smile. "But before that, we'll have to deal with that Inui bloke, won't we."

If it were so easy to "deal with" him, we would have done it already. They all groaned and fell silent. Before they knew it, the King of Sweden and Professor Karl Krantz sat facing each other in the opposite corner of the shabby little restaurant, blinking as they surveyed the scene around them.

"They're here!" Atsuko said in dismay.

Inui's malevolence had found its way into Noda's dream. No – perhaps it had originally been Noda's dream, but now it was unclear whose dream it was. For all they knew, they could all have been dragged back into Inui's dream.

"I've started to sense a loathsome black thing inside, outside, inside my insides," said Noda. "It's sharp-edged and prickly. There's nothing like that inside me."

The group were transported from the corner of the *okonomi-yaki* restaurant to the middle of a dense jungle. For some reason, Kuga was missing. The jungle was alive with Inui's febrile energy. But it clearly wasn't Inui's dream. Noda thought they were on the island of Doctor Moreau; that thought was immediately relayed to the others. Vaguely familiar with the story, Jinnai pulled out his knife and gripped it in battle readiness. *You're right. It's the final confrontation*, thought Atsuko, now transformed into Paprika. *It's good. We have a lot of friends here.*

Himuro appeared before them wearing a mud-covered lab coat. He was gigantic, so tall that they had to look up. "I might be dead," he said pitifully, observing them with his little round eyes, "but I haven't forgotten my bitterness at being killed. These are the last scraps of my consciousness as I lay dying. There are lots of them lying around here."

Tokita howled in terror and crouched in the undergrowth.

Jinnai hurled his knife at Himuro's eye, but it had no effect in a dream. It merely made Himuro's face look even more grotesque and Tokita even more terrified. Noda remembered those fights with old classmates in his dreams, and the feeling of emptiness that accompanied them. "*Be gone!*" he yelled as he performed a wild lunge at Himuro. Called up by Noda's mind, a number of humanoid creatures dressed in rags emerged from the undergrowth, together with Takao, Akishige and Shinohara, to join in the attack on Himuro.

Himuro turned into Inui for a moment, then vanished. Inui must have been shocked to be attacked by those hideous humanoids, creatures that not even he had imagined.

They were inside a cathedral bathed in a dark-red light. Now Jinnai was missing; he'd either been unable to enter, or someone had shut him out. Torataro Shima joined them in his place.

"There's danger here," said Shima. "We're in Inui's dream now, no doubt about it. He's brought me here many times. I detest this place!"

"All right, let's go back, to my dream, back to my dream," Noda invited the entourage, resisting his own impulse to fall into a deep sleep. "See, it's like going on a journey, isn't it? I'll be happy, to take you with me. I'll drive the Marginal."

They were in an old-style inn, under the blue sky and sunlight of early afternoon. Farm fields could be seen from the window. It looked like Toratake's inn. Shima and Tokita had disappeared; now only Paprika and Noda were in the tatami-floored room. Perhaps the others had all returned to their own dreams, but what about Tokita? Had he been forced back into Inui's dream? A paper screen slid open on both sides to reveal Nobue Kakimoto in the next room, sitting sideways in a cotton kimono. She gawked at the pair, with hair hanging horribly to one side and her sagging labia exposed.

"Transient illusion of love. It was a sorrow I brought on myself. I wish I could bite you to death!"

This was the kind of phantom Noda found most abhorrent. Shrinking from the ghastly obscenity of the scene, he ran to

341

the window. Namba was selling vegetables in a field outside. "Heeeeelp!" called Noda. "I'm scared! Namba Namba Namba, come and help me, help me please!"

But Namba just laughed and shook his head, climbed onto a giant tomato and flew off down the road into the distance, floating about three metres above the ground.

"I know," said Paprika. "This is my fear. The Vice President is using it to his advantage."

"All right. Come on, Torao." For some reason, Noda called his son's name. He'd shouted "Torao", but in his mind he saw the image of Takao Toratake. An enormous tiger appeared from the tokonoma alcove and went to attack Nobue. Her already crumpled body collapsed entirely, turning into an indeterminate lump of flesh that clung to the tiger, then was eaten by it and bled profusely.

Paprika could see what was really happening. An intense battle with Inui was in progress. At that moment, the contest was evenly matched, but she was nowhere near defeating him. What could she do to "deal with" him once and for all? Would she have to destroy his stubborn ego? And how could she do that?

Yes. How could she do that?

She was inside the cathedral again. The inner sanctuary was deserted; Paprika was alone. A moment's slip in concentration, and she'd been transported back to Inui's dream. But this time, the cathedral looked uncannily like the concert hall where the awards ceremony had been held. A life-size image of Christ on the cross stood in the centre of the altar. His near-naked body was contorted with pain, fresh blood flowing suggestively over his smooth white skin. Why did Paprika find this image of the dying Christ so alluring? Paprika gasped. It was not Jesus Christ but Morio Osanai. That was why the sight of his freshly flowing blood, his face beautifully distorted in suffering seemed so erotic to her. It must have been the image of Christ in Inui's mind, the object of his adoration.

Inui's hoarse voice rang out. "Damn you, woman! Damn your impurity! Your meddling in other people's lives! Driftwood! Viper! Scum! May you be crushed! May you be sliced up into little pieces! Then I will offer up your remains on this altar!"

A window shattered, and fragments of stained glass came flying at Paprika. There was nowhere she could run. She tried to duck under a chair, but the floor started to undulate, presenting further danger. She could feel Noda, Tokita, Jinnai and Kuga desperately trying to help her. Inui had removed them from his dream, and was now homing in on Paprika, his first victim.

Noda twisted his body to break through an invisible membrane, and somehow forced his way through to Inui's dream on the other side. He had been spurred on by that unrealistic bravery that always existed in his dreams, together with an almost indecent passion towards Paprika, and had used them to come to Paprika's rescue. He appeared just below the altar. Instantly, layers of Inui's subconscious entered Noda's vision through gaps in the shell of his preconscious, cracked by the combined violence of love and hatred. Noda would now start his attack on Inui, using a logic that could only exist in dreams.

He jumped onto the altar and whipped off the loincloth from the figure of Christ, the embodiment of Morio Osanai. The result was just as Noda had strongly willed it to be, using the power of dreams. There were female genitals between the saviour's legs.

"Wahahahahahahahahahahaha!"

Inui's insane laughter filled the sanctuary. The ceiling peeled off and shards of stained glass danced through the air. They turned into dead rats, German dictionaries, wineglasses, fountain pens, scorpions, cats' heads, syringes and a motley jumble of other objects that filled the space, flying around madly, swirling like a whirlwind, surging like a raging sea.

"He's lost his mind!" shouted the voice of Kosaku Tokita, unseen.

But the madness was short-lived.

343

The cathedral disappeared, whereupon all returned to their respective dreams and their respective realities. Except for Inui, that is. It wasn't clear what had happened to him.

This was the moment Kuga had been waiting for. He'd been standing by, having diverted the power of his dreams to make time go backwards. He'd done so by focusing his mind on dreams in which the dreamer wants to return to the past, and had thereby tried to reinstate a specific time in his dream. He had succeeded in his attempt, but the sheer effort of it had drained every last drop of his energy, both mental and physical. He lost consciousness.

Professor Karl Krantz started to speak in English. "Doctor Kosaku Tokita and Doctor Atsuko Chiba, for your invention of psychotherapy devices in the treatment of mental illness, and your considerable achievements in their clinical application, it is an honour and a privilege to convey to you, on behalf of the Royal Swedish Academy of Sciences, our warmest congratulations on winning the Nobel Prize in Physiology or Medicine…"

26

P.S. I Love You echoed around the dark-brown interior of Radio Club. In a spacious booth at the back of the bar, the one that was like a private room of its own, a quiet celebration was in progress. The participants were looking back over weighty events that seemed to have taken place only a moment ago, and were rejoicing in their safe conclusion.

"Amazing that such a place existed," Torataro Shima said with an air of lament. "None of us knew about it. He must have been sleeping there the whole time. He must have starved to death in his sleep."

Seijiro Inui's emaciated body had been found in one of the forgotten detention rooms, in the second basement of the hospital attached to the Institute for Psychiatric Research.

"He must have been hiding there, building up his psychic power for the day of the awards ceremony," Toshimi Konakawa said with a sigh of disbelief, slowly and repeatedly shaking his head. "He knew very well that it would ultimately destroy him, yet he was still wearing the DC Mini. It was embedded so deep in his skull that a layer of skin had grown over the base. Such was the depth of his malicious vindictiveness."

"And you think he died just after that last confrontation?" asked Tatsuo Noda.

"Probably. There were no more appearances after that, until they discovered his body. Either in our dreams or in reality." Konakawa nodded. "That last battle must have used up all his remaining energy."

"I thought he'd gone mad for a moment."

"He did go mad," Tokita said before turning to Konakawa. "Did Osanai know the Vice President was down there?"

"If anything, I think it was Osanai who put him there. And I reckon they kept Himuro there as well."

Morio Osanai had been charged with Himuro's murder.

"Himuro. And Hashimoto. Poor blokes." Tokita hung his head, revealing his inner torment. "They all went mad from the beginning. We all did, me included."

The others showed a certain discomfort with that notion, and shifted uneasily in their seats. The residual effects of the DC Mini. No, that wasn't all. The anaphylaxis effect, which could but increase. The immune hypersensitivity, which could but grow more hypersensitive. It was a fear they all felt but could not express. If only someone could make them forget it. Anyone.

"But at least Tsumura and Kakimoto are on the way to recovery," Atsuko Chiba said cheerfully as she patted the back of Tokita's hand. She felt proud, at that moment, of her ability to appear nonchalantly light-hearted for Tokita's sake.

"More drinks, anyone?" Kuga stood beside Atsuko, a huge crescent-shaped smile occupying the whole of his face.

"That's right! We haven't had that toast yet!" Noda exclaimed, turning to Kuga. "Yes. The same all round, if you would."

"The same all round. Coming right up." Kuga bowed low in a state of great joy.

"And have you recovered now?" asked Shima.

Kuga gave another polite bow. "Oh yes. The collapse was only temporary. Now I'm just as you see me," he declared, spreading his arms wide.

"He says he's fatter than before," Jinnai called with a laugh from behind the counter.

"By the way, it's been known for married couples to win the Nobel Prize, but I don't think two prizewinners have ever married each other before," said Noda. "When do you plan to tie the knot?"

"Well, once all this hullabaloo has died down a bit," Tokita said sheepishly. "Quietly, no press conferences or anything like that."

"We're really so very sorry," Atsuko said with her head bowed.

They all laughed at the faintly immoral implication behind Atsuko's words, which only they could understand. Drinks were brought. Jinnai and Kuga also helped themselves, whereupon all raised their glasses in a toast to Atsuko and Tokita, winners of the Nobel Prize and now engaged to be married.

"And that's the end of Paprika, too," Atsuko said emphatically, surveying the men's faces as she did. "Whatever happens from now on, Paprika will not be working again."

"True," Shima concurred sadly. "Inevitable, really. So that sweet, lovely girl is really dead now?"

"She's dead," Atsuko said with a smile. "She no longer exists."

"No, that's not true," said Noda, straightening up from the back of the seat. "Paprika is still alive. Just like any idol, she will live on for ever in the hearts of those who met her. I will never forget her, for one."

"But we won't be able to meet her," said Konakawa.

"Yes, we will," Noda contended with some conviction. "If we want to meet her, we can always find her in our dreams. If we really want to meet her, we need only wish sincerely to see her, and she will always join us there. I really believe that. She will be an independent personality. She will smile at us and talk to us, just as she has until now. I'm sure she will. With her incredible beauty, her delicate gentleness, and her great intelligence coupled with unbending courage…"

27

P.S. I Love You echoes around the dark-brown interior of Radio Club. There are no customers in the bar. Jinnai is wiping glasses behind the counter, Kuga is standing by the door. As always.

What was that? Jinnai tilts his head. It's almost as if he can hear some customers in the booth at the back of the bar, enjoying a quiet conversation and good-natured laughter.

They're fondly remembered, those customers, a group of really decent people who often used to meet, both in reality and in dreams. *I wonder if they'll ever be back*, thinks Jinnai. *How long is it since they were here?*

He looks up to see his old friend Kuga standing by the door with his back to him, completely motionless. As always.

Jinnai can no longer resist the urge to call out. "Hey. We were fighting, weren't we?"

Kuga doesn't turn, but the trace of a smile on his lips broadens a little. "Yes. We were fighting," he replies. He almost looks as if he's asleep.

Jinnai nods twice before going back to his wiping. He smiles in satisfaction; his mouth seems about to break into a chuckle. He waits a moment, then, as if to confirm what he heard, calls out to Kuga once more. "And we were courageous, weren't we?"

"Yes. We were courageous," Kuga replies with a groan.

Jinnai looks happy as he increases the vigour of his wiping. But there's something he still finds hard to comprehend. He remembers what it is and the smile leaves his face. He mumbles a question, neither to himself, nor to Kuga.

"So – it was all a dream, was it?"

Kuga doesn't answer. His back is still turned. His eyelids are closed, as if he were deep in meditation. It's not certain whether he knows the answer or not. The smile on his face makes him look more and more like an image of Buddha.

Born in Osaka, Yasutaka Tsutsui is particularly well known for his science fiction. Winner of various awards, including the Izumi Kyoka Prize, Kawabata Prize and Yomiuri Literary Prize, he has been decorated as a *Chevalier des Arts et des Lettres* by the French government.

Yasutaka Tsutsui
Salmonella Men on Planet Porno
978-1-84688-068-1 • £7.99 • 288 pp.

Defying the commonly held perceptions of time and space, and escaping any easy classifications, Yasutaka Tsutsui's stories centre on the folly of human desire. Most of his characters suffer awful fates as a result of their own foolishness, which usually takes the form of greed, lust or vanity. With influences as diverse as Darwin, Freud and the Marx Brothers, his writing displays a mixture of pathos, slapstick and psychological insight, shot through with bolts of Kafkaesque inventiveness.

Tsutsui's quirky imagination, and his ability to construct new and striking realities, threaded with a dark-edged, menacing humour, make him a truly unique literary voice, and ensure that *Salmonella Men on Planet Porno* is hard to put down and impossible to forget.

Yasutaka Tsutsui
Hell
978-1-84688-046-9 • £7.99 • 192 pp.

Hell is a place where three days can last as long as ten years on earth, and people are able to read each other's minds and revisit the darker details of their former lives. Yuzo can now look his murderer in the face. The actress Mayumi and the writer Torigai are chased by the paparazzi into a lift that drops to floor 666 beneath ground level.

The vivid depiction of the afterlife in *Hell* includes the traditional horrors, but subjects them to Tsutsui's unique powers of enchantment. Witty, amusing, unparalleled for its poetic style and the wizard-like light touch of the author's shifting focus, *Hell* is a masterpiece of surrealist literature.